The City of Lights is never so romantic as it is on New Year's Eve—and for Carrie Mae agent Nikki Lanier, it's never been so deadly.

Still reeling from her break up with CIA agent Z'ev Coralles, Nikki is tracking a Basque anarchist who may be planning to kill fellow Carrie Mae operative Camille Masters. Nikki's search leads her to Camille's son, bad-boy pop star Kit Masters, who is traveling to Paris on tour. When Nikki receives a picture of Z'ev with another woman, Kit is happy to help mend her broken heart—but first, they'll have to fend off masked gunmen so Kit can arrive safely at his New Year's Eve concert.

When dissension in the ranks of Carrie Mae gets Nikki fired from the mission, she defies orders and recruits her friends to help solve the case. But staying alive long enough to protect Camille—while untangling her increasingly messy love life—will be the hardest thing Nikki's ever done.

Also by Bethany Maines

Bulletproof Mascara

COMPACT WITH THE DEVIL

a novel

BETHANY MAINES

ATRIA PAPERBACK
NEW YORK LONDON TORONTO SYDNEY

ATRIA PAPERBACK
A Division of Simon & Schuster, Inc.
1230 Avenue of the Americas
New York, NY 10020

This book is a work of fiction. Names, characters, places, and incidents either are products of the author's imagination or are used fictitiously. Any resemblance to actual events or locales or persons, living or dead, is entirely coincidental.

First Atria Paperback edition April 2011

ATRIA PAPERBACK and colophon are trademarks of Simon & Schuster, Inc.

For information about special discounts for bulk purchases, please contact Simon & Schuster Special Sales at 1-866-506-1949 or business@simonandschuster.com.

The Simon & Schuster Speakers Bureau can bring authors to your live event. For more information or to book an event, contact the Simon & Schuster Speakers Bureau at 1-866-248-3049 or visit our website at www.simonspeakers.com.

Manufactured in the United States of America

10 9 8 7 6 5 4 3 2 1

Library of Congress Cataloging-in-Publication Data

Maines, Bethany.
Compact with the devil : a novel / by Bethany Maines. — 1st Atria Paperback ed.
p. cm.
1. Women spies—Fiction. 2. Anarchists—France—Fiction. I. Title.
PS3613.A34964C66 2011
813'.6—dc22
2011001206

ISBN 978-0-7432-9279-5
ISBN 978-0-7432-9280-1 (ebook)

COLOMBIA I

Rocking Around the Christmas Tree

December 24

Nikki Lanier popped open the hood of her small red Fiat and stepped out onto the sun-washed, dusty Colombian road that tumbled away in a series of jogs and bends in either direction. The far side of the road was a mass of greenery from which issued an occasional lonesome birdcall and the repetitive chirp of insects. The near side was a wall of clay bricks broken only by a set of tall iron gates and a smaller wooden door a few yards away. A scrawny calico cat sunned itself on top of the wall, ignoring Nikki, who was pretending to examine the inner workings of the engine. The blast of hot air from under the hood added to the sheen of sweat covering her skin. The monotonous tick of the cicadas should have made her feel alone; instead it simply seemed to underscore her feeling of being watched. She held still and listened for a sound behind the insects.

Her cell phone buzzed against her hip bone, vibrating in her pocket. Fireworks of adrenaline burst in her chest, shooting sparkles of fire down her arms. They were supposed to be in the communication blackout phase. Had something gone wrong with the team? Nikki checked the phone's face. Her boyfriend's picture blinked next to "incoming message."

Against her better judgment, she pressed the accept button.

"Call me. We need to talk," was all the message said.

Nikki froze. In the entire history of man, nothing good had ever come from the phrase "we need to talk." A grating noise pulled her back into the moment.

Turning, she saw the small door in the wall slowly opening. Nikki whipped back around and looked at the engine again, stuffing the phone into her purse. She put Z'ev firmly out of her mind. It was time to concentrate on the mission. The team depended on her.

She heard the crunch of footsteps as two men emerged from the doorway. They were wearing jeans and T-shirts, with guns slung across their shoulders. Nikki knew at a glance that the black, snub-nosed machine guns were TEC-9s. Nikki waved happily at the two men, who remained expressionless.

"Boy, am I glad to see you guys!" she chirruped, trying to look as harmless as possible.

"*¡Usted no puede parquear aquí! ¡Usted no puede estar aquí!*"

"Sorry, fellas," said Nikki, jutting out one hip and sounding as American as possible. "*No habla español.* I don't suppose y'all *habla* car?" She made little steering motions with her hands and then broke the imaginary wheel. The men exchanged looks.

"*Americana estúpida.*"

"*Sí, pero está buena.*"

"*Justos, ayudémosla a arreglar su coche así se va más rápido.*"

The second man shrugged. They both slung their guns behind them and approached Nikki's rental car. Nikki beamed.

"You can see it's just busted all to fooey," she said, holding the smile and resting a hand on the upraised hood.

Both men ducked under the hood and peered at the engine workings. Nikki maintained her smile, put both hands on the hood, and then slammed it down on their heads. There was a satisfying *whonk* sound, and when she raised up the hood both men fell, unconscious, onto the roadway.

"*No todos los americanos son estúpidos, mus amigos*," Nikki said in perfectly clear Spanish, looking down at the bodies. "But it's nice to know you think I'm hot." She collected the guns and pulled the guards to the side of the road, pushing them into the underbrush.

Moving quickly, Nikki went through the door in the wall and walked briskly down the path as if she had followed it a hundred times before. The path led to a small, round building that overlooked the gate and the main house. She slithered through the doorway, letting the TEC-9s lead the way. The caution proved needless since the hut was empty except for blinking TV screens that showed various black-and-white viewpoints of the grounds, including a middle-gray version of Nikki's Fiat and a small delivery van arriving at the back gate.

"Right on schedule," she said, checking her watch. Her rescue plan was moving smoothly through phase one and into phase two—extraction.

Nikki flipped the switch that opened the back gate, and the van pulled through without even stopping. Reaching under the console, Nikki ripped out a series of wires, and one by one the TV screens went blank. Then, taking a tool kit out of her purse, she climbed on the console and inserted a bug into the junction of wires where they emerged into the room. When a repair crew came in, all they would see was the mess of ripped-out wires under the console; meanwhile, Nikki's team would be able to see everything going on in the Alvarez compound. Climbing down from the console and dusting off her hands, Nikki frowned.

"We need to talk," she muttered to herself. "There's nothing to talk about!"

Nikki jogged toward the main house, still carrying the TEC-9s. But her mind was racing faster than her feet, considering the things Z'ev might want to talk about. Two days from now they were supposed to meet in Mexico for two weeks of Christmas fun, sun, and making out on the beach. And probably lots of those little drinks with the umbrellas in them.

Nikki liked this plan; it was a good plan; had lots of good points to recommend it. Avoiding one more depressing, obsessive holiday with her mother, for one thing. And it was convenient since she was already in South America on "business," anyway. Not that Z'ev needed to know that. And had she mentioned umbrella drinks and making out? Nikki approached the house with a worried expression that had nothing to do with the looming oak doors. Z'ev had canceled this vacation before. Twice before, in fact.

Nikki kicked open the front door and quickly scanned the room. In one corner was an enormous fake Christmas tree that had been decorated with a Martha Stewart–like pathology. The rest of the room boasted a mix of traditional Colombian and totally drugged-out *Miami Vice* decor. It was Colombian eighties. Nikki paused her scan at the fireplace; there was a large fertility god on the mantel, large in a way that required the kind of hand gestures fishermen usually reserved for the best fish stories. *No, really, it was* this *big.* While Nikki was taking a moment to consider why men felt the need to decorate with their penises, a maid ambled into the room accompanied by the slow *sluff, sluff* sound of her house slippers on the tile floor.

"*Buenos días,*" said the maid, shutting the door and ignoring the fact that Nikki was carrying not one but two submachine guns. Nikki smiled uncertainly.

"*¿Puedo tomar su bolso?*" the maid asked, gesturing to Nikki's purse. For lack of anything better to do Nikki handed over her purse, shrugging it awkwardly over one of the guns.

"Where is Mrs. Alvarez?" asked Nikki, momentarily forgetting her Spanish.

"*La señora no está aquí,*" said the maid placidly, and Nikki stared in dismay.

"*¿No está aquí?*" repeated Nikki, feeling a cold fear creep into the pit of her stomach. What did the woman mean, "not here"? Nina had to be there. Isolated from her family and married to the abusive head of a drug cartel, Nina Alvarez needed help. The mission was to extract Nina and install monitoring devices in the house to help them bring down her husband, who was funding revolutionaries throughout the region. That was the plan. But in order for the plan to work, Nina had to be there.

"*Los hombres están allí,*" said the maid, pointing through a large archway.

Nikki looked through the archway and felt a gust of wind that chilled the sweat on her skin. Hearing the loud *pop, pop* of gunfire coming from the same direction, she took a big gulp of air and ran toward the noise. She paused at a corner and risked a glance before sharply pulling her head back. Her team had three guys pinned down, but the men were behind a big cement planter. Nikki swore under her breath.

The team had deviated from her plan. Nikki remembered the briefing; she was pretty sure she'd been extremely specific about the east entrance. The guards patrolled east to west. Entering on the west put them directly in front of the guards; entering from the east put them behind the guards and in perfect position for an ambush. Entering from the west meant that they were more likely to be spotted and get into a time-consuming and dangerous shoot-out . . . like they were doing now. This was exactly the sort of thing Nikki had been trying to avoid. She ground her teeth in irritation and calculated her next move.

Between the hard pops of gunfire she heard the *sluff, sluff* sound of the maid approaching. Nikki glanced over her shoulder and saw the maid shuffling quickly toward her, apparently talking on Nikki's cell phone. Nikki gaped in disbelief.

"Get back," she hissed urgently at the woman, making desperate "go away" hand gestures.

"*Sí, señor, Lucy Ricardo. Esa pelirroja loca. Aquí está.*" She handed Nikki the phone with a smile. "*Es el señor.*" Nikki took the phone, wondering what else could go bizarrely wrong today.

"Nikki, finally! Where are you? That sounds like gunfire." Z'ev sounded irritated.

"I'm at Mrs. M's," lied Nikki. The number of times she was mysteriously hanging out at her boss's house was growing improbable. She was going to have to come up with a new place to be. "Some kids are lighting off fireworks."

"Wow, they're loud."

"I know," said Nikki. "Can you hold on a sec?" She didn't wait for his reply but held the phone to her chest, muffling the speaker, and leaned around the corner, firing a spray of bullets at the men behind the planter. There was a yelp from one of the men, and Nikki heard Camille yell at them to put their guns down. She picked up the phone again.

"I think the gardeners are yelling at them now," she said,

hoping that would cover any yelling he might hear in the background.

"Oh, good. Look, Nikki, about our vacation plans . . ."

Nikki felt her neck muscles tense. "No, Z'ev! No. You've canceled twice already."

"It's not my fault, it's work."

Nikki bit back a reply that involved swearing and glanced around the corner in time to watch Jenny take a running dive over the planter and take out one of the guards. She pulled her head back and leaned against the cool adobe wall.

"Well, you can tell them to go take a flying leap off a cliff!" she said fiercely. It was the best she could do without a diatribe of cuss words that she couldn't quite bring herself to say with the maid watching. "I haven't seen you for more than two days in a row in two months."

"I know, I know, but these things just happen."

"They don't just happen, Z'ev. You let them happen! I rearrange my work schedule for you." She pushed herself away from the wall and walked out into the courtyard. Jenny had a grip on one of the guards; the other was wrestling with Ellen.

"Well, forgive me, but I think my work is just a little more important than yours." Nikki thought of Nina Alvarez's bruises and got mad. Ellen lost her grip, and the man slithered out of her grasp and ran toward Nikki, still looking at Ellen.

"My work is just as important!" she yelled into the phone. Forgetting about the TEC-9 dangling from her shoulder, she punched the guard in the face. He went down like a sack of potatoes.

". . . you work for the Carrie Mae charity foundation," Z'ev was saying with irritating calm as she put the phone back to her ear. "And outside of that one time in Thailand, world peace doesn't exactly depend on you."

Nikki clenched her fist around the phone. She couldn't decide which infuriated her more: his attitude about her job or the fact that she couldn't tell him what her job really was. The Carrie Mae Foundation, charity subsidiary of the at-home-cosmetic-sales giant, was a widely acknowledged force for women's rights; that they also happened to use force was less well-known. Very few people outside the foundation knew about the all-woman spy network. What worried her was the creeping suspicion that even if Z'ev knew she was an operative for a secret agency focused on women's rights, he'd have the exact same attitude.

"Well, I may not work for the CI—"

"Nikki!" Z'ev interrupted sharply. Talking about his job on the phone was forbidden.

Briefly, Nikki took stock of the year that they had been dating. Weekends mostly, and occasional weeklong visits in between missions, his and hers respectively. She'd always tried to get time off or schedule things around his visits. He'd never even invited her to his apartment in Chicago. He had never made her a priority.

"I may not work for your 'company,'" Nikki said, "but if you read the news these days, it's a pretty good guess that in the world peace department, you guys suck!"

There was an angry silence on the other end of the phone, and Nikki made a quick status check; the team looked fine. No one was bleeding. Jenny was hog-tying the guards.

Nikki walked toward Nina's room; she had a mission to complete, but her legs felt rubbery. She couldn't believe he was doing this to her. Ellen was a few steps behind her.

"Nikki, I'm sorry, but this is the way it has to be," he said at last. There was an angry finality about his tone that she hadn't heard before.

Nikki opened the door and looked around the room. He had a

drawer in her apartment and a job in the CIA and Nikki suddenly realized that was how it was always going to be. The room contained a lot of things, but none of them was Nina Alvarez. She blinked back tears. This was a disaster.

"Well, in that case, Z'ev Coralles," said Nikki, reverting to her mother's habit of using full names when truly pissed, "next time you want to call up and cancel plans with me, don't bother, because we don't have any." And she hung up the phone.

COLOMBIA II

Well, I've Never Been to Spain

"Did you just break up with Z'ev?" asked Ellen, taking off her ski mask and mopping her face with it. Nikki felt sick. Ellen's comfortably middle-aged face held an expression of concern, and she patted Nikki's back in soothing little circles.

"He'll call back," Nikki said, breathing hard.

They both looked at the phone in her hand, which was noticeably not ringing.

Camille stalked into the room, snatched the phone out of Nikki's hand, and threw it against the wall. Nikki watched as her phone splintered into a thousand tiny pieces and fell to the floor with a clattering plastic noise.

"Hey," protested Ellen. Nikki's voice was stuck in her throat along with her heart.

"Oh, I'm sorry," said Camille, grinding the phone into dust with her heel. "I didn't mean to interfere with Nikki's personal life. Perhaps when you've dealt with your boyfriend issues, you'd like to join the rest of us in doing our job!" Camille's sarcasm stung, and Nikki flinched. The petite brunette didn't wait for a reply but swept out of the room. Nikki gathered up the pieces of her phone, hoping that the memory card was intact.

"She isn't here," yelled Camille, her crisp British accent echoing off the walls of the courtyard, her personality sweeping everyone along in a tidal wave of anger. "Everyone back in the van. You too, Lanier."

"That is not the plan," said Nikki, but Camille cut her off.

"Well, the plan was that she would be here, and she isn't. Ellen can drive back to the rendezvous. Give her the keys."

Nikki thought about arguing; she was the leader of this mission. But Camille was her superior. She looked at Ellen, who shrugged and grimaced apologetically. Nikki looked around the room, feeling a little lost, and spotted the maid peering through the bedroom doorway, still carrying Nikki's purse. Nikki sighed in resignation and took her purse back, handing the keys over to Ellen.

"It's out front," said Nikki. "Look out for the two guys in the underbrush." Ellen nodded and jogged away with the keys. Nikki smiled wanly at Ellen's easy burst of activity. When they had first met in training over a year ago, Ellen had been struggling to run a mile.

The drive back to the rendezvous was accomplished in silence—a humid and slightly embarrassed silence from the team; icy fury from Camille. Meanwhile, Nikki's mind alternated between the failure of the mission and her failure as a girlfriend. Nikki rubbed her temples, dislodging sweaty red curls from her ponytail.

Besides the ludicrous amount of chemistry between them and the ridiculous fascination that Z'ev held for her, they actually worked well together. During her first mission in Thailand they had operated as a team, albeit a strange team, where she knew he was CIA and he knew nothing about Carrie Mae. But in the year since then it seemed that he'd managed to convince himself that her behavior had been a fluke—as if Nikki's occasional brushes with death and willingness to tote heavy artillery were simply character flaws. He had reverted to treating her like just a girl.

An hour and a half later the van jerked to a halt and the team slowly exited, hauling their gear behind them.

"Operations room, twenty minutes," barked Camille, pushing through the double doors of the office building that was Carrie Mae's Colombian headquarters.

"Nikki, y'all are so getting screwed over this," said Jenny, watching Camille walk away. Jenny and Ellen were two-thirds of the team that Nikki had brought down to Colombia to help with this mission. Presumably Jane, the third, was inside being briefed on Nikki's shortcomings.

"Thanks, Jen, that's really helpful," said Nikki sarcastically. Jenny had a talent for stating what everyone else would prefer to leave unsaid.

"It wasn't your fault," said one of the Colombian girls with a shrug.

"Camille's just like that," said another.

"She's a good boss if you can just keep her from interfering in the day-to-day stuff," said the first girl.

"I think she misses the action," said the second thoughtfully. "But she's too busy to go to the briefings and then she won't listen to anyone who has. Not your fault."

"It wasn't your fault," agreed Jenny, "but that woman is going to try to kick your ass six ways from Sunday." Jenny, a true born Southerner, was constantly forcing her gracious, Georgia-peach accent to wrap itself around the hard-nosed aspects of her personality. Hearing her speak was like being mugged by someone really nice. "You know how else you're going to get screwed? Your mom is going to be absolutely gonzo if she can't reach you on the phone."

"I told her last night I was going to be missing Christmas and she yelled at me and then hung up. And usually after the yelling she gives me the silent treatment for a week. That's why I didn't call her till last night," said Nikki, feeling the familiar twinge of guilt.

"You mean you mentally manipulated your own mother!" exclaimed Jenny. "I don't know whether to be horrified or impressed."

"What? I wanted some vacation time with Z'ev to myself without her calling. I just figured that timing was everything, as Mrs. Merrivel says."

Jenny shook her head, looking both amused and disgusted.

"Let's just get this over with," said Nikki with a sigh, and started toward the building.

"Did you really break up with Z'ev?" asked Jenny as they walked.

"He canceled vacation plans, again," said Nikki.

"That's not good," said Jenny. "You don't think it had anything to do with . . ." Nikki shot her a warning look as they entered the building and Jenny changed the topic. "Well, can't you just keep him around for sex?"

Startled, Nikki tripped over the carpet in the entryway and careened into a passing office worker. The woman gave her a nasty look, and Nikki smiled apologetically.

"Jen!" protested Nikki when the woman was out of earshot.

"What?" demanded Jenny. "I've seen that boy; he's hot. I mean, steam actually rises off of him."

"Don't be silly."

"I'm not being silly; there was steam."

"It was just that one time," said Nikki with irritation. "We were running and it was cold out. Our sweat was warmer than the air, therefore you get steam. Natural phenomenon."

"It ain't natural to be that fine, but I guess you can delude yourself if you want," Jenny said, seeming cheerfully unconcerned.

"Thanks, I think I will," said Nikki as they arrived at the Operations Room. "Because he may be fine, but that doesn't stop him from being an ass."

"Fatal flaw of all men," said Jenny with a grin as she opened the door.

The room was walled with whiteboards that were pasted over with blueprints, diagrams, and intel sheets. In the center of the room was a long conference table that had been laid with manila folders set perpendicular to the table edges, so that each seat was the picture of businesslike precision. At the head of the table sat Nikki's boss, Miranda Merrivel, a dark-haired woman of nearly seventy with a serene, professional appearance. Nikki sharply sucked in a breath of freon-cooled air, and Jenny flinched a little. They had been expecting a ranting Camille, but finding Mrs. Merrivel waiting for them meant that they were in for a whole new level of getting chewed out.

Jane entered the Operations Room from the opposite door. Nikki looked for some sign from Jane as to Mrs. M's mood, but Jane avoided eye contact and handed a folder to Mrs. Merrivel. Jane preferred the chic-punk-rock look and today was working a safety-pinned black T-shirt that bore the words WHITE WRITING ON A BLACK SHIRT. She had paired it with Donna Karan slacks and black jelly bracelets. Mrs. M, as usual, appeared oblivious to Jane's costume and simply accepted the folder with a nod.

"Come in, girls," she commanded. "Camille's been telling me about the mission." Nikki and Jenny exchanged looks. Mrs. M could go either way; there was no telling if she was pissed or not. As they entered the room fully, they noticed for the first time that Camille was leaning against the wall, fuming.

"Mission?!" snapped Camille. "Maybe you should explain the concept of a mission to Nikki and her boyfriend. We're working our tails off and she's chatting on the phone like she's getting her nails done. She completely blew it."

"The maid answered my phone," protested Nikki.

"You could have hung up!" Camille pushed herself away from the wall and began to pace. "Why she's a team coordinator I'll never know—the girl's incompetent!"

"Really, Camille," said Mrs. M, "your temper hasn't improved any with age. You're still as quick to judge as ever." Jane gave a small cough and handed Mrs. M another sheet of paper. Mrs. Merrivel examined it briefly. "According to the initial reports you violated the mission parameters, which resulted in a time-consuming and dangerous firefight. Perhaps you should have followed Nikki's plan, hmm?"

Camille turned a brilliant shade of red, but Mrs. M continued ignoring Camille's impending explosion.

"It also states that Nikki fulfilled all her mission parameters while breaking up with her boyfriend. Not ideal, perhaps"—she gave Nikki a piercing stare, and Nikki squirmed—"but hardly the fault of the team coordinator. Now, won't you all please sit down?"

Camille continued to glare, but Mrs. M held the woman's angry gaze calmly. Camille didn't move, but Nikki knew Mrs. Merrivel well enough to know who would win the staring contest. Ignoring the battle as if it were already over, she went to a seat at the table.

"I had to make a judgment in the field!" said Camille defiantly.

"I'm sure you did. These things happen. Please sit down; we need to discuss a matter that will concern you particularly."

Camille sat down gracelessly, arms folded across her chest in a pout. Nikki eyed the fiftyish British woman in dislike.

Ellen entered a moment later, talking quietly to Rosalia, Camille's second-in-command. Rosalia was a competent woman who, in Nikki's estimation, was picking up a lot of Camille's slack. Mrs. M gestured for them to sit down.

"We have decided to suspend this mission," said Mrs. M, and Nikki sat upright in surprise.

"But we don't have a location on Nina Alvarez," said Nikki. "She could be in trouble. We can't just leave her."

"Shortly after your team entered the compound we received information that indicates that Mrs. Alvarez may be in CIA custody," said Rosalia. "Unfortunately, we weren't able to confirm this until after your team had committed."

Nikki looked to Jane, who nodded miserably. Nikki avoided looking at Jenny and Ellen. They would discuss this later.

"Why would the CIA be involved?" asked one of the girls.

"Why don't we ask Nikki's boyfriend?" Camille said, sniping at Nikki.

"They're working with the DEA agents, who we know have been keeping tabs on Alvarez," said Rosalia. "Apparently his foray into funding revolutionaries has been enough to raise his threat level."

"Well, that complicates matters," said Nikki, "but I don't trust the CIA." Mrs. M shot her a keen look that Nikki couldn't interpret. "They're not going to be interested in protecting Nina. They're only interested in her husband. We shouldn't abandon the mission."

"I concur," said Mrs. Merrivel, "which is why the mission is merely being suspended. We will use long-range surveillance to monitor the situation without engaging. We won't abandon Mrs. Alvarez."

Nikki frowned. It was a compromise and she didn't like it. She'd promised Nina that Carrie Mae would look after her. She didn't like breaking her promise.

"The other reason we've pulled the team in is that we have received news that just over thirty-six hours ago the Spanish prison of Puerto 1 experienced a prison break."

Camille's arms dropped to the arms of her chair, where her fingers curled over the sides in a white-knuckled grip.

"This has been reported by various sources, and we have independent confirmation from an agent on the ground. I also expect that the European news community will be reporting it shortly."

Camille made an abortive gesture, as if she wished to hurry Mrs. Merrivel along but reconsidered the wisdom of that maneuver.

"The files in front of you contain details of the escape, but in short, two men in a helicopter landed in the prison yard and used a grenade launcher to blow out a wall of the isolation units. Four men emerged from the cells. Three were shot by guards; one managed to make it to the helicopter and was transported from the scene. This touched off a riot inside the prison that the guards and Spanish army are still trying to put down."

"Who?" Camille was leaning forward, eyes wide. "The man who escaped, who was he?"

"Initial reports indicate that the escaped prisoner is Antonio Mergado Cano, the Basque separatist."

Camille went white, the color dropping from her face like a sheet from a work of art.

"I have to go," she said, standing up, two spots of red blossoming high on her cheeks.

"Sit down, Camille," said Mrs. M firmly.

"I have to go. My son is touring in Europe!"

"Kit is in no immediate danger. Sit down."

Camille sat down as if her knees had given out.

"For those of you unfamiliar with Mr. Cano, we have tangled with him before. He first crossed our path in 1977 as part of the Basque separatist movement, and he was also selling guns to the IRA. Mr. Cano used Carrie Mae cosmetics packaging to smuggle guns. Naturally we were a little upset about this, and thanks to Camille, he was put behind bars for the first time. I say for the first time since, over the last thirty years, Mr. Cano has proved to be something of an escape artist. This is his third escape from a European prison."

"Well, no offense to anyone, but why do we care?" asked Jenny. "I mean, he's obviously a bad man," she said hastily, as Camille looked ready to explode, "but it sounds like the proper authorities are handling it, so what's our interest?"

"He's a murderer!" snapped Camille.

"Mr. Cano has knowledge of Camille and the Carrie Mae Foundation," said Mrs. Merrivel calmly, ignoring Camille's outburst. "When Camille effected his last arrest, he made certain threats against Camille, her family, and the foundation. We are anxious that he not follow through on any of them. We also have a strong interest in making sure he doesn't share knowledge of our organization or members with any news sources."

"He's not going to get the chance," said Camille. "I've gotten him before." She looked around the table defiantly. "I can do it again. He is not going to hurt my son."

"No, he is not," said Mrs. Merrivel. "But you are needed here.

Nikki will be handling this." There was a stark silence in the room. It was the kind of silence that usually followed the sound of something expensive breaking.

"No," stated Camille at last. "Cano is too dangerous."

"Camille, I sympathize. But Nikki will eliminate Cano before he even gets near Kit. Your family will be in no danger." Nikki tried to hide her surprise; Mrs. M was making a lot of promises in her name. She hoped she could live up to it, and she wondered who this Kit was.

"What about the Nina Alvarez matter?" asked Rosalia, breaking in. "Our unit is fine with one-on-one extractions, relocations, and so forth, but an extended campaign against the head of a drug cartel is a little out of our league. I thought Nikki's team was going to help with that."

"Jenny and Ellen will be staying to coordinate and train with your team," said Mrs. M, pivoting slightly in her chair to focus on Rosalia. "Nikki will be heading to Europe, and Jane is scheduled for a required vacation."

"I don't need a vacation!" Jane said in protest.

"You haven't had more than two days off in a row for over a year, Jane," said Mrs. M. "It's company policy. Without needed time off, even the best of us can slip up."

"This really isn't a good time."

"In my experience it's never a good time." Mrs. M continued before Jane could object further. "Since the Alvarez matter is now in a reassessment phase, it's as good a time as any. Nikki will be proceeding to Europe."

"I should go with her," said Camille forcefully.

"Camille, you don't seem to realize that you are no longer a field agent," said Mrs. M. "Branch managers are not supposed to insert themselves into field operations, and in light of your recent decision-making skills in the field, I think we can all see why."

Camille went red again.

"Nikki isn't familiar with Cano," said Camille through gritted teeth, showing more self-control than Nikki had thought she was capable of. "I am."

"True. Which is why she will be reviewing your old reports. But I'm afraid that you are too emotionally involved to be objective and clearheaded. The matter is decided, Camille; I'm sorry. Nikki will be going to Spain."

COLOMBIA III

Clockwise Witness

Nikki fidgeted in the limo seat. It was now well into evening and she had the twitchy feeling of too much caffeine and not enough sleep. It had been a hard few weeks putting together the Nina Alvarez strike, and instead of having a well-deserved rest, she was on her way to the airport. On Christmas Eve, no less.

"I don't have a phone or any of my gear," Nikki said, pouting.

"Rachel will send you a care package. Until then you'll have to make do," said Mrs. Merrivel.

"I don't have the right clothes. I'm not packed for Spain in winter."

"You can buy whatever you need when you get there."

Nikki pictured the number of forms that purchasing an impromptu winter wardrobe on the company dime would require.

"Don't worry, I'll get everything approved," said Mrs. M, reading Nikki's expression.

"I don't like leaving Nina Alvarez alone with just the CIA," she said, knowing that she was repeating herself.

"Yes . . . about that," said Mrs. M, cocking her head slightly, "you didn't happen to mention Nina Alvarez to Z'ev, did you?"

This was a moment of choice—like a Choose Your Own Adventure book. Left or right. Tell the truth. Get Jane in trouble. Get them all in trouble. Lie. One little lie. Mrs. Merrivel was smiling. That was not a good sign.

"No," said Nikki. "Why would I do that?"

"We've been in place for two weeks with no hint of CIA involvement and then they suddenly drop out of the sky. Call me suspicious, but your abrupt breakup seemed interestingly timed to their arrival."

"He canceled vacation plans again," said Nikki. "What's the point of being with a guy who doesn't want to be with me?"

"Relationships and careers are hard to balance," said Mrs. Merrivel, nodding sadly. "Meanwhile, you'll at least have this new mission to take your mind off things."

Nikki was silent; she didn't want a new mission. She wanted to stay here. She searched her mind, trying to find other objections that would carry more weight than "I don't wanna."

"You know tomorrow's Christmas, right?"

"John has reminded me of that fact several times," said Mrs. M without looking up. Nikki felt a guilty pang. Mrs. Merrivel had been married for far longer than Nikki had been alive. Being separated on Christmas couldn't be easy for them. Mrs. Merrivel opened her briefcase and pulled out a thumb drive.

"Here are the old files on Camille and Cano. They include a dossier on her son, Kit, who I believe is gaining some notoriety as a singer."

"Do you think Cano is actually a threat to him?" asked Nikki.

"Cano has made very strong threats against Camille, and if he's aware of Kit then he would be a good means of hurting

Camille. I suggest reviewing the files on the plane; you'll understand more about Cano."

"She really seemed to hate him," said Nikki.

"I believe the feeling is mutual; he blames her for his abandonment by the Basques and IRA. He may have a point, I suppose. After he killed her husband, I believe she went out of her way to make sure he was persona non grata among the European separatist groups."

"Killed her husband? No wonder she wanted to come along."

"Yes, well, it's exactly why I didn't want her along. Camille has her good points, but she can be extremely emotional, particularly about her husband and Cano, and especially around this time of year."

"Anniversary of his death?" asked Nikki, and Mrs. Merrivel nodded.

"Some wounds never quite heal, and she loved Declan more than anything, even if he was IRA."

"Her husband was IRA?" asked Nikki, scandalized.

"You don't have a lot of room to talk, young lady," said Mrs. M tartly. "Between your CIA agent boyfriend and your unnatural insistence on keeping Val's name on the Consultants of Note plaque . . ."

"That's different! Val . . ." Nikki remembered Val falling toward the water, her face pale and her sleek, black hair puffing out as the wind caught it. Nikki trailed off, trying to capture the enigmatic, acerbic, capricious, and ultimately treacherous person that had been Valerie Robinson, her first and only partner at Carrie Mae. Val had been a hero to a lot of agents, and her betrayal of Carrie Mae for a man—a gun-smuggling slave trader no less—had left them all reeling. But somehow her death hadn't been satisfying to Nikki—she couldn't work up the righteous wrath. Val had helped her become a stronger person. "Val was different." Nikki finished lamely.

"Valerie was extremely different, on many different levels," Mrs. M said in agreement. "But my point is that pots should not call kettles black. It's best to reserve judgment until you know the whole situation."

"Mmm," said Nikki, deciding not to comment, since she had nothing nice to say. "What about Cano?" asked Nikki, changing the subject. "What's our goal? Kill or no kill?"

"Kill if you think it's necessary," said Mrs. Merrivel. "I would prefer to have him returned to the proper authorities. It would keep things so much tidier for us, but if the situation does not permit . . ." She shrugged to finish her sentence, and Nikki nodded. She was becoming used to these conversations. She had been issued case-dependent kill authorization not long ago, and it worried her. So far she hadn't had to use her authorization powers, but somehow that just made the tension of wondering which case and when it would be even worse. Being the decision maker on who lived or died was unpleasant. Her only safety net was Mrs. M, who made the decision on which cases she would be granted kill permission. She wondered if it bothered Mrs. Merrivel the same way or if it was something she had gotten used to.

"Aside from Camille," said Mrs. M, "I thought the team operated quite well."

"We're really starting to click," agreed Nikki enthusiastically. "And some of the Colombian agents were figuring it out, too. If we could just start training branch teams before an emergency mission comes up, things might go a little more smoothly."

"I know." Mrs. M nodded. "But the council has to be persuaded in increments. Assault teams were not in Carrie Mae Robart's vision for the foundation."

"With all due respect to the founder, she probably just couldn't envision a world full of terrorist cells and ridiculously powerful small arms."

"You're preaching to the choir," said Mrs. M drily. "We'll get there; you just have to keep the faith. In the meantime, I think this mission will be good for you."

"Every time you say that it never means what I think it means," said Nikki bitterly.

"I try to send all my girls where I think they can do their best," she said, smiling her Buddha smile, but Nikki frowned. "Everyone needs to get out of her routine periodically."

"Well, why can't I take Jenny and Ellen with me?"

"Besides their being needed here to keep an eye on Nina Alvarez and our CIA friends, I think it would be good to split up the team for a bit. Doesn't do to get too complacent."

Nikki eyed Mrs. M suspiciously. She trusted Mrs. M—she really did—but the longer they worked together, the more Nikki started to think of her as a clock: a clear, easy-to-read face, but inside, so many little gears and cogs whirring away in a much more complicated process.

"Oh," said Mrs. M as Nikki exited the car. "Be sure and call your mother before too long, hmm? We don't want another incident like in the Congo, do we?"

Nikki blushed. Besides being known as the agent who had brought down Val Robinson, she was also known as the agent whose mother called the cops if she went undercover for too long.

"Yes, Mrs. M," she muttered, and hurried into the airport, wondering if Mrs. M knew. She couldn't know. It wasn't as if they'd done it on purpose.

COLOMBIA IV

How It All Went Down

It had started innocently enough. Six months into dating Z'ev she'd started to feel the ping of guilt each time she lied to him about work. With no clear thoughts on the matter, she'd turned to her sounding board.

"I'm thinking about telling Z'ev," she'd said as they sat on their bags, waiting for a bus.

"You can't," said Jenny, fanning herself with the useless Bolivian bus schedule. "It's totally against the rules. If Mrs. M got wind, your ass would be in the crapper in no time."

"I know," said Nikki, "but I hate lying to him all the time."

"Do you think you can trust him?" asked Ellen, dabbing her cleavage with a damp handkerchief.

"No, she can't trust him!" exclaimed Jane.

"You sound like my mother," said Nikki disparagingly.

"Do you think this bus is ever going to show?" asked Jenny.

"Relax—the mission's over," said Nikki. "We're not in a hurry."

"Yeah, I thought you Southerners didn't mind a slower pace of life," said Ellen, her eyes twinkling at Jenny over the top of her sunglasses.

"If there was a patch of shade and a mint julep, the bus could be as slow as it liked," Jenny shot back. "Meanwhile, I think you could fry an egg on this road."

"You're not the one wearing all black," said Jane. "I think my eyeliner's melting, and this heat cannot be good for my computer." Jane was wearing a recently purchased fedora-like hat resembling those worn by the traditional Uros women. She looked like a Goth Frank Sinatra.

"I told you not to wear pencil liner in this heat," said Jenny. "And Nikki didn't answer the question. Do you think you can trust him?"

Her three friends stared, waiting for her reply. Nikki bit her lip.

"I want to trust him," she said at last.

"Not good enough," said Jane, shaking her head. "You can't trust boys."

"That is ridiculous," objected Nikki. "That's just like saying women can't do math or any other misogynistic nonsense. We have to start judging people as individuals."

"I hate to agree with our resident feminazi," said Ellen, "but Jane's right. It's not good enough to want to trust him. If you were going to break the rules . . ."

"Which I do not advise," said Jenny, interjecting.

"You have to be absolutely certain," finished Ellen.

"Well, isn't it an act of faith at some point?" objected Nikki. "I mean, how am I supposed to be absolutely certain?"

But she'd wanted to be certain, and a few months later, back in California, she had felt a surge of confidence when Z'ev finally made vacation plans for the two of them.

"We're going on vacation!" said Nikki. "To Mexico, over Christmas."

Jenny stopped rummaging in Nikki's fridge and looked over the door.

"What? Again?"

"Can't be again," said Ellen. "They haven't actually been yet."

"Didn't you lose your deposit last time he canceled?" asked Jane. "I would have been soooo pissed." Kickboxing class had evolved into nacho night at Nikki's place.

"He paid me back," snapped Nikki, irritation coloring her voice. "And this time, he's the one who asked me. He wouldn't cancel his own plans, right?"

"You want to listen to yourself on that statement, hon?" asked Jenny from inside the fridge. "Is this ground turkey still good?"

"Should be. I just bought it a couple of days ago," said Nikki, leaning over the door to see what Jenny was digging into.

"Yeah, why should his plans be more important than plans you've made?" asked Jane, rinsing lettuce in the sink.

"I've been thinking about the 'tell him' issue," said Ellen, taking out a pan.

"We're calling it the Big Reveal," said Jane. "Like a makeover show." Ellen snorted.

"Okay, the Big Reveal. What you need is a test."

"A test?" repeated Nikki skeptically.

"You need to tell—sorry, reveal—some secret, and if he tells his company then you'll know."

"That dog might hunt," said Jenny, looking thoughtful.

"I don't know," said Nikki uneasily. "I don't have any secret—other than my job."

"I'm sure we could come up with something that the CIA would be interested in," said Jane. "I think you should do it."

"What happened to 'I hate men'?" asked Nikki, laughing.

"I don't hate them," protested Jane. "I just happen to think that, as a group, they're unreliable. But you've been upset about this for a while, and I can see how having a relationship where one of you is being honest and the other isn't could impair things a bit. There's got to be a solution. So, if you think you can trust him, maybe you ought to put him through some sort of beta testing. It's only logical."

"Thanks, Mr. Spock, but the fatal flaw with the theory is, what would be a secret that I, the charity foundation employee, could plausibly know?"

The girls looked thoughtful as the smell of sizzling meat filled the air.

"Well, I'm not coming up with anything, I'll admit," said Jane, opening drawers randomly. "But I still think it's worth considering. Where's your cheese grater?"

Two months later in Colombia, and only two days away from her promised vacation, Nikki was having doubts. She hadn't shared them with the girls, but privately she had decided against the test. Ellen and Jenny quietly let the subject drop, but Jane had apparently not forgotten the idea.

"I've got it," said Jane, her voice tinny in Nikki's earpiece.

"Got what?" murmured Nikki, looking through binoculars into the Alvarez compound.

"How to beta-test Z'ev," answered Jane.

"Oh, for crying out loud," said Nikki. "I'm not going to test Z'ev! It doesn't make sense! I promise I won't tell him about Carrie Mae, but we're just going to have a nice vacation, OK?"

"But I've got the perfect idea!"

Nikki sighed, knowing that Jane would just keep bringing it up till she listened.

"What's the idea, Jane?"

"Tell him about Nina Alvarez. No, this could work," she continued, overriding Nikki's squawk of outrage. "Tell him she's a foundation contributor who wants to leave her husband, but her husband is a drug kingpin who finances revolutionaries. Then tell him not to tell."

"That won't work. Alvarez is totally a DEA case; we've been ducking them for weeks," said Nikki.

"Just tell him about the fact that he's funding revolutionaries that could potentially destabilize the entire region," said Jane blithely, clearly having thought of everything.

"No," said Nikki, annoyed at herself for leaving Jane room to argue. "Besides, if the CIA got involved it would put Nina at risk."

"You're extracting her on Thursday," said Jane. "The CIA can't move that fast, particularly if they have to do a smash-up with the DEA. So if he gives you up, then they'll be there after we're gone, and if he doesn't then you have a perfectly nice vacation."

"It's an ongoing Carrie Mae investigation," said Nikki firmly. "It's too risky. There's no way I'm going to tell him about that."

Later that night, Nikki had nearly forgotten about Jane's idea when Z'ev called.

"Hey, Z'ev!" said Nikki, picking up Z'ev's call. Jane was in the shower, and Jenny and Ellen had gone for ice. It had been two weeks of nearly constant drills, but the Colombian team was finally ready, and with extraction set for forty-eight hours and counting Nikki had decided everyone could use an early night.

"Hey, babe," said Z'ev, a smile clear in his voice. "You all packed for Mexico?"

"Sure," said Nikki. "I packed today. I bought a swimsuit."

He chuckled. "You're going to pack like you usually do, aren't you?" he asked. "Throw everything in a bag the morning of your flight."

"Gee, Mom, maybe I should pack like you?" Nikki asked sarcastically as Jane exited the shower, humming.

"No, that would take all the entertainment value out of it for me," said Z'ev. Jenny and Ellen returned to the room, laughing at some joke.

"Tell Jenny your theory again," Ellen called out to Jane. "I'm not sure I got that right."

"Is that the girls?" asked Z'ev.

"Yeah, we're all going to aerobics in a minute," said Nikki, moving past Jane and heading for the patio, where it would be quieter. Z'ev thought she was still in California and she saw no reason to disabuse him of the notion.

"Oh!" exclaimed Jane as Nikki opened the sliding door. "I think Nikki should tell Z'ev about Nina Alvarez!"

Nikki froze and pivoted back to Jane, her eyes wide, praying that Z'ev hadn't heard Jane's comment. Jenny and Ellen froze, seeing Nikki's expression.

"Who's Nina Alvarez?" asked Z'ev, his voice echoing from the phone into the silent room. Jane went white and clapped both hands over her mouth.

"Oh!" said Nikki, and laughed. It almost sounded real. "Jane just has an overactive imagination. One of our foundation contributors is South American. Jane is convinced she's married to a drug kingpin."

"Probably," said Z'ev callously. "Why does Jane want me to know about him?"

"We think she wants to leave her husband. Jane, of course, made up some wild fantasy about his being an antigovernment revolutionary and thinks you should arrange to save her. It's all irrelevant anyway. Her donations are supposed to be confidential; I really shouldn't be discussing this with you at all."

"Nikki, you haven't been discussing my . . . business, have you?"

"No!" said Nikki, as if that was the farthest thing from the truth and she was shocked that he would say such a thing. "I told them what I told my mom—you work for the state department doing human rights stuff."

"Nikki . . ."

"No, seriously, I haven't said a thing. It's not my fault Jane thinks you're Superman."

"Well, OK," said Z'ev.

Twenty minutes later, Nikki finally eased her way out of the conversation. Jane was sitting on the bed in tears.

"I thought you were talking to your mom!" she wailed. "I came out of the bathroom and you said, 'Gee, Mom.'"

"Even if I was talking to my mom, how does that make it OK to bring up a mission?" said Nikki, trying to calmly express her anger, without yelling. She wanted to explode.

"It doesn't," sobbed Jane. "I just . . . I wasn't thinking." Jenny hugged their friend and grimaced at Nikki over Jane's head.

"Do you think he's going to investigate?" asked Jenny.

"I don't think so," said Nikki cautiously. "He was more worried that I'd been discussing his job with all of you. With any luck he'll forget all about it. But let's just keep this between the four of us, huh?"

"No worries there," said Ellen. "I don't really feel like getting fired."

COLOMBIA V

Devil May Care

On the plane, Nikki saw that the usual menagerie of grumpy airline passengers had been replaced with a surprisingly numerous and cheerful crowd of vacationers and last-minute homeward-bound commuters. Even the stewardesses were smiling more genuinely and wearing jaunty Santa caps. With every happy face, Nikki found her own mood worsening. The prospect of a thirteen-hour flight made the looming post-breakup blues seem even worse. She didn't want to be here, and she resented everyone who did. She wished Mrs. M had let Camille take the mission; then she could have at least crawled home to her mother.

She rejected the complimentary eggnog and yanked down the shade as they rose above the clouds and into bright sunshine. Ignoring Mrs. M's directive to review the files, she wrestled the provided blanket into place, punched the pillow, and tried to sleep, eventually nodding off. She shook her head as she awoke, trying to clear it, and tossed off the now too-warm airline blanket. The boisterous holiday spirit had cooled somewhat—a natural reaction to being cooped in a flying metal sausage with limited leg room. Nikki felt her own spirits take a perverse lift as she looked around at her companions' now dismal expressions.

Giving a self-satisfied yawn and stretch, Nikki reached for the remote control connected to her armrest and turned on the TV embedded in the back of the seat in front of her. Flipping through the channels, she found an American blockbuster that she hadn't wanted to see the first time around, a Euro art-house flick, a string of Christmas specials from various sitcoms, and a rotating schedule of entertainment news, interviews, and music videos.

None of the channels holding her interest, Nikki left the TV on the music video channel and pulled her laptop from under her seat and flipped it on, plugging in the thumb drive Mrs. M had given her. She stared out the window as it booted, dimly aware of the music videos still playing on the TV.

Nikki restlessly flipped through the files on the drive, feeling vaguely like a voyeur. Pictures of a much younger Camille smiling with her arm wrapped around a beefy Irishman went past. She didn't want to know about Camille's past. She didn't really even want to know about Camille in the present. With a sigh, she dug into a section that had Cano's name in it.

"In an attempt to form alliances with other terrorist groups, the Basque separatist Antonio Cano has approached the IRA through Declan O'Deirdan and his brother, Matthew. The consultant Camille Masters believes Cano to be the leader of the group using Carrie Mae packaging to smuggle weapons. The consultant continues her mission with the IRA but believes that we should develop an independent profile of Cano. Consultant Masters believes that O'Deirdan is becoming disenchanted with the IRA. Next meeting is scheduled for . . ."

The dry tone of the intel officer's report left a lot of information between the lines. Why was Declan becoming disenchanted? In retrospect, with the knowledge that he and Camille would be married, the answer was obvious. But the report writer hadn't seemed to know or care. Jane would never have posted a report like that.

Nikki flipped back to Camille's service record. The marriage was included. There was the record of Declan's death. A yearlong hiatus for Camille followed it.

"Declan O'Deirdan, former IRA, and Consultant Masters pursued Cano to his home country of Spain. Receiving a tip-off, Consultant Masters attempted to corner Cano at an abandoned farmhouse on the road to Aramaio."

"'On the road to' . . . ," muttered Nikki in disgust. Where was the address? The GPS coordinates?

"Mr. O'Deirdan was already at the farmhouse when the consultant arrived. Initial reports suggest that Mr. O'Deirdan may have arranged the meeting. Consultant Masters currently rejects this conclusion."

Nikki rolled her eyes.

"Cano refused to surrender, and when Consultant Masters attempted to effect arrest, Cano blew up the farmhouse, killing three of his own men, as well as Declan O'Deirdan, and severely injuring Consultant Masters. Consultant Masters was removed to a nearby hospital for medical care. Mr. O'Deirdan's body was returned home to Ireland."

The report was unsatisfying. She could understand Camille's grudge against Cano, but it didn't really explain how Cano had knowledge of Camille or her family. At the thought of family, Nikki frowned. Reopening Camille's service record, she scanned down the page until she found the section she was looking for—

the section on Declan. There was a picture of Camille and Declan in their IRA days, all woolen sweaters and AK-47s.

Next of Kin: Christopher (Kit) Masters—son
Tessa E. O'Deirdan—mother
Matthew D. O'Deirdan—brother, location unknown

The picture for Christopher showed him in an overly posed publicity shot of a boy band. Nikki shook her head and chewed her lip, pondering the vagaries of Camille's file. She wondered if Camille had made her son's surname Masters to protect Kit from Cano or to protect him from his family's past.

Beyond her computer screen music videos were still playing. She focused on the TV, her attention snared by the flashing colors. She'd never heard the song before, but the video had all the hallmarks of a big pop hit. The singer was wearing a wicked red suit and walking down a flight of stairs—a hip-hop version of "New York, New York." Dancing girls slinked after him dressed in skimpy red leather outfits and wearing horns.

The scene cut away to a backstage area, the camera zooming across roadies and a door that had a star with the words KIT MASTERS printed on it. Startled, Nikki plugged in her headphones. The scene cut back to the music video.

The camera zoomed in as the refrain started, and the singer turned a pair of startlingly blue eyes to the camera and winked.

"The devil may care," he sang, "but I don't."

He had a generous mouth that curved into a roguish smile, and Nikki felt an answering smile tug at her own lips. It was hard to resist someone who was having that much fun. Nikki scrutinized the singer. He had a boyish face, round nose, mischievous eyes, and that flashing smile that was more cute than handsome. Nikki squinted, covering half of his face with her hand; he did look sort of like Camille.

"Welcome, everyone," said a voice-over as dancing girls shook their groove thing, "as TransAir goes behind the scenes at the Kit Masters Hotel Hell tour."

You say you're gonna leave,
But I know you won't,
Sweet sin, slipping in,
The devil may care, but I don't.

"With *UNCUT Magazine* calling him the next big thing," said the voice-over, "Kit Masters is poised to leave his boy band roots behind and become the biggest star in Europe."

Nikki's eyebrows rose in disbelief. She would never have believed in Camille's ability to produce a charismatic pop star, but the proof was singing to her from the TV screen. She tried to picture Camille as a proud stage mom and utterly failed. In all their interactions, Camille had come across as extremely derisive of anything remotely related to popular culture. She'd actually chided one of the other agents for watching YouTube on her lunch break.

The camera panned the backstage area again. It was clearly stock footage that had been re-edited for the convenience of the airline. Roadies were running around; the band milled about their instruments like racehorses waiting for the starting gates. They were studies in stereotypes. As if someone had put together a band from a checklist.

Item: one crazy drummer—check. He wore a Union Jack wrestling singlet and had dyed his hair into leopard spots. He wore Doc Martens over knee-high Pippi Longstocking striped socks and seemed happy about it. Nikki watched as he beat out a rhythm on a stagehand, then on the stage, then on the keyboard, until the keyboardist pushed him away.

Item: one heroin-thin guitarist—check. This one topped off his gelled coiffure with a tiara and wore a torn Def Leppard T-shirt over his tight black multizippered pants and enormous boots. He was smoking and slouching insolently over his guitar, in the union-approved pose of guitarists everywhere.

Item: one slightly dorky but trying-for-chic keyboard player—check. Looking straight out of an eighties video, he wore a skinny tie and button-up shirt with the shirtsleeves rolled up, and a fedora pulled down low over one eye. He was running his fingers over the keys nervously, as if afraid that Crazy Drummer had injured them.

Item: one silent but funky bass player—check. They had gone against type here and cast a black woman. She had a couple swirls of glitter on the left side of her face, but the rest of her costume consisted of a white tank top and pair of well-used jeans over flip-flops. Her funkitude was all in her accessories: a devil-horn headband was wedged into her long braids, and she sported a heavy silver cuff on one wrist and a reggae-colored sweatband on the other. She had a second sweatband farther up that same arm, and Nikki realized that these were on her playing arm and were probably useful rather than stylish.

The final item—sexy backup singers—had been assembled in fine style. The girls were wearing red leather skirts and thigh-high boots. Horns had been attached to their heads, possibly with super glue, and much of their exposed bits had been covered in red body paint. Nikki watched as they ran through a few of their moves; she wondered if they got paid as much as the rest of the band. Probably not.

Nikki sighed and rubbed her temples. So much for Cano being unable to locate Camille's son; this guy had gone and put himself in a giant spotlight—literally. They had probably even heard of him in a prison like Puerto 1. She had been planning to hit the ground running in Germany. Connect with the local consultants. Track Cano to wherever he was going and figure out how to bring him down. Angrily, she yanked the headphones out of her ears. She couldn't afford to split her efforts trying to protect a rock star. Why hadn't Mrs. M emphasized how popular he was? No wonder Camille was beside herself.

Nikki leaned back in her seat and closed her eyes. This was definitely not the way she had planned to spend her Christmas. Of course, she also hadn't planned on spending her Christmas on a plane. She had planned on spending it with Z'ev, and now she wasn't at home and she wasn't with Z'ev. She pictured the way his brown eyes crinkled up when she made him laugh and felt homesick. She wondered if this was what it meant to be grown-up—wanting things that didn't exist anymore. On second thought, it probably wasn't being grown-up; it was probably just being old.

She opened her eyes again and looked at Kit Masters. He finished his song with a wink of his ice-blue eye and the video blanked out. He didn't look like the kind of person who let real life push him around. He looked like someone who took on the world headfirst and laughing. She envied that.

"Rock star . . . ," she muttered to herself. Rock stars were the kind of people who had security. They had paid babysitters on staff. She turned back to the computer and skimmed his file. She raised an eyebrow over a few drug/alcohol arrests for various kinds of mischief but relaxed at the detail that he did indeed have security. Relieved, she shut down the computer, promising herself that she'd review the files more carefully later. For now, she wouldn't let Kit Masters change her plans. She had to keep her eye on the objective—Cano.

GERMANY I

Your Time Is Gonna Come

December 26

Nikki slung her backpack over her shoulder and pulled her inadequate cardigan more tightly around her. The digital clock told her that it was December 26 and seven PM. She had managed to miss Christmas.

At the Barcelona airport, she'd been met by an excited young agent with a message from Mrs. M. Cano had been spotted crossing into Germany. She was to go directly from Barcelona to Berlin and meet a German operative named Astriz Liebenz. So much for seeing Spain.

The layover had taken hours, and her first flight had been canceled. Not many people flew on Christmas Day. Once again her career as a superspy seemed slightly less than advertised. James Bond never had to wait for a layover. But what was she supposed to do? Even if she rented a car and drove straight through, where was she going? Without intel, the safest thing to do was stick to the plan. Once in Berlin, she'd found a message waiting for her from Astriz Liebenz. The message politely assured Nikki that, while picking her up was of utmost priority, due to circumstances out of human control she was not to be picked up until 7 PM. Nikki had crumpled the note up and thrown it in the garbage can. Astriz might as well have written, "I'm busy doing my job and will get to you when I've got time."

She'd ended up calling her mother and getting the answering machine. The cell phone had also gone to voice mail. Either her mother was *that* mad or she had gone to visit Grandma. Cell reception was weak on Grandma's farm, since the neighbors (all two of them) had rejected an offer to put up a cell tower. With nothing else to do, she spent the time playing solitaire and trying, unsuccessfully, to not think about Z'ev.

The sliding glass doors of the Stuttgart airport opened on a sleetish rain covering the world in dirty film and admitted a gust of cold wind into the airport that broke Nikki from her thoughts of Z'ev, warm California nights, and salsa at Club Caliente. Daylight had long ago faded from the sky. She was definitely going to hold Mrs. M to her promise about approving any winter wardrobe purchases. A newer-model Mercedes pulled into a cab space and a woman got out, giving the European two-fingered salute to a cabbie who had the nerve to comment. Taking a deep breath, Nikki walked out into the elements; this had to be her ride.

"Nicole?" said the woman, surveying her uncertainly.

"Astriz?" replied Nikki. There was a silent moment where they measured each other, and then the woman nodded. She was about thirty-five and wore a pair of black slacks with suspenders over a crisp white button-up shirt. A beige trench coat, black driving gloves, and newsboy cap completed the ensemble. Her blond hair shot out from under the cap in defiant spikes.

"This way," Astriz said, jerking her head at the car.

"You're not what I expected," said Astriz in German-accented English once they were on the road.

"Well, I'm sure you were expecting someone with a coat," said Nikki, holding her fingers in front of the heater. She knew what was coming next, but she was hoping to avoid it.

"Heh, yes," said Astriz, lighting a long thin cigarette and cracking the driver's-side window an inch. "But also, I thought you would be taller and perhaps a little older." She blew smoke out the side of her mouth toward the open window and cranked the heat with one hand. "I worked with Valerie once, you know?" the woman said.

"No," said Nikki, pausing slightly, "I didn't."

"She nearly got me killed."

"She shot me in the chest," said Nikki, trying to keep her tone neutral. "Twice."

"Then it is probably a good thing she is gone," said Astriz with a laugh.

Nikki shrugged and continued to rub her hands together over the vent.

"But, uh, I hear you made them keep her name on the wall?" Astriz glanced at her sidelong, only taking her eyes off the road for a second.

Nikki leaned back in her seat. Talking about Val was one of her least favorite things. But she was getting used to this particular conversation. Val had been the stuff of legend, and the circumstances of her death had spread like wildfire through Carrie Mae. Astriz wasn't the first person to think Nikki would be taller or older.

"I don't think how she died should negate how she lived," said Nikki.

"She wasn't always bad," said Astriz, a little sadly.

"Not always," agreed Nikki.

"But she wasn't always very good either," said Astriz, suddenly grinning at her. "If we have time, we will drink to her memory and spit on her grave for the number of times she punched us in the face!"

"That might be a lot," said Nikki.

"Yes!" exclaimed Astriz.

"We have a job to do first," said Nikki, laughing.

"Ah, yes, Cano. I was surprised that they sent you. It is a European problem."

"He has a violent history," said Nikki. "I have training in how to handle such cases."

"Ah, the young American hotshot." Astriz seemed gleeful to have a label to put on Nikki.

"Just looking to help," said Nikki self-deprecatingly. "Tell me about Cano."

"A strange man. Doesn't he know that the Basques are out? It is the Muslims who are in right now."

"I don't think terrorists think of themselves as a fad," said Nikki dryly, and Astriz shrugged.

"Well, Cano might not, but the old associate he contacted last night in Villingen certainly did. Wilmer has a niece who is with us. Wilmer's statement was that he was too old for that sort of nonsense. He sent Cano farther up the road just to get him out of his house."

"Where did he send him?"

"To another 'old friend' who might have a 'project' that Cano would like. A Gypsy named Voges. Our operative arrived just in time to see Cano leaving the Voges' abode."

"Abode?" repeated Nikki, struck by the word.

"'Abode' is not right?" asked Astriz, looking faintly embarrassed.

"No, it's fine. Just unusual," said Nikki, sorry she'd brought it up. Astriz shrugged and took a long drag of her cigarette. "Do we know where Cano was heading?"

Astriz shook her head. "Voges and a house full of his family are too much for a single agent to take on. But we have a tail on Cano now."

"Seems like you've got a handle on the situation."

"*Ja,*" said Astriz in agreement.

"That's great. I'm really just here to support your efforts." It was a bullshit statement. She was there to get the job done, and they both knew it, but it was the kind of thing to say when you were trying not to pee on someone else's tree. "Do you have a sniper?"

"Er, no. The Stuttgart branch is not equipped for assassinations." Astriz looked embarrassed again, and a little irritated this time. "The closest sniper is Paris."

"OK," said Nikki, feeling a pang of the old frustration. Carrie Mae just wasn't equipped for twenty-first-century badness. "Well, in that case, what's your plan for containment?"

A sour expression crossed Astriz's face. She didn't like being questioned.

"We were thinking . . . car accident," said Astriz, spreading her hand out over the words 'car accident,' as if to give them a special glow. "I've got a girl who's good with explosives. We just have to locate his vehicle."

"OK," said Nikki. That was more like it.

There was an electronic burble, and Astriz plucked her phone from the cupholder, driving now with her cigarette hand. They were pulling off the freeway now into an industrial-looking area. In the distance, a sports stadium loomed.

"*Ja?*" There was a pause and some chatter from the other end. "Oh? Uh . . . *Ja.*" Astriz frowned, shaking her head, and extended the phone to Nikki. "It's for you."

For a second, Nikki held out hope that Z'ev had managed to track her down, then she put the phone to her ear.

"Nikki?" said Jane's hopeful voice.

"Jane?" answered Nikki, perplexed. Then she started to think of all the reasons that an on-vacation Jane would call her. None of them were good. "Jane, is something wrong?"

"I . . . I . . ." Jane was stumbling over her words. Nikki's hand tightened on the phone.

"Jane, what's wrong?" She tried to keep her voice flat and neutral, so as not to add additional panic to the situation.

"I had to call," said Jane. "I had to apologize. This is all my fault! We're being punished because I couldn't keep my big mouth shut."

"Jane," said Nikki, relaxing. "You've apologized enough already. It's not your fault. I mean, you didn't intend for the CIA to show up and we don't even know it's because of you anyway. We're not being punished."

"Then why did Mrs. Merrivel break up the team?" demanded Jane. "Why did she make me go on vacation?"

"Vacation isn't a punishment," said Nikki reasonably.

"I'm on a beach!" wailed Jane. "I'm on a beach and I hate it. I don't tan! I'm Goth."

"So go to a Goth club and mosh out to some angry metal music or something."

"You have no clue what Goth is, do you?" asked Jane.

"Sure I do," said Nikki. "They wear a lot of black and think the world is pointless?"

Jane sighed in apathetic disgust. "It's a lot more than that."

"OK, so go do something Goth-y then. You're on vacation!" Nikki tried to sound cheerful.

"Why? The world is pointless," retorted Jane bitterly. Nikki laughed.

"Jane, I would love to help you find something to do, or at least point out that I've seen you wear brown and even jeans sometimes, but I'm in Stuttgart. We've got a lock on Cano and we're going to try to put him down before he hurts anyone."

"Stuttgart?" said Jane, suddenly perking up. "What's the date over there? You should go to the Kit Masters concert!"

"You listen to Kit Masters?" asked Nikki, surprised.

"Er . . . no. I mean, maybe some of my friends in the European branches sent me a song or two. I looked him up when we started working with Camille."

"Uh-huh. I don't think he's very Goth, Jane."

"Whatever," said Jane with a sniff.

"Yeah, whatever," said Nikki, smiling. "Look, I've got to go."

"No, wait," said Jane. "Don't you think you could use some help? Don't you definitely need to send for your intel officer?"

"Sorry, Jane," said Nikki. "You're just going to have to sit on that beach a while longer."

"Whatever," said Jane gloomily. "Bye."

"Bye. Enjoy yourself!"

"Be careful!" said Jane as Nikki hung up.

"Your friend wanted to chat?" asked Astriz with a hint of sarcasm, taking the phone.

"My intel officer. She doesn't want to be on vacation," explained Nikki. Astriz raised a questioning eyebrow; Nikki shrugged. Explaining Jane, the CIA, and Z'ev to Astriz was last on her to-do list, especially since it would turn into defending Jane rather than explaining.

The phone rang again; this time Astriz checked the number before answering it and Nikki pulled her mind back to the present.

"*Ja?*" There was some chatter on the other end, and Astriz nodded.

"Wir sind fast am Ziel," she said, and paused again. *"Ja. Ja, ja,* bye." She hung up and looked at Nikki. "Almost there. Cano is in a café near the stadium. I have a surveillance post set up."

Nikki thought they had been driving at a good rate of speed but felt her head jerk back as Astriz put her foot down on the accelerator. She took a sidelong look at Astriz, her long cigarette and driving gloves, and nodded to herself. What was she? Six, seven years younger than Val? Just young enough to think Val was the coolest agent ever when they had met. Nikki didn't blame her; she remembered the feeling. But sitting next to the German woman, it was clear to Nikki that Val had shaped Astriz just as much as she had shaped Nikki. She wondered if Astriz was aware of it; then she shook her head. It didn't matter; it just meant that Nikki was going to have to be careful. Val would never have welcomed a foreigner on her turf.

Astriz wound her way through an industrial neighborhood, slowing as they neared their destination. Down side streets, Nikki could see the bulk of the Gottlieb-Daimler-Stadion. And as Astriz parked the car, Nikki realized that they must be in the kind of commercial area that sprang up around stadiums and mostly catered to fans of one variety or another.

"This way," said Astriz, leading her toward a corner building, her trench coat billowing behind her. Nikki buttoned her cardigan, shivering. First chance she got, she was going to buy a jacket.

They were entering an office building that appeared to be closed. Astriz breezed past the janitors and headed for the back stairs. Nikki followed Astriz upstairs to a conference room, where what looked to be an espionage picnic was laid out for them. Binoculars, a mark-7 remote listening device, two sandwiches, and a thermos sat on the table.

"Loni is kind," said Astriz, smiling at the sandwiches. "What do you see?" she asked as Nikki picked up the binoculars.

"Mmm . . ." Nikki scanned the café, looking for Cano. "Got him! Corner booth. He's with someone." The signage from the café obscured the head of Cano's dining partner, but Nikki saw that both their hands were resting clearly on the tabletop, where no sudden moves could be made.

"He's got backup," said Astriz, pointing away from the coffee shop to a building kitty-corner from the office building. A man leaned against a wall by a bike rack, smoking. Nikki nodded and went back to Cano.

"Do you have any idea who he's meeting?" asked Nikki, handing the binoculars to Astriz.

"We think it's a contact from Voges," answered Astriz, zooming in on the pair across the street. "Voges is a fixer; he can supply anything for a fee—guns, mercenaries, new identity, money. Whatever Cano's planning, Voges can help him set it up. I can't make anything out." Astriz handed the binoculars back and Nikki refocused them to take another look, scrutinizing the table. Cano was easy enough to identify from his pictures. He had a suntanned complexion, a scar across his left eye, and a wild shock of black hair. His hands were wide, hirsute, and the knuckles were flattened and scarred. The other person had smaller hands, one of which was clenched around a cell phone; the other held a plastic-looking rectangle. He, or she, Nikki couldn't be sure, was dressed in a gray jogging suit.

"The other person is holding something in one of his hands," said Astriz.

"I'm trying to figure that out now. It has a picture of a devil on it," said Nikki, squinting and trying to get a closer look at the plastic card in the hands of the gray-suited figure.

"A devil?" repeated Astriz. "What's that got to do . . . oh *scheisse*." Nikki heard the thump of Astriz's fist on the glass and refocused the binoculars. Across the street, a woman on a motorcycle revved the engine.

"It's Camille," said Nikki, recognizing the woman as she pulled on a helmet and flipped the visor down. Together they watched as Camille drove straight through the plate-glass window at the front of the café.

Nikki pounded down the stairs, Astriz behind her. Her thoughts tripped through her head, colliding with each other before leaving. She didn't have a gun. She never told Z'ev that she loved him. Astriz had better have a gun. Camille was going to get them all killed.

They exited onto the street in time to see Cano's backup charging into the café, gun drawn, and from the back of the café Nikki could see the person in the gray jogging suit, hood now up, running down the street. Astriz hesitated, clearly torn.

"I've got the contact," yelled Nikki. "You go after Cano, and for God's sake, get Camille out of here!" Astriz gave her a thumbs-up and ran toward the café.

Nikki sprinted after the gray tracksuit. The dark streets were the perfect cover, and Nikki could only catch glimpses of the person whenever they were illuminated by an errant streetlight or pair of headlights. Dodging cars, Nikki slid on the wet, slushy pavement and rounded a corner, just in time to see her quarry scramble over a chain-link fence.

Swarming over the fence, Nikki dropped down, seconds behind Tracksuit, in a parking lot. The enormous bulk of the stadium squatted across the asphalt from her, looming over the packed parking lot. There was a dull thrumming in her ears and she shook her head, only then realizing it was the sound of music emanating from the stadium. Tracksuit had ceased to dodge and weave; he was now in a full-out sprint for the back of the stadium. Nikki gave chase, sweat pouring down her face.

Tracksuit dodged some roadies and ran up a ramp leading to an intake bay. A large security guard lumbered into view as Tracksuit flew past.

"Hey!" he yelled, apparently not seeing Tracksuit but spotting Nikki right off. He was a large man, standing a good six feet, six inches tall, with a neck thicker than his head and hands the size of dinner plates. Nikki dove under one of his meaty paws, but he was quicker than he looked and managed to make contact with the other, sending her crashing to the floor. Spinning onto her back, Nikki took aim at his groin and thumped her foot upward. The security guard grimaced and hesitated before falling to one knee. He was hardly out for the count, but it was all the time Nikki needed to get back up and send a roundhouse kick whistling into the side of his head. Continuing forward without waiting to see the results, she heard the crash and smiled as the security guard hit the floor behind her. Someone yelled for her to stop, but she was already running. She didn't have time to turn around and look.

Turning a corner, she was faced with a crowd of roadies and backup dancers.

"Gray tracksuit, which way?" she yelled. There were a handful of startled stares. "Which way!" yelled Nikki again. A half-naked girl in devil horns and body paint pointed left. Nikki ran left through a door and stopped. The cavernous room was packed with clothing and makeup; it was a disaster zone of nooks and crannies and had no visible exit. There was a groan from the floor to her left, and Nikki saw a pair of legs emerging from under a toppled chair.

Nikki moved the chair and found herself staring into the woozy blue eyes of an older woman with huge bouffant hair. She was also wearing an older-model Carrie Mae necklace. Rachel had one displayed in her lab. It was the first 100 percent reliable knockout-gas model—a real breakthrough in Carrie Mae technology.

"Whahappen?" asked the woman, rubbing her head.

"I'm with Carrie Mae," said Nikki, speaking rapidly. "Is there a way out of this room?"

"Carrie . . . Did Camille send you?" The older woman's face brightened at the idea.

"What? No. Is there another way out?"

"The back door," said the woman, pointing vaguely. "But, why . . ."

Nikki dropped the woman and pushed her way through the racks of costumes. Sure enough, a back door stood open, revealing the expanse of backstage area. Tracksuit was nowhere in sight.

GERMANY II

Maxwell's Silver Hammer

"Bastard piece of shit!" exclaimed Nikki. It was one of Z'ev's favorite swear phrases.

"I don't think that's appropriate Carrie Mae language, dear," said the woman, peering over Nikki's shoulder.

Nikki pivoted slowly to look at the woman.

"Who are you?" she demanded, thinking of a few other examples of un–Carrie Mae–like language.

"I'm Trista," said the woman, patting absentmindedly at her towering hair. "Who are you? What are you doing here if Camille didn't send you?"

"I'm asking the questions," snapped Nikki. "What's your mission?"

"I'm not on a mission," said Trista primly. "I retired from Carrie Mae. I'm now the head makeup artist to Kit Masters."

"Son of a bi—"

"Young lady!" exclaimed Trista. "I just do not know what is

happening in Carrie Mae these days that they would hire women who use that kind of language."

Nikki took a deep breath and counted to ten.

"What concert is this? Where am I?"

"It's the Hotel Hell tour," answered Trista. "Kit Masters?" she added when Nikki's expression tightened.

"Kit Masters, Camille Masters's son?"

"Yes," said Trista. "Is there some kind of trouble? Who are you?"

"Nikki Lanier," said Nikki. "Antonio Cano escaped from prison; I've been sent to apprehend him."

"Oh God," said Trista, going pale and clutching the nearest clothing rack for support. "Please tell me he's not here."

"I was chasing someone he was talking to," said Nikki, withholding the information that the meeting had been interrupted by Camille.

"Oh God!" exclaimed Trista again, her hand dramatically covering her heart. "We have to do something! That's too much; Kit can't know about that."

"No one's telling him anything yet. Doesn't he have security?" asked Nikki impatiently.

"Of course, but he's just come out of rehab, and he doesn't know anything about Cano or Camille's job. You can't tell him!" Trista was wide-eyed in horror.

Somewhere an alarm went off, beeping in a rapid rhythm.

"Oh!" exclaimed Trista, jumping slightly at the noise. "Oh! We have to go. It's time!"

"Time for what?" asked Nikki.

"Uh . . . uh . . ." Trista was hurrying around the room, collecting bits of clothing and strapping on a tool belt full of makeup. "Just . . . come on. I'll explain it on the way."

They walked rapidly through the backstage area, passing a strange desk full of switches, manned by an overfed roadie in a tour T-shirt and a donut clasped in one hand. A panoply of wires connected the desk to what looked like an air compressor, which ran hoses for pneumatic mechanical legs that rose into the dark recesses above their heads.

"That's the elevating stage," said Trista, noticing the direction of Nikki's gaze. "The band's up there, and when Kit comes out after intermission, he'll get on that." She pointed to a small platform that was ringed with an iron railing. "It'll shoot him up on the stage. Then he'll get on the elevating stage with the band, and then they'll all rise another twenty-five feet in the air and hover while the fireworks go off."

"Great," said Nikki, feeling that some sort of response was called for. She wasn't sure where they were going or why. She needed to question Trista about likely suspects for Tracksuit's identity, but instead Trista seemed to be giving her a tour. They climbed steep, corrugated metal stairs, the concrete floor beneath them disappearing rapidly.

"We need to focus on Cano," said Nikki, feeling that she was losing control of the situation and raising her voice over the music that was getting louder as they approached the stage. "Assuming Cano's targeting Kit, who on the tour would meet with him?"

"No one," said Trista. "Everyone loves Kit."

Nikki rolled her eyes. "Well, someone met with Cano. Someone I chased back here; someone who conked you on the head."

"No one would want to hurt Kit." Trista's face folded into an angry pout.

"All these people 'love' Kit?" asked Nikki skeptically, gesturing around ascurrying roadies. "No one would give up security details for a fat lot of cash?"

"Duncan vetted everyone," said Trista.

"Who's Duncan?" Nikki asked.

"Duncan Kilkenny, Kit's bodyguard," said Trista, looking distracted as they came out into the wings of the stage. "He takes care of all the security matters. Here, hold this." She pushed a pile of clothes at Nikki.

"No, really," said Nikki, fumbling the clothes. "I don't have time for this. I have a mission. Cano—"

"That's why you have to stay!" exclaimed Trista. "You have to protect Kit."

"He's got bodyguards. You just said."

"What's he doing?" asked Trista, checking her watch. "He should be offstage by now."

Onstage Kit Masters was screaming lyrics into a microphone, leaning way out over a speaker. His sleeveless T-shirt was soaked through and clung to his body. The square stadium was jammed with people. Banners littered the swarming pile of fans. As the band jammed, Nikki craned her head and watched sweat fly off the drummer in post-bath-dog shakes of his flailing arms. Kit finished the song, throwing up his hands in exultation. The fans screamed in reaction, and Kit stepped back from the microphone and looked around, seeing who was with him. He lifted his hands and made small patting, shushing movements. The stadium quieted to a mountainous whisper. Kit hitched up his pants with an almost embarrassed movement.

"Now, look, people, ordinarily at this point in the show I go sponge myself off, but we are having such a good time that I think we need to do one more song. Which one do you think we should do? What do you think, guys?" He turned around to look at the band.

"One more song," muttered Trista. "He must be having a really good time. He never does an extra song. He's always prompt about his halftime break."

Out onstage, Nikki could hear the band shouting suggestions.

"'God Hates Elvis,'" said the guitar player; the bass player shrugged.

"'Less Than Second,'" said the keyboardist, and then the drummer yelled, " 'Heaven-Sent!'"

Kit laughed. He turned back to the microphone.

"Burg wants to do 'Heaven-Sent.'"

There was a terrific roar of approval from the crowd. Kit shook his head in disbelief. The guitarist began playing a riff, a little tease of music. Kit laughed and the bass player joined in, her braids swinging with the *thunka-thunka* bass line. The guitar players exchanged glances and then began the chord again, a little more seriously this time. Kit looked between the two of them and then shrugged. With a sly grin he turned back to the microphone. Burg, the drummer, started the drums with a light tap.

"He's not really . . . ," said Trista, turning to Nikki.

"Not really what?" asked Nikki, mystified

Kit began—"Girl, you are my shining star . . ." then stopped, laughing. "God, I haven't done this song in ten years. I don't think I can sing this on my own; let's try it again with your help."

"Girl, you are my shining star . . ." He leaned the microphone out to the crowd.

The stadium shouted the words along with him, incomprehensible in their multitude.

"It's an @last song!" yelled Trista as the music swelled. "He always swore he wasn't ever going to sing those songs again!"

Kit and the stadium hit the bridge and finally rocked into the chorus, the words becoming clearer as the crowd became more synchronized.

> Oh my sweet angel, my heart, my dear . . .
> Baby you've been heaven-sent
> Yeah you've been heaven-sent . . .

"But I'm in hell without you here!" Kit sang a little before the beat, his voice carrying above the noise. Nikki knew the song was ridiculous boy-band nonsense, but somehow the way he sang, the way his voice soared, nearly took her breath away.

They finished the song, and Kit leapt in the air, pumping his fist in Tom Cruise–like enthusiasm. He bounded offstage, and the backup girls came circling down to the front to take his place. Trista handed him a bottle of water. Kit chugged most of the bottle in one gulp and poured the rest over his head.

"Who's she?" he demanded, pointing at Nikki.

"Never mind her," answered Trista, yanking off his shirt. "She's helping me." She shoved a towel into his hand and pushed him down the stairs.

Kit began walking down the stairs, toweling himself off. At the midway landing a small entourage awaited him, spearheaded by a woman in a headset, gray slacks, and a white blouse. In one hand she clutched a clipboard and phone. Her bottle-blond hair was slicked back in an overly gelled bun and Nikki frowned at her. Tracksuit could have been a woman. Was it gel or was her hair simply wet?

"Mike and the sound guys say—" she said, but Kit cut her off.

"I don't give a shite what the sound guys say," he said.

Two men completed the waiting group. One was another headset-clad man who looked to be following the woman around. The other was a large man with a handlebar mustache and blue eyes peering out from bristling eyebrows. He faded to the back of the group immediately upon seeing Nikki, but she was aware of his presence all the same.

"Fix it or do it or don't do it, just don't bother me with it," Kit said, handing the towel back to Trista. Trista tossed the towel to Nikki and began to unbuckle Kit's belt.

"Who's she?" demanded headset girl, pointing at Nikki.

"She's helping Trista," said Kit as Trista slid his pants down.

"Shoes," Trista commanded. Kit stepped one foot on the heel of the other and stepped out of his shoe, then reached down to yank off the other.

"She's not on my list," said the blonde, rifling through the papers on her clipboard.

"Do I look like I care?" shouted Kit, and the woman blanched.

"Uh, no, sorry."

He was down to his Jockeys and socks by this time and heading for the spring-loaded platform that would shoot him back up to stage level. Singing and dancing for two hours a night had given Kit a sports-star physique, and Nikki was unprepared for the surge of pure physical attraction she suddenly felt. Nikki tried to look somewhere else that didn't involve a mostly naked, glistening Kit Masters. No one else seemed to care, but she felt she was crossing some professional boundary line—as if it were impolite to notice that the emperor had no clothes on. She glanced back and caught Kit's eye; he winked, clearly enjoying himself, and Nikki looked away again, blushing.

"Pants!" Trista snapped at Nikki, who dutifully handed over the rough-grained leather pants. "Step," she said to Kit. Kit stepped into the pants, and the mustache-wearing man and Trista grabbed at the waistline and yanked upward until he was fully in the pants. Shoes came next, but when Nikki held out the shirt Kit waved it away.

"It's blistering under the lights, don't need it."

"Fine," said Trista, and set about powdering him. He stood for it, but impatiently. "You're going to be great," she said, pinching his chin and smiling. Kit was nodding before she'd even finished.

"I've got to get back out there!" Kit said to Trista, grinning from ear to ear. "The crowd is awesome tonight!" He stepped onto the platform, squatting a little before nodding to the technician, who pushed a button. The platform shot upward, and Kit was gone.

Nikki checked her watch. The entire change had taken less than four minutes. She scanned the area for mustache man; she wanted another look at him.

"Trista, if you're going to have guests you need to clear it with me or Mr. Dettling," said the girl in the headset.

"Well, thank you for that information, Angela, but I believe that it's Kit's tour, not Mr. Dettling's," snapped Trista. "And Kit knows that I bring in anyone who helps me get the job done. Now, why don't you go do your job?" Trista took Nikki by the elbow and swept back toward the dressing room. Angela's face was frozen in a scowling mask of fury.

The mustache man was standing between them and the dressing room.

"I don't care if you clear it with Kit or Brandt, but new hires get vetted through me. I want her info in my hands by the end of the night."

"No problem, Duncan," said Trista, smiling tightly. "It's just a last-minute thing."

Duncan didn't return the smile and instead gave a curt nod before stalking away. Trista muttered something Nikki didn't catch and continued to drag Nikki back to the dressing room. Nikki watched him go. He was far too tall and broad-shouldered to be Tracksuit, but he still set off little alarm bells.

"I need to borrow your phone," said Nikki.

"My phone?" repeated Trista.

"To call my team," said Nikki, holding out her hand.

"Ooh, you have 'teams' now, do you? In my day, all a Carrie Mae lady had was her wit, her charm, and herself."

Nikki threw her eyes heavenward and counted to ten. "Well, these days we try not to leave anyone stranded. Phone?"

Reluctantly, Trista handed over the phone. "I'll just give you some privacy then, shall I?" she asked rhetorically, exiting quietly.

Nikki waved distractedly and stared at the phone, only then realizing that she had no way of contacting Astriz. Without a company phone or a computer, she was out here on her own. So much for her pep talk about teams. Frowning, she dialed a number that she knew by heart.

"This is Jane," said Jane after two rings. She sounded very businesslike and slightly annoyed.

"Jane, it's Nikki. I need your help. You still bored enough to come in off the beach?"

"You better believe it!" exclaimed Jane. "What's up?"

Briefly Nikki recounted her evening's adventure, backtracking periodically to answer Jane's questions.

"OK," said Jane at the end. "So you have several problems here."

"Lay it on me," said Nikki. This was Jane's usual method: assess, dissect, offer methods of attack.

"Cano and this guy Voges . . . Just who and what did Voges set him up with? We'd know a lot more about Cano's intentions if we knew what kind of stuff he'd picked up."

"I agree," said Nikki. "But Astriz seemed to think Voges was too much for one agent to take on."

"It's the twenty-first century," said Jane. "We don't need to take him on. We need to take on his computer."

"OK. Let's just say we're in agreement on the solution for problem number one, but since I'm not a computer whiz and you're on vacation, we're going to have to table it for right now."

"Mmm," grunted Jane, clearly dissatisfied with that answer. "Problem two. You need to reconnect with Astriz, figure out where Cano is, and then smack the crap out of Camille."

"Sort of a three-part problem, but yeah."

"I've got Astriz's number here now. Got a pen?"

"Uh-huh," said Nikki, digging through Trista's equipment for a piece of blotting paper and a stick of eyeliner to jot down the numbers Jane recited.

"I think I'll make a few calls when we're done," said Jane abruptly after finishing. "Astriz may have phoned in to her home branch. Won't hurt to check it out."

"You're supposed to be on vacation," protested Nikki.

"Whatever," said Jane. "Anyway, problem three is Kit Masters. Do you think he's really Cano's target?"

"At this point, yes," said Nikki. "Cano has knowledge of Carrie Mae and Camille, and whoever was wearing that gray tracksuit had a backstage pass and came directly here."

"So what are you going to do? Chase Cano or chase Tracksuit?"

"I'm not sure," answered Nikki. "I feel like Tracksuit is still here. Which makes Tracksuit an easier target than Cano." Nikki sighed and rubbed her head. "I need to talk to Astriz, see what her situation is."

"Good thinking."

"Thanks for talking to me, Jane."

"No problem. It's what I do. Ooh, wait . . . final question," said Jane.

"OK, final question," said Nikki tolerantly.

"How hot is Kit Masters in person?"

"Very hot," said Nikki. "You should see him in his underwear."

"Underwear?" shrieked Jane.

"Gotta go, Jane, duty calls," said Nikki maliciously, and hit the "off" button.

Before she could dial Astriz, the phone began to buzz violently. Scrambling to stop the buzz, Nikki hit the "view" button on the incoming text message.

"Call me after," was the entire message, and with a shock, Nikki realized that it was from Camille.

"Everything all right?" asked Trista, reappearing in the doorway.

"Uh . . . yeah," answered Nikki. "Just making one last call." She dialed Astriz's number.

"Hallo, hier ist Astriz. Bitte hinterlassen Sie eine Nachricht nach dem Piepton." Grumbling, Nikki hung up the phone and dialed again; the phone went to the answering message.

"Astriz," said Nikki. "It's Nikki. Call me back at this number. I chased Cano's contact to the backstage of the Kit Masters concert. I'm with a former Carrie Mae agent. Call me." She hung up the phone and tapped her fingers on the countertop of Trista's work space. If Astriz was as much like Val Robinson as Nikki thought, there would be no call back.

She needed to find Tracksuit, which was going to be difficult. She needed to see more of the crew and stage area. Nikki sighed and went to stand beside Trista in the doorway.

"What are you going to do now?" asked Trista.

"I'm going to wait for my German contact to call me back and then we'll see." Nikki hoped it wouldn't occur to Trista to ask what she would do if the German contact never called.

"But you have to stay and help protect Kit!" exclaimed Trista.

"I'm going to help Kit by finding whoever was meeting Cano," answered Nikki. "I can't spend a lot of time worrying about the internal politics of a rock concert. He's got bodyguards, right? Let them do their job and I'll do mine. I'm going to have a look around, see if I can spot Tracksuit. I've got your phone. Call me if you see anything suspicious."

Trista opened her mouth, but Nikki didn't give her a chance to speak, walking away before the makeup lady could protest.

GERMANY III

Tilt!

Nikki toured the perimeter, trying to make sense of the scene in front of her. The mechanical stage apparatus took up the center of the room with a snaking octopus of wires that all fed into a central panel manned by the plump, donut-eating tech she had noticed earlier. She could see Kit and the band on a small TV monitor at the currently unmanned desk; the tech was back at the craft services table. Taking a deep breath, she sidled up to him.

"Hey," she said, "I'm Nikki. I'm helping Trista out." Donut Eater nodded and wiped his fingers on a napkin to shake hands. "Am I the only new person on board today?" She added a winsome smile.

"Well," said the tech, looking around as if he wasn't sure she was talking to him, "there's the walk-on help."

"What's walk-on help?"

"Them," he said, waving at the black-clad men currently carrying equipment toward the loading bay. "The tour can't bring enough people to really do just labor, so we hire out. Some towns are better than others. The Germans, at least, seem to live up to their reputation for efficiency. Things are going pretty well tonight."

"What about—"

The tech's watch beeped, interrupting her. "Time to start the prep for raising the stage," he said, pivoting on his heel and leaving without another word.

Nikki watched him leave and shook her head. Nerds . . . so smart and yet so stupid. Why were the technologically savvy so frequently undersocialized?

She followed some of the walk-ons, keeping a wary eye out for security. Somewhere there was a large man who would be pissed at her when he woke up.

A groupie was waiting by the back entrance, a backstage pass dangling from her neck and a cigarette from her fingers. Nikki leaned against the wall and scrutinized her; she'd never seen a real live groupie before. Plaid mini and spike-heeled boots that left the pale expanse of her thighs exposed for all admirers to see. A cascade of pale blond hair that fell down her back in a straight curtain of corn silk. A thin, youngish man in a dark suit, his blond hair in a faux-hawk, approached her and the two talked for a moment before he escorted her outside.

The way in which the man rested his hand on the small of the girl's back reminded her of Z'ev. Z'ev's fingertips would rest with the lightest of touches on her spine as they walked through restaurants or onto the dance floor. Nikki could never quite figure out if she liked it as an old-fashioned gesture of courtliness or disliked it as a patronizing gesture of ownership. She couldn't quite shake the idea that he thought she needed his guidance to do things, as if she couldn't take care of herself.

Even when he had proof otherwise, he still didn't seem capable of accepting it.

"What the hell was that!?" demanded Z'ev, slamming the door on the apartment. "You go out for butter and forty-five minutes later I find you answering questions from the cops."

"I was helping," said Nikki.

"You were helping?" repeated Z'ev. "The policeman said you did a flying side-kick across the counter and beat the guy unconscious with a brandy bottle."

"Don't be ridiculous," said Nikki. "It was tequila. Longer neck, better grip."

"Nikki!"

"What? What do you want me to say, Z'ev?" asked Nikki, heading into the bedroom to take off her sweatshirt. Z'ev followed after her. "Poor Mr. Singh was getting robbed. What was I supposed to do? Just stand there?"

"You could have called the cops!" suggested Z'ev, glaring.

"Yeah, and by the time they got there Mr. Singh could have been dead and definitely would have been out all the money in his till. He's putting his son through college, saving for his daughter's dowry, and sending money back home. He can't afford that!"

"Nikki, you are not bulletproof! You could have been killed."

"Meh. That guy didn't know what he was doing."

Z'ev sighed and sat down on the bed. "You are not a professional. You can't keep doing things like this," he said, reaching out his hand for her, and she went to him. "One day you won't be so lucky."

What did he mean, "lucky"? She hadn't been lucky; she'd been good. Clearly he hadn't seen the surveillance footage. Although, she decided, she should call work in the morning and get that quashed. Mrs. M wasn't going to want to have that appear on one of those reality clip shows.

He put his arms around her and buried his face in her stomach. Her anger dissipated and she wrapped her arms around him tightly, wanting to hold on forever.

"And besides," he said, leaning back to look her in the face, "you're going to give me a heart attack." Nikki laughed and leaned down to kiss him.

"Cut back on red meat," she suggested.

Shaking her head, Nikki made her way back to Trista, trying to forget about Z'ev. She knew she'd better face facts: she and Z'ev were broken up and she'd lost Tracksuit entirely.

Trista was standing by the stage tech's desk, watching the concert on his monitor. On the little TV, she could see Kit was surrounded by the dancing girls and had wrapped himself in a red feather boa that someone had managed to toss onstage. She didn't understand the girls who did things like that—losing it over a celebrity defied her comprehension. The stage rose higher and even at this level Nikki could hear the swell of cheers and applause.

"So what happens now?" asked Nikki.

"Fireworks," said Trista, and, as if on cue, fireworks shot in arcing streams of light across the crowd-filled soccer pitch.

The technician rolled smoothly from one side of the table to the other and began flipping switches, ignoring the TV footage.

"Cool," said Nikki. The fireworks were blowing out the contrast on the tiny screen.

The platform was nearly five feet up from the main stage, and more than twenty from the cement floor and the machine that powered the pneumatic arms that lifted the stage into the air, when there was a sudden grinding jerk and it tilted dramatically to the right. One of the drummer's drumsticks flew out of his hand and hit the bassist in the head. Next to her, the keyboard player clutched his keyboard in a full-body hug. The guitar player and Kit, who had been in the midst of moving, both fell and slid toward the edge of the platform. From the other side of the stage, Duncan, the bodyguard, hurtled through the flames and landed on the stage.

Trista made a helpless whimpering noise, her fingers clenching and unclenching in fists at her sides, but she was apparently frozen otherwise.

"Hey!" yelled Nikki to the technician. Donut Eater was talking on the phone as he poked underneath a panel. "The platform's tilting; get it down now!"

"Tilting," he repeated, sitting up and looking at her seriously. "That's not a funny joke." He surveyed his array and shook his head. "No, that would cause an alarm on my board. See, no alarm."

Nikki spun the monitor around and shoved it at him.

"Tilting!" she yelled, and the technician went white, beads of sweat suddenly standing out on his forehead. Nikki looked down to the floor, then picked up a coiled piece of cord and jammed it into the empty slot on the board. The board lit up in a blinking cascade of red.

"Jesus, Jesus, Jesus," yelped Donut Eater, and began thumbing controls in a rapid-fire sequence.

"Get it down!" yelled Nikki. "There are people up there."

"Jonesy, Jonesy, kill the goddamn pyros!" he yelled into his headset. Crewmen were running upstairs toward the stage. "Jesus, Jesus." Donut Eater prayed some more. He stood and was yanked back into his seat by his headset. "It won't come down!" Donut Eater shouted in terror at Nikki as he fought the headset.

"Why not?"

The technician scanned the octopus of black wires and air compressors.

"It's jammed!" he yelled, and Trista moaned in horror, still frozen in place, covering her hands with her mouth. Nikki followed his pointing finger, tracing cords up the riser where a wrench, locked around one of the air tubes, had literally been stuck into the works. At a certain height the wrench had pinched the hose, cutting off power to the piston that pushed the telescoping arms of the stage mechanism into the air.

Nikki sighed in exasperation. This was not her night. Taking a deep breath, she ran toward the scaffolding, climbing hand over hand until she reached the level of the wrench. Extending her arm, she found the wrench just out of her reach. She took a long look at the grease-covered arm and then jumped. Grabbing the wrench, she slid down until her feet connected with the next section of the piston. She felt her shirt pull up and winced in disgust as she felt grease cover her skin. The floor was less than six feet away, so she jumped, landing in a low crouch and covered in a black film of grease. She stayed there a minute, panting, as the ragged edge of adrenaline started to take its toll.

Donut Eater was already pushing buttons as she landed, and, with a sucking noise from the compressors, the platform righted itself and began to descend. Nikki watched anxiously as the platform sank down into resting position. The bodyguard had made it through the flames mostly unharmed—his mustache looked a little singed. He had one beefy arm hooked around Kit and the other holding the guitarist by the belt. The bassist and the keyboard player had their arms wrapped around the firmly anchored keyboard and Burg, the drummer, had a white-knuckled grip on his snare drum. As the stage touched down, no one moved for a long second.

"Bloody hell," muttered the bassist, standing swiftly and walking shakily to the edge of the stage. Nikki reached up a hand to help her down, but she shook her head.

"Help Hammond," she said, gesturing to the keyboard player. "He's afraid of heights."

"Holly, Holly," whispered Hammond, "don't leave me."

"Here," said Nikki, extending a hand. He crawled to her as if not wanting to remove more than one limb from the ground at a time. The bodyguard lifted Kit and the guitarist to their feet and then began to stalk toward the stage technician.

"What the hell did you do?" bellowed Duncan. Behind him, Kit and the guitarist clung together.

"Duncan," squealed Trista, but whether in protest or fear Nikki couldn't tell.

"Oi! It wasn't me!" shouted the technician. "Some cowboy's been messing with the machinery!"

The keyboardist was still on all fours and the bassist was patting him on the back, murmuring encouraging things. The drummer finally lurched off the stage and stumbled toward the pair. Kit grabbed him as he went by, looking him over as if for damage.

"Hey now," said a smooth voice. "What's going on?"

"Brandt Dettling," roared Duncan, "what the hell kind of show are you running?"

They all turned to look at the new arrival, and Nikki recognized him as the man she had seen talking to the groupie. Nikki eyeballed the suit and estimated a designer label and a designer price tag. At the moment Brandt's square face and hazel eyes were set in an expression of determined patience, but there was a strong suggestion of clenched teeth in the muscles along his jawline. Behind Brandt, a white-faced Angela clutched her clipboard to her chest as though it were armor.

"You tell me!" Brandt yelled back. "What the hell is all this? What's everyone doing down here? We've got a show to do!"

"To hell with the show!" said Kit, shaking himself loose from the group hug the band had melded into. "I'm not going back out there!"

"The stage malfunctioned," explained the bassist, still comforting the keyboardist. "We all could have fallen to our deaths."

Brandt surveyed the scared faces as if assessing how far he could push them.

"Look, I know it was scary. We'll fire the stage guy. You"—he pointed at the technician—"you're fired. Now, we'll send the instruments back up and you all can go up through the stairs," said Brandt soothingly.

"Like hell we will!" yelled Kit.

"Kit, you have to do over half the scheduled show time or we have to pay a default to the venue."

Next to her, Trista gulped audibly. Nikki glanced over and saw that the older woman looked genuinely scared, but whether it was of Brandt or of the idea of defaulting on a venue, Nikki couldn't tell.

"Screw the venue!" said Kit savagely. "I'm not going back out there, and neither is anyone else!" Kit glanced around, gathering the band to him with a look.

"Kit, you can't do this," said Brandt desperately. "Just do one more song, say good night, and then we'll go."

"No, Brandt. No."

"Yes, Kit," answered Brandt. Kit gazed into Brandt's eyes and this time he didn't flinch.

"He did an extra song," said Nikki into the silence, tossing her words like stones. "Before the break. He did an extra song. That ought to put him over the halfway mark."

"Right," said Kit, looking at Nikki in surprise. "I sang my extra song and we're going."

"The bus is this way," growled Duncan. Kit fell into step after Duncan, gathering the band to him with a look. They closed in around Kit like a human wall and they walked without talking, as if getting to the bus were more important than whatever anyone had to say. Angela trailed after them protesting in sputtering half sentences, but after a few feet she gave up, stymied by the wall, unable to gain access. Nikki looked back over her shoulder and saw the controlled and regimented woman stomp her foot in childish anger.

The group proceeded forward, crossing the gray concrete floor, hurrying as they felt the first chill sting of outside air.

The groupie was there waiting for them by the backstage door, her blond hair swinging in the breeze. Her miniskirt if anything looked shorter than the first time Nikki had seen it. Nikki squinted in dislike; she'd thought Brandt had escorted her out, but apparently she'd come back in.

"Hello," she called out to Kit with only the faintest trace of a German accent.

Kit stopped. He was still shirtless, draped in the red feather boa, tattoos exposed, still reeking of adrenaline and fear. A few floating feathers had glued themselves to his skin; his eyeliner was sweat smudged and his leather pants seemed molded to his legs. Energy crackled off him like electricity. He was as hot as she was cool.

They stared at each other until the air between them sizzled like water on a hot burner.

"Hi," he answered. He took off the feathered boa and tossed it around her neck, catching the ends and drawing her close. And just like that the deal was closed. As if the girl's voice had been a trumpet call, the wall fell apart. Stances altered, eyes lost their single-minded focus. The drummer gave an all-over body twitch. They had gone from being a single entity to a cluster of individuals. The groupie didn't appear to notice the change in atmosphere; she was running her hands over Kit's chest. Nikki blinked. Talk about turbo-slut.

"Say good night, everyone," said Kit, looking around with a faint smirk. "Elvis has left the building."

GERMANY IV

Honest, I Swear

"You'd better come with us," said Trista as the band disembarked from the tour bus.

"You're going to need some new clothes," said the bass player, following Trista and Nikki.

"Yeah," said Nikki, looking around, wishing Astriz would magically appear with her luggage. The grease from the stage was starting to permeate her pores. She felt like an oil slick. "I don't think I have any."

"We'll dig you up some," said the bass player. "I'm Holly, by the way. Thanks for saving our lives."

"Sure, no problem," said Nikki awkwardly, uncomfortable with being thanked.

"Sorry about Brandt and all the shouting," said Holly as Trista unlocked a hotel room.

"Brandt?" said Nikki, and Holly grimaced.

"Man in the suit. The one who pulls all our strings," said Holly bitterly.

"What do you need in the way of clothes?" asked Trista, interrupting.

"Whatever I can get?" said Nikki, looking in dismay at her grease-covered clothing.

"I'm sure Holly can lend you something," said Trista. She looked hopefully at Holly, who snorted in derision.

"Not likely. She'd be swimming in all of my kit. What are you, a size zero?"

"Do I look like a fourteen-year-old? I usually run a two or a four."

"Same difference from where I'm standing," said Holly. "I'll check with the backup dancers and see what they've got."

"Is there anything else you need?" asked Trista as Holly left the room.

"Just some privacy," said Nikki, holding up Trista's phone. "Sorry," she added.

She really needed to get a replacement phone ASAP. "As soon as I get in touch with the German agent, we'll make a plan," said Nikki reassuringly, flipping open the phone.

Trista nodded, looking as if she wanted to stay but knowing that she shouldn't. "I'll just go check on Holly," she said with enforced cheerfulness, bustling from the room.

Nikki found the recently dialed numbers and redialed Astriz as she looked around.

Trista was organized and tidy, as befitted a former Carrie Mae lady. Baggage kept to a minimum, equipment laid out within easy reach. A hair had even been placed across the latch on Trista's bag; should anyone search it, the hair would be disturbed and reveal the intrusion. Nikki pondered the implications of this as the phone rang. Either being a Carrie Mae agent had left Trista with an ingrained mistrust of all other human beings or she had reason to suspect that someone might search her bag.

The phone went to voice mail and dejectedly, Nikki left another message. Chances were good that Astriz had no intention of returning her calls or in fact returning for her at all.

There was a knock on the door, and then it popped open to reveal Holly.

"I cadged some stuff off the backup girls."

"Thanks," said Nikki.

"Got tights and tunic." Holly held up a pair of black, footless tights and a blue smock-type shirt with a green geometric pattern.

"No jeans?" said Nikki weakly.

"Sorry," said Holly sympathetically. "They all wander around in shite like this and Ugg boots. It's what they had. Your shoes were pretty trashed too, so I got you some replacements."

"Not Ugg boots?" said Nikki, fearing the worst.

Holly laughed. "No, I doubt I could pry an Ugg boot out of their skinny little fingers if I tried. Reject shoes, I'm afraid." She pulled out a pair of what to Nikki looked like wrestling boots—flat soled and reaching midcalf, they were lace-up and electric green.

"Oh God," said Nikki, horrified. "I'm going to look like Madonna circa 1984."

"Don't you know?" asked Holly. "The eighties are back. It's, uh . . . very Kanye."

"But I don't even like Kanye West," muttered Nikki woefully, and reached for the clothes with a sigh. Beggars could not be choosers. The smock at least had long sleeves and might be slightly warmer than her tank-top-and-cardigan combo had been. But the shoes . . . they were kind of embarrassing.

Once dressed, she washed her face and used some of Trista's makeup to make herself presentable. Stepping back to look in the mirror, she had to admit that the outfit wasn't as bad as she had feared, but it still was a little too boho chic for her comfort level.

She tried Astriz again, and it went straight to voice mail. Trista still hadn't returned, and Holly was puttering around her side of the room, plucking at piles and humming.

"The guy running the raised platform," said Nikki, giving in to her own curiosity.

"Ewart?" answered Holly, looking puzzled.

"Do you know where he is?"

"Brandt fired him. Why?"

"I want to talk to him about the accident."

Holly sat down on the bed, looking serious. "You're going to ask about the accidents? I'm not sure that's a good idea."

Concentrating on her mascara, Nikki raised her head like a bloodhound scenting an escaped prisoner. "Accidents?" she repeated, emphasizing the plural. "There have been others?"

"Uh . . ." Holly stalled, looking worried.

"This could have killed all of you, Holly," said Nikki, putting the mascara wand firmly back in the tube and turning to watch Holly more closely.

"It couldn't have been Ewart," said Holly, avoiding eye contact. "Not for the others anyway. Besides, they're just accidents. These things happen."

"You don't believe that," Nikki said. "You're worried about these accidents. How many have there been?" Nikki could tell this was the point where Holly decided whether or not to trust her; she tried to look sympathetic and harmless. Holly took a deep breath and held it, then let it out in one long gust.

"I don't know. One of the bus tires blew. They said it was just one of those things, but my brother used to slash tires, as a prank," she added hastily, aware of Nikki's raised eyebrow. "I know what slashed tires look like. Louis said that if we'd been in an older bus it might have flipped over. Fortunately, brakes work really well these days."

"What else?"

"The helicopter," said Holly. "Kit, Duncan, and Brandt were in a helicopter; it almost ran out of gas. They set down in some farmer's field all right, but it could have been bad. It's why Kit's so firmly attached to the buses now. And then there was the crewman who broke his leg. Slipped down some stairs just ahead of Kit. I saw those stairs later; one of them looked clean. Like maybe something was on it and had been wiped off."

"These don't sound like just accidents," said Nikki.

"I know, but we can't talk about it," said Holly, her eyes pleading. "The tour's been really stressful. Kit's just barely got his fingernails dug into sobriety and then there's his writer's block. And these accidents are getting . . . well, they're making things worse. People are starting to say the tour is cursed. Plus, Brandt's really pushing Kit—trying to get him on the international level. Which I think Kit wants too, but man, it's a lot of pressure. Sometimes he talks about giving it all up to become a shoe repairman."

"A shoe repairman?" asked Nikki in disbelief, and Holly shrugged.

"Or an accountant—it's what he always says when the stress gets to be too much. If he thought someone on the tour was actually trying to hurt him . . . I think it might break him. Something like this could push him right back to the bottle."

"We need to talk to Ewart then," Nikki said again, and Holly shook her head.

"Ewart's an idiot, but it can't have been him."

"I don't think it was Ewart either," Nikki said soothingly. "He broke out in a flop sweat the second I pointed out the problem, but not before. You can't fake that kind of reaction. Do you think we could find him?"

"Probably," said Holly, looking worried, "but I don't know . . . Brandt sacked him. And once Brandt sacks someone, it's bad to be seen with him. Brandt takes that shit personally."

"Who's Brandt again?" asked Nikki. "And why do we care?"

Holly's eyes widened in shock. Brandt was apparently one of the deities of this world.

"He's Kit's manager. And they're best friends. They were in @last together."

"Trista mentioned that. What's At Last?"

"@last?" Holly looked more shocked, if that was possible. "They were a boy band in the nineties. You know, 'at' symbol, 'last.' It was really novel at the time. They kind of imploded I guess, but Kit and Brandt formed Faustus Records. Nobody thought Kit was worth much, but he and Brandt showed them all wrong. Kit's going to be the biggest thing in Europe."

"So Brandt used to sing and now he runs a record label and is Kit's manager?" asked Nikki, trying to get the progression straight. Holly nodded. "And apparently he's kind of a prick if he won't let you talk to people who've been fired."

"Well . . ." Holly hesitated, then nodded. "He is a bit of a bastard." The relief in Holly's voice spilled out with the words. "It's just that things are so tense right now. I don't want to upset the apple cart."

"Well, if we stop the 'accidents' things would get less tense, wouldn't they? And that would be good."

Holly nodded but still looked miserable. "I guess. The roadies will know where Ewart went. Come on."

Holly led the way outside to the tour buses, from which the crew had strung Christmas lights and a disco ball. Inflatable palm trees stood or sagged between the buses, and German techno pumped through an impressive sound system. Around them, heat blowers brought the temperature up to a comfortable level. The crew and their guests crowded the area, dancing. It seemed impossible to find anyone, but Holly led the way through the crowd as though she had a compass.

"What are they celebrating?" asked Nikki, watching the dancing throng.

"Celebrating?" asked Holly, puzzled, as they arrived at the bus.

"It's always like this," said the drummer, coming out of the bus and pausing on the step above them to mime picking lice from Holly's hair. "Who's she?" he demanded of Holly.

"Burg, this is Nikki. Nikki, this is Burg. Our drummer. He thinks he's a monkey."

"Ape, darling, ape," he said, as he shook hands with Nikki, and then responded to Nikki's question. "The crew throws the best parties all the time. People think it's the rock stars, but it's the crew that really rocks the house."

"Good booze, too," said Holly, shoving a plastic cup at Nikki. Nikki sniffed it cautiously; it smelled like fruit-flavored nail polish remover. "Have some Jungle Punch."

"I think I just lost a few nose hairs," she commented, but took a small sip anyway. She had discovered in high school that refusing a drink made people dislike you. It made them feel like they were doing something wrong.

"So what can I do for you fine folks?" asked Burg, sitting down on the stairs and sipping from his own cup.

"The guy that was running the platform . . ." began Nikki.

"Ah, the dearly departed Ewart," said Burg, shaking his head and scratching his armpit.

"I don't suppose you know where I can find him?" asked Nikki.

Burg stopped pretending to pick lice and looked at her. "He's down at the battle cruiser getting comprehensively banjoed."

Nikki blinked and tried out the sentence in various formations on the big screen in her head.

"Sorry," she said at last, "you're going to have to try that again with different words."

"Uh . . ." Burg looked flummoxed, linguistically stuck in a groove.

"He's getting drunk," Holly said at last.

"Down at the pub," said Burg.

"Which one?"

"Why do you want to find this guy?" asked Burg curiously. "He screwed up; he was sacked."

"He's been doing this job the whole tour, right? And this is the only mistake he's made?"

"Ook! Hell of a mistake!" answered Burg.

"Someone stuck a wrench around one of the hoses," said Nikki.

"It was a wrench?" asked Holly.

"Yeah," said Nikki, nodding. "Trust me, I was nose to nose with the thing."

"Well, even if it wasn't his fault, there's nothing we can do about it now. Brandt fired him. When Brandt fires people, they stay fired," said Burg with a shrug.

"Even if it wasn't his fault?" asked Nikki, trying to make them actually hear the words.

"Brandt doesn't really admit mistakes," said Burg. "He just sort of keeps rolling forward."

"He's like the Adolf Hitler of the music industry," interjected Holly.

"Well, let's just pretend I'm Russia in winter and I actually do have the power to stop Adolf in his tracks. Can you take me to Ewart?"

"I suppose," said Burg, "that I could do that. But, well, if shit goes down, then we pretend I'm Switzerland. Brandt can get vindictive when challenged."

"Switzerland it is."

Burg led them, occasionally pausing to leap on things, through clean, well-lit streets to a small pub. They entered the bar and spotted Ewart the Donut Eater almost immediately. He was sitting with his head on the bar but twisted sideways to watch soccer on the bar TV. At his feet were a number of bags and backpacks, presumably everything he owned at the moment. He was wearing some regrettable red stretch jeans and an even more unfortunate yellow-ochre T-shirt. Nikki slid into the seat next to him.

"Hey, Ewart," she said. His eyes flicked from the screen to her.

"I know you," he slurred.

"Sure you do, Ewart," said Nikki easily, and waved to the bartender. "One for me and my friends, and another for my friend Ewart."

Ewart looked down the bar at Holly and Burg.

"I didn't do it!" he moaned, burying his face in his arms.

"Shh, Ewart. Here's your beer."

The bartender placed a frosty brown beer in front of each of them, the suds streaked down the sides. Nikki paid the silent bartender and slid the beer toward Ewart. "You want your beer, don't you?"

"I didn't do it," he said again, but put out a hand and pulled the beer close to him.

"I believe you, Ewart."

He raised one eye above his elbow and looked at her hopefully. "You'll tell Mr. Masters that?"

"Yes. But I need something more to tell him. Do you know who put the wrench there?"

"I didn't do it!" he wailed, and buried his head again.

"Why don't you just tell me about the evening?" asked Nikki, taking the beer back. That brought his head up slightly.

"I set up my equipment and the guys built the platform." He reached for the beer.

"Then what?" asked Nikki, pulling the beer just out of reach of his grasping fingers.

"Then the show started. Everything went fine." His fingertips slid off the wet glass, unable to gain enough traction to bring the glass closer to him.

"Then what?"

"Trista came down from the upper stage and told me there were donuts on the craft services table. So I got a donut and hung out with some of the guys. Then Miss Angela came by to check on me. Mr. Dettling showed up and asked me about the specs for the Paris show. Wanted to know if the smaller stage size was going to be a problem. I told him no. They went away. You ran by. I got another donut."

"Who's Miss Angela?" hissed Nikki to Holly.

"The tour manager; she used to be Kit's personal assistant. She and Brandt are like this." Holly wrapped two fingers around each other.

"What did you and Angela talk to each other about?" asked Nikki, turning back to Ewart.

"She was looking for Mr. Dettling, like I said. She seemed in a hurry. Course it was time for her to meet Mr. Masters, so she'd probably been running."

Nikki let him have the beer. He swallowed thirstily.

"She looked like she'd been running?" asked Nikki. Tracksuit could have been a woman.

"Well, hurrying," said Ewart with a shrug. "Duncan was the one who looked like he'd been running."

"Kit's lead bodyguard," said Burg. "Big moustache, ook."

"He ran by while I was talking to Miss Angela."

"Could you see your table the whole time?" asked Nikki.

"No, I guess I wandered around a bit. But who would want to hurt Kit?"

Nikki sighed; Ewart was fairly useless.

"Duncan did come and fiddle with stuff earlier, though," said Ewart suddenly. "I saw him. He walked around the whole thing and touched stuff. I saw him. I was getting some ties from my gear bag."

"When was that?" asked Nikki.

"Earlier. Between when Kit went onstage the first time and the break. Before Trista told me about the donuts."

"Was it unusual for Duncan to do that?"

"Who knows what's unusual for Duncan? He doesn't answer to the likes of us." Ewart gave a piqued sniff.

"Then what?"

"Then the second half started, and it got all ballsed up!" He rubbed his eyes sorrowfully, like a grown-up boy with his bottle.

"If you didn't leave the wrench there, then who did?" snapped Holly, and Nikki shot her a warning glance.

"I don't know," said Ewart grumpily, and clutched at his beer. "It wasn't me."

"I know that," said Nikki soothingly. "Who do you think it was?"

"One of those idiot German hire-ons, most likely," he said. "I don't know. It could have been anyone."

He nursed his beer and Nikki drank some of hers, considering the matter; even Burg was quiet down at the end of the bar. "Holly, where does the tour go next?" Nikki asked.

"Paris. We're doing a New Year's Eve show."

"Ewart, do you have a ride to Paris?" asked Nikki.

"Why would I go to Paris? I haven't got a job there."

"Well, you will if I get your job back."

"No chance of that," said Ewart sulkily. "Mr. Dettling doesn't go backward."

"But Kit would hire you back, wouldn't he? If he knew it wasn't your fault?"

"Yeah, yeah, he would." Ewart agreed eagerly, a light shining in his beer-dimmed eyes. "Mr. Masters is a real gentleman. He'd take me back."

"Well, you meet us in Paris for the show and I'll see what I can do."

"Really?" asked Ewart, looking at Nikki in disbelief.

"Sure," she answered with a smile.

"Well, that's a bit of all right then." He grasped her hand in both of his and shook it enthusiastically. "Can't thank you enough."

"Wait till I pull it off before you get to thanking me," answered Nikki with a wry smile.

"No, you'll do it right enough. I saw you go up the scaffolds and come down with a wrench. You're the kind of person who prods buttock and takes nomenclature. You'll come through, right enough." Nikki smiled at the compliment, but another thought occurred to her.

"What would have happened if I hadn't gotten the wrench? Would the stage have kept tilting?"

"Oh no, it's got a tilt sensor. If it goes past fifteen degrees it freezes. It wouldn't have gone up too much farther on its own."

"Hmm. Well, thanks, Ewart. We'll see you in Paris."

"We don't really think Duncan put the wrench there, do we?" asked Holly as they exited the bar. The puddles in the street were frozen, and it smelled like snow.

"We don't think anything just yet," answered Nikki, "except that I'm freezing. Let's get back to the hotel."

"I didn't know you were the one who fixed the stage," said Burg as they walked.

"You thought I just did a face-plant into some grease?" asked Nikki.

"I didn't know what you did. I just thought . . . I didn't think about it at the time. Anyway, for what it's worth, thanks." Burg offered a hand and Nikki shook it, surprised.

"It's what I'm here for," said Nikki with a shrug.

"Actually," said Holly, "what are you here for? Where did you even come from?"

"I'm . . ." Nikki hesitated. "I'm with Carrie Mae. I'm assisting Trista."

"Sure you are, love," said Holly. "You're everything I expect from a Carrie Mae lady."

"We're multitaskers," said Nikki.

"Well, you are a woman," said Holly, laughing. "And women can do anything."

"Just about."

"Damn female liberation," said Burg good-naturedly. "Why couldn't you just stick to running things from behind the scenes?"

"You looked like you were having too much fun," answered Holly with a grin.

"What are we going to do now?" asked Burg. "If someone put that wrench on the stage on purpose then that means someone's trying to sabotage Kit. What do we do about that?" Holly nodded and then turned to Nikki, awaiting a response.

"We're going to stop it," said Nikki. "But first we're going to talk to Duncan." She hoped that was the right answer.

Nikki could hear the thumping bass from the roadies' party as they walked to the hotel, but it was the distant screech of tires on pavement that drew her attention. A silver Mercedes rounded the corner behind them; Nikki recognized Astriz as the car sped past.

"Damn Germans," muttered Burg.

The Mercedes reached the intersection, slid to a halt, and then began reversing toward them, still at full speed.

"Damn!" exclaimed Burg, scrambling onto the sidewalk with Holly right behind him, but Nikki held her ground as Astriz came to a stop inches from Nikki's toes. The window silently descended and Astriz tossed a cigarette butt on the sidewalk.

"Not real subtle," said Nikki, stepping on the cigarette.

"What happened to your clothes?" asked Astriz.

"There was an incident," said Nikki.

"*Ja?*" Astriz did not appear interested as she lit up a fresh cigarette. "Who are they?" She waved her cigarette at Holly and Burg, who were huddled together.

"They're . . ." Nikki hesitated.

"We are with the band," said Holly stiffly. Nikki smiled. She was really starting to like Holly.

"Ah," said Astriz, stepping out of the car. "It seems that happenings have occurred."

"That's one way of putting it," said Nikki. "Let's take a walk; I'll fill you in."

Astriz shrugged and matched Nikki's stride as she walked away from the band members.

"What happened after I went after the person in the tracksuit?" asked Nikki.

"Things did not go well," she said, pursing her lips in frustration. "Cano had a second backup waiting outside. Camille hit the café, and the backup pulled up in a truck and sprayed some bullets while Cano made a run for the vehicle."

"OK, well, did you at least get Camille locked down?"

Astriz cleared her throat and squinted up at the streetlight. "She got away."

"So what have you been doing since I left?" asked Nikki, trying not to sound annoyed.

"I managed to plant a tracking device on the truck." Astriz paused, and Nikki's face brightened. "But I think it got damaged in the escape." Nikki's face fell. "The signal is not very strong. I had to go back to headquarters to see if I could find a way to boost the signal."

"So we've got the possibility of a location on Cano, Camille is in the wind, and Kit Masters is a sitting duck."

"I don't know what that means," said Astriz bluntly. "Why is Kit Masters a duck?"

"It's an expression derived from hunting, meaning that he is an easy target. As in, a sitting duck is easier to shoot than a flying duck," said Nikki without breaking stride, and Astriz nodded thoughtfully. "I chased Tracksuit straight to the backstage area, and someone may have tried to kill Kit tonight. And the tour has been hit with several unexplained 'accidents' in recent weeks."

"You think Cano is behind it?" Astriz asked.

"It's a possibility," said Nikki. Astriz grunted in reply. "And I think Tracksuit is here."

"It would be consistent with what I read in the file. Cano did make threats against Camille and her family. He may have been planning a strike against Kit," said Astriz. "It's unfortunate that Camille's son is such a public figure; it only makes him more attractive to a terrorist like Cano."

"My instinct is if we stick with Kit, Cano will come to us," said Nikki.

"Use him as bait?" asked Astriz, and Nikki shrugged. "But no," said Astriz. "We've got a shot at Cano. We should pursue him directly."

Nikki could tell by the way Astriz set her shoulders that she was willing to fight for her point.

"You're right," said Nikki, and watched Astriz's shoulders drop in surprise. "As long as we've got a direct link to Cano we should pursue it. But with what you said about the damage to the tracking device, I'm worried we'll lose him and leave Kit exposed to danger."

"Well . . . *Ja*," said Astriz. Nikki frowned, trying to parse her way through the situation. She would have given anything to have Jenny, Ellen, and Jane with her.

"I hate to split up," said Nikki, "but we may have to. You stick with Cano; I'll take Kit."

"You're not what I expected, Nikki," Astriz said.

"Yeah, I know, you thought I'd be taller."

"I thought you'd be a bitch," said Astriz. "But you care about the mission, don't you?"

"It's my job," said Nikki, not sure where Astriz was taking the conversation.

"Mine too. OK, we split up. What about Camille?"

"The next time you see Camille, hit her with a shot of freesia KO."

Astriz chuckled. "I love that scent. So much better than the orchid-plum knockout gas."

"I know!" exclaimed Nikki. "What were they thinking?"

"It smelled cheap," said Astriz in agreement, walking back to her car. "You will be all right on your own?" she asked.

"What are you talking about? I've got my crack team to back me up." She jerked her thumb at Burg and Holly. Astriz laughed again.

"Check-ins twice a day?" said Nikki. "Ten and sixteen hundred hours?"

Astriz nodded. "Perfect. We'll bring Cano down yet." She slammed the door and threw the car into gear. Nikki felt a sinking feeling as the car drove away.

"You don't look happy," said Holly. "Who the hell was that?"

"And can I have her number?" asked Burg.

"No," said Nikki, ignoring Burg. "I'm not happy at all. My luggage is in the trunk of her car."

GERMANY V

Groupie Chick

"Are you really planning on questioning Duncan?" asked Holly as they approached the hotel.

"Ook, ook," Burg said in low-voiced distress.

"No reason to wait," replied Nikki.

"Ook! Questioning Kit's nearest and dearest is above my pay grade," said Burg nervously.

"You don't have to come," Nikki said, surprised that they were even contemplating going along and taken aback to hear that a bodyguard was counted among Kit's inner circle.

"I'm in," said Holly. "You're better than the usual after-party high jinks."

Burg scratched his armpit and then shrugged. "What the hell? You only live once."

"OK," said Nikki, nodding, "great. Does anyone know where Duncan actually is?"

"That guy lives in Kit's shadow. So penthouse is my guess," said Holly.

"OK." Nikki headed for the elevators. If she could track down the accidents or the link to Cano tonight, she'd be able to backtrack to Cano himself. Problem solved. And then it was back to L.A. Her brain added "and back to Z'ev" before she could stop herself. She'd been doing so well—almost four hours without thinking about him.

Once in the elevator, Burg attempted to poke the buttons of random floors while Holly smacked at his hands. Nikki wasn't sure if it was playful or not; they both seemed very serious. Maybe Burg just liked negative attention.

Arriving at the penthouse level, the elevator doors slipped apart, and the three occupants stared down the hallway. Duncan was in front of them, looking over his shoulder at Kit, who was marching the groupie down the hallway as she tried to scramble back into her clothes.

"Duncan, perhaps you would be kind enough to escort this young lady out of the hotel," said Kit icily. His furious disdain suddenly reminded Nikki of Camille.

"Pig!" spat the girl as Kit shoved her into the elevator.

Holly, Nikki, and Burg edged into the hallway, out of the way of the groupie, as Kit threw the girl's jacket into the elevator. As he did, a small plastic bag containing a white substance fell onto the floor.

"And take your drugs with you!" shouted Kit, throwing the bag after her.

"You didn't tell me he was crazy," the girl hissed at Duncan as the doors closed.

"So," said Holly when the silence had become uncomfortable, "it looks like you have a free evening." Kit threw back his head and laughed.

"Yes, and now I need to do something with it."

"You know," said Burg, picking up the feather boa that had gotten left behind, "I never find these things sexy. It's like Big Bird is in the room with me."

They all turned to stare at Burg, who looked back seriously.

"Well, I mean, could you have sex with Big Bird in the room?" he asked defensively.

"Big Bird? That gives me an idea," said Kit suddenly. "Come on."

Nikki looked back at the closed elevator doors. Her plan was getting hijacked. Holly tugged on her and gave a wide-eyed "hurry up" look. With a sigh, Nikki followed after the two band members. Maybe it wouldn't hurt to find out a little about Kit.

"So you're helping Trista?" asked Kit, handing out drinks from the bar.

"Er, yes," said Nikki, realizing the question was directed at her.

"She's the one that got the platform down," Holly put in helpfully. "Saved our lives, she did." Burg nodded in support.

"Welcome to the family, then," said Kit, clinking his seltzer water against her glass.

He disappeared into the bedroom to call room service and was back a moment later.

"Did you—" He was cut off by the ringing of his phone.

"Mum!" said Kit, answering his phone cheerfully. There was a pause as he listened to Camille speak. Nikki tensed, wondering if it was about her. Had Trista called Camille? She should have clarified that with Trista.

"No, Mum, I'm fine. How'd you even hear about that?" Kit paused, listening to Camille's explanation. How had Camille known about the platform debacle? Had Trista told her? And why was she taking time out of her busy chasing-Cano schedule to call Kit? Nikki considered taking the phone away and talking to Camille herself.

"Well, the news got it wrong as usual. It was just a mechanical error. Duncan got things under control in a blink." Nikki could hear the tiny whine of Camille's voice on the other end. It went up a fraction in tone as if Camille had asked a question. "Duncan's my bodyguard. I'm pretty sure I've mentioned him before," said Kit. "I can't help it if you haven't met him." There was more chatter and Nikki glanced at Holly and Burg; they had the practiced blank stare of subway riders pretending not to eavesdrop.

"Well, I trust him. Nan's met him and she likes him. Yes, he had excellent references. What is this, the third degree?" asked Kit. "I am capable of hiring good people, Mum." There was more chatter and Kit heaved a sigh of frustration. "Well, maybe if you ever came to one of my shows you'd have met him," said Kit tartly.

The volume increased from Camille's end and Kit's jaw clenched.

"Yes, I know you're busy. No, I'm not suggesting you just drop everything and come attend to me. I'm just saying you've never come to one of my shows."

"She's never been to one of his shows?" whispered Nikki to Holly, who shook her head.

"I get the impression that she doesn't approve."

"I think it's a bit beyond her approval at this point," said Nikki, and Holly shrugged.

"From what Kit says, Camille is the type of woman who thinks she has the final say on everything," Burg said. Nikki grunted in agreement as he continued. "But Kit . . . he's got to sing, you know? She'd know that if she ever came around." He added the last part bitterly and Nikki nodded, feeling a surge of sympathy for Kit.

"Well, you know absentee parents," she said, remembering her own father. "Can't live with them . . ."

"Can't live without them?" asked Holly, trying to complete the phrase.

"No," said Nikki, "just can't live with them. Because they're not there."

"Agh!" said Kit, slamming the phone shut. "She drives me absolutely spare!"

"Is she in town?" asked Nikki casually.

"Who knows?" said Kit with a shrug. "She travels a lot. I'm a freaking international rock star, or at least I will be after this tour, and she's still not happy. Wants me to settle down and get a real job. Does anybody else have this kind of problem with their mother?" he asked, looking around in bewilderment.

Nikki raised her hand. "Which reminds me. I haven't called her in two days, which means she's probably about this far from reporting me as a missing person."

"Want to borrow my phone?" asked Kit, holding out his phone and smiling sympathetically.

"It's international," she said, and he shrugged as if that didn't matter in the least. "Thanks," said Nikki, taking the phone and dialing. She walked away from the couch, quickly dialing her own mother. "Lanier residence," said her mother, sounding suspicious. It was her formal greeting for when she didn't know who was calling.

"Hey, Mom," said Nikki, staring out the window at the driving rain. She'd forgotten to calculate time zones. Hopefully, she wasn't waking her mom up in the middle of the night. There was a sharp knock on the door and Kit rushed to answer it.

"Oh," said Nell, the formality dropping from her voice. "I thought you might be your father." Nell was starting off with a strong serve—bringing up Nikki's father was a surefire fight starter. Nikki frowned, trying to concentrate on the match with her mother as two bellboys opened large cardboard boxes filled with nothing but red feather boas. Another bellboy was carrying a box of Elmer's glue. They deposited their burdens, received their tips, and departed with carefully expressionless faces. Kit began tossing boas out left and right until the floor was mounded with heaps of feathers.

"Why would Dad call?" asked Nikki impatiently. "You've been divorced for twenty years." Nikki volleyed back, trying to push the fight to Nell and ignoring the fact that Kit, Holly, and Burg were divvying up the boas and glue.

"How would I know?" asked Nell. "He's the only person I know who travels overseas." Total willful ignorance of Nikki's life; high lob over the net.

"Mom, he can't possibly be the only person you know. Besides, I've been at my job for over a year now; you know I travel." Burg was climbing on the bar and beginning to glue the boas to the woodwork.

"Which is why I bothered to answer the phone," retorted Nell, and Nikki sighed. "You're lucky I answered the phone anyway." Nell continued, the sound of grievance building in her voice. "Where have you been? I've called you four times and it won't even go to voice mail." Point to Nell—15 love.

"I called you on Christmas. I left you a message. I told you; my phone got broken." Quick return from Nikki. Holly was decorating the lampshades now; Kit seemed to have fixated on the television.

"Did you leave it on my cell phone?" asked Nell sharply, hitting back.

"No, you told me not to. I left it on the home phone."

"Oh, well, you know I don't check that every day." Thirty-love to Nell.

"Well, I'm calling you now. Do you know how much this phone call is costing?" Blazing return from Nikki.

"I didn't ask you to call," Nell said, attempting a strong tone.

"No, I'm pretty sure you said, 'Make sure you call,' before I left." Score! 30–15!

"Well, maybe. How's Z'ev and Mexico? You know, it's funny, but the area code on the phone you're calling from is British." Nell's job at an international business development firm had given her an easy familiarity with most of the international calling codes.

"Er . . . ," said Nikki. Fault! Advantage Nell; score 40 to 15. "There was a last-minute assignment at work," Nikki mumbled.

"You're missing out on your vacation and Christmas with me for work?" demanded Nell.

"Vacation kind of got canceled." Weak return from the challenger!

"What? Why? Did he cancel it? Didn't you say he'd canceled twice already?" It's all over! Winner Nell Lanier. "Nikki! Didn't I teach you to stand up for yourself? If I were you, I'd tell him to drive straight or hit the road."

"Kind of did," said Nikki, wishing she could change the subject. "We broke up."

"Oh," said Nell, startled into silence. "I'm sorry, honey," she said at last. "I know you really liked him. I don't suppose there's a chance you two could work things out . . ."

"I don't really want to talk about it, Mom."

"Okay," said Nell, lapsing into silence. Emotional moments were not her forte. "Well, so is this new assignment good?" Nell's cheerfulness sounded a little forced.

"Uh, yeah," said Nikki, looking around at Kit, Holly, and Burg.

Burg was attempting to swing from the glass rack above the bar. Kit looked up from feathering the remote and made a face; Nikki smiled in response. "It's got its perks."

"Well, if they picked you for an emergency last-minute assignment then they must think you can get the job done."

"Mrs. M seemed confident, but I have to admit I'm not as convinced," said Nikki, eyeing Kit and wondering just how much trouble his mother was going to be.

"Oh, you can do it," said Nell with easy confidence. "Don't be a whiner."

"You're a real confidence booster there, Mom," said Nikki sarcastically.

"I'm just saying women can't be whiners in the workplace. We have to be go-getters if we want to get ahead."

"Yeah, you're right, Mom. And I guess I should probably go get them, so I can get ahead."

"That's the spirit," said Nell, somehow missing the bitterness in Nikki's voice. "Make sure to call again soon."

"Sure," replied Nikki, since there wasn't much else to say. "Talk to you soon. Love you."

"Love you too, sweetie! Bye!"

"Bye," said Nikki, hanging up. "Thanks," she said, handing the phone back to Kit.

"Sounds like our mothers should be in some sort of group," said Kit, taking the phone back with a grimace.

"How about an asylum?" suggested Nikki.

"There's a plan," said Kit with a laugh.

"What's with the boas?" asked Nikki, looking around. The room was quickly taking on a feathered quality.

"Kit's a hotel artist," explained Holly.

"You don't think that maybe it's a bit juvenile?" asked Nikki, looking around in disbelief. Holly's eyes widened in horror, as if she couldn't believe Nikki had just said that.

"Well . . . yeah," said Kit. "Of course. But I have to; it's in the rock and roll bylaws. Johnny Cash once painted an entire hotel room black. Aerosmith used to get long extension cords so they could leave the TVs plugged in when they threw them into the pool." Nikki must have looked confused because he added the explanation moments later. "They explode that way. Then there's Keith Moon's birthday food fight extravaganza that ended up in an arrest, a car in the pool, a trip to the dentist, and twenty-four thousand dollars in damages. And those were 1967 dollars."

"Yes, but"—Nikki frowned, trying to nail down her objection—"I'm pretty sure all those people were high."

"I know," said Kit, nodding. "That's the problem. When I was using, I was always too high to do anything really artistic. And I don't see why, just because I'm sober, I should be banned from juvenile and stupid behavior."

"Uh," said Nikki. It was strange and weird, but it did have a certain logic.

"Now, what do you want to glue?" asked Kit, holding out more boas.

"I wouldn't know where to start," she said.

"Just pick someplace and start gluing," he said. "You can't really get it wrong." He was smiling at her. It was a lopsided smile, but it seemed as if he was assuring her that everything was all right.

"Well," said Nikki tentatively, "I would kind of like to try the fireplace. But that could take a lot of boas."

"There's more where these came from," he said with a wink. Nikki smiled back and took her boa to the fireplace. It seemed very bad. Some interior decorator had spent a lot of time and energy on this suite. The glue was not going to be easy to remove. She wondered what Z'ev would do in this situation. She was having a hard time picturing Z'ev getting himself into this mess in the first place. Maybe that was the problem with them anyway. She was always in these situations. Her life was one long situation, and where did Z'ev fit into that?

"I love it!" said Kit, popping up from the other side of the couch a few minutes later.

"Really?" she asked, concerned he was merely being polite.

"Yes," he said, nodding enthusiastically. "It's like the Vietcong conquered the fireplace."

"I would need punji sticks for that," she said, testing the tautness of one of the trip wires/boas.

Kit laughed, and she was about to turn the conversation, casually but purposefully, to Duncan when there was a scream and a crash from the other end of the room. Nikki dropped her boa and stood up. Burg was lying, legs up in the air, below the bar.

"Are you all right?" asked Kit, hurrying to help him up.

"No, I bloody well am not," said Burg. "I just fell off the bar!"

"He was swinging from the glass rack again," said Holly, not looking the least bit sympathetic.

"I'm an ape," said Burg primly. "You can't expect me not to swing."

"Hm, well, aside from that," said Kit, clearly ignoring Burg, "what do we think? Are we done?"

"It's nice?" said Nikki tentatively. "It's like a bird whorehouse."

"Ook, ook! It's not nice," exclaimed Burg in some agitation. "It's like Big Bird exploded. I'm going to need therapy."

"You already need therapy," said Holly.

"Yes, but now I'll have something to talk about besides you."

"Maybe you ought to talk about your monkey fixation," said Nikki.

"What monkey fixation?" replied Burg.

"I don't feel quite done," said Kit, getting up and walking to the doorway. He looked around as if trying to gauge the impact it would have on a first-time visitor. A sudden sparkle leapt into his eye; walking swiftly to the phone he brushed aside the feathers and dialed the front desk.

"Yes, hello, this is Kit Masters in the penthouse. I need two dozen pink lawn flamingos and a box of lingerie." He listened for a moment. "No, I don't care about color. Whatever you can get is fine. Bird whorehouse," he said to the other three as he hung up. "We'll get them set up and then we'll get out the camera."

"I think the one over the bar is starting to come down," said Nikki, pointing.

"Oh, ook," said Burg. "I'm not going back up there."

"Don't worry," said Nikki, laughing and hopping up onto the bar. She was surprised that she actually was having a good time. "I'll take care of it."

"Don't go Burg on us," said Kit, hovering below her as she affixed the final piece.

"No worries," said Nikki, preparing to get down, but Kit reached up and lifted her by the waist, helping her down from the bar. He was surprisingly strong and Nikki landed with a soft jolt and unusual feeling of breathlessness as she looked up at him. He started to speak, but whatever he'd been about to say was interrupted by a knock on the door. Kit ran to crack the door and peer out.

"We saw them carrying flamingos," said a voice, "so we figured they had to be coming here."

"That's Hammond, the keyboardist," whispered Holly to Nikki.

"Yes, tip them and I'll let you in," replied Kit, looking excited but still not opening the door to its full extent. There was the sound of rustling pockets.

"I'm not sure what we've got," said a second voice.

"Richie, lead guitar." Holly identified him as if narrating.

"What does one tip for flamingos?" asked Richie.

"Just give it to them," said Kit impatiently.

There was a clink of coins and the sound of bellboys departing.

"Well?" asked Hammond. "They've gone. Now what have you done this time?"

Kit flung open the door and stood back.

"Dear God," said Hammond, entering the red-lit, feather-draped room. "It's like . . . I don't know what it's like. I love it."

"It's a bird whorehouse," said Kit proudly.

"Ah," said Richie. "That explains the flamingos."

"Yeah, help me set them up."

"I'll get the lingerie!" said Holly, reaching for the bag that Hammond was now bringing in from the hallway.

Kit snapped pictures while they set up flamingos and draped garter belts around them. Nikki picked up a particularly stretchy bit of lace and on impulse snapped it like a rubber band at Burg's face.

"Oook!" yelled Burg, pounding his chest in rage.

"Oh, it's on!" said Richie, reaching for more lingerie ammunition. Laughing, Nikki dove for a garter belt and fired back. The fight might have escalated from there if Duncan had not appeared in the doorway.

"Lovely," said Duncan. Kit glanced at him, and a sudden shift in mood spread across the room. It was if the parents had returned.

"Well," said Hammond, clearing his throat and removing the garter from around his head, "we've all got to get up early in the morning. I suppose we should turn in."

"Yes. Really lovely room, Kit," said Holly, following Hammond to the door.

"See you in the morning," said Nikki inanely, making her own exit, with Burg and Richie close on her heels.

"Anyone want breakfast?" asked Burg as they entered the elevator. "I'm starved."

"Well, to tell the truth, I've been up for over twenty-four hours and I could use the sleep," said Nikki, checking Trista's phone; it was nearly three thirty AM. She had lost track of home time vs. Colombian time vs. German time, but she was very clear on the fact that she was tired.

"We generally sleep on the tour bus," said Hammond. "It helps, really, since there's nothing to do on the bus besides sleep and get in fights. Plus, Kit's got an interview in the morning. There will be lots of lovely uninterrupted sleep on the bus while we're waiting for him."

"I'll just take you back to the room," said Holly with a wry smile, eyeing Nikki's doubtful expression.

GERMANY VI

Green T-shirt Blues

December 27

"'Kit Masters in Concert Debacle,'" read Richie, unfolding the morning paper.

"That wasn't a debacle, that was a death trap," Hammond put in.

"'Has Kit returned to his old gig-ditching ways?'" Richie continued.

"He's ditched before?" asked Nikki from her seat on the bus, and Holly nodded. She had been rousted from her bed mere moments before and then herded onto the double-decker tour bus. Nikki had tried to talk to Trista, but Trista had ducked straight into a limo with Kit, Brandt, and Angela. With nowhere else to go, Nikki had followed the band dutifully onto the bus. They were now going to the TV station, where Holly had promised that they would all be settling back down to sleep. Instead they were reading the review of last night's show.

"Last tour he walked out on five shows. No reason. Or at least no good ones. It's why people were a little leery of booking us this time," answered Holly.

"'The Masters management at Faustus Records cited unsafe machinery as the reason, but disappointed fans demand full-price refunds.'"

"That's so unfair," said Burg vehemently. "He's been a rock this tour and the one time he walks out—with good reason—he gets absolutely pilloried."

Nikki sighed. After talking to Ewart, the possibility of Kit or the band actually dying seemed small. On the other hand, the safety mechanisms didn't seem to be common knowledge; someone may have intended death.

The bus slowed for a long turn into a parking lot and stopped, idling.

The television studio was an unimpressive cube of concrete populated by people in business suits. Kit's limo door was being opened by station personnel and Trista was exiting as well. Suddenly Nikki was tired of waiting. She had important things to do; she could not be waiting on the vagaries of a rock star.

"Be right back, guys," she said. And without waiting for their response, she galloped down the bus stairs and dashed over to the car.

"Nikki!" exclaimed Trista as Nikki appeared at her elbow. "What are you doing here?"

"I needed to talk to you," said Nikki.

"We can't talk now," said Trista. "I have to prep Kit for his interview."

Nikki glanced at Kit. He was shaking hands with a number of stuffed suits and as if feeling her gaze, he looked over his shoulder and flashed a brilliant smile, as if to say, 'I know this is ridiculous, but I have to do it, try not to laugh.' Nikki found herself smiling back.

"Trista, you and Nikki coming?" he asked, yelling a little across the top of the limo.

"Be right there!" chirped Trista, then turned to Nikki. "We'll talk after I get his makeup done. You should go back to the bus."

"I think I'll go see what a TV interview looks like. I was invited, after all." With a Mrs. Merrivel–like smile, Nikki brushed past Trista and followed Kit and his entourage into the building. Duncan was the last in, holding the door for everyone. He scrutinized them as they entered, as if his eyes were an X-ray machine.

"We need to talk," said Duncan as she passed him. Nikki's eyes flicked up to meet his, but he was looking out into the parking lot. She glanced away and nodded.

"After the interview," she said, and he gave his own nod.

She followed the parade of people as they entered the offices. Kit, accompanied by Brandt and Angela, made the meet-and-greet rounds, while Trista made a beeline for the greenroom. After watching people fawn for a few minutes, Nikki followed her.

Trista settled into the greenroom, setting up her own stock of brushes and makeup. With nothing better to do, Nikki perched on the couch and looked around, only then noticing that one of the side tables held a chilling bottle of champagne.

"Should that be here?" asked Nikki, pointing to the champagne.

"Oh, for the love of . . . !" exclaimed Trista, clearly angry. "He was always so fond of champagne. Don't they know he's trying to stay sober? Can you find someone to give it to?" Nikki nodded and toted the champagne out into the corridor, looking for someone to direct her. She could see Kit's entourage down the hall; secretaries and other worker bees were swarming forth from their cubicles to look at him.

"Hey," she said, snagging the first passing drone. "Is there someplace I can put this? He doesn't want it." She jerked her head in Kit's direction.

"Is it the wrong kind?" he asked, a worried crease forming between his eyebrows. "We got what was on the list."

"List?" she asked.

The man produced a clipboard with a fax sheet on it; it was titled "Greenroom Requirements." Scanning the list, Nikki saw that champagne had been added by hand just below M&M's; Nikki spared a thought to wonder if someone had gone through to pick out the brown ones à la Van Halen.

"See? It's on the list."

"Why is it handwritten?" she asked. The man frowned, clearly confused by the language difference.

"It's not typed," she said, miming writing.

"Ah," said the man, comprehension dawning. "Someone called to request."

Nikki cocked her head to the right, her face remaining expressionless. "Do you know who? Who called?" she asked, saying the second sentence slightly louder and then feeling stupid about it.

"A woman," said the man. "It is not the right kind?"

"No, it's fine," said Nikki, "but he doesn't want it now," she said. The German frowned, trying to wrap his brain around the concept of a rock star not wanting alcohol. "He might want it later, but not now," she added, hoping to smooth things over.

"Ah," said the man, as if he understood. "I will put it into icebox, yes?"

"Yes, perfect," said Nikki, dropping the ice bucket into his hands and returning to the dressing room. Trista was lighting a small purple candle that smelled like lavender. Nikki raised her eyebrows.

"He likes the smell," said Trista. "Lavender is very soothing."

"Uh-huh," said Nikki, not really listening. Someone had purposely requested alcohol for a recovering alcoholic. A woman—and that narrowed the pool of suspects a bit. Not that a man couldn't have a female accomplice. Duncan entered and quickly surveyed the room, leaving the door open. He moved with the efficient smoothness of a professional. Outside the door, she could hear the swell of voices as Kit and his entourage got closer.

Angela, Duncan, and Kit all swept into the room accompanied by the most persistent autograph seekers among the office staff. Kit signed the proffered papers with a practiced hand, and just as easily Duncan shoved them out the door. Nikki admired the big man's adroit manner of bullying individuals without actually making physical contact.

When the room had been cleared Kit flopped onto the couch next to Nikki and Angela took a seat in the makeup chair. The producer made ass-kissing noises until Duncan politely asked him to leave.

Nikki critically examined Angela; a woman had called to ask for the champagne to be added to the list, and Tracksuit could have been a woman. Beside her, Kit was playing with the zipper on his hoodie, running it up and down to his own internal rhythm, until it sounded like a DJ scratching.

Angela was twentysomething and tall in her high heels. Long and slender, she was the kind of woman whom other women love to hate. But Nikki was startled to realize that she didn't. Like someone being shown how a magic trick worked, Nikki could spot all the tricks Angela was using to look like an alpha female. High heels, lacy undershirt peeking from the décolletage of her power suit, black-rimmed glasses to offset the sexiness, bleached hair pulled up into a French twist. Nikki had worn that very outfit at least twice to go undercover. She wondered what Angela looked like on a dateless Saturday night. She was willing to bet it was sweats, a ponytail, and a pint of Ben and Jerry's all the way.

Angela was still on the phone, speaking halfway-decent French, but she was having trouble coming up with the French vocabulary to describe stage assembly parts. Angela flipped through her day planner and then covered the phone's receiver with one hand.

"Does anyone know the French for 'black nylon'? I'm on the phone with the supplier." Everyone stared blankly at her, and Kit waved his hands as if warding off an oncoming plane.

"*Tissu en nylon noir,*" said Nikki.

"Uh-huh," said Angela, narrowing her eyes at Nikki, and then went back to the phone. "*Non, non.* I need thirty meters of *tissu en nylon noir.*" While Angela harassed the supplier, Nikki became aware that she had drawn the attention of everyone in the room. Nikki smiled awkwardly; when was she going to learn to keep her mouth shut?

"Brilliant," said Kit, looking impressed. "You'll come in handy."

"Everyone's met Nikki, right?" asked Trista, clearing her throat somewhat reprovingly. "She's going to be helping out for a few days, and then she's going to fill in for me when my granddaughter's born. I know she didn't get properly introduced last night, but it was rather last-minute." Nikki sighed in annoyance; they should have gone over her cover story together before Trista just blurted it out to the assembly.

"Hi," said Nikki.

"But you're American," rumbled Duncan, as if he didn't approve of multilinguists, and Nikki winced. One word and she'd managed to reveal herself.

"Who's American?" asked Brandt, slipping through the

door. "It is a mob scene out there! They love you, Kit!" Kit shrugged. Brandt scanned the room and seemed to see Nikki for the first time. "You must be the American; I know all these other bums here." He stepped forward to shake her hand. "Brandt Dettling."

"Nikki Lanier," said Nikki, and shook his hand. His was a firm handshake—not firm enough to crush and not weak enough to insult her either. He added a raffish grin to the handshake, turning on the charm. "I'm going to be helping Trista for a few days."

"Great! The more the merrier, as someone said." But she could tell that he was disappointed; he'd wasted his smile on a mere makeup lady. "Well," he said, turning back to the room. "Let's get this show on the road. Kit, you're not really going to wear that, are you?"

Kit was lighting a cigarette and stopped with the flame of his lighter still flickering.

"I'd been planning on it," he said grimly, flicking the lighter closed.

"You look like you just got up!"

"I did," said Kit, taking a drag. "When you schedule these things last-minute, you get last-minute fashion."

"Would you two stop fussing?" clucked Trista, flapping her hands at Angela, who vacated the makeup chair but didn't get off the phone. "You know I'd never let my boy go out looking less than his best." She patted the canvas seat invitingly and Kit grinned his charming smile that probably made girls of all ages trip over their feet.

"Of course you wouldn't," said Kit. "I can't imagine what we were thinking." He stood up, stretching his hands over his head, before moving to the makeup chair, unlit cigarette still dangling from his lip. Trista started vigorously brushing his hair; Kit seemed unperturbed.

Angela handed Brandt a piece of paper, jabbing it at him to get his attention, since she was now arguing about the cost of an additional electrician. Brandt took the paper reluctantly and looked over it.

"The question list from the producer is in," he said casually. "Usual stuff—who're you sleeping with, how's the sobriety going, new album."

"The new album is off the list," said Kit.

"Kit, we need to generate excitement for it now, so that when it drops we've got the kids waiting in line."

"Brandt, what am I supposed to talk about? There is no new album. I haven't written anything worthwhile in two months."

"You're just stressed out," said Brandt. "You'll come around in time."

"Maybe," said Kit. "And maybe I won't, but I'm not going to talk about my writing with some German twat of a television host."

There was a long, uncomfortable moment of silence, and then Brandt crumpled up the sheet with a loud crackling noise.

"Fine," said Brandt, shooting the paper ball into the wastebasket with a surprising athleticism. "It's off the list."

Trista began applying cleanser and unzipped Kit's hooded sweatshirt to reach his neck, *tch*-ing over the ratty KISS T-shirt underneath.

"I stole it from Richie."

"Richie should invest in some new clothing," said Brandt severely.

"It was either this or his Rainbow Brite shirt," said Kit cheerfully as Trista applied moisturizer to his face.

"Well then I'm glad you went with Kiss, but you couldn't find something without holes?" asked Trista, trying for a lighthearted note.

"In Richie's bag? No."

"She's right, Kit, you're moving onto the international stage here. You could at least dress the part," said Brandt, looking vaguely around the room as if he'd misplaced something and rattling a few M&M's in his hand. Kit's face twitched in a paroxysm of annoyance, but his voice was relaxed when he spoke.

"I don't tear down your suits, Brandt. Leave me my T-shirts."

"No need to get all stroppy," replied Brandt. "It's your career, after all. I'm just trying to be helpful." Brandt tossed the M&M's in his mouth.

Nikki was certain that Kit would blow a gasket here, since he hadn't actually been getting "stroppy"—whatever that was. Instead he picked up one of the lids from Trista's bottles of goop and screwed it into his eye like a monocle.

"I would like to speaken to ze manager!" said Kit in a terrible German accent.

"I am ze manager," Brandt responded, but half-reluctantly.

"Please to tell ze singer he must wearen ze pants!"

"He says you have to wear pants, old boy," answered Brandt, smiling in spite of himself.

"But I am wearing pants!" exclaimed Kit, popping the monocle/lid out to speak in his own voice and then popping it back in to use his German accent. Brandt joined him for what was obviously the punch line of the joke.

"But they are not on your bottom!"

Brandt gave a chuckle that filled the room; Kit grinned and let Trista take the lid back.

"The rules never said we had to wear pants on our legs,"

said Kit around Trista's makeup sponge. "I really think we were unfairly treated. We should sue. Remember that old man's face? I thought he was going to have an apoplexy."

"He was a bit red in the face. That was a good night!" Brandt's nostalgic smile held a trace of sadness.

"If I could remember more of it, I'm sure I would agree," said Kit.

"Ten minutes," said a headset-clad woman, popping her head in the door. Kit waved his acknowledgment as Trista finished, applying some powder. Smearing hair gel between her palms, she spiked his hair with expert fingers, giving his makeover the final touch. Nikki had to admit that in a matter of minutes, Trista had somehow managed to take Kit from frazzled and sleepless to trendily dirty.

Brandt and Angela disappeared shortly after Kit went onstage, leaving Trista and Nikki to watch the show from the greenroom. There was some banter from the host in German, which Nikki didn't understand, and then Kit came out to massive cheers from the audience and the host switched to English.

"They'll subtitle it later," said Trista.

"The champagne's on the fax sheet of dressing room requirements," answered Nikki, following her own train of thought.

"What?" asked Trista.

"I gave the champagne that was in here to someone, and he showed me a faxed list of dressing room requirements. Someone called in and added it to the list."

"This is the third time that's happened!" Trista began to stack her brushes and bottles back into their purple Carrie Mae case, slamming them down harder than necessary.

"Well, he's made it this far," said Nikki practically. She wasn't sure how far "this" was, but he seemed to be coping.

"And it's been longer than any of his other dry spells," said Trista, "but that's why I'm worried. How much longer can he hold out? Especially since he's not writing."

"Not writing . . . ," Nikki repeated, unclear on the connection.

"Songs. He's blocked. And I don't think he's ever written anything sober—not a whole album anyway. I don't know, maybe Camille's right. Maybe he isn't cut out to be a rock star."

On the TV, Kit was smiling his rock star smile and lying through his teeth.

"The new record? No, it doesn't have a name yet. But, yeah . . ." Kit ran his hand through his hair; Nikki caught only a tiny flash of anger before he smiled and answered. "Yeah, it's going great."

"I don't know . . . ," said Nikki, thinking of the hotel room. "He seems rock starrish to me. Why wouldn't Camille want him to be a singer?"

"Besides the obvious danger of exposing him to people like Cano?" asked Trista sharply. "Or the fact that it has led him to a nearly fatal level of addiction? Besides all that, I can't think of a single reason."

"Maybe you should tell me more about these 'accidents,'" said Nikki, deciding not to argue. Trista sighed loudly, still annoyed. "I talked to Holly about them last night."

"You talked to Holly? Well, I'm sure she covered it then." Trista loosened up and then retightened a bottle lid.

"I'd rather get your professional opinion." Sucking up never hurt.

"They're nothing really that big; probably just accidents. I think everyone's just been a little on edge. A tire blew out on the bus. And you might think that would make the bus flip over, but Louis, the bus driver, says buses don't work that way anymore . . ."

"And maybe it was somebody who didn't know enough about

bus tires to know that wouldn't make a bus crash. What about the helicopter?" Nikki asked, and Trista shrugged uncomfortably.

"Someone didn't do their job, and the helicopter got fueled incorrectly. They had to make an emergency landing. Which is why Kit's taking the tour bus everywhere now. It was rather tense for everyone on board, but Brandt and Duncan were with him. He was never in any real danger." Nikki was about to ask how they could have possibly protected him from a helicopter crash when Trista glanced at Nikki and then back at her makeup bottles. Nikki's instincts pricked up their ears; Trista was about to say something interesting.

"I'm a bit worried about Duncan, to tell the truth," said Trista. "He's always around when these things happen."

"He's security," Nikki said, playing devil's advocate. "Presumably he's always around."

"Yes, but like that groupie last night. Duncan vetted her. He always does. So how did she end up with drugs?"

"Mmmm," said Nikki, choosing not to comment on the groupie. The existence of the groupie kind of grossed her out, but she knew she'd sound naïve if she said so. "You think he's behind the accidents?" she asked, returning to the subject of Duncan. Trista shrugged in response.

Nikki thought about Trista's theory; she didn't think Duncan could be Tracksuit. Their physiques were quite different in her memory, but she supposed it was possible. Ewart had said that Duncan had been lurking around his machinery. Motive was a bit of a mystery, although in her experience, money proved to be all that most people needed.

"So why haven't you investigated these accidents?" asked Nikki. Trista was ex–Carrie Mae; she should have been able to handle a few mysterious happenings.

"I've got a job to do, you know!" Trista exclaimed. "I can't be haring off after unexplained accidents that might not be anything more than accidents."

"Well, I'm just assuming that Camille made Kit hire you as extra security. I figured you'd both be concerned."

"Why would anyone want to hurt Kit?" asked Trista.

"You don't think the accidents are intentional?" Nikki scratched her head; Trista wasn't making any sense.

Trista shrugged again, her back still to Nikki. "With so many people running about, something's bound to go wrong on a tour. Like I said, no one would hurt Kit."

"Even Cano?" asked Nikki. She couldn't really understand Trista's mind-set. She wasn't worried about the accidents, but she was worried about Kit. She didn't make sense.

"Well, Cano would," said Trista, turning around, eyes wide. "Cano would in a heartbeat. He hated Camille. He hated Declan and . . . all of them. He thought they were traitors to the cause. He'd off Kit as soon as a blink."

"Why did Cano hate them?" asked Nikki.

"They were quitting the IRA. Well, Declan was quitting. Camille never really was IRA. And after Declan's death Camille burned him with all the groups in the region. But it wasn't just them. The world was changing. People weren't supporting violent movements anymore."

"Violence is not a sustainable political tactic," said Nikki, and Trista shrugged.

"Cano blamed Camille; he would try to hurt Kit. I suppose he could be responsible for the accidents." Trista sounded as if the thought had just occurred to her.

"Yeah . . . " said Nikki. "I thought so too. But the more I learn about the accidents the more they sound sort of . . . half-assed.

Scary, sure, but not really dangerous. Cano sounds like more of a whole ass."

"That platform could have fallen and killed everyone!" exclaimed Trista.

"There's an emergency brake on it. It won't tilt past fifteen degrees without shutting down. I talked to Ewart last night."

"Oh," said Trista. "I guess—" Whatever she had been about to say was cut off by the ringing of a cell phone, causing both women to jump.

"It's an unlisted number," said Trista, handing her the phone. "It's probably for you."

"This is Nikki."

"Nikki?" said a voice, and Nikki recognized Astriz's German accent. "I'm checking in. I'm still on Cano's trail, but I keep losing the signal and must back the track frequently. Have you had any luck?"

"Not much," said Nikki. "Where are you now?"

"Reims," said Astriz.

"France?"

"*Ja*. I think Cano is heading for Paris—away from Mr. Masters. What do you want to do?"

"The tour goes to Paris next, right?" asked Nikki, looking up at Trista.

"Yes. There will be a few days off for everyone, and then the New Year's Eve show."

"Hm," said Astriz, overhearing the conversation. "It might be coincidence."

"Or Cano may be planning to meet the tour," said Nikki.

"Plausible. We will meet in Paris?" asked Astriz.

"Sounds like," Nikki said. "Keep in touch."

"*Ja*," said Astriz, and hung up.

"Exactly like Val," said Nikki, shaking her head. "Would it kill people to say good-bye before hanging up?"

"Who's Val?" asked Trista.

"Nobody," Nikki lied. "Where do you think Duncan is?"

"Interview's almost over; he'd be securing the exit, I guess," answered Trista with a shrug.

"Great," said Nikki, "I need to talk to him."

"Mmm . . . ," said Trista. It was a peculiar noise, sort of Marge Simpson–ish. "I'm not sure . . . Duncan is . . ."

"Duncan is what?" asked Nikki. "I thought you said you were suspicious of him."

"He's very devoted to Kit," said Trista, looking faintly embarrassed.

"Right," Nikki said sarcastically. "And no one would ever hurt Kit. I'll meet you at the bus."

Duncan was in the parking lot. He appeared to be returning from the bus, and he checked his stride when he saw Nikki.

"You talked to Ewart," he said without preamble when they were near enough to speak.

"Yes," said Nikki, surprised by his bluntness.

"You told him to come to Paris, and you would talk to Kit about getting his job back."

"Yes," said Nikki with a shrug. "He was fired without reason. That stage was rigged."

"Yes, I know," said Duncan. "But you will not be talking to anyone about that. Christopher does not need to know that the stage was more than an accident." It was the first time she'd heard anyone call Kit by his full name.

"Shouldn't you be more worried about who's causing these accidents than covering them up?" said Nikki.

Duncan rolled his eyes. "If you're going to pretend to be helping Trista, don't you think you should have packed some luggage?" he fired back.

"It got misplaced," she said lamely, and he shook his head.

"I don't need any more Carrie Mae women around here," he said, emphasizing his words with a pointing forefinger. "You tell Camille that Christopher is going to keep on singing." Before she could respond, the doors swung open and Kit exited with his entourage in tow.

"All right, buddy boy," said Brandt as they kissed the TV station execs. "I'll see you in Paris. Have fun on the bus."

"Aren't you coming?" asked Kit, looking surprised.

"I can't follow you around the whole tour like the old days, Kit," said Brandt.

"No, I know. I just thought you were riding to Paris with us."

"We're taking the helicopter," said Angela. "We've got to be in Paris early to set up for your press junket."

Kit blanched slightly, but whether it was from the mention of the helicopter or the press junket, Nikki couldn't tell.

"All right. I guess I'll see you there, then."

GERMANY VII

You Can Get What You Need

"Are you reading that crap?" asked Kit as he entered the bus and noticed Richie's newspaper.

"Actually, I was thinking about putting it into the loo for personal use later," said Richie, folding the paper down again.

"No, seriously," said Kit, snatching the paper out of Richie's hands and crumpling it into a ball. "I don't like seeing that shit."

"Yeah, sure," said Richie, slightly sullenly. "Sorry."

"I'm going upstairs to get some sleep," said Kit. "I suggest the rest of you do the same."

Nikki felt confused by Kit's suddenly diva-like behavior. He'd seemed so easygoing last night. Why did he just assume that he could boss people around like that?

There were general murmurs of agreement as he climbed the stairs to the bus's upper floor, but no one followed him except

Duncan. Everyone else began to curl up on the far less comfortable downstairs bus seats. Nikki shook her head.

With nothing else to do, Nikki found a blanket in one of the overhead compartments and followed the suit of her traveling companions. The morning was turning into a dark, wintery afternoon when Nikki awoke, bleary-eyed, to look out the window. Periodically a small village passed by in the distance. For a while, Nikki was content to watch the scenery drift by and listen to the steady rhythm of the road. The weather was cold and bleak and made her long for the warm days of California. In her head, California was always summer and beaches and all those nonnative palm trees that had somehow become iconographic of the place. That's what she'd wanted her Christmas to be—warm and beachy.

Nikki lay perpendicular to Z'ev with her head on his stomach. The sun beat down on them, making a dew of sweat form in Nikki's joints and cleavage. Frisbee Man ran by for the bazillionth time. Nikki buried one foot in the sand and then, being too lazy to hold it there, watched the foot flick upward, sending sand into the air.

"Man, those Frisbee guys are making me feel lazy. We should get up and go do something."

"We should," said Z'ev, moving only his lips.

There was a long pause. Nikki listened to the distant screech of gulls and children overlaying the faint buzz of voices and machinery from the Santa Monica Pier.

"I don't actually *want* to do anything. I just feel like I should," commented Nikki.

"Did you pack my gun?"

"Yeah," answered Nikki around a yawn. "It's in my bag." She waved negligently toward the pink straw bag that matched her flip-flops.

"Hand it to me; I'll shoot the Frisbee players and then you won't feel guilty anymore."

Nikki chuckled and rolled to the side and bit him lightly on the stomach. "This is a no-shooting-people day, remember?"

"Oh, right; my bad."

"Can you hand me the sunscreen?"

Z'ev, moving only his arm, reached down, fumbled for the bottle, and started to hand it across his body to Nikki, when he caught sight of the label.

"SPF fifty? Jeez, babe, you're never going to get a tan."

"He thinks I tan," laughed Nikki as she applied another layer of sunscreen. "I'm a redhead, Z'ev. I have two colors: Day-Glo white and lobster red. Not all of us were born as lucky as you." She poked him in his latte-colored side with her index finger. "Can you put some on my back?" she asked, holding up the sunscreen.

"Well, at least I know you'll never come home that weird orange fake-bake color," he said, smearing sunscreen haphazardly on her back. "You're just always going to be my little vanilla cookie." He added the last part in a Cookie Monster voice that he knew always made her laugh and faked gnawing on her shoulder. Nikki giggled, twisting away from his ticklish lips. "Now I'm hungry," he said in his normal voice. "You want to go get some ice cream?"

Under the corner of her towel Nikki felt her phone vibrate. She faked a yawn-and-stretch, covering the motion of her phone.

"Ice cream sounds wonderful. I think you should go get it," she said.

"You think I should . . . Lazy bum."

Nikki stuck her tongue out at him. "If you want boyfriend privileges, this is the price you pay."

He laughed and flicked at her nose with one finger. "Whatever, wife." It was their oldest joke, and Nikki grinned at it. "What flavor do you want?" he asked, standing up and shuffling into his flip-flops.

"Vanilla, what else?" said Nikki, as he pulled on his shirt and reached in her bag for his wallet.

"Does that mean I have to get chocolate?"

"Cappuccino, maybe," suggested Nikki.

"Mocha swirl," he shot back over his shoulder, and Nikki laughed.

As soon as he was out of earshot, Nikki grabbed her phone and hit "call back."

"Jane, I told you I've got Z'ev this weekend. I'm totally Do Not Disturb!"

"I know, I know," said Jane, "but we've got a little situation here. Mrs. M wants you to come in."

"And how am I supposed to explain that to Z'ev?" demanded Nikki.

"Tell him there's an emergency with the event you're coordinating. The florist ordered the wrong flowers and no one can figure out where the invoices are or something."

"Yeah, OK, what event am I coordinating again?" Nikki asked, rolling her eyes. How long was Z'ev going to keep buying this crap?

"Uh . . . the Women's Symposium Breakfast," said Jane.

"We really need to come up with better names," said Nikki.

"Sue me," said Jane. "You can name the next one."

Another hour passed, which Nikki filled with memories of Z'ev. The warm sunshine in her memory made her present feel even colder. A general restlessness set in—eating and sleeping had lost their entertainment value, and everyone settled into the serious business of irritating the crap out of each other.

Richie was sorting through his laundry based on smell. Hammond was jotting things down in a notebook, and Holly was laughing at the good bits of her book but wouldn't tell anyone what the joke was. Burg beat a steady tattoo on the back of the seat in front of him, punctuating the rhythm with an occasional belch.

"Damn it, Burg," yelled Richie, chucking dirty socks at Burg's head. "Can you stop that infernal racket? I can't hear myself think!"

"I'm bored out of my mind; why should you be able to think? Where are we, anyway?"

"Someplace near Kehl, I think," said Hammond.

"Really?" asked Burg, looking out with more interest. "I knew a girl from there once." There was a thoughtful pause while they watched the buildings and hedges go by. A nativity scene flashed by on the other side of a hedgerow. "I should look her up and apologize." There was another pause, but this time everyone was considering what action the perpetually naked, belching, expectorating, and farting Burg would think worthy of an apology.

"Burg," said Holly, closing her book, apparently bowing to the inevitable. "What's your real name?"

"It's Burg," said Burg without looking around.

"No, it isn't," said Hammond. "I saw your paycheck; it said F. Harris."

"It's short for Fredericksburg," he said, looking around with a smile only faintly tainted by embarrassment.

"Like Fredericksburg, Virginia?" asked Nikki, puzzled.

"That's the one," said Burg, nodding happily.

"Why would anyone name their child after a city in Virginia?" asked Richie.

"Well, my brothers are named Chicago, Dallas, and Denver."

"Fredericksburg isn't exactly in the same league with those. Shouldn't you be named something like Seattle or Miami?" asked Nikki.

"It was a compromise," said Burg. "My dad wanted to call me Frederick after Granddad, but Mum wanted to stick with the city theme."

"Ah," said Nikki. Burg's oddity was starting to seem a product of genetics.

"Hey, speaking of names," said Burg. "You know what we need?"

"A mute button for you?" replied Hammond genially.

"No, don't be silly; I'm at least as annoying in mime. No, what we need is a band name. We can't just be the Band."

"That one's taken anyway," said Hammond.

"Dead Mimes," suggested Holly.

"Purple Weasels!" exclaimed Richie. "I've always wanted to call a band the Purple Weasels."

"We could be the Egregious Philibins," said Burg. "That's a name that's too silly to be anything other than a band name."

"Hey, Louis!" yelled Holly to the bus driver. "What should we name the band?"

"The Dental Philosophers," yelled Louis from the driver's seat. That got another laugh.

"What's everyone yelling about?" asked Kit, coming down the stairs, looking more rested and in a happier mood.

"We're trying to come up with band names," said Holly coolly when no one else jumped in. "So far we've rejected the Purple Weasels, Egregious Philibins, and Dental Philosophers."

"Well, one look at the lot of you and I'd think it'd be obvious," said Kit affectionately, leaning on the back of a seat. "It's got to be the Mongol Horde."

"I kind of like that," said Richie, shaking out a Care Bears T-shirt.

"I like Communist Synthesizers," said Hammond.

"You would, you damn keyboarding Commie," said Burg. "How about Sherpa's Union?"

"What about the Rhythm Method?" said Nikki, and Holly burst out laughing, rocking back and forth, her braids swinging.

"I don't get it," said Burg.

"It might be kind of a girl thing," said Nikki apologetically.

Hammond's puzzled frown cleared. "Oh, dear," he said.

"Oh," said Kit and Richie at the same time.

"We'd never get away with it," said Hammond.

"I don't know," said Kit, grinning. "That's kind of tempting."

"I still don't get it," said Burg.

"And you probably never will," said Kit, laughing. "Richie, come upstairs and play some whist with me."

It wasn't so much what he said as how he said it that bothered Nikki. There was no question in his tone. There was just the command to go upstairs. It wasn't delivered with any sort of malice; it was just the base assumption that Richie would obey. Nikki frowned. She couldn't decide whether or not she liked Kit. One minute he seemed vulnerably disarming, the next he seemed like the lord of the manor. He was like a sore tooth that she couldn't stop poking at.

"Whist?" asked Richie, looking pained. "Nobody plays whist anymore, old boy. You're going to lose your rock star privileges if you play games that went out of fashion with your grandmother."

"My grandmother is very fashion-forward, I'll have you know," said Kit impudently. "You too, Nikki, come on." He bounded up the stairs without waiting for Nikki's reply. Nikki gritted her teeth; Trista beamed at her. Richie got up to follow.

"Playing cards—this will be nice," Trista said happily, and Richie turned a questioning look her way.

Nikki shook her head. "That's all right. I don't feel much like playing. You go ahead."

Nikki became aware that the entire bus had turned to look at her.

"But you've got to," said Trista in dismay. "He asked for you specifically. That means he likes you, and he doesn't like everyone."

"Well, I don't like everyone," said Nikki, "but I don't always get to play with my favorite people."

"Come on," said Richie from the stairs. "Don't leave me alone with the whist. I'll never figure out what I'm doing on my own."

Nikki sighed, knowing already that she was going to give in.

"Please, just go upstairs and play cards with him," pleaded Trista. "What's wrong with playing cards?"

"This is ridiculous," muttered Nikki. "Normal people do not just get to demand that people play with them."

"He's not normal," said Trista. "He's Kit."

"You can't always get what you want!"

"But if you try sometimes . . . ," murmured Holly without removing her face from her book. Nikki shook her head and grudgingly got up.

"I'm doing this for Richie," said Nikki, frowning at Trista's anxious face. "I'm hoping to win his Oasis shirt off of him."

"Ook. Good luck with that," said Burg, adding a belch for good measure. "Oasis is his favorite."

Nikki trudged up the stairs, following Richie, and found herself wondering if Richie would fit into her jeans or if he would find them too big. Why were rock guys always so skinny? Were only skinny guys attracted to the guitar? Or did you become skinny by spending so much time playing the guitar?

"Nikki says she's going to try to win my Oasis shirt off me," reported Richie as they reached the second story.

"Strip whist. Now there's a thought," said Kit, twisting an imaginary villain's mustache. "And wait, you own an Oasis shirt? Heretic!"

"It's vintage!" protested Richie good-naturedly. "From their '98 tour!"

"I'm not sure if that makes it better or worse," said Kit, throwing himself onto one of the bench seats.

Nikki looked around the padded interior of the second story. Near the stairs were two rows of traditional bus seats. Beyond those, couches lined the walls and formed a U shape at the front of the bus. There was a low coffee table at the bend of the U; Kit took the seat on the other side of the coffee table, a solitary spot of subdued blue jeans and navy hoodie against the crimson plush. There were metal poles sunk into the floor, and Nikki leaned against one as the bus swayed around a corner.

"What's wrong with Oasis?" she asked.

"Nothing, except they're complete shite," said Richie, taking a seat next to Kit.

"Can we play with odd numbers?" asked Nikki.

"There are four of us," said Duncan in a quiet voice, showing a disconcerting ability for sneaking up on Nikki. He'd been sunk down behind one of the seats, but she still should have spotted him. Duncan pulled a foldout chair from one of the overhead bins and unfolded it with a magician's snap, placing it opposite Kit at the coffee table. Then he sat opposite Richie, effectively forcing

Nikki into the folding seat. Nikki frowned; she didn't like being surprised, out maneuvered, or having her back to a door.

Kit took two decks of well-thumbed cards out of his sweatshirt pockets.

"I'm not sure I'm qualified for a two-deck card game," said Nikki, not moving from her spot against the pole.

"You just keep one at the ready," said Duncan, taking one and shuffling. "The dealer's partner shuffles it and puts it to the dealer's left. It speeds things along." He shuffled the cards long edge to long edge and then jammed them together with a forceful shove. Kit copied the shuffle in an exact duplication of his movement.

"So who's partnering with whom?" asked Nikki.

"Who's partnering with whom," repeated Richie mockingly. "Who says the Americans can't speak English?"

"I give, who does say that?" responded Nikki.

"The English," answered Duncan. "I'll take Richie; you get Kit."

"What if I don't want him?" asked Nikki, peeved at having her decisions made for her.

"Everyone wants me," answered Kit, half-serious. "I'm a rock star."

"I'm not spoiled. I'm not, I'm not, I'm not!" murmured Nikki, taking her foldout seat. That got a chuckle from Richie and a reproving glance from Duncan.

"With whist," said Kit, skillfully ignoring something that might upset him, "you simply deal all the cards out. Partners sit across from each other. The last card dealt is the trump card. Person to the dealer's left starts the play; all other players must play a card to match the first card's suit. If you don't have a card of that suit, then you can play any card. Once a trick is all played the person with the highest card of that suit or the highest trump card takes the trick. The person who wins the trick starts the play on the next one. When all cards have been played, the team with the most tricks taken wins. But you don't start scoring until after you win six tricks. First team to five points wins."

"What kind of game doesn't count the first six points?" asked Nikki, slightly outraged.

"Whist!" replied Duncan and Kit in unison. Nikki shook her head and picked up her cards. She had a feeling that whist had been invented in a century that didn't have television.

Whist was surprisingly more complicated than it looked, and the first few hands were spent in intense concentration. Nikki frowned as Duncan took another trick; she wasn't sure when she had acquired such an intense aversion to losing, but the fact that Richie and Duncan were one winning hand away from actually starting to count points was bringing out the sore loser in her. She hadn't always been so competitive, had she? Nikki couldn't remember; she wondered if it was a habit she'd picked up from Z'ev. Now, there was a competitive man.

She played the three of clubs while picturing Z'ev's solid form, his crisp white shirt setting off brown skin with a sly smile in his deep cocoa-colored eyes.

"Nikki!" Kit scolded her as Richie scooped up the cards with a grin.

"Damn, sorry," said Nikki guiltily. "I was thinking about something else."

"Keep thinkin', darlin'; it's doin' fine for me," said Duncan cheerfully, and Nikki looked at him thoughtfully as his English accent slipped slightly sideways, but it hadn't lasted long enough for her to place it. "I like to win," he said, the accent coming back full force, and Nikki wondered if it had just been a trick of her ears.

Nikki organized her cards according to suit and rank while Richie finished shuffling, plunked the deck down next to Duncan, and then picked up his own cards. It was an odd system, but the waiting second deck did speed things along; she wondered idly what other card game the second deck could be applied to.

Kit opened with a low heart; Richie countered with the nine of hearts. Grinning, Nikki played the trump card and Duncan threw down the five of hearts in disgust.

The second round continued, and Nikki and Kit evened up the score while Germany floated by outside the window, a blur of white snow on black everything else, eventually turning into France. Kit triumphantly played the final card as his phone began to ring; it took a moment before Nikki recognized the @last song that Kit had sung at the concert.

"Damn Brandt," muttered Kit, rummaging through the seat cushions for his phone. "Never did have any sense of timing." He flipped open the phone and answered with an almost normal-sounding cheerfulness.

"Hey, Brandt," said Kit. "What's new?" Nikki watched Kit's face go slowly still and become tired. She felt a surge of sympathy. He never really seemed to get a break. "No, Brandt. Yes, Brandt. No, I haven't read the paper."

Brandt could be heard talking again, and Kit made unconscious hurry-up moves with his hand. Abruptly he pulled the phone away from his ear to look at the screen.

"Hold on, Brandt, Mum's on the other line. I'll be right back. Mum," said Kit, switching lines. Nikki tensed. "No, Mum, I can't talk. I'm on the other line with Brandt." Kit paused and the tiny sound of Camille's voice was audible as a strident whine to the other listeners. "Mum, I am so going to call you back. No, I don't know. Ask Trista or Nikki." Kit rolled his eyes as Camille continued to talk. "Nikki, Trista's assistant; she's new. Seriously, Mum, Brandt's on the other line. Call Trista. Yes, all right, Mum, all right. I'll talk to you in a minute."

He flipped back to Brandt and Nikki started counting. On number fifteen Trista came trudging up the stairs, a panicked look in her eye and the phone to her ear. Nikki sighed and went to meet her at the top of the stairs; she should have known Kit would spill the beans sooner or later. She held out her hand for the phone and silently Trista passed it over.

"Trista's new assistant, I presume," said Camille, sounding to be in an icy fury.

"Hi, Camille," said Nikki, dropping into a seat, out of earshot but where she could keep an eye on the rest of the upstairs inhabitants.

"What the hell do you think you're doing?"

"I'm protecting Kit," said Nikki. "Isn't that what you wanted?"

"You are supposed to go after Cano! I don't want Kit having anything to do with us."

"Well, I guess that explains your hands-off approach to mothering." There was a gasp of outrage from Camille and Nikki wished she'd kept her mouth shut. It wasn't any of her business and Camille already hated her.

"Since you can't hold on to a man long enough to procreate, your opinions don't really matter to me!" Camille shot back.

"What do you want, Camille?" asked Nikki, sighing. "Can't you follow orders for once and let me do my job?"

"Not a chance," snapped Camille.

"It doesn't worry you that Kit's been the target of several mysterious accidents?"

"I know all about those; they're just accidents. He should stop playing at being a singer and get a real job. Cano is the real threat.

And since you're clearly never focused on the task at hand, I will have to do it myself." Camille's disregard for Kit's safety and his career choice was shocking and Nikki found herself gesturing in disbelief even though Camille wasn't there to see it.

"And maybe we'd already have Cano if you hadn't blown it for us in Stuttgart. Your emotions are getting in the way of the mission, just as Mrs. M said they would. If you're not working with the team, you're working against it."

"Do not presume to lecture me about the mission," said Camille. "I have been doing this job since before you were born. I don't need you or your precious team."

Nikki gulped back rage. She needed to get Camille under control, and arguing wasn't going to get the job done.

"Camille, we have the same goals. Why can't we work together?"

"Because you're not good enough," said Camille, and hung up the phone.

Nikki felt a hot flush of embarrassment on her face as she went back to the card table. Kit was still talking to Brandt. She began to shuffle the cards, giving her fingers something to do. She shuffled them short end to short end, then bridged the two stacks between her hands until they fed back on themselves and became one stack. Her thoughts followed the movement automatically, watching the blue intertwining leaf pattern on the card-backs blink past.

What had Camille meant when she said she knew about the accidents? How could she be so sure they were just accidents? And what if Camille was right—what if she wasn't good enough?

"Jeez! How do you do that?" exclaimed Richie as she shuffled again.

"You can't do that?" asked Nikki, blinking in surprise.

"No. What are you, some sort of card shark?"

"It's just a stupid human trick. Here." She grabbed the second deck and handed it to Richie. "You divide the stack and shuffle end to end. Then you sort of press your thumbs down and flex your fingers in." Richie flexed, and the cards exploded outward.

"And then you play fifty-two-card pickup," said Duncan with a chuckle.

"Damn it!" yelled Kit, jumping up and pushing cards off his lap. "No, Brandt, I'm not yelling at you. The idiots I live with are just making a mess."

Nikki narrowed her eyes in irritation, her previous sympathy erased. Richie hurried to gather the cards in again.

"Look, Brandt, can we go over this later?" said Kit, stepping on the table and then walking across to the other side. Duncan followed Kit with his eyes. "You know, I can't get these things without pictures."

There was a pause, and from the first floor of the bus Nikki could hear the laughter of the band and crew. The laughter of Terry, the Scottish packing chief, boomed like a foghorn in the distance, and Burg's monkey noises filled in the spaces between the notes.

"Cleaning up my mess? My mess? This isn't my mess. I didn't walk out! I'm not paying them anything. They ought to be thanking their lucky stars I'm not suing. Screw the fans!" shouted Kit, and even Duncan blinked at that one. "No! *No.* I'm hanging up now. Fine. We'll talk about it in Paris." Kit slammed the phone shut. "Have you got anything better to do than stare at me?" he snapped at them.

"No, not really," said Nikki, feeling contentious.

"Don't worry about it, man," said Richie. "They don't know what they're talking about."

"I didn't walk out on that concert! I mean, I did, but . . . I was right to. It was dangerous."

"Seriously," Richie said in agreement. "We could have died. The papers are just looking for a story. It's a load of twat and everyone knows it."

"I don't think you actually would have died," said Nikki practically.

"That's easy for you to say!" protested Richie. "You weren't staring death in the eye. Any more tilt on that stage and we would have come crashing down."

"Actually, it wouldn't have tilted any more. I talked to Ewart, the platform tech. At most you would have had another few inches before it shut down."

"You talked to the tech?" demanded Kit. "When?"

"Last night, before we decorated your hotel room."

"No one asked you to do that!" snapped Kit.

"Didn't realize I had to be asked," said Nikki. "The poor guy was drinking himself into oblivion at a bar. He really liked his job." She glanced at Duncan. He'd talked to Ewart too; he must have come to the same conclusion she had—that someone, someone besides Ewart, had rigged that stage. She was half expecting him to back her up, but instead he sat mute, his face looking as if it had been carved from stone.

"Then maybe he shouldn't have screwed it up," yelled Kit.

"He didn't," replied Nikki, trying to keep ahold of her temper. "Someone rigged the stage. It wasn't an accident."

"Bullshit!" cried Kit. "He screwed up; he gets fired. Everyone pulls their own weight around here. Stop telling me this stuff!"

"I don't get it," said Nikki, shaking her head. "Are you just stupid, or do you honestly not want to know what's going on? And if we're talking about pulling your own weight, then what about you? The papers have a point. Those fans paid a lot of money to only see half a show." Nikki knew it was a low blow. She didn't actually disagree with his decision to walk out of the show, but she was mad.

"Don't start with me!" said Kit savagely.

"Why not? Because you're a rock star? There's the bullshit!" yelled Nikki. "You are a working professional. You get paid to sing; if you're not singing, what are they paying you for?"

"I did sing! I sang an @last song, for Christ's sake! But they don't pay me to risk life and limb just so some German teenager can throw her knickers at me."

"Well, she was throwing them at you last night!"

"She was an adult and I can do what I want!"

"Oh yeah, I forgot. You're a rock star; you can do whatever the hell you want. Grow up! You cannot always do what you want. You cannot always have everything you want!"

"Where do you get off! You're just some little makeup girl. You've been here two days. You don't know anything about my life!"

They were standing inches apart now. Nikki was dimly aware that Duncan and Richie were hovering in the background, but mostly she was aware of Kit's blue eyes boring into hers. He smelled of the ginger breath mints he'd been eating and the underlying scent of cigarettes. She was also aware of a crackling heat passing between her and Kit.

"What is going on?" exclaimed Trista, coming up the stairs, breaking the moment.

"Nothing," snapped Kit. "Your understudy is just overestimating her value and my ability to replace her."

"Yeah, 'cause I'm really worried about keeping this job," answered Nikki sarcastically, and pushed past Trista, stomping down the nearly vertical stairs to the first floor. She wasn't surprised when Trista didn't follow.

She surveyed the spacious seats. The band members and crew had spread out across them in her absence. The only remaining empty seat was directly behind the driver. Nikki remembered enough of her junior high experience to know that this was the seat reserved for complete losers but sat down anyway. Loserville was better than the city of Losing It Completely and Killing a Rock Star.

"Hey," said the bus driver over his shoulder as she sat down.

"Hey," she answered, staring at the passing scenery. The road was a slick black ribbon of licorice against the heavy layer of fondant snow. They rounded a curve, the bus working hard to drag them up the hill. Ahead of them on the next switchback, Nikki could see a semitruck coming toward them. As the truck came into view, it seemed to speed up.

"Damn idiots," muttered Louis, eyeing the oncoming semi.

The road belled out in an oxbow curve, and the semitruck took the turn wide, well into the bus's lane. Louis sounded the horn, but the truck just kept coming, swerving closer to the tour bus. Louis yanked the steering wheel, and the bus began to slide. Nikki could hear screaming, but she couldn't tell if it was her fellow passengers or the brakes.

"Oh . . . ," said Louis, yanking harder on the wheel.

"Shit." Nikki finished for him, taking a firm grip on her seat.

At the last possible second the semi veered slightly, avoiding a head-on collision, clipping the front corner of the bus. The impact sent a jarring shudder throughout the entire frame of the two-story land yacht, and for a moment everything was perfectly balanced and still, then with incomprehensible speed the bus tipped over and began to tumble.

FRANCE I

Fiery Crash

"Shit," repeated Nikki when the world had stopped moving. The black in front of her eyes faded, turning her view to a sort of jumbled grayscale. And it looked sort of fabric-ish. She blinked and realized that someone's luggage had landed on top of her; she pushed it off and took stock of things.

She was on the floor, wedged between the seat and the back of the driver's booth. She could hear people crying and cursing. The sound grated on her nerves and reminded her that there was work to be done. Always more work to be done.

The bus was tilted at a forty-five-degree angle, leaning against the hillside, and the interior was a jumble of bodies, luggage, and broken bus fixtures. Louis was lying, unconscious, in the aisle and against the seats. Nikki could see a large gash across his forehead and nose; his knuckles were bloody where they'd been hit by flying glass. She knelt down and pressed two fingers to the soft spot under his jawbone. The steady *thrum-thrum* of his pulse against her fingertips was reassuring.

"Louis," she said, tapping the bus driver gently. "Are you OK?" Nikki swung her head back and forth, trying to clear the cobwebs.

"Louis, talk to me. Time to wake up, Lou."

"Bus," he said, groggily opening his eyes.

"That's right," said Nikki encouragingly. "We're on the bus."

"Bus fell over," he said.

"Yeah, it did. Easy," she commanded as the bus driver struggled to sit upright.

"I'm all right. I'm sort of all right," he said as the realities of physical pain slowed him down. Louis leaned against the tilted seats and wiped the blood out of his eye. He took a deep shuddering breath and winced.

"You all right enough to stay here while I check on everyone else?" asked Nikki, pulling her hands away from Louis slowly. But he stayed upright and even nodded.

"Go check on Mr. Masters," answered Louis. Nikki frowned but didn't respond. Mr. Masters was last on her list.

Making her way to the back of the bus, Nikki saw that most of the band members were righting themselves and responded dazedly but affirmatively to her repeated "Are you OK?"

She half crawled up the stairs, slipping on guitars and suitcases. Once she was on the second floor, the drunken angle of the bus was even more distinct. Nikki clung to the ceiling rail that was now at waist height, precariously stepping from seat edge to seat edge. She could see Duncan's feet protruding from one seat aisle. Kit was ahead of her, kneeling on the couch, and he looked up at her, his face a mask of wide-eyed desperation.

"Help me," he said, "she won't wake up."

Nikki felt her heart contract at the fear in his voice and stumbled forward.

Trista was slumped on the couch, blood trickling from her

mouth, one of her legs bent at an unnatural angle. Nikki knelt down next to Kit and felt for Trista's pulse; it was weak but there. There was a groan from Duncan.

"*Gabh suas ort féin,*" spat Duncan, jerking upright. The big man paused for a moment, his mustache bristling like a set of dog whiskers as he oriented himself; Nikki tried to work out what language he'd been speaking. "Where's Kit?" he asked, attempting to stand.

"I'm here," said Kit, making his way back to Duncan. Duncan seized Kit's shoulder, sizing him up in one measuring glance, then surveyed the bus's interior, noting Nikki and Trista. "Bus crash," he said, as if answering some internal question.

"Come help Trista," said Kit, pulling at Duncan's sleeve.

"No. Let's get you off the bus—someplace safe."

"Bollocks," said Kit, shaking his head. "Help Trista." Nikki shook her head, trying to draw on her linguistics background to figure out what language Duncan had been speaking, but the urgency in Kit's voice was making it hard to concentrate.

"One of you call an ambulance," interjected Nikki. "Argue later."

Kit pulled out his phone with a gunslinger's quick-draw reaction, then halted.

"I'm not getting any reception," Kit said, looking at them with questioning eyes. "Call box!" he exclaimed with a snap of his fingers, and made for the stairs.

"Kit!" snapped Duncan, reaching after him but snagging only air.

"Be right back!" Kit yelled, bouncing down the stairs and over the luggage like a pinball.

"Well, you wanted him off the bus," said Nikki, gingerly feeling Trista's leg. She was certain that it was broken but hoped that the leg was the worst of the damage.

Duncan looked back at Nikki and growled before heading after Kit.

The ambulances arrived shortly. First one, then two more as the paramedics assessed the damage. Trista was hurt the worst, but the bus driver needed stitches and an X-ray, while the sound guy and one of the other security men had broken arms. The number of whiplash cases was steadily rising, and Nikki was kept hopping back and forth between patients, translating for the paramedics. Kit matched her in an opposite orbit, checking on everyone but stopping every few minutes to place or answer phone calls.

"I'm trying to rent a bus to come get us," said Kit, slipping across the snow toward her, his phone outstretched, "but my French is terrible. Give us a hand."

Nikki took the phone, her nearly numb fingers brushing along Kit's equally cold hand. He grabbed her free hand and held it close to his mouth, breathing on their fingers. She smiled at him as she talked and he grinned. The bus manager was skeptical, but a promise of cash got a promise to be there within minutes.

The police cars arrived next, with their penetrating sirens and tires splashing snowy slush onto the already grimy scene.

"*Bonjour, mesdames et messieurs,*" said the sergeant, flashing his badge and putting a halting hand on the gurney carrying Louis toward a waiting ambulance. "*Quelques moments de votre temps, s'il vous plaît, vous devez répondre à quelques questions.*" Everyone turned to Nikki.

Nikki pulled her smock a little tighter around her and wished she had a coat; her green sneakers were soaked and she had stopped being able to feel her toes several minutes ago. With a sigh, she straightened her posture. No sense in letting everyone see that this was hard work.

"He wants—" Her voice, raspy from the amount of recent

translating, squeaked on "wants." "He wants to ask everyone some questions."

"Bollocks," snapped Kit, returning from an excursion into the bus. He dropped someone's overcoat onto her shoulders. "My people are cold, tired, and hurt. You can ask all the questions you want at the hospital."

"And you are, *monsieur*?" asked the sergeant stiffly in resentful English.

"Kit Masters!" exclaimed the younger policeman getting out of the car.

"*Qui est* Kit Masters?" asked the sergeant, still glaring at Kit.

"La star du rock anglaise!"

"Pleased to meet you," said Kit, cupping his hand around a cigarette and lighting up with effortless cool. "Now get the fuck out of the way. My man Louis needs to get to the hospital."

Nikki watched the sergeant's lips purse into a wrinkly rosebud of instant dislike. The newly rented bus chugged into view and parked on the other side of the orange cones that the paramedics had set out.

"All right, my children," said Kit, turning away from the policemen and projecting his voice to the widespread group with impressive ease. "All those who aren't in an ambulance are in the bus. We're going to follow the ambulances to the hospital, and unless the paramedics gave you an absolutely clean bill of health, I want everyone to get checked out by the doctors. If we could have all those with healthy hands help with loading the luggage into the new bus, we can be under way shortly."

Nikki stared at Kit in confusion. He was commanding the entire tour bus with ease and bullying the police with aplomb. It was as if more people made him less shy. Not to mention giving him a rather sexy disregard for authority.

"*Non, non, monsieur,*" said the sergeant, shaking his head. Kit nodded to the ambulance driver, who began to load Louis into the ambulance.

"*Oui, oui,*" mimicked Kit. "You can question us at the hospital. Terry? How're we doing?"

The perpetually harried Scotsman turned from his chivying of cold and traumatized volunteers as they unloaded the tipped-over tour bus and hauled the luggage onto the new one.

"Your band dinna know how to load for shite! They'd never make it in my line o' work."

"They're musicians; give them a break!" answered Kit, grinning.

"Lift with your legs, son!" Terry screamed at a startled Burg. Nikki had a sudden flashback to Carrie Mae training. Give Terry a ponytail and a set of falsies and he'd fit right in with the other instructors.

"Duncan, have you got ahold of Angela yet?" Kit yelled to Duncan, who shook his head as he jogged over to them. "No, her phone's off."

"Yeah right," said Nikki sarcastically, and saw Duncan frown.

"Maybe the battery died. What about Brandt?" asked Duncan.

It was Kit's turn to shake his head. "It keeps going to voice mail. Is this the right thing?" he asked Duncan suddenly. Duncan stared at him blankly, and Kit swung his gaze to Nikki. "Am I doing this right? It's Angela that does the arranging of things."

"You're doing great," said Nikki honestly.

"Swearing at the copper wasn't too much?"

"Probably, but hopefully he didn't understand enough English to get that."

"Everyone knows that one," muttered Duncan.

"Probably true," said Nikki distantly, watching the sergeant argue with his junior officer. "I'll be right back," she said, sliding her arms into the jacket sleeves. "Just keep getting everyone on the bus."

The sergeant was red in the face, and the junior officer was looking a bit pale as Nikki approached. Nikki took a deep breath and considered her approach. The junior officer was on her side already; it was the sergeant she had to worry about. She knew her accent was more Canadian than proper French, which wasn't considered a good thing. On the other hand, it was French, which was eons ahead of English, and she was a girl and she was cute, which frequently counted for a surprising amount.

Z'ev was so much better at this than she was. He'd say something about sports, and suddenly they'd be best friends. Or grandkids. For some reason people were always showing Z'ev pictures of their children. She raised her chin defiantly. She was not going to be outdone by Z'ev, particularly when he wasn't even here. She yanked her hair out of its ponytail and plastered a smile on her face.

"*Bonjour,*" she said breathlessly to the policemen, smiled a little extra wide, and tried to look doe-eyed.

"*Bonjour,*" replied the sergeant, eyeing her suspiciously.

Fifteen minutes later, the sergeant loaded the final bag onto the rental bus and helped Nikki up that treacherous first step.

"*Nous vous rencontrerons à l'hôpital,*" she said with her smile in place, and bent down to exchange the customary double kiss.

"Oui, mademoiselle," said the sergeant, and waved as the bus doors closed and pulled away in a fog of diesel fumes and evaporating snow flurries.

She stepped up into the main cabin and looked for a place to sit. The band and crew burst into applause.

"That was just impressive," said Kit, scooting over and making room for her in the geek seat behind the driver.

"I've never seen anything like it," said Hammond.

"I have," said Duncan, giving her a cold stare.

"Did he really show you pictures of his grandchildren?" asked Holly from a few seats back. She had a bandage over one eyebrow, and it gave her a cockeyed look.

"Uh, yeah. He's got a daughter who married a Canadian, so he was showing me where they lived."

"Sorry, you've lost me," said Hammond. "How does Canada matter in the slightest?"

"I'm Canadian," explained Nikki. "I don't really speak French. I speak Quebecois, so he knew I was Canadian, and then of course he wanted to know if I knew his daughter."

"I thought you were American," said Holly.

"I am. I'm just also Canadian."

"Can you do that?" asked someone farther back.

"Mike's right. I don't think that's allowed," said Hammond. Everyone stared accusingly at Nikki.

"Uh, sorry. You'll have to take that up with my parents."

"Well, she's got a point there," said Kit. "My old fella was Irish, and there's not a thing I can do about it." Nikki caught a flicker of movement from Duncan as the rest of the bus laughed. He was frowning heavily into his mustache, apparently unamused by Kit's Irish parentage.

"I hope Trista's all right," said Kit as the bus trundled into a small town. "The paramedics didn't seem . . . Well, they took her first. That's not very good, is it?" He turned his dark-fringed baby blues to Nikki, looking for reassurance.

"That just means that she got there first," said Nikki. "She had regained consciousness by the time she left, so that's good."

"But her leg . . . ," said Kit, looking a little ill at the memory of Trista's leg bending in unnatural directions.

"I'm sure they'll set it and it'll be fine."

He nodded nervously and didn't smile. Nikki glanced back and encountered Duncan's gaze. He flicked his sun-bleached blue eyes away before she could read his expression, but she had the distinct impression that it hadn't been a happy one.

The hospital was tiny and straight out of the fifties—completely undeserving of having a busload of rock and roll freaks dropped into their lap. Word of their coming had been sent on ahead, and the admitting personnel were polite and efficient, much to Nikki's relief. She wasn't sure she could pull another Sergeant Herault. How many other people could possibly have daughters in Canada? A stern-faced doctor chased away the loitering nurses clearly hoping to catch sight of Kit and marched up to their group.

"You are Monsieur Masters?" inquired the doctor. His dark face looked as though it had been carved out of teak and was a perfect antithesis to his crisp white coat.

"Yes, my friend Trista . . ." Nikki noted the use of "friend" over "employee."

"Yes, Trista Elliot."

"Can we see her?"

"Actually, I'm afraid she has to go in for surgery. We've just given her anesthesia."

"Is she all right?" Kit asked, going pale.

"Her leg was broken in three places and we need to set it with pins. Ordinarily, we wouldn't let anyone see her at the moment, but she's been extremely insistent."

"I'll go immediately," said Kit.

"No, she's been asking for someone named Nikki. Nikki Lanier." Kit stared at Nikki.

"That's me," she said, feeling a blush rise. "Shall I go now?"

"Yes, this way," answered the doctor, leading the way. Nikki walked past Kit with an apologetic smile.

"She'll be out soon," said the doctor, pulling back a curtain, revealing Trista covered in a white sheet and hospital gown. "So you'll have to be quick."

"Nikki," said Trista hoarsely, and reached out a clawing hand. Nikki took her hand and leaned down to hear the makeup woman's message.

"Nikki, you have to stay with him," whispered Trista, and licked her lips. "Duncan—"

"I know. Don't worry; I won't let Duncan hurt him."

"No," said Trista. "Duncan won't hurt him. He wouldn't want you to know; he's afraid. But you've got to know." Her voice was getting smaller, and Nikki leaned closer. "Don't let Camille know."

"Know what?" demanded Nikki, leaning closer.

"Duncan . . ." But whatever she had been going to say slid into muttering silence as her eyelids drifted closed and Trista slipped into unconsciousness. The nurses appeared as if on cue and popped up the metal frames on the sides of the bed.

"Pardon, mademoiselle," said one, politely shoving Nikki out of the way.

Nikki didn't notice. She had too much to think about. What would Duncan be afraid of? Duncan wasn't afraid of anything but Kit and a bottle of booze. Slowly, she wound her way back out to the reception area. Kit was waiting impatiently for her, Duncan a solid shadow behind him. She looked from Kit to Duncan and realized that Trista had been right—Duncan was afraid. He was afraid of her.

FRANCE II

Dirty Laundry

Nikki sat in the minuscule bathtub at the hotel and tried to regain some warmth. Her shoes were drying on top of the radiator. Trista's luggage had been brought to her room. Nowhere better to put it, she supposed; at least she could raid it for additional clothing, and more importantly, she could borrow Trista's phone.

She dialed Jane and added more hot water while waiting for her to pick up. When it immediately kicked into voice mail Nikki frowned and redialed.

"Uh, hey, Jane," said Nikki as the voice mail beeped. "Give me a call when you get this. Uh . . . hope you're enjoying your vacation." Nikki hung up, feeling stupid. She had been counting on Jane to answer. Jane did have a right to enjoy a work-free vacation, but she'd seemed happy to help before . . . Nikki chewed her lip and then dialed Jenny.

"Hello, this Jennifer," said Jenny, using her professional voice.

"Hey, Jen, it's Nikki."

"Nikki!" exclaimed Jenny, all pretense of formality leaving her voice. "How y'all doing? I was going to call you, but you don't have your phone. Camille's gone AWOL. We think she's gone after Cano."

"Believe me," said Nikki, "I'm aware."

"Uh-oh," said Jenny, laughing at Nikki's tone. "What happened?"

"I wouldn't know," said Nikki bitterly. "I've managed to sideline myself."

"Is that Nikki?" asked Ellen in the background.

"What do you mean?" asked Jenny.

"Is that Nikki?" repeated Ellen.

"Yes, shhh," said Jenny, turning away from the phone.

"You'd better put it on speaker," Nikki said. "Otherwise, I'll just have to go over it all again with her."

"Oh, good point. Uh . . . hold on." There was a click, and then the background noises took on a tinny quality. "Are you still there?" asked Jenny anxiously. Jenny was notorious for accidentally hanging up on people. For her, hold, transfer, and speaker were mysterious functions.

"Still here. Where are you guys?"

"At a bar in Colombia," said Ellen. "We gave the bartender a twenty to vamoose for an hour, though, so speak freely."

"How's the Nina Alvarez situation?" asked Nikki, belatedly remembering the case and feeling guilty.

"We're still trying to confirm CIA involvement."

"What are you going to do if the CIA is involved?" asked Nikki.

"General consensus is sit back and keep tabs on their op and on Nina. If there's no CIA, then we'll replan the extraction and go. Today's the first day she's been out of the house. We've been following her; Jenny has a brown wig on as part of her disguise. It's hilarious."

"It's hot, is what it is," said Jenny. "I think I need an ice pack."

"Don't mention ice packs," said Nikki. "I'm freezing."

"Freezing? What happened?"

"Well . . . ," said Nikki, trying to remember how far back to start. "I left there on Christmas Eve and landed in Germany the day after Christmas. I'm still a little bitter about that."

"Understandable," said Ellen. "My daughters were surprisingly upset about my missing Christmas, too. Which is funny; I didn't think they'd notice."

"My family didn't even call," said Jenny sadly. "But I called Jane! She said we should wait to exchange presents until we're all back in L.A."

"Yeah," said Nikki, "that was my plan. All your presents are back at the apartment."

"We're getting distracted," said Ellen. "We were catching up with Nikki."

"Wait, I need a soda," said Jenny. There was shuffling and then the crisp noise of a beer bottle top. "'Kay, continue."

"You didn't bring one for me?" asked Ellen.

"You didn't say anything while I was over there," said Jenny in protest. Ellen sighed. There was more shuffling and a second bottle-top sound.

"And the story resumes on Boxing Day in Germany," said Ellen. Ellen had weaned herself off soaps but had never quite lost the taste for lurid tales of adventure.

Nikki recounted her story, adding in her phone calls with Jane.

"Well, something is definitely going on with the Kit Masters tour," said Ellen when she had finished. Nikki put her own phone on speaker and exited the bath, wrapping herself in a towel.

"But is it related to Cano?" asked Jenny.

"And what's with Duncan?" said Ellen.

"Yes, I'm worried about him. That conversation outside the television studio . . . 'I don't need any more Carrie Mae women.' That sounds like he knows more about Carrie Mae women than he should. And why is he covering up the accidents if he knows they're not accidents? And why is he scared of you? Is he causing the accidents?" Jenny had the same questions Nikki did.

"I don't know. I feel like I'm missing something. Trista keeps insisting that no one would want to hurt Kit, but she did sort of hint that she thought Duncan was a bit off. I feel like there's something else going on . . . I just can't put my finger on it." Nikki rummaged through Trista's luggage looking for clothes that she could wear without hiding her face in shame.

"Well, it could be any one of the band or crew," said Ellen.

"Can't be the band," said Nikki. "They were all onstage when I was chasing Tracksuit."

"That doesn't mean they can't be responsible for the accidents," said Jenny. "Tracksuit and Cano may have an accomplice or they may not be related to the accidents at all. And what better way to throw off suspicion than to be part of the accident?"

"Oh great," said Nikki bitterly. "Just when I have my suspect pool narrowed down, you gotta stick your two cents in. But I have to say these accidents aren't as simple as I thought. Trista keeps insisting that no one would want to hurt Kit, and after the crash today, I'd almost agree with her. I just don't see a motive for hurting or killing him."

"What do you mean?" asked Ellen.

"Oh, his people. They kept asking about him. I'd go try to get someone off the bus and they'd ask if he was OK. Trista's right;

his people love him. And they are literally his people. They'd follow him anywhere."

"Sounds like that kind of bugs ya," said Jenny, and Nikki sighed in response.

"It's just weird. He says jump; they say how high. It's so . . . feudal."

"You're just not used to a power structure that doesn't include you at the top," said Ellen.

"I'm nowhere near the top!" exclaimed Nikki, shocked. "I'm a drone in the Carrie Mae army!" There was a snorting noise from the other end of the phone, and Ellen laughed.

"Sorry, Jenny tried to breathe soda through her nose. Honey, you may not have noticed this, but for the last year or so you've had a bunch of women following you around doing what you tell them to do. It's called being a leader."

"We're a team," muttered Nikki, blushing. "Besides, you don't tiptoe around and kowtow to my every whim. Which frankly would be a nice change from all of you bossing me around and telling me not to use the zip line!"

"I stand by my opinion. It was a bad idea in that instance," Jenny said. "The angle was all wrong and the Congolese would totally have spotted you coming out of the tree."

"Probably," said Nikki, skipping over the old argument, and pulled out a plain white T-shirt that looked unobjectionable, "but my point is, I want more tiptoeing, damn it! Other people get tiptoeing." She shook out the shirt and from the folds dropped a medium-sized roll of fabric. It looked like a rolled-up travel jewelry kit, but Nikki knew instantly that it wasn't. She undid the knot and unrolled it, feeling her heart beat faster. Trista had clearly not abandoned the Carrie Mae way entirely.

"Well, if you're looking for a motive, I say follow the money.

Find out who benefits from his death financially. I'd go talk to that Angela girl. She's sounds a little suspect—go find out about her."

"I could stand to know a little more about all of them," said Nikki.

"Room search?" suggested Jenny.

"How's she going to search rooms?" objected Ellen. "She doesn't have any equipment."

"Actually, I do," said Nikki. "I guess Carrie Mae retirees don't entirely give up the life."

"Trista's packing?" asked Jenny gleefully.

"Lock picks, a small fingerprint kit, knife, and an early version of knockout gas perfume."

"Ha!" said Ellen. "Once you're Carrie Mae, you are always Carrie Mae."

"So it would seem," said Nikki, pulling on her mostly dry bra and reaching for the T-shirt. "Although . . . I know I didn't ask for this stuff, but I'm pretty sure that their existence is something that I should have been told about. I'm not trying to step on anyone's toes, but I'm starting to feel like I'm not being taken seriously." Nikki knew she was drifting off into whining, but it had been a bad day.

"Nonsense," said Ellen. "We take you seriously."

"Yeah, but you like me. I'm starting to think that everyone else just sees me as some redheaded . . ." Words failed her and she reverted to the one thing she was afraid she'd always be labeled. "Cheerleader. I mean, I'm not like Z'ev. He looks solid and reassuring and people just assume that he knows what he's doing. Or Val. Well, mostly people were scared Val was going to shoot them, but people still did what she told them. Or Kit. He just smiles and suddenly people want to take care of him and be with him. But I'm just some twenty-six-year-old Twinkie. Nobody's even questioned that I could be a makeup artist; they think it's totally reasonable."

"That is ridiculous," scolded Ellen. "You are not a Twinkie. You are a smart, kick-ass woman. And you're undercover; no one is supposed to question whether or not you could be a makeup artist."

"It's just kind of hard," said Nikki. "Did I tell you about the groupie? She looked like a six-foot-tall supermodel and he kicked her out. I mean, she had drugs and everything, but it's just hard not to feel a little . . . short."

"You like him," said Jenny, and Nikki could hear the smirk in her voice.

"No, I don't," snapped Nikki.

"Yes, you do. You have a crush on the rock star. You're not mad that people trip over themselves when he smiles; you're mad because you trip over yourself when he smiles."

Nikki drummed her fingers on the bedside table.

"Maybe," she said, admitting it finally. "But that is irrelevant to my point about leadership. And besides, he has bigger issues than I do, which is a serious red flag. Plus, I just broke up with Z'ev."

"Yes, and you seem to be taking that awfully well," said Jenny.

"I haven't had time to think about it," said Nikki, fighting the lump that unexpectedly welled up in her throat. If she thought about Z'ev she would break down and cry. And crying, even in front of Jenny and Ellen . . . Well, she just couldn't do it. Better to not think about the bad stuff, as her mother said. "This isn't really the time to think about me anyway," said Nikki, trying to reroute her emotions before they became dangerous. "I've got a job to do. Got to figure out just what the hell Camille and Cano are up to and save the rock star from whoever's trying to kill him, yadda yadda yadda. And I get to do it all on about four hours'sleep."

"Oh, stop your pity party," said Ellen with good-humored acerbity.

"See?" said Nikki, smiling. "I don't want to hear that. People don't tell the leader that."

"Yes, they do," said Ellen. "That's one of your problems with Kit—no one is telling him the truth, and he's not insisting that they do. It's hard to be a leader when all you hear is the echo of your own voice. But that's not you. You thrive on collaboration and information. It's part of what makes you a good leader."

"I'm a leader without a pack," said Nikki plaintively.

"OK, fine," said Ellen, "lone-wolf it then. You're suspicious of Duncan; you think someone is attempting to sabotage Kit's sobriety and you're pretty sure Cano's trying to kill him. Time to get busy. What are you going to do?"

"Trista knows something," said Nikki, giving in. "I'm going to search the rooms tonight and then talk to her in the morning."

"Well, call us back afterward," said Jenny. "I want to hear what you find."

"Probably a lot of dirty laundry," said Nikki realistically.

"That's what we're hoping for!" exclaimed Jenny, mistaking the actual laundry in Nikki's mind for a metaphor.

"Signal!" said Ellen suddenly.

"Ooh! That's us. Gotta go. Talk to you later, fearless leader!"

The line went dead, and Nikki sighed again. She wished her friends were with her now. Things always seemed so much more manageable when they were around.

Nikki found a pair of Carrie Mae purple sweats that had faded almost to gray in Trista's bag and put them on, rolling the top down several times. Then, packing Trista's roll of bad-girl tools into a bath towel, Nikki stepped out into the corridor, hoping she just looked like a guest searching for the hot tub.

FRANCE III

Say It Ain't So

With everyone else still at the hospital, Nikki set out to search the rooms. Trista's tools were archaic, but fortunately, so was the hotel. They still operated off of actual keys and locks, even at the penthouse level—her first stop. It was on the top floor, but Nikki had the impression from Holly that it was below Kit's usual standards. She bypassed Kit's luggage and went directly to the phone and dialed the front desk.

"Hullo," she said. Her English accent wasn't perfect, but it would fool a French person. If the phone call ever came under suspicion the limited number of French speakers on the tour would make her a suspect. But a random British female widened the pool significantly.

"Yes, hullo, I'm part of the Kit Masters tour and I need a record of what rooms the Kit Masters tour is currently occupying." She listened to the person on the other end of the line, as she searched the desk drawers. "Yes, I'm afraid we're all a bit confused and no one can find anyone. If you wouldn't mind just running down the names and numbers of our rooms, that would be smashing."

Turning up nothing of interest other than stationery and a fax machine, Nikki waited impatiently for the clerk to finish looking up the room numbers.

She had just finished jotting down the numbers when she heard a key in the door. She ran into the hall, ducking into the bathroom just as the front door opened.

"This is it?" asked Angela disdainfully. "This is the penthouse? God, I don't even want to see our rooms."

"Well, we must make do with what fate hands us," said Brandt, sounding as if he was only half listening.

"It ought to be your room anyway," said Angela. "You're the head of a major record label. He's just an *artist*."

Nikki blinked at the major sucking up from Angela.

"Just drop your stuff," said Brandt. "We're not staying that long. We'll see what Kit's doing at the hospital and get out of here as soon as possible. Probably tonight."

"I don't know . . . ," said Angela. "He's awfully attached to that stupid Trista. He's not going to leave."

"Well, he'll have to," said Brandt, sounding more stern. "He has contractual obligations, which I will remind him of."

"This wouldn't be a problem if he were boozing again," said Angela. "We could just feed him a bottle of Jack and some E and pack him on a plane to Paris."

"Yes, his sobriety has been surprisingly long-lived," said Brandt, not sounding in the least perturbed by Angela's suggestion. "Who would have thought he'd develop willpower at this stage in his life? Maybe he'll take one of your little hints one day."

There was the sound of bags being put down as Angela laughed nervously.

"The champagne was just a joke," said Angela, clearly defensive. "I thought you'd be into it."

"Leaving a bottle of champagne in every greenroom? Hilarious. But don't worry about it," said Brandt. "Between Duncan and Trista he hasn't seen one of them. You're really going to have to try harder." Brandt didn't sound mad—just annoyed in a distant way.

"Do we really have to go to the hospital?" asked Angela in the uncomfortable silence that followed.

"We don't want to seem rude," said Brandt. "It's expected, after all. And besides, we need to get Kit out of there and back on the road."

"Those people hate me," said Angela bitterly. "I've done nothing but run an efficient tour and they all hate me."

"They don't hate you," said Brandt.

"Yes, they do," said Angela. "None of them will sit next to me on the bus."

"Why would you want to sit with them anyway?" asked Brandt. There was the sound of the door opening and then closing over Angela's whining reply.

Carefully Nikki exited the bathroom and surveyed the bags left by Brandt and Angela.

"Let's do yours first, peaches," said Nikki, reaching for the Louis Vuitton carry-on bag that she presumed to be Angela's. Carefully she unpacked the bag on the coffee table, laying everything out in the order she removed it. It was a boring collection of items. Designer brush, designer soap, designer underwear, all packed in separate designer pouches.

Nikki didn't know how much tour managers made, but she was pretty sure that at any salary a designer life was still going to stretch the budget. The remaining item of interest was a binder filled with clipping after clipping from Kit's career.

The clippings dated back to his @last days. There were the basics, founding, highlights, implosion, death of the lead singer in drug-fueled car accident, predictions of a similar death for Kit. Brandt was mostly missing in those articles—usually listed under "other members." Then there was the founding of Faustus Records—MASTERS AND DETTLING PARTNERS! Apparently that article had gone for the double entendre about the gay rumors surrounding Kit and Brandt's close friendship. Then there was Kit's first number one single. KIT MASTERS CAUGHT IN SWISS MISS MAYHEM! The picture showed a sprightly blonde in braids and lederhosen. Nikki skipped that article. A recent article about Brandt was headlined FAUSTUS SUES ISLAND RECORDS. Artist poaching seemed to be the problem in dispute. A short article about the helicopter incident rounded out the collection. With a shrug, Nikki was about to shut the notebook when it fell open to the back cover.

The back pocket of the binder was stuffed with letters. Nikki might have dismissed them as fan letters had she not caught the word "kill" in the midst of one of the sentences. Pulling out the letters, Nikki scanned them. They were all threats of some kind. One raving anti-fan blamed Kit for the breakup of his relationship and threatened a whole list of bodily damage. The last letter in the stack seemed the least crazy but disturbed Nikki the most.

"Your very existence is proof that the world has become like an obese man eating ever more while his neighbors starve. You should be put down before you poison the world with the corrupt culture you represent." The letter was signed AMC. Antonio Mergado Cano? The letter had a Spanish postmark, but she had no idea what the postmark from Puerto 1 would look like. If the letter was from Cano, then it seemed clear that Cano had abandoned the Basque cause for a general hatred of Western culture. And it seemed equally clear that he was aware of Kit's existence.

Neither was a particularly good sign. She shuffled through the letters again. Angela hadn't appeared to give AMC's any special attention, but it was a connection, however tenuous. And Angela had admitted to leaving the champagne in Kit's greenrooms. Angela was looking even more likely as the figure in the tracksuit, but Nikki couldn't be sure.

She moved on to Brandt's luggage—a slim-line Nava briefcase and small overnight bag.

The overnight bag held basic necessities and a small .38 pistol. Nikki contemplated the gun with interest. There was no smell of cordite to indicate a recent firing, but the piece had been oiled and cleaned not long ago. Tucking the contents back in the overnight bag, she turned to the briefcase. It was locked but yielded easily to Trista's lock picks.

The briefcase was a mess of paperwork. If Angela was precision itself, then Brandt was an explosion of restless disorder. She removed a notebook containing tiny, chicken-scratch writing and doodles; several artist contracts; and a spreadsheet that she couldn't make heads or tails of. After further digging, she found a copy of Kit's contract. Nikki checked her watch and mentally cursed. She didn't have time to go through the legalese and still search everyone's room. They would all be getting back from dinner and the hospital soon.

Acting quickly, she went back to the desk and opened the bottom drawer, pulling out a fax machine. It took several minutes to fax the entire contract to Jenny and Ellen, but she thought it was worth the effort. Getting the staple back in the exact same holes, however, taxed her patience to the utmost.

Sliding out of the penthouse, she moved on to the other rooms on her list. She went through the band's rooms first. They had enough physical proximity to Kit to be a threat, but they had been onstage during the collapse, which made it unlikely that they were behind the accidents or in league with Cano. But Nikki didn't cross them out entirely. From there she turned to the road manager and top crew members; nothing suspicious appeared. Duncan's room was last since he was still at the hospital with Kit and was least likely to return without warning.

Turning toward Duncan's room, she began to hurry. Trista's semicoherent rambling and Duncan's own suspicious behavior and knowledge of Carrie Mae had put him at the top of her suspect list until she'd seen the letter in Angela's carry-on.

Nikki opened the door to Duncan's room and looked around. His bags, all two of them, had been placed on the bed. Not surprisingly, since she didn't think he'd left the hospital, nothing else had been touched.

She took the first bag off the bed and placed it on the floor. The main portion of the bag contained clothes, an incongruous but well-worn pair of cowboy boots, and what looked like a hand-knitted sweater of oatmeal-colored wool. The other pockets contained a well-worn bulletproof vest and toiletries, a netbook computer, and a fat novel by Neal Stephenson. The second bag contained an expensive black suit and dress shoes.

And that was it. Necessities and entertainment. Nothing personal. The guy was a blank slate.

"He ought to have more equipment," she muttered to herself. A bodyguard needed equipment, didn't he? Maybe he was wearing all of it, so it wouldn't be in his suitcase, but there ought to be something. "OK, start again," she told herself.

She ran her hands along the lining, feeling for lumps and looking for gaps. She finally found a small slit in the lining near the base of the bag. Reaching inside, she withdrew a flat piece of folded cardboard fastened with electrical tape. Inside the cardboard was a hand-honed ceramic knife. No chance of setting off a metal detector, and near the spine of the bag, it probably blended pretty well in an X-ray.

Next she inspected the wheels and handle. She pulled the handle out to its full extension. A second's worth of effort pulled the handle off entirely. Inside, she found a piece of piano wire, bundled neatly and taped to the inside.

"Garrote," she said, "check."

When the suitcase revealed nothing further, she went back to the clothing, starting with the off-duty outfit. The cowboy boots were from Austin, Texas, according to the label, and revealed a spring-coiled sap hidden in the heel. So much for being weaponless. Carefully replacing the sap in the heel, she turned her attention to the sweater. It was definitely hand-knitted, but by a skilled knitter.

She opened the netbook and immediately checked the history on the browser—nothing of interest. She poked around some more and eventually found his e-mail account, but his password eluded her. She thumped the netbook closed in frustration. She needed Jane. She snatched up the novel, preparing to repack it, and dropped it in her anger. The book immediately flopped open to a page bookmarked with a photo.

Picking up the photo, Nikki read the back first. The lone description scrawled on the back was "1971," and flipping it over Nikki was shocked to see a young Camille Masters smiling back at her. Next to Camille was her husband, Declan. Except for the AK-47 machine guns they carried, the couple looked as though they were out for a Sunday hike in boots and backpacks. Duncan wasn't in the photo, but that would make sense if he took the picture. She flipped the picture over and read the inscription again. It was definitely during the time period that Camille had been undercover in the IRA. Did Duncan know Camille and Declan? And if he didn't, how had he gotten the photo?

Damn, she needed Jane. This would be so much easier if she had any equipment. A simple scan and upload, a few inquiries, and she'd have more intel than she could shake a stick at. She thought about using Duncan's netbook to log on to the Carrie Mae site but rejected the idea as too risky. Reluctantly, she rezipped the luggage and placed it back on the bed. She had gone looking for answers and come away with more questions.

She considered searching further, but tour members were beginning to return to their rooms. She thought about going to her room, but a growl from her stomach made her detour toward the hotel bar.

She was halfway through a mediocre omelet when Hammond entered. His left hand and wrist were bandaged. She waved and he smiled weakly.

"Hey, Nikki," said Hammond. "Didn't recognize you in those sweats—gray isn't really your color. I was going to get a drink. Would you care for anything?" He made eye contact with the bartender, who came out from behind the bar, with a desultory air.

"Gray?" repeated Nikki, glancing thoughtfully down at her sweats. In the half-light of the bar, they did look gray.

"Gin and tonic," said Hammond to the bartender, and they turned inquiringly to Nikki.

"Vodka and cran," Nikki said, and watched the bartender's mouth purse up. "Vodka and tonic?" suggested Nikki, guessing that he was trying to figure out how to tell her that they did not carry "cran."

"Holly says," said Hammond, seating himself, "that you are some sort of private detective that's here to solve the mysterious accidents. That you're not really here to replace Trista."

"And what do you think?" asked Nikki.

"Part of me hopes you are a private eye. This tour needs help," he said glumly.

"And the other part?" asked Nikki.

"The other part of me doesn't want to know," said Hammond. "Because if the accidents aren't accidents then it's sabotage, and that means it's one of us. I'm not really sure I could take that. I'm not sure I want to know which one of my friends is trying to kill Kit. Because it has to be Kit, doesn't it? None of the rest of us is worth killing. We just happen to be in the way." Hammond sounded only a little bitter.

"I'm not sure the accidents were supposed to be deadly," said Nikki.

"Then what are they 'supposed' to be?" asked Hammond. "I can't come up with a motive, other than killing Kit or stopping him from singing. And who would want that? You'd have to be crazy to want either. And how are we supposed to tell if it was one of the stagehands or . . . or someone I actually know? It could have been anyone on the tour."

"Not anyone," said Nikki.

"We all have access to the equipment," said Hammond. "I don't see how you can narrow the pool at all."

"They have to be the kind of person who can think of it, and then they have to be the kind who can execute." The bartender returned, set down their drinks, and departed again.

"You'd have to be daffy-headed to think of it," answered Hammond.

"What's different about this tour?" she asked, deciding not to argue.

"Besides the accidents?" demanded Hammond, setting his glass down forcefully.

"Yeah," said Nikki, taking a sip.

Hammond shook his head as if trying to clear it. "Kit's sobriety," he said at last. "But I don't know what that's got to do with anything."

"Mmm," said Nikki. Hammond looked miserable and guilty. Having searched his room, she thought she knew why.

"You want to tell me about the book?" she asked.

"You know about that?" His face was a mask of panic.

Nikki shrugged, implying that nothing was secret from her. Hammond gulped his drink.

"The publishing company wants me to include Kit, but I . . ."

"You don't want to?"

"I see their point. I mean, what's a tell-all book if you don't tell all, but I just . . . The publishing company might drop me if I don't include him, but all the dirt I have on him is from when he was using, you know? And he's been working so hard on his sobriety. It just seems like if I put him in the book with the others that it would just be tossing it back in his face. Although it might be better for him if he did start drinking again." Hammond sighed heavily.

"What do you mean?" she asked.

"Brandt's hounding him to get back in the studio, and Kit keeps saying he's working on songs, but I saw his notebook. Maybe Kit should listen to his mum—go get a real job. He's got nothing. He can't write sober."

"Oh," said Nikki, feeling a sudden click in her head. "No, that can't be right."

"It is," said Hammond. "He had twelve pages of crap and a bunch of doodles."

"I believe you," said Nikki. "I was thinking of something else."

"You know something, don't you?" demanded Hammond.

"I think something, and that's a separate thing entirely," said Nikki.

"You know, some of the others are thinking of leaving the tour. They don't think they can take another 'accident.'" Hammond made finger quotes around the word.

"There won't be another accident," said Nikki. "You can tell them that from me."

Hammond took a deep breath and leaned back. "For sure?"

"Pretty sure," said Nikki, hedging her bet. "You can stop worrying."

"About dying anyway," said Hammond, going back to his personal hell.

"Maybe you could ask him," said Nikki. "He might be OK with you talking about his past."

"Not likely," he said, shaking his head.

"Put the sobriety in," she said suddenly.

"What?" asked Hammond.

"This tour doesn't have high jinks, but it does have drama. Describe the bus crash and Kit's heroic behavior afterward. That'd sell some books, wouldn't it?"

"Maybe," said Hammond, sitting up a little straighter. "Maybe! Counterbalance some of the bad stuff. Keep the bad stuff funnier."

"Sure," said Nikki. "It's all in how you tell it."

"Thanks, Nikki! I'm going to go write some notes on that. You're giving me an idea."

Hammond rushed from the room and Nikki held up her drink in a silent toast to his back.

"Gave me an idea too," she said. She finished her omelet and hurried to return to her room. She needed a closer look at Trista's luggage.

FRANCE IV

Interrogation

December 29

On Monday morning, Trista was still unconscious and Kit was still unwilling to move. The rest of the band had cheerfully taken the day off while Brandt and Angela huddled in Kit's suite stewing. By the next morning, Trista was well enough for visitors and the band was starting to prepare to hit the road again. Opting out of the preparations, Nikki made her way to the hospital, pushed her way through the throng of fans, and headed for Trista's room.

Halting on the threshold, Nikki felt a surge of uncertainty. Her theory seemed appallingly low on facts in the harsh light of day. Trista was sitting up in bed and looking very pale. Kit and Brandt were sitting on opposite sides of the bed, with Duncan hovering in the background. As usual, Kit looked as if he'd slept on a park bench. He was staring vacantly at the pattern on the bedspread and absentmindedly twirling the bit of hair at his temple that Trista typically spiked up as devil's horns. Brandt looked as if he'd just stepped off the pages of a men's magazine.

"Kit," Brandt was saying, "be reasonable. You can't stay here. You have obligations and a much better hotel waiting for you."

"I don't want to leave Trista or anyone here," sulked Kit.

"Well, you can't stay," said Brandt, his tone making it clear Kit was being childish. "If for no other reason than because this town just isn't equipped for us. I'm surprised the hospital hasn't asked you to leave already."

"The hospital doesn't mind," said Trista. "I asked the doctor. They all think it's very exciting."

"Yeah, well 'exciting' becomes 'pain in the arse' after two days," said Brandt.

"We could use a break," said Trista. "Missing a show wouldn't be the end of the world."

"Not for you," retorted Brandt.

"We'll just stay until everyone's back on their feet," said Kit.

"Well, most of them can come back to work now, but Trista can't be moved. Doctor's orders," said Brandt with businesslike indifference.

"I don't want to leave Trista by herself," Kit said, reiterating with a frown.

"She won't be by herself," said Brandt heartlessly. "Louis is in the next room, and didn't you say your daughter would be out in a few days?"

Trista nodded reluctantly.

"You see, Kit?" said Brandt, nodding. "She'll be fine and you've got to get to Paris for the show."

"I don't give a damn about the show in Paris," said Kit forcefully, and Nikki watched Brandt's jaw clench.

"Well, you might not, but there's a lot of crew and people who do. Not to mention the fans in Paris and on TV," said Brandt with a deceptively easy tone.

"It's a hell of a way for a man to spend his New Year's," muttered Kit bitterly.

"Yes, surrounded by one of the biggest parties of the year, with some of the hottest stars in the EU."

"Yes, the perfect place to find drugs and alcohol," said Trista.

"You know," said Brandt, ignoring Trista, "I'm getting a bit tired of this 'poor me' routine. We have worked damn hard to get here. And now you're acting like you don't want it."

Kit shifted uncomfortably and shrugged. "I want it. I just . . . maybe Mum's right. Maybe I'm not cut out to be a star."

"Well," said Trista, and Nikki sensed she was picking her words carefully, "maybe a break could be just the thing for you. Get those creative juices flowing again."

"Look Kit," Brandt burst in over the end of Trista's sentence, "this is the last big push. Then you can take a bit of a break. Sure, Trista's right. I can see that. You need a bit of a break to get that album together. It's hard to concentrate in the middle of a tour. But not right now. A lot of people watch the *Bonne Année* show every year. Some American stations are going to be broadcasting portions of it. This is what we need to put you over the top."

Nikki saw a spark in his eyes at the mention of America, but still he chewed his lip indecisively.

"I didn't want to do it without Trista," he said plaintively.

"Well, you heard what the doctors said: it'll be at least six weeks till she's up and about. But you've got . . ." He hesitated and then snapped his fingers, pointing to Nikki in the doorway. "Nikki. You've got Nikki now. And Trista will be back as soon as she's up on her feet."

Kit nodded and she could see that Brandt had won. Brandt had played Kit perfectly. Nikki wondered how much the Paris show mattered to Brandt. She glanced at Trista, who reclined weakly against the pillow. She looked defeated.

"It's all right," said Trista, smiling sadly. "Nikki will take care of you. Duncan will look after you. This is what you always wanted—to be number one. You can't stop now, just because of me."

He sighed and then ducked his chin and came up with a grin. "Well, all right, but only for you."

"Good," said Brandt, standing up. "I'll have the bus brought around in a bit. Do you want to sign some autographs?"

"Yeah, sure, a few. Do we have to leave so soon?"

"It'll be better," said Brandt. "Get you to Paris. Do the press junket, maybe get some time in a studio if you've got a song done." There was the slightest hesitation and when Kit didn't leap in with assurances about completed songs, he shrugged and continued. "Don't worry; we'll let the techies comb over everything before you go onstage. We don't want any more accidents, do we?"

"No," said Kit tiredly.

"No, we don't." Brandt agreed in a distant tone of voice that indicated that he was already thinking about something else. He stood up, collecting his things, preparing to leave.

"Brandt," burst out Kit, "I'm sorry about yelling at you like that on the phone. You know, before the accident yesterday. I just don't think I was wrong to walk out."

Brandt shrugged. "Forget about it. What's done is done. On to the next challenge." He patted Kit on the shoulder and Kit smiled back with relief.

"I just realized that if we'd died in that bus crash, that yelling at you would have been the last time we talked. I don't want anger to be the last thing to pass between me and my best mate."

"Sure, your mate," said Brandt with a smile, "but your manager could be foaming at the mouth and you wouldn't give a damn."

"It's a good thing you don't foam—you wouldn't want to mess up that suit!" Kit laughed.

"I'll remember you said that next time I'm foaming," answered Brandt easily. "Angela will call you in a couple minutes when the bus gets here." He nodded to the room in general and walked out. Nikki slid into the room to clear the doorway for him; Brandt swept by without acknowledging her existence.

Nikki surveyed the room. Kit and Duncan looked as if they weren't planning to move any time soon. Kit smiled, but he looked genuinely pleased to see her.

"Hi," said Nikki, suddenly shy. "I, uh, came to see if Trista had any makeup information she wanted to share with me." Trista nodded weakly. For the first time Nikki noticed the dirty yellow and green bruise on her temple and puffed-up eye. Trista had taken a major beating from the bus. She felt another pang of doubt.

"All of my equipment was on the bus, so I'm sure Terry's packed it up safely. I have a notebook with most of the details on everyone's allergies and moisturizer requirements."

Kit shook his head.

"Moisturizer . . . This sounds like something that will only confuse and confound me. I'm going to pop over to Louis and see how he's doing." Trista nodded and waved feebly as Kit stood up to go.

"I'll see you down on the bus?" he asked, touching Nikki's hand briefly as he passed, and she nodded in response.

Trista continued as the door closed. "The notebook also has everyone's show faces detailed. The hardest part will be the backup girls. It would be a good idea if you could get some practice in with the spray brush before the show."

Nikki looked at Trista in disbelief. The question had been an opening for her to kick Duncan and Kit out—not actually talk about makeup.

"They can practically do it themselves these days, though," said Trista reassuringly, mistaking her appalled silence for job-performance anxiety. "Terry has my call sheets for who I see first. Just stick to that order, and everything should come out all right."

"Right," said Nikki. "As incredibly fascinating as that is, I would actually like to talk about something slightly more important. I searched everyone's rooms last night."

"Searched . . . why?" asked Trista.

"That semi hit us on purpose, as I'm sure the police reports will show. These accidents are getting more serious. We need to figure out who's behind it."

"No one on the tour would want to hurt Kit," repeated Trista tiredly.

Nikki agreed. "God no. He's the goose who's laying the golden eggs. No one would want to hurt him. Maybe just shake him up a little."

"It's not like that," said Trista, looking hurt. "We all love him."

"Did you know that Richie is packing enough pharmaceutical-grade pot to open his own shop in California?"

"Oh . . . I thought that was Burg, honestly."

"Nope. Richie. I think it's why he packs so many shirts. I don't think he wants to wear any of the ones that smell like pot around Kit."

"Well, you see," said Trista brightly, "he's only thinking of Kit."

"Yeah," said Nikki, "real sweet." Trista wasn't going to be easy. "Then there's Angela, calling ahead to all the interviews to get champagne put in the greenrooms."

Trista flushed with anger. "I don't like her! Lord knows I've tried! She's very efficient, but I just don't like her. I think she's mad because we don't all worship her instead of Kit."

"Probably. Did you know that Hammond is writing a tell-all book about his life on tour with various rock stars?"

Trista shifted uncomfortably in her bed, tugging at the blanket. "I'm sure he wouldn't actually include Kit," she said weakly.

"It's a retirement book," said Nikki. "It's the kind of thing that an author hopes to make a million off of and retire, because he knows once he exposes everyone's dirty secrets he'll never work again. As a retirement plan, it's probably better than Carrie Mae's."

"Better than being a makeup lady, you mean?" asked Trista, skewering Nikki with a steel-eyed glare.

"Better than being dead," said Nikki, and Trista sank back into the pillows.

"Dead or makeup. Hell of a choice."

"I thought you liked this job," said Nikki.

"I do," said Trista, but her eyes slid away, and she looked down.

"Do you really?" Nikki pressed her, and once again, she caught the restless flash of anger in Trista's gaze.

"I love Kit," Trista said at last. "The job is . . ." She raised her hand and fluttered it on a horizontal axis. "I thought it would give me the excitement. You know, the buzz, like Carrie Mae. But it's a lot of routine and late nights." Trista sighed. "It doesn't matter. You wouldn't know what it's like. You're still in. But there's going to come a time . . . You're going to want kids, or maybe you'll just get tired of wondering who's on the other side of the door when someone knocks and calls your name. But once you quit . . . What are you supposed to do? There aren't many places for a retired secret agent who only has Carrie Mae on her résumé. It's not like the CIA, where you just have to show your future employer a résumé with a bunch of blacked-out bars and they hire you on the spot. And God forbid you actually have to sell makeup. Have you ever tried to do that? That's . . . that's scary."

"Yes," said Nikki, remembering the evening she'd tried to force-feed an unruly client a tube of lipstick. "But while you may all love Kit, you all have lives outside of Kit. Forces that drive you."

"I just don't think anyone would hurt him . . . ," Trista said weakly.

"I searched your luggage too," said Nikki quietly, and Trista blanched. It wasn't ever going to be admissible in court, but for Nikki, it was all the confirmation she needed.

"Why would you do that?" asked Trista with a brittle laugh.

"Well, I started to wonder just what was driving you. I found your tool kit. And under the lining of your bag was the manual for the stage assembly. The flat on the bus—that was you too. Too bad you hadn't investigated bus braking technology since 1970. You might have actually succeeded with that one. And the helicopter—you must have bribed someone, right?"

Trista was breathing in rapid, shallow breaths.

"I might not have bought it even then, because unlike everyone else, you really do put Kit first. But then there were those text messages from Camille. She put you up to it, didn't she?"

"No!" exclaimed Trista, but she was unable to make eye contact.

"That's how she knew about the accidents. She was so certain they were just accidents. What was she thinking? That Kit would just get scared and quit?"

"I told her it wouldn't work," said Trista with a sob. "But she kept insisting. She visited him in rehab and he was so . . . wiped. She said if he kept going he was going to die. She didn't think he could stay sober and be a rock star. She said I had to scare him into taking time off, that I'd be saving his life." Tears trickled down her cheeks. "I never wanted to hurt him."

"And it didn't occur to either of you that maybe he could stay sober?" asked Nikki incredulously.

"Do you know what the odds are on that?" asked Trista.

"What about the semitruck?"

"Semi?" asked Trista, confused, then her eyes widened in apprehension. "I swear, that wasn't me," she said earnestly. "I'm not crazy; someone could have been killed! I know I haven't got a leg to stand on, but honestly, I didn't arrange that. It really was an accident!"

"I was sitting behind the bus driver," said Nikki. "The semi hit us on purpose. I mean, what? None of your plans worked, so you thought you'd call in Cano? Don't you think that's a bit like using a nuclear weapon to hammer a nail?"

Trista gaped speechlessly.

"What are you talking about?" asked Trista.

"Oh, come on," said Nikki. "It was you in the café. You were the one who met with Cano. I thought your sweats were gray, but they were really just your faded old Carrie Mae set. I chased you back to the stadium. The security guard wouldn't stop you, but he would stop me. And then while I was dealing with him, you changed out of your sweats and threw yourself on the floor as though you'd been knocked unconscious."

"It wasn't me," said Trista, her eyes wide, her breath coming in gasps. The beeping of her heart-rate monitor began to speed up. "You have to believe me! I would never . . . I didn't know Cano had escaped! I would never . . . ," Trista sputtered, lost among a morass of half-sentences. "Cano would kill Kit in a heartbeat. I would never collaborate with him. That's why I wanted you to stay with the tour. I wanted you to protect Kit!"

"If it wasn't you, then who was it?" said Nikki, sitting back with a frustrated sigh.

"I don't know," said Trista. "I really don't. Killing Kit doesn't help anyone."

"What about Duncan?" asked Nikki, and Trista shook her head.

"I just tried to use him to keep you away from me. He loves Kit, and he would never work with Cano."

"Hm," said Nikki. "Well, maybe you can explain why Duncan has a picture of Camille in his room. It's a picture of Camille and her husband, back when they were still IRA."

"I . . . I think you're going to have to ask him."

"Trista," said Nikki dangerously, "do not mess with me. The pieces fit—it could have been you with Cano. I'm trying to believe you, but since my first partner with Carrie Mae turned traitor, let's just say I'm not exactly buying this story hook, line, and sinker."

"I had to rig the accidents," protested Trista. "Camille said it was the right thing to do. Maybe I was wrong, but I thought . . . I thought I was helping. But Cano, the bus accident, that wasn't me. I wouldn't ever do that, not in a million years!"

Kit poked his head into the room. "Angela just phoned up. Time to get a wiggle on. I hope you've got all of her secrets out of her!"

"The route's been cleared," murmured Duncan, pushing open the door all the way. "We need to go now."

"Yeah, yeah," said Kit, entering the room. "Bye, Trista," he said, leaning down to kiss her. "We'll see you when you're better?"

"I wouldn't miss it for the world," she answered with a smile, looking at Nikki hopefully.

"I'm sure she'll be back to her old self in no time," said Nikki.

"I'm sure there won't be any more accidents." She raised an eyebrow at Trista, who gulped.

"Better than my old self," promised Trista, and Kit smiled.

"That's what I like to hear! I don't like to be without you," he said. "And I don't know what I'd do if you weren't around to look after me."

"Well, you've got Nikki till I get back," said Trista. "She'll take care of you."

Kit beamed and Duncan glowered. Nikki wasn't sure what to make of either look.

FRANCE V

Care Package

Nikki followed Kit and Duncan out to the waiting bus. It was slow going; Kit stopped every few feet for autograph-seekers.

"Can you sign this for me?" asked one girl, presenting a *Hotel Hell* CD. She was a blushing seventeen with a wrist full of bangles and too much eye makeup.

"Sure," he replied easily. "What's your name?"

"Oh, it's not for me. It's for my little sister . . . Rochelle."

"Uh-huh," said Kit, and Nikki could see he didn't believe her. He signed the CD with a flourish and handed it over. "Here you are, Rochelle."

"*Merci,*" she said, and then her face froze as she realized she'd been caught. Kit moved on and Nikki smothered a laugh. Kit looked back over his shoulder and winked.

"Is Burg OK?" asked a boy holding out a CD for signing. "He's my favorite."

"Yeah," said Kit, a look of pleased surprise on his face. "He just got a couple of bumps and bruises. I'll tell him you asked."

"I made this for you," said a girl of about fifteen, thrusting a teddy bear at Kit. Nikki saw that its fur had been clipped and colored to match Kit's tattoos. Kit solemnly took the bear without comment.

"I've seen you in concert three times. I really love you."

"Thank you," he said, and kept moving.

"I love you!" she called after him, starting to cry. Nikki couldn't tell what emotion the tears sprang from: love, disappointment, hysteria. It all seemed jumbled together in one sobbing teenage face. Nikki wondered if she'd ever been like that.

The crowd in front of the bus was massive, and Duncan was using a fair amount of muscle just to bully a path through the press of bodies. Nikki tried her best to keep the path clear, but she was no six-foot security dude. Lacking mountainous bulk, she resorted to the pointed use of elbows.

"Thanks for coming out, everyone," said Kit, climbing onto the bus stairs. "I appreciate your-well wishes and I know my band and crew do too." There was a cheer from the crowd and a wave of flashes from a few press members. "I would also like to thank the doctors and staff at the St. Denis hospital for their patience and expert care." This got another cheer from the hometown crowd. "Thanks again and I hope to see you in Paris!" Kit waved and let the bus driver close the door. "All right," he said, tossing the teddy bear to Nikki. "Who's for whist?"

"Are you sure that's the best idea?" she asked. "It didn't go very well last time."

"I'm stubborn," he said, flashing a smile. "I keep trying till I get it right."

"Actually," said Angela, her clear voice sounding suspiciously parental, "we need to go over a few things before Paris."

"Fine," he said with a shrug.

"I'm sitting just here," she said, pointing to a seat near the front, and turned her back to Nikki, effectively blocking her from joining in. "I don't know why you got a single-story bus," she said peevishly. "It's like working in a madhouse."

"How dare you insult the troops of Napoleon Bonaparte!" exclaimed Kit, thrusting his hand into his jacket and striking a Napoleonesque pose.

"Funny," said Angela with a tight smile. Seeing as there was no room for her in Angela's seat, Nikki made her way back toward where the band was sprawled out.

"Hey," she said, dropping down next to Holly.

"Hey," replied Holly. "Have you made any progress on our mysterious happenings? Hammond seemed to think you had things wrapped up."

"Sort of," said Nikki, making a face. "Things are never as tidy as you want them to be."

"Anything you want to share with the class?" asked Holly hopefully, but Nikki shook her head. "Play it close to the vest, then," said Holly with a shrug, and ducked back into her book.

Nikki leaned her head back into the seat and thought about things she knew and things she didn't know and things she suspected. She heard Kit pass by and heard Burg make a wet farting noise. She opened her eyes and looked around. The bus trundled on through town, and Nikki surveyed the passengers and luggage with a sinking feeling.

"We're not going back to the hotel, are we?" Nikki asked Holly.

"No, why?"

"I don't suppose you checked me out and got Trista's luggage loaded?"

Holly winced, seeing what was coming. "Uh, no. Sorry, didn't know I was supposed to. Angela was hurrying us all and getting everyone rounded up. She had a checklist of tour members; maybe she got Trista's stuff?"

"Yeah, maybe," said Nikki doubtfully. "I'll ask."

She moved up the bus to where Angela sat sorting through her day planner.

"Hey, Angela," Nikki started to say, but the woman held up a shushing finger and then entered a series of numbers into her iPhone.

"Yes, Nikki isn't it? What can I do for you?" Angela stretched her lips into an upward-tilting line that might have passed for a smile if someone didn't know better.

"I went over to the hospital this morning to check on Trista. I don't suppose you collected her luggage when you checked everyone out? I was using her stuff." Nikki maintained her calm and suppressed the urge to punch the other woman.

"Oh, I'm sorry. Everyone was responsible for their own luggage." Angela flipped her day planner to an employee list, and Nikki saw that her name had been added and then circled.

"But you got me checked out?" asked Nikki, suddenly aware that she was the target of a great deal of female hostility. She could tell because Angela was showing all her teeth, which were beautiful displays of the dental art, practically gleaming with a white neon glow. It was very un-British.

"Of course," said Angela, showing even more teeth. A couple of years ago, Nikki would have slunk back to her own seat. Angela was class president material and Nikki was the ditzy cheerleader. She knew that by all rights she should absorb the slight and go away. Instead, she found herself slightly bored. The fact surprised her.

"So you knew I wasn't there?" she asked, wanting to be perfectly clear.

"I made an announcement; I can't be responsible if you weren't there."

"You didn't answer my question, Angela," said Nikki softly.

"I don't know what you mean," Angela said, breaking eye contact.

"If you have a problem with me, I'd like to hear it," Nikki said, marveling at the calm in her own voice.

"You know," said Angela, her voice rising, "I've looked and I can't seem to find your hiring packet. I really think that when we get to Paris, we're going to have to have a little discussion about your job. I don't think I can let Kit have an unqualified replacement for Trista."

"Trust me, Angela, I'm the only qualified replacement you're going to find," said Nikki, feeling amused.

Angela's nostrils flared, and she tossed her hair back angrily. "Who do you think you are? I'm the tour manager and you are just some stupid makeup girl. You think just because you know Trista that I can't have you fired, like that?" She snapped her fingers, making a sharp clicking noise. These were dire threats; even as little as a year ago Nikki would have started to panic and apologize. Instead she smothered a laugh as the woman continued, her soft features sharpening into bitterness. "We've been with Kit for years. If you think you can just walk in and change how things are done, and instantly become a part of the inner circle, you've got another think coming."

Nikki tried to come up with an appropriate answer. Something witty and devastating, something Val Robinson would say.

"Hey, Nikki," yelled Kit from the back of the bus. "Come back here. We're going to watch Burg light something on fire!"

"You hold that thought, Angela," said Nikki with a smile as genuine as Angela's had been fake. "I'm going to join that little inner circle over there, and afterward, if Kit doesn't want to do something new and routine-breaking, I'll get back to you."

"What joy?" asked Holly as Nikki made her way down the aisle.

"None, I'm afraid. I'm luggageless once again. And it had my 'good' outfit from the backup dancers in it. Not to mention Trista's phone."

"Oh, that's too bad. We were planning on going out tonight. Now you won't have anything to wear."

"What's this?" asked Kit, looking up.

"Nikki's luggage got left at the hotel," explained Holly.

"I swear that happens at least twenty times a tour," answered Kit. "Do you want to borrow my phone and call the hotel?"

Nikki started to shake her head and then stopped. "That would be great, actually. If you don't mind?"

"Of course not. Call whoever you need." He handed over the phone, just as there was a burst of flame and a cheer from the back row of seats. "Oh damn! I missed it! Do it again!" yelled Kit. He scrambled over the top of the seats to land on Richie and elbowed his way into the circle. Holly and Nikki exchanged unanimous glances of female confusion over the male fascination with farting.

"What hotel are we staying at in Paris?" asked Nikki.

"The Paris Hilton."

"You're kidding." Holly grinned and shook her head. Nikki shrugged and, taking the phone, went into the small bathroom. The bathroom smelled of astringent covering other odors. She sat on the sink with her feet on the toilet lid, trying to get above the smell, and dialed the international number for Carrie Mae.

"He took his vorpal sword in hand: Long time the manxome foe he sought," she quoted to the voice-recognition computer; there was a whirring click as it processed her through the switchboard.

She listened to the various options and selected one for English, four for live operator assistance, and two for an unsecured line.

"*Bonjour,*" said a pleasant-voiced woman, interrupting the music. "You've reached the Carrie Mae Foundation, Paris branch. To whom am I speaking?"

"Nicole Lanier, Los Angeles branch."

"Nicole, how can we help you help the world?"

"I need a care package," answered Nikki, ignoring the tagline. "I'm arriving in Paris later today and I have no phone, clothes, or equipment. I'm also expecting contact from Astriz Liebenz from the Stuttgart branch and I . . . no longer have the phone I was using to reach her."

"Oh, that's unfortunate," the operator cooed sympathetically. "I'm sure we can arrange a delivery for you. Can we have your Paris location?"

"The Paris Hilton," answered Nikki, feeling a bit silly for even saying it.

"Which one?"

"There's more than one?"

"There's the Paris Hilton and then there's the Hilton Arc de Triomphe."

"Hold on." Nikki stuck her head out the bathroom door and looked around. "Anybody know which Hilton we're staying at?"

"The Hilton Arc de Triomphe," yelled Kit over his shoulder. There was a gust of flame and a strange burning smell that Nikki didn't care to investigate.

"The Hilton Arc de Triomphe," she reported to the operator.

"Ooh," chirped the woman, "Kit Masters is going to be staying there for his New Year's Eve show! Maybe you'll see him."

"Maybe," said Nikki. "But he might be too busy lighting things on fire."

"What?"

"Nothing. We'll be getting into Paris later this evening. Can I get something by tonight?"

"I'm forwarding your color chart, measurements, and preferred equipment list to our *prêt-à-porter* department. We can have a complete package together by six o'clock tonight."

"Great. I'll be registered under my real name."

"Do you require anything particular or in addition to the list?"

"They said something about going out later, so probably whatever one wears to a Paris club these days."

"Of course."

"Oh, and if you can get me a manual on airbrush makeup techniques I'd appreciate it." There was a pause on the other end of the line.

"Now, when you say the airbrush manual you're referring to . . ."

"Oh, uh, the real one. I've got a slight makeup crisis to deal with."

"Of course," answered the operator smoothly, regaining her momentum. "It will be included."

"And I've been out of contact with the office for a few days. If you could include any e-mail, phone messages, or information uploads to my file that would be great."

"I was already adding it to the list! Anything further?"

"Nope, I think that's it."

"Very well. *Bonne chance, mademoiselle!*"

"Thanks," answered Nikki, and hung up. "*Bonne chance* indeed," she repeated to herself with a small laugh. She hadn't had much *bonne* luck since Colombia.

PARIS I

I Love Paris

Nikki sat across from her EU counterpart and felt blobby and gross. The girl was tall, blond, slightly younger than Nikki, and impeccably dressed in a twill skirt, coordinating pumps, purse, and overcoat. Over everything she had draped an elegantly folded scarf pinned in place with a Carrie Mae butterfly. It looked a bit as though she'd put on her older sister's clothes, but Nikki couldn't fault the attire, since it also looked as if she had showered recently and slept more than eight hours in the last two days. Unhampered by luggage, Nikki had gotten off the bus first and dashed into the lobby, where she had immediately recognized her contact; Carrie Mae women always attained a look that was beyond reproach. Nikki felt a stab of guilt over letting the team down with her grubbiness and winced when she saw the girl scan her sweats-and-T-shirt ensemble with a faintly raised eyebrow. Nikki pretended not to notice, and they exchanged *"bonsoirs"* and air kisses while the entire hotel staff made a mad dash for the tour bus.

Svenka was Swedish but working with the Paris branch. She

appeared unaware of the raucous arrival of the band but was very excited to assist Nikki. Svenka continued her introduction and delivery of equipment in rapid-fire but accented English, dragging a set of matching rolling suitcases forward. Nikki seated them behind some enormous potted palms for a bit of privacy. The suitcases were beautifully styled pieces of leather luggage that would have made any bellboy swoon, and Nikki wondered just how much paperwork they were going to cost her.

"You didn't have to come out yourself," said Nikki, still confused by the girl's excitement. "You could have just left the luggage at the desk."

"I wanted to!" exclaimed Svenka. "I don't get to do the proper agent things very often. I'm new, and everyone has to start at the bottom." She ended on a quasi-hopeful note, and Nikki frowned. There was something sort of puppy-doggish about Svenka. If the puppy were a giant blond Viking that had no idea it was going to grow up into a supermodel. Nikki wondered if Svenka had any idea she was gorgeous or could crush a man's skull with one hand.

"Plus, I heard that Kit Masters, the British pop star, was going to be staying here," Svenka said, leaning forward conspiratorially.

"I heard that too," answered Nikki evenly, wishing she could dunk her head in a bucket of ice water to wake her brain up a little. She had a gritty feeling between her ears, as if she'd spent all day buried in beach sand.

"I was kind of hoping that I would see him while I was here. This is why I arrived early."

"There's always a chance," said Nikki.

"We weren't sure what you'd be looking for in terms of luggage. We went with a classic style. This one's for clothes." She gestured to the suitcase on the left with Vanna White–like grace. "We included basic lingerie needs, casual wear, club wear, and dress wear, as well as four shoe styles. These include boots, heels, flats, and trainers."

"Thanks," said Nikki simply; she was having trouble following Svenka's accented English. She had spent too many hours trying to decipher Englishman's English, and it had warped her ears. The rhythms were all wrong.

"We picked colors from your color chart, but you didn't have any color preferences specified, so I'm not sure you'll like everything we pulled for you." Svenka looked up nervously and tugged at her scarf slightly.

"Yeah, I've been meaning to do that. I'm sure it will be fine," Nikki said reassuringly.

"The second case contains your equipment. Standard-issue hairspray, lipstick, perfume, etc., all in your scents and colors. We've also included some of the recent Paris branch innovations!"

Svenka unzipped the second case and displayed the neatly organized interior.

"The belt." She pulled out a leather belt that had a curious stiffness to it. "The steel cable running down the center creates an ideal whip, with added weight for impact. The snakelike construction permits flexibility and added snap while still being light enough for day-to-day wear."

Nikki nodded, suitably impressed.

"These are from our outdoor accessory line." She held up a pair of gloves. "Made of a Kevlar-rubber blend, these extremely warm gloves can't quite stop bullets, but they're slice-proof and allow you to handle live electrical current."

"Because I do that so frequently," said Nikki.

"But now you can!" exclaimed Svenka cheerfully, packing the black gloves away into their proper spot and rezipping the suitcase.

"Oh . . . good," said Nikki. Rachel, her own techno-wizard, frequently made similar statements. Since she invariably never saw the point of, say, slice-proof gloves, Nikki never knew quite what was expected of her in response. It was her estimation that people like Rachel and Svenka had bigger imaginations than she did. For them, everything had the potential to be something else, and they never saw any reason those things shouldn't be.

"Oh, and here is your phone." She produced a phone from her pocket; it was plastic-wrapped and sealed. "We were told we could not retrieve your phone messages. Apparently, your phone is in repair? We gave you an unassigned Carrie Mae phone as a loaner. Just mail it back to us when you're done. We also included a manual for airbrush makeup techniques." Svenka paused, a frown wrinkling her brow. "Did you really mean to have the actual makeup manual?"

"Yeah, I've got to do a bit of body-painting on some devil girls," said Nikki.

"Oh." Svenka's forehead furrowed even further. Devil girls were apparently not on the list of common problems for a Paris Carrie Mae agent. "They must give you the really difficult assignments," she said at last. "To tell the truth, I thought you'd be taller."

"I get that a lot," said Nikki.

"Hey, Nikki," said Kit, making a beeline toward her from the front counter. Out of the corner of her eye she saw Svenka's jaw drop. "You're rooming with Holly; she said that would be cool. Here's your key. Can you come up to my room as soon as you're settled in? I think Brandt has some plan about reporters and studios and I might need reinforcements."

"Yeah, sure," said Nikki. "Kit, I'd like you to meet my company rep, Svenka. She's dropping off some clothes for me. Svenka, this is Kit Masters." Svenka closed her mouth and mustered her composure.

"It is a pleasure to meet you, Mr. Masters. Welcome to Paris."

"Thanks," said Kit, shaking hands. "I guess Carrie Mae really takes care of their people."

"Indeed," replied Svenka breathlessly. "We certainly try. Nikki is one of our top consultants."

"Oh," said Kit, clearly unsure of what that meant. "Well, she's certainly gone above and beyond for us." Kit added one of the brilliant smiles that made people fall in love with him, and Nikki watched in disgust as Svenka beamed back at him. "See you upstairs, Nikki?" he asked.

Nikki nodded. "Be up in a minute."

"Oh my," said Svenka, fanning herself and dropping back into her chair as Kit walked away. "He is so handsome! I thought I was going to faint! And so nice!"

"He has his moments," said Nikki.

"Wait until I tell the girls! They are never going to believe me. Did you know he's the son of one of our very own agents?"

"Yes," said Nikki dryly. "I'm aware."

"You are so lucky!" said Svenka. "If you need anything else from us just call the number programmed into your phone."

"That's me. Ms. Lucky." Nikki sighed. She was being grumpy. And worse than grumpy, she was feeling a wave of sniffly, self-pitying wanna-stay-home-and-snuggle-with-the-boyfriend-she-didn't-have-anymore wash over her. She had been doing so well. This was not the time to succumb to the breakup blues.

"I don't suppose you've heard from Astriz?" she asked. If Valerie Robinson had been saddled with a partner she didn't request who then subsequently disappeared, Val would have continued on without a second thought and certainly without stopping to collect Nikki. Nikki suspected that Astriz was not going to be any different. She was going to be on her own when it came to catching up with Astriz and Cano.

"Not yet," said Svenka. "But we programmed your current caseload alerts onto the phone. If she checks in, you'll get a text. And if we hear anything about Cano, we'll immediately contact you."

"What about Camille?" asked Nikki, feeling another wave of fatigue sweep over her. Dealing with rogue Carrie Mae agents seemed to be half her life. Shouldn't she just be dealing with the bad guys?

"Camille Masters?" asked Svenka, her head cocking to one side like a bird. "I did not know that she was in Europe. Is she visiting her son?"

"Not sure," said Nikki, hedging, "but she is in Europe, and I need to find her before she does something stupid."

"I could add her to your watch list, I suppose," she said.

"Thanks, Svenka," Nikki said, making an effort. "I really appreciate your helping me out."

"Of course," Svenka answered with chipper confidence. "We are Carrie Mae. What else would we do but help you help the world!"

"Yes," said a Teutonic voice laconically, "what else would we do?"

Astriz dropped into the seat between Nikki and Svenka. Nikki smiled in surprise.

"Welcome to Paris, Nicole. I see that you have managed to get reequipped."

"The Paris branch is being friendly," said Nikki. "Svenka, meet Astriz. Astriz, Svenka."

"I like friendly," said Astriz, giving Svenka a once-over. "Do they have any leads on Camille?"

"They didn't realize she was in Europe," said Nikki. "Do you have any leads on Cano?"

"One," said Astriz. "I nearly had him in Reims, but Camille ran me off the road. It was a . . . what does your military say? A cluster-screw?"

"Not quite, but same meaning," said Nikki.

"Camille is a highly respected agent," said Svenka, looking uncertainly from Astriz to Nikki. "She's friends with our director. Why would she run you off the road?"

"She's not thinking clearly," said Nikki. "We need to find her."

"I'll see what I can do," said Svenka doubtfully.

"Speaking of the Masters family," said Astriz, "what have you found about Herr Masters?"

"Well, apparently most of the accidents were an attempt to make Kit reconsider his career choice. Show him that stardom isn't so great and maybe get him to take a break from it all," said Nikki, choosing to leave out the person who caused the accidents. "It was for his 'own good.'" Nikki made air quotes around the last phrase. "No connection to Cano."

"Very strange," said Svenka.

"However, the most recent incident—a truck deliberately crashing the tour bus—wasn't connected to the other accidents. So I have to assume it's connected to Cano. And we're back at square one in terms of figuring out who on the tour is in cahoots with Cano."

"Cahoots?" repeated Svenka, and belatedly Nikki remembered that they were both non-native English speakers.

"Collusion, alliance, in league with," said Nikki, waiting for the lightbulb moment.

"Ah!" said Astriz at last. "Well, it would have to be someone who could alert Cano or the truck driver to the tour bus's exact location."

Nikki nodded. "Someone with an ax to grind, who doesn't want Kit to succeed."

"You have someone in mind?" asked Svenka.

"I have two top suspects. Angela—the tour manager—has been leaving alcohol in Kit's greenrooms. Or there's Duncan, Kit's bodyguard, who has a picture of Camille and her husband from the IRA days and was covering up the accidents."

"But what does either of them gain from killing Herr Masters?"

"I'm not sure," said Nikki. "Angela seems bitter and angry now that Kit's sober and making his own decisions. And I know Duncan is hiding something. I just don't know what."

"Kit doesn't have very much family," said Svenka helpfully. "Just his grandmother and Camille. Maybe he left either Duncan or Angela money in his will?"

"Pulled his file, did you?" asked Astriz.

"*Maxim* magazine interview," muttered Svenka, blushing.

"So . . . just Camille and his grandmother," repeated Nikki, staring off into space.

"Who would presumably inherit," murmured Astriz. Nikki shared a look with her.

"Well, thank you, Svenka," said Nikki, standing up and holding out her hand. "You have been very helpful." Svenka looked confused but stood also.

"Of course," she said, "I am happy to help." Svenka shook hands with Nikki and Astriz and walked out of the lobby, pausing to wave at the door. Astriz watched her all the way.

"Cute ass," said Astriz as the revolving door spun back around empty. "Too bad that she's not so"—she tapped her forefinger against her temple—"smart."

"I think she's just young," said Nikki, sitting back down and putting her feet up on the coffee table. "You don't think Camille would really hurt Kit, do you?"

"It seems implausible," said Astriz, "but you had the same thought or you wouldn't have sent our little friend packing."

"The person who was creating the accidents was the retired Carrie Mae agent Camille had watching Kit—Trista Elliot. Trista's been following Camille's orders to scare Kit into leaving the rock star life."

"So maybe Camille wants to kill Kit for money, but going to Cano . . . I don't think even Camille . . ."

"I don't buy it," agreed Nikki. "She's terrified someone will hurt Kit. I'm not saying her decisions are rational, or even smart, but I do think she's trying to protect Kit the best way she knows how. I don't think she gives a damn about money."

"Back at the beginning then," said Astriz glumly.

Nikki laced her fingers behind her head and stared at the ceiling. "Svenka's right. I need to look at Kit's will. Cano wants to kill because of his history, but whoever's working with Cano wouldn't have that history. It has to be something basic, something simple, like money."

"What about Camille?" asked Astriz.

"She may be off her rocker, but we have to proceed like she's on our side."

"She wrecked my car," said Astriz. "She is not on my side."

"Point taken," said Nikki. "But you can't shoot her."

"Punch her in the face?" asked Astriz.

"Sure, sounds great," said Nikki. "But we need to get her and Cano under control."

"We have word that one of his associates may be at a club later tonight," said Astriz. "I was planning to either follow him or capture him and force him to tell us where Cano is. I can pick you up when we go."

Nikki nodded. "That will give me some time to question Kit about his will."

"Then we have a plan," said Astriz, standing. "I will call for you at ten." Nikki nodded and Astriz strode off with the briefest of waves.

"Val-like and yet not," said Nikki thoughtfully to herself.

PARIS II

Something's Wrong

Nikki waited in the lobby for Astriz with a feeling of self-satisfaction. True, she hadn't been able to get the details of Kit's will, but she had managed to lend a little anti-Brandt support and talk Kit into having dinner with the band. And more important, Kit had endured the entire hour of dinner with drinkers without even breaking a sweat. Seeing the occasional glass of wine on the table had not sent Kit reaching for the nearest bottle, and the band had been glad to see him. Even Duncan had cracked a smile when Hammond told a story about an Amsterdam lounge singer, dueling pianos, and Kit parked on top of a piano like Michelle Pfeiffer in *The Fabulous Baker Boys*.

Which was a far different mood than Duncan had been in when she'd first arrived in Kit's room. Brandt had been pushing Kit to let the press follow him around.

"So they can, what? Snap pics of me napping? No bloody thanks!" exclaimed Kit as Duncan let Nikki into the room, his face grimmer than usual.

"Well, then let them come with you to the AA meeting tonight," said Brandt.

"Absolutely not." Brandt appeared caught off guard by the stark refusal in Kit's voice, and Angela lifted her head in surprise. "Meetings are private for a reason. The people there give me support and understanding, and I am not about to exploit them just to give myself good press. Being who I am already makes it hard enough for people to open up. My meetings stay anonymous, do you hear me?"

"Yeah, sure, Kit, we can do it your way," said Brandt coolly.

"It's the second A, for Christ's sake!" shouted Kit, as if just realizing what AA stood for.

"Fine!" snapped Brandt. "I said we wouldn't do it, already." It was Kit's turn to look surprised at Brandt's outburst. "But we have to do something." Brandt ran his hand over his hair, feeling the gelled ridges but not disturbing his coif. "If you're not going to do it tonight, then it'll have to be New Year's Eve, the day of the concert—maybe you can take some press to the studio."

"I really don't want to," said Kit distinctly, his jaw clenched. "I'm not ready to take anything into the studio, let alone complete strangers. You need to stop pushing me."

"Look, if you say you don't want to do it, then you don't do it. Simple as that." Brandt snapped his fingers in emphasis, but Nikki frowned. Brandt was giving in too easily. Had he had a change of heart? Or did he just have some other plan up his sleeve? "So the schedule is: meeting for you tonight, press junket tomorrow, take it easy day of the thirty-first. Just some sound checks and run-throughs on the day of."

"Yeah, no problem," said Kit with a dismissive wave.

Brandt and Angela had left then, Angela shooting her a look of poisonous dislike. Kit had looked up at her as if he couldn't remember why she was there and Nikki felt ready to sink into the floor. The one time she actually answered his call, and now he didn't want her.

"Hey," said Nikki, feeling a blush starting around her collarbone. "I was going to dinner with the gang. Thought you might want to come along."

Kit hesitated. "I have to go to this thing tonight."

"Yeah, I heard. No biggie."

"But wait, wait." He glanced nervously at Duncan as if for reassurance. "Maybe I can stop by for a few minutes."

"Yeah, that'd be cool."

"OK, let me get my jacket." Kit grinned and dashed into the bedroom.

"What do you think you're doing?" hissed Duncan as soon as Kit was out of the room.

"I'm inviting him to dinner."

"You can't just treat him like he's a normal person! He's an alcoholic and a rock star. You can't just invite him to things."

"He's going to have to see people drinking eventually," Nikki retorted. "And besides, he's going to a meeting right afterward. Seems like this would be the perfect opportunity to test the waters."

"Ta-da!" said Kit, jumping out of the bedroom and posing. "Don't I look smashing?" He flipped up the collar of a suit jacket he'd put on over his blue hoodie. "Brandt left it here. I think it looks rather good on me." He did a spin and threw his hands up in a rock star pose.

Nikki laughed. "Absolutely smashing! Can we go?"

"But of course, darling, but of course." He had offered her his arm, and Nikki had taken it, suppressing the urge to make a face at Duncan.

Nikki was still reveling in her triumph over Duncan when

Astriz pulled up in a beat-up Yugo, looking miserable. Laughing, Nikki stepped out to the curb.

"What's the matter, Astriz?" asked Nikki, leaning down to talk through the window. "This car doesn't match your self-image?"

Astriz's fingers tightened on the steering wheel. "It's all that was available on short notice, but it does not produce good speed," said Astriz stiffly. "It is not adequate."

"But it gets good gas mileage," said Nikki, trying not to laugh.

"I don't care!" snapped Astriz. "The car is ugly!"

Nikki turned an impending laugh into a cough as she was getting into the cracked vinyl passenger seat and patted Astriz on the shoulder.

"It's OK. No one will ever believe that Serbo-Croatian engineering is really your thing. You'll be back in a Mercedes soon."

"*Danke,*" said Astriz with a small sniff.

"What's the plan?" asked Nikki.

"We have an informant who says that Cano is meeting a supplier tonight at Club Jupiter. I thought we would run the same plan as last time. Wait for him to meet his supplier, seize him on the way out, and then call the cops on the supplier."

"And hope that Camille doesn't interrupt this time?" asked Nikki.

"At least now we know to expect her," said Astriz. "Perhaps this time we can stop her before she ruins our trap."

"What are we packing?" asked Nikki, eyeballing the black duffel bag in the back.

"I remembered what you said about snipers," said Astriz. "But I didn't think you would want to ask for one from the Paris branch."

"Mm," said Nikki in nonverbal agreement. Svenka had seemed helpful, but she was worried about her comment about Camille and the Paris director being friends; keeping demands on them to a minimum might be preferable. People talked with annoyance about good ol' boys' clubs and their glass ceilings, but very few understood the ice-age type of freeze that could be instituted by a well-organized sorority of hatred.

Astriz continued. "So I just got some basics. Two MP5s and two Kimbers."

"And silencers," Nikki said approvingly, opening the bag to take a peek.

"*Ja,*" said Astriz. "Camille is too loud for my tastes. I thought we should stick to something quieter."

"Camille is not the target," Nikki said, reminding her.

"But if she happens to take a bullet in the toe, then accidents happen. She killed my car," said Astriz bitterly, and Nikki laughed.

"Ricochets happen," said Nikki in agreement. "But remember, our primary target is Cano. If you get a clean shot, take it. I'd love to tie him up neatly and leave him for the police, but let's face facts. The man's a killer, and he's not going to stop."

"We're authorized?" asked Astriz, glancing at her.

"I'm authorizing," said Nikki.

"I didn't know you could authorize," she said, and Nikki couldn't tell if she was impressed or annoyed.

"I have case-dependent kill authorization. In this case I've been authorized."

"Huh," said Astriz. "Well, I guess that's why they pay you the big bucks." Nikki snorted at that.

Fifteen minutes later Astriz pulled up in an alley and turned off the car. Nikki passed out the handguns, tucking hers into her waistband and pocketing the silencer. The guns were Kimber Raptors with three-inch barrels on aluminum frames—easy for concealment. Nikki preferred the old standard 1911, but Kimber produced solid guns with reliable performance; she had no complaints.

"I think someone should wait here with the car, as backup," said Astriz, and Nikki sighed. "Someone" was a linguistic substitute to make a request more socially acceptable. "Someone" never meant the speaker; "someone" invariably meant the person being spoken to.

"I think you should go out front," said Nikki directly; she didn't have time to worry about offending anyone. "I will cover the rear exit from the inside, while you cover the front from outside."

"Why you?" demanded Astriz.

"Cano doesn't know me."

"He doesn't know me, either," Astriz said in protest.

"Three days following him around and you think he hasn't got a clue what you look like?" asked Nikki. "If he's half as good as Camille says he is, then I find that unlikely."

Astriz made a grunt that wanted to be disagreement but didn't quite make it.

"I'll have you on speed dial," said Nikki. "If I buzz you, don't bother to pick up, just come running."

"*Ja*," said Astriz, nodding. "I will approach from this end of the block; there's a café I can watch from."

"I'll circle around and approach from the opposite side," said Nikki.

The rain was turning into tiny, stinging snowflakes as she approached Club Jupiter. Nikki could see that it was not much of a club, at least not in the sense of dancing and flashing lights. It seemed more of a low-key drinking establishment designed to draw an older crowd. The bouncer was sitting just inside the door. He looked big enough, but he was sipping wine and nibbling from a plate at his elbow; he barely looked up as she entered. It was hard to look tough with a cheese platter.

She skirted the edge of the room, scanning the tables for Cano. It was a dimly lit place with candles in jars on the handful of tables and seating at the bar. No one looked suspicious, and she settled into a seat at the bar with her back to the wall.

The bartender returned from delivering drinks to a table and took her order for the house red. Nikki checked her watch and then the door; it was only half an act. Women alone in bars were not especially common in any culture. She needed to look as though she were waiting for someone. Minutes ticked by, and then she checked her watch for real. She hated stakeouts. Another ten minutes stretched into infinity and Nikki checked her watch again. The door opened and Nikki tensed as Svenka entered with the brusque, businesslike look of someone who was there for a purpose. Nikki frowned, her eyes narrowing. She had noticed, in her short tenure with the company, that Carrie Mae women tended to look as though they were always there for a purpose. It was a look she tried to coach out of her team; it made them too easy to spot in a crowd. Nikki relaxed against the wall, letting herself merge with the shadows from an overhanging shelf.

She had two choices: approach Svenka or wait to be approached. It was not a big bar; eventually she would be spotted. Before she could decide, Svenka had seen her and was marching across the room to plant herself defiantly in front of Nikki.

"You're blocking my sight lines," said Nikki. Svenka's defiant pose wilted slightly, but she forged ahead.

"You must come with me," she said.

"Sorry, honey, working," said Nikki. "No time." "Honey" was a word that implied that Nikki had higher status and power, and Nikki used it intentionally.

"But you must," said the girl. "I am supposed to insist. The Paris director requires you," said the girl, beginning to look frustrated. "I will use force." She pulled aside her coat and displayed a Taser. Nikki sighed.

Nikki thought about ways to disable Svenka. She thought briefly about shooting her in the foot and shook her head at that bad thought. All her options involved fighting or doing what she was told. Neither was appealing or would advance her goals.

"Svenka, sweetie"—Nikki used the diminutive like a weapon—"you transferred to Paris because you wanted to be posted somewhere urban and classy, didn't you?" Svenka nodded. "But the Paris girls just use you for muscle, don't they?"

"They make cow sounds when I eat lunch," Svenka said quietly, her shoulders dropping dejectedly. "It's because I'm big."

"No, it's because they're lazy bitches who don't want to break a nail. Carrie Mae is about women being able to stand up for themselves. If they want to be Carrie Mae they should stop hiding behind you, and you need to tell them."

"I can't!" exclaimed Svenka, widening her eyes in shock but nodding in spite of herself.

"Sure you can." Nikki scooted the bar stool next to her closer to Svenka. "Pull up a chair," she said. "You can help me on my stakeout."

"That's not what we're supposed to do," said Svenka, leaning toward the seat.

"Whatever," said Nikki, and waved to the bartender. "Who's 'we' anyway?"

"Suzette," said Svenka, sitting down. "She's waiting for us."

"So why'd she send you in?"

"Because I had met you already; they thought you might come

with me. But Suzette's in charge. Maybe we should go out. She is going to be angry," Svenka said fretfully.

"It'll be character-building," answered Nikki callously. She was too busy wondering how to communicate her predicament to Astriz to worry about Suzette's feelings. Nikki's phone rang and she picked up immediately.

"Yeah—Svenka, I know. She's here with me at the bar."

There was a long pause.

"Nikki, this is Jane."

"Jane, where have you been? I called you a couple of times."

"I flew to Germany."

"What? Why?"

"I like the beer?" said Jane, but there was a crack in her voice.

"Very funny. Want to tell me what's really going on?"

"Remember how you told me about that guy Voges—the fixer who helped Cano?"

"I remember Voges," said Nikki dryly. "What's the connection?"

"Well, you said the Germans couldn't go up against him because they didn't have a team and he was too dangerous. And I thought that you didn't really need an assault team, you needed someone with a computer."

"Oh God," said Nikki, seeing where Jane was headed.

"Well, it is my vacation," sniffed Jane defensively. "And I thought I really owed you after Colombia."

"I told you to forget about it!" exclaimed Nikki.

"How am I supposed to forget about it!" wailed Jane. "I had to do something!"

"So you decided to spend your vacation cracking the computer system of a German arms supplier?" asked Nikki sarcastically.

"Well, yes. Only . . ."

"Only what?" demanded Nikki.

"Well, he's got some pretty severe systems and a couple of isolated drives that I had to have a land connection to. And, well, I guess I'm not a very good field agent . . ."

"Jane! You got caught?"

"No, at least not yet. They have my hotel staked out. I haven't left the hotel all day and I'm not sure how much longer I can hold out on German room service. The food is terrible!"

Nikki paused, pondering her next move.

"Nikki?" asked Jane nervously when the silence had gone on too long. "I was joking about the room service. The guys outside are scary. I was just trying to help."

"I know, Jane, and if you actually got something out of Voges's computer, then all is forgiven."

"I did! I got all of it!" said Jane. "I'm going through it now. I can call you the second I know something."

"Good. Meanwhile, I'm going to put you on with Svenka while I make a few plans. Svenka, talk to Jane for a minute," said Nikki, handing over the phone. "And lend me your phone."

"No, I'm supposed to take you out to Suzette," said Svenka, but she was already handing Nikki her phone.

"We'll go see Suzette in a minute," said Nikki. Svenka's problem was that she was too obedient. Of course, had she been any different on her first assignment?

Astriz answered Nikki's call cautiously. "This is Astriz."

"It's Nikki. We've got a problem."

"*Ja*." said Astriz. "Looks like a Paris field agent just parked in front of the club and Svenka went inside. Cano will never come inside with them parked there. I was going to go in after you. I thought calling would either be pointless or draw attention to you."

"Don't bother," said Nikki. "I have something else I need you to do." Briefly she filled Astriz in on Jane's situation.

"Voges is a nasty piece of work," said Astriz. "Your Jane sounds . . ."

"Foolhardy?" suggested Nikki.

"I was thinking ambitious," said Astriz. "So you want me to go to retrieve your Jane?"

"Yes, if you don't mind."

"It is no bother, but what about you?"

"I'm going to go have a chat with Suzette out in the car there and see if I can get a face-to-face with Camille, since she's got to be the one behind this."

"I suggest that you kick her in the knee. Possibly also some eye gouging."

"I'll keep it in mind," said Nikki, laughing. "Good luck!"

"*Ciao,*" said Astriz, sounding not in the least Italian.

Nikki hung up; Svenka was now laughing at something Jane had said. She signaled the bartender for the tab and charged it to her Carrie Mae account. They owed her on this one. Svenka finally noticed Nikki was off the phone and handed her cell back as Nikki was signing the receipt.

"Those Paris girls don't sound very nice," said Jane.

"Not very," said Nikki.

"I'm adding Svenka to my friend list."

"Just what you need—another e-mail correspondent."

"Whatever," said Jane, sounding more like her usual self. "Just because you think e-mail is a government conspiracy to help your mother keep tabs on you doesn't mean the rest of us can't enjoy it."

"Damn that Al Gore; he never should have invented that Intraweb." Jane giggled as Nikki had hoped she would. "I've sent

Astriz to help you out. She should be there in about five to seven hours, depending on whether or not she ditches the Yugo. Can you hold out that long?"

"No prob," said Jane firmly. "I have Astriz's number from before, so maybe she can translate the menu and help me order something that isn't sausages."

"We can only hope," said Nikki. "Catch ya later."

"See ya!" replied Jane cheerfully.

"OK," said Nikki, turning back to Svenka. "Let's go find Suzette."

"She's going to be mad," said Svenka glumly.

"I am already angry," said a sharp Parisian voice. Suzette stepped through the back entrance, dressed in a fur coat and hat and black leather gloves. She also wore a bracelet and gold ring on the outside of the gloves; the outfit seemed slightly over the top to Nikki.

"We were going to come out," said Svenka guiltily, getting out of her seat.

"No, you were having a glass of wine," said Suzette. Nikki was about to speak when Suzette reached out and slapped her on the back. Too late, Nikki realized that the ring was not simply fashion; it was the knockout-injection ring from last season's line of specialty items. Nikki felt the world go foggy, and she started to slide from the chair. She was only dimly aware of Svenka catching her. It was a good thing that Svenka was big.

PARIS III

There's No Place Like Home

Nikki woke up with a mouth that tasted like that time in third grade when she'd challenged Rory Henderson to a glue-eating contest. She waited, eyes closed, hoping to catch some clues about her situation before her captors were aware of her consciousness. She was slumped in an armchair, and she could hear the sound of a crackling fire—it was sucking all the heat in the room toward it and not giving much in return.

"You were supposed to gently but firmly request that she join us here," said an annoyed English voice.

"Svenka got carried away," replied a second voice that Nikki's hazy memory thought might be Suzette's. There was a slight protesting noise from the other side of the room. "She should be waking up soon; the injection only lasts a couple of hours. We'll just tell her she slipped and hit her head on the ice."

"She's not going to believe that," said Svenka, sounding surly.

"Nobody asked your opinion," snapped the English voice again, and this time Nikki recognized it as Camille's.

"I'm going to go with Svenka on this one," said Nikki, yawning and stretching.

She was in an antique room with antique furnishings. A heavy wooden desk was in front of her, the fireplace to her left. Camille sat behind the desk in a fashionable coat; her hat and gloves lay on the desk in front of her, as if she had just removed them. There was a sparkle of melted snow on the felt hat. Suzette stood by the desk. Svenka leaned against the far wall. No door was in sight, which meant that it was behind her.

"I'm not going to believe it," said Nikki, "because it didn't happen."

Camille's smile was small. Botox was a factor in the size of the expression, as was the fact that she clearly didn't mean it.

"Welcome to Paris, Nicole," said Camille, giving her a hard glare.

"Thanks," said Nikki, waiting for the argument to begin. Camille continued to stare. "Well," said Nikki, refusing to be intimidated, "I assume you brought me here for a reason. What can I do for you?"

"I read your file," said Camille, and Nikki felt a touch of nervousness. "You've never operated in the European theater before." Nikki shrugged. "There are a few things that perhaps you should have been warned about before thrusting yourself into a situation that was none of your business."

"I was assigned to the mission," said Nikki. "You were there. Frankly, if I'd had my way, I wouldn't have left Nina Alvarez."

Camille snorted softly, as if amused. "You were trying to undercut me from the beginning." Nikki gaped in astonishment. "I've met your kind before—always climbing over your betters. And maybe I could have let that go if you'd just minded your own business, but you should have known better than to get between a mother and her son."

"Camille, get a grip. This isn't some showdown. I'm not trying to get between you and Kit. In fact, I think it would be great if you spent more time with him."

"Don't tell me how to parent!" snarled Camille.

Nikki took a deep breath. "I know you're upset about Cano, and I promise you, I will stop him, but you have to trust me," she said, trying to sound conciliatory.

"I have a letter here from Madame Feron, Paris branch director," said Camille with a small triumphant smile.

Nikki sighed. She'd known there was going to be trouble the second Svenka had mentioned Camille and the head of the Paris Branch were friends.

"Due to the fact that you have entered Paris without obtaining permission from her—"

"You know domain permissions are no longer required," Nikki said, interrupting.

"Do not lecture me on what I do or do not know!" hissed Camille. "Domain permissions are still on the books in Europe. You are in violation."

Perhaps it was being knocked unconscious by her own team, or her lack of sleep, but Nikki's temper finally rose to the surface. "I'm on an assignment and you're interfering with the completion of it. I will stop Cano and I will protect Kit, and I'm not going to be sidelined by some paranoid hack who won't admit when she's in over her head." Nikki enunciated each word clearly, and she could feel her face get cold as the blood drained from it to her rapidly thumping heart.

"The Paris branch will be handling Cano from here on out. You are no longer required. Suzette and Svenka will escort you back to your hotel, where you will collect your belongings and leave. Read it and weep," said Camille, as if Nikki hadn't interrupted. "I don't need you. Kit doesn't need you. You aren't wanted here."

Camille slapped down the letter on the desk and Nikki felt a helpless rage; she had been outmaneuvered. Refusing to cave, she took the letter and read it. It was just as Camille said. She crumpled the letter into a ball and tossed into the fireplace. She couldn't disobey an order from a director, but she'd be damned if she'd go without a fight.

"Nice," Nikki bit out. "If I want this countermanded I have to call Mrs. Merrivel. Meanwhile, you have the run of the field."

"Glad you appreciate it," said Camille with a genuine smile.

"I'll have this lifted by morning," said Nikki, standing.

"Feel free to try," said Camille.

Nikki stomped to the door and slammed it satisfactorily behind her. She stood in the hallway and realized belatedly that she had no idea which way to go. The door opened, and Nikki whirled to face it. Svenka gingerly shut the door and jerked her head to the left.

"I am to drive you back to the hotel," said Svenka as she walked. "I'm sorry about"—she waved her hands in the air—"all of this. The director is very big on etiquette."

"I'm sure she is," Nikki said, and Svenka looked at her worriedly.

"Do you think you can get the order reversed?"

"Yes," said Nikki with more confidence than she felt. Mrs. Merrivel could be a miracle worker, but Camille seemed like someone who had probably tucked a lot of favors away over the years. It might be a tight match.

"I've never seen anyone stand up to a director like that," said Svenka, impressed.

"You should get out more," answered Nikki, feeling that she hadn't stood up at all.

Once in the car, she dialed the home number and waded through voice checks and helpful on-duty intel officers to get to Mrs. Merrivel.

"Sorry, Nikki," said the leader's personal secretary, "Mrs. Merrivel's in a situation. She can't be disturbed."

"OK," said Nikki, biting back a string of swear words, "here's the situation." She ran down the problem, and she could hear the secretary typing as she spoke. The report would go to Mrs. M directly, at least.

"Sorry, Nikki, I'll try to get Mrs. M on it as soon as possible."

"Thanks," said Nikki, and hung up.

"Not lucky?" asked Svenka, and Nikki shook her head. Dawn was edging into existence over the eastern edge of Paris. Beams of muted sunlight crept across the Champs-Elysées with the sparkling grace that made the poets talk about Paris and sigh. Even the lines of cars crowding the Champs managed to look glistening and romantic. In the near distance, the Arc de Triomphe anchored the skyline with the massive dignity of coffered stone. Nikki turned bleak eyes away from the view—the romance was lost on her. She wanted to go home. Home where there were hugs after a bad day. Home where there were snuggles on the couch. Home where Z'ev made dinner. Home where she could look forward to salsa on a Thursday night. She realized with a sinking feeling that Z'ev had come to equal home, and Z'ev wasn't there anymore. And really, who did she think she was fooling? He wouldn't have been there much longer. Even after he'd made plans for Mexico, he still had one foot out the door.

Z'ev was listening to Tricky, which was better than old-school Portishead. Nikki stood with her key in the lock, listening to the thumping bass of the gravelly-voiced Euro trip-hopper's music through the door of her apartment. Nikki preferred Portishead, but as an indicator of Z'ev's mood level, Tricky was definitely better. Portishead was for serious depression; Tricky was for irrational grouchiness. She finished unlocking the door and kicked off her shoes, ditching her sunglasses and purse on the table by the door.

Z'ev was in the kitchen, cooking. She watched as he chopped small red potatoes with short, vicious strokes of the knife.

"Have the potatoes been bad?"

"Your knives suck," he said without looking at her. "I'm buying you new knives."

"OK," said Nikki.

He threw the knife into the sink and dropped the potatoes onto a cookie sheet. Olive oil went on top of the potatoes in angry shakes, followed by bits of rosemary, salt, and pepper.

"So what are we having for dinner?" asked Nikki, leaning against the counter.

"Black bean salad, rosemary potatoes, and grilled chicken. Flan for dessert."

This was a bad sign; he had been watching the Cooking Channel again.

"Honey, do you want to go to the gym later?" she asked. The man clearly needed to hit something. The potatoes were not helping.

"Don't call me 'honey,'" he snapped, slamming the oven closed on the potatoes. "You only call me 'honey' when you're being patronizing."

Nikki folded her arms across her chest. She had tried several methods of dealing with a Tricky mood in the past: joking, soothing, and understanding. Nothing seemed to work. She could just walk away and let him stew in peace, but his mood seemed to follow her around the apartment. It was time to get tough.

"Z'ev, if you are angry about something, please tell me so you can stop being so aggressive with my cooking utensils."

He yanked open the refrigerator. "I'm not angry." He took out a dish of marinating chicken breasts and stomped away.

"You're not?" she asked, following him out to the deck, where her barbecue was heating.

"No," he said through gritted teeth. He flopped the chicken onto the grill and the marinade splattered up, splashing his shirt. "Damn it!" He barged back into the house, stripping off his shirt. With a sigh, Nikki followed him into the bedroom. He was digging through his drawer for a clean shirt.

"Did I do something to upset you?" asked Nikki, picking up his chicken-splattered T-shirt from the floor and carrying it into the bathroom.

"No!" he yelled.

"Then why are you yelling at me?" It was one of his favorites—bright yellow with a picture of a matador on it. Personally, she thought the shirt was hideous.

"I'm not yelling at you!" he yelled. She started to rinse it out in the sink; the sound of Tricky's "Cross to Bear" filled the apartment. Z'ev was still rummaging in the drawer.

"If you want to wait, this will be clean in a minute and we can dry it out on the deck."

"Don't want to wait," he grumbled, standing in the door of the bathroom.

"But I like it when you go topless," she said, looking at him in the mirror. That almost got a smile, but he clearly wasn't ready to relinquish his mood. She washed the shirt while he watched from the doorway.

"I got that shirt in Spain," he said, but he still sounded slightly surly. Nikki nodded.

"Travel shirts are kind of irreplaceable." The spot had disappeared to her satisfaction and she twisted the shirt, wringing it out. "There you go," she said, unfurling the shirt with a wet slap, "good as new. Just have to dry it out."

He pushed the shirt out of the way to kiss her.

"Mmm. I told you I liked topless," said Nikki. He laughed, backing her up against the sink to kiss her again. Water from the shirt in her hand ran into her blouse as she put her arms around his neck. The scent of rosemary filled the air and the oven timer began to beep incessantly.

"Ignore it," Z'ev said, and Nikki laughed, breaking away.

"The last time we ignored it we almost set the kitchen on fire," she said. "I really don't want to have to explain that to the maintenance guy *again*!"

"Fine," said Z'ev, rolling his eyes and jogging to the kitchen to rescue the potatoes while Nikki took his shirt out on the deck to hang over the back of one of the chairs.

"So," she said when dinner was through and the last of even the burned potatoes had been eaten. "Are you going to tell me what you were upset about?"

He grunted in response. Nikki ran it through her Z'ev translator and decided it most closely resembled "Yes, but don't push me." She waited.

"Doesn't matter," he said after a while. "It was a work thing."

"That you can't talk about?" Nikki asked, squelching a surge of annoyance. He grunted again; this time she guessed that the grunt meant, "Yes, let's not have this conversation again."

"I don't like coming here when you're working," he said suddenly. "There's nothing to do and I end up cleaning."

"Works OK for me," said Nikki, attempting a joke, but he shot her a sour look.

"I end up thinking of all the stuff I should be doing at work."

"Ah," said Nikki, sensing they'd reached the real crux of his bad mood.

"'Ah'?" he repeated, looking suspicious.

"You were mad at me because you were here when you felt like you should have been at work."

"I never said I was mad at you," he said.

"You didn't have to. Your moods tend to permeate."

"I wasn't mad at you," he repeated. "I was mad at the situation."

Nikki wanted to point out that she was the situation, but she didn't have the courage. Instead she stared at the setting sun and wondered when he'd break up with her.

PARIS IV

Z'ev's Dead, Baby, Z'ev's Dead

December 30

When they reached the hotel Nikki had every intention of leaving the younger girl on the sidewalk, but Svenka called her back.

"The director, Madame Feron, said I should give this to you," said Svenka, reluctantly taking an envelope out of her pocket. "In case your conversation with Camille wasn't productive. Those were her words. I don't know what's in it." Svenka looked worried and guilty.

"It's probably just another copy of that damn letter," said Nikki with a shrug, tucking the envelope into her jacket.

"I could give you a ride to the airport," said Svenka halfheartedly. Nikki gave her a speaking look and Svenka nodded. They both knew she wasn't going to the airport.

"I'll see you later, Svenka," said Nikki, and headed into the hotel.

Tiptoeing into her room, she could hear Holly softly breathing and considered what to do while she waited for Mrs. M to call.

A few hours later she woke with a start, reaching for the gun that she didn't have, as Holly walked past the bed.

"Late night?" Holly asked, looking at her strangely.

"Yeah," she said, realizing she was still wearing her clothes and shoes.

Holly returned from the bathroom, brushing her teeth, and they both stared at the ever-brightening sky.

"Paris is one of those places, isn't it?" said Holly after a while.

"Yup," said Nikki, and Holly giggled.

"Now there's an American word. You-up."

"Yup."

"You-up."

"Yup."

"You-up."

Nikki shook her head with a laugh, and Holly grinned.

"I'm going to go find some breakfast—want to come?" asked Holly, pulling on jeans.

"No, thanks, I've got a few errands to run." Nikki said the words automatically, although at the moment she couldn't think of what she possibly had to do.

"Oh. 'Kay."

Holly returned to the bathroom while Nikki sat on the bed and thought about taking off her shoes. What did she have to do? She had been derailed from her intended destination, and now the effort to reorient herself seemed Herculean.

"You sure you won't come to breakfast? You look like you could use a decent meal," said Holly, coming out of the bathroom, applying a smear of lip gloss. "Actually, you look like you could use a decent night's sleep, but that never happens on tour."

"Thanks, Holly, but I really do need to take care of a few things."

Holly shrugged again and headed for the door, picking up her jacket as she left.

The loaner phone buzzed; Nikki picked it up and groaned as she recognized her mother's phone number.

"Mom, how did you even get this number?" asked Nikki, picking up.

"I called your company and was annoying until they gave it to me," said Nell. "The power of annoyance is amazingly strong."

"Mom, why couldn't you just wait until I called you?"

"That'll be the day," said Nell with a snort. "Besides, it was slow at the office and I wanted to talk to you. I've been thinking about the ambassador boy."

Nell was under the impression that Z'ev worked for a U.S. embassy somewhere. Nikki had given up trying to correct her, figuring that explaining that he really worked for the CIA probably wouldn't go over very well. "I told you to bring him home for the holidays, but no, you thought Mexico was going to be better. Thought you needed couple time. Should have listened to your mother, now, don't you think?"

"Mom, did you just call to tell me how much I suck at relationships?" asked Nikki. "I figured that out on my own; don't really need the reinforcement."

"You don't suck," said Nell, cutting short the "mother knows best" tirade. "Men are just stupid. That's why I called."

Nikki laughed. "Mom, you wasted what was probably hours on the phone to get my phone number to tell me that men are stupid? Seriously?"

Nell sighed, managing to breathe the idea that Nikki was a remarkably stupid daughter into one single sound.

"You really liked him, didn't you?"

"Yes," said Nikki glumly. She didn't want to explain that what she had felt went well beyond "like." Then again, maybe her mother knew.

"Well, I was thinking that if you apologized he would probably come back."

"I'm not apologizing!" exclaimed Nikki. "He should apologize to me! He was treating me like I was an accessory to his life!"

"Look, I'm not saying you're wrong. I'm just saying that men sometimes don't learn too quickly. They get all goal-oriented and job-focused and don't realize that no one's going to give a crap about them when they're eighty if they don't start giving a crap about someone now. But they figure it out eventually."

"I don't think I can hang in there till he's eighty, Mom," said Nikki.

"No, it really only takes a year or two. You just have to get them used to the idea. I see it all the time. So if you call and apologize, he'll take you back and then by this time next year he'll be proposing."

"And you get some grandbabies?" asked Nikki suspiciously.

"That might be a pleasant side effect, yes," said her mother, as if the idea had never occurred to her.

"You spent Christmas with Grandma, didn't you?" asked Nikki.

"That has nothing to do with it," said Nell sharply.

"You only start bringing up grandkids when you go to see Grandma," said Nikki.

Nell sighed again, but sadly this time. "She's out there on that farm by herself. I mean, the woman annoys the crap out of me, but . . ." There was a pause and Nikki wondered what to say. Nell hardly ever got sentimental about her mother. "We used to be a big family, you know? But your father left, and Dad died, and the cousins moved back east. It's just the three of us now, Nikki, and that's kind of sad."

"I know," said Nikki, not knowing what else to say. "But I'm not apologizing to Z'ev. I can't trick him into thinking I'm important to his life. He's got to think it on his own."

"That'll be a long wait," said Nell dryly.

"Thanks for the encouragement, Mom."

"Just saying . . . Men are stupid."

"Not any stupider than women," said Nikki, feeling a crushing sense of depression.

"Probably true," said Nell, "but think it over."

"'Kay," said Nikki.

"Love you," said Nell. "Don't forget to call."

"I won't," answered Nikki. "Love you too. Bye."

Hanging up the phone, Nikki scrubbed her hand through her hair. Her mother possessed awesome powers for creating annoyance, depression, and low self-esteem. She was like a walking women's magazine. Nikki knew she should immediately get up and do the important things she'd told Holly she was going to do, but she felt drained of energy and coherent thought. Instead she went into the bathroom and washed her face. She thought about simply going back to bed. She had been ordered off the case, after all. Who was going to care if she took the day off to wallow in misery?

Kit's face sprang unbidden to her mind, and with a sigh Nikki began to reapply her makeup. For all his foibles, Kit was trying very hard to put his life together. A life that was at risk from Antonio Mergado Cano. She couldn't abandon him—no matter what Camille and her letter from the director of the Paris branch told her to do.

She dialed Astriz's number and got voice mail.

"Astriz, it's Nikki. Camille got the Paris branch to order me off the case. I'm appealing it, but it'll take a little time. You may need to lay low for a bit. Call me when you've got Jane."

She tossed the phone down on the bed next to her jacket and pulled on a new shirt from her luggage. She couldn't wallow. She had things to do. She had to . . . Nikki paused, trying to formulate her checklist. She had called Astriz—check. She had to read the airbrush manual—those devil girls weren't going to paint themselves. And she had to call Z'ev. Nikki winced in a physical reaction to her own thoughts.

She'd been trying to avoid thinking about Z'ev for almost a week now, but it hadn't made things any better. She was going to have to call him and say something. He deserved better than an angry hang-up. Besides, she wasn't really sure she wanted to break up with him anyway. But what did she want?

"I want a vacation," she grumbled out loud to herself, picking up the airbrush manual. She flipped through the pages. The concept seemed simple enough, but she suspected the actual practice would be a different matter. Holly had also brought up Trista's notebooks. As befitted a Carrie Mae lady, Trista's notes were obsessively detailed when it came to color mixing and sequence. Sketches, fabric swatches, and neatly smeared samples filled a notebook. She had half-expected personal notes to be scattered among the information, but the notes were strictly business. Trista had apparently lived for the job and Nikki grimaced in fear.

"I don't want a vacation," muttered Nikki, "I want a life."

Maybe that was what she needed to tell Z'ev. Living in separate cities, spending vacations and weekends together, wasn't working. They needed to have an actual life together if they wanted to succeed as a couple. That's if they wanted to succeed. Her phone wasn't exactly ringing off the hook with messages from Z'ev.

Thinking of her phone, she stood up and went to the bed. She spotted it, half-hidden in the folds of her jacket, and yanked the jacket off the bed. As it lifted, an envelope fluttered onto the floor.

Nikki sighed and picked up the Paris director's mysterious envelope, belatedly remembering Svenka's message about having a productive conversation with Camille. Whatever that meant; Nikki snorted in irritation. She ripped open the sealed envelope and pulled out several sheets of paper.

> Do you want to explain to Mrs. Merrivel how your boyfriend knew about Nina Alvarez? Or do you want me to? Leave Paris.
>
> Madame Feron.

Nikki frowned—there was no way Madame Feron could have known about Jane's gaffe. There was no proof. Camille might have told her some suspicions, but they had to be bluffing, and Nikki wasn't about to fold over a bad bluff. Setting aside the note, she turned to the next sheet of paper.

It was a printed e-mail, addressed to Camille from Rosalia, Camille's second-in-command at the Colombian branch. Nikki frowned and checked the heading again. It was a routine update report, nothing unusual there. She skimmed through the parts she already knew.

Nina Alvarez, the wife of an international drug dealer and victim of spousal abuse, had desperately begged for their help. Her parents had been afraid to even call her, and with no access to any money of her own, Nina Alvarez had effectively become a prisoner in her own home. The only person she had regular outside contact with was her Carrie Mae lady. Fortunately for Nina, knowing a Carrie Mae lady was more useful than knowing the Marines. Carrie Mae had sent in the troops, only Nina hadn't been there. With frustration Nikki remembered how their month of planning had gone down the drain at the exact same moment as Nikki's relationship.

She went back to the report. Nina had returned to her husband's house. The Carrie Mae assault had been blamed on rival drug dealers, which had touched off a minor drug war, and Nina had been moved to the Alvarez beach property, where she had been seen canoodling with a young man. Nikki laughed at the use of "canoodling." The word was probably entirely accurate, but it smacked of either translation or the fact that English was Rosalia's second language. Nikki flipped the page to see a photo of the young man in question.

The photo filled the entire page. But even in black and white laser print, Nina looked like Jennifer Lopez in her brief period of Latina glamour between P. Diddy and Bennifer. Nina had lustrous copper skin and waves of obsidian black hair; she was all curves and sex appeal. She might as well have had "Most Wanted" tattooed on her ass. But next to Nina was number one on Nikki's top ten list: Z'ev Coralles. And worse than simply being next to her, which was enough to make Nikki hyperventilate, his lips were actively involved with Nina's. Z'ev Coralles, her boyfriend, was kissing Nina Alvarez.

PARIS V

The El Nina Effect

Nikki jumped to her feet, scattering papers everywhere. Scrambling to shove the e-mails back into the envelope, she found herself sobbing in dry, gasping coughs. The waterworks came a moment later in big, fat blobby tears that ran down her nose, messing up her foundation. Nikki shoved the envelope into her luggage and locked it, only then noticing that the picture of Z'ev and Nina had slipped elusively under the bed.

Nikki ignored it, reaching for her boots, yanking them on with fingers made clumsy by the jumble of emotions twisting in her gut. She had to get out of this room. She had to get away. She stood with her hand on the doorknob for a long moment, then, hanging her head, she ran back and scooped up the picture, shoving it into her pocket.

Nikki walked angrily throught the front doors of the Hilton, brushing tears off her face. How could he? Nina's image floated across her mind and she wondered how she could think he wouldn't. Nina was perfect, and with her sad eyes and sob story any man would be aching to rescue her. And Z'ev was good at rescuing. Nikki sniffed fiercely and blinked back fresh tears.

What had she been thinking? How could she have thought that she could possibly hold on to a guy like Z'ev? Who did she think she was?

Someone bumped into her with a muttered "Excuse me." It was the voice that caught her ear. It was over-the-top, imperfect American—a foreigner's idea of what an American should sound like. Acting on instinct Nikki reached out and caught the man's arm. Her pull swung him around, and Nikki found herself looking into Kit's blue eyes. He had a knit cap pulled down low over his forehead, and he was bundled into a scarf and windbreaker over a sweater.

"What do you think you're doing?" Nikki asked.

"Going out," he said haughtily.

"Where's Duncan?"

He hunched one shoulder and looked away. "I don't need Duncan."

"Yes, you do," said Nikki.

"Look, I've got to get out of there. The press guys Brandt set me up with . . ." He shook his head in frustration. "They're driving me starkers. I just want to get out and breathe a little."

"I don't know what 'starkers' is, so I'll assume it means crazy," said Nikki. "And I get that, but take Duncan with you."

"I don't need a babysitter."

"Not a babysitter, backup. In case something goes wrong."

"OK, I'll go with you. You were going out, right? You can be my backup." There was a devilish light in his eyes Nikki didn't trust.

"You can't go with me," said Nikki firmly. "Go back and get Duncan."

"Why not?"

"Because I'm going to a bar," answered Nikki, starting to walk away. He followed her, almost skipping.

"So?"

"So, you're a recovering alcoholic; you aren't supposed to go to places like that." Nikki realized she was sounding like Duncan but didn't really care. Maybe Duncan was right. Maybe Camille was right. Maybe everyone was right. Everyone but Nikki. Nikki picked up her pace; she didn't care. She just had to get away. "And I'm going to get really drunk."

"I'm not supposed to drink. I can still go out. That's what we talked about at my meeting last night." He stopped, tugging on her arm until she stopped also. He checked his watch, fumbling to get his mittened hands under the layers of windbreaker and sweater. "But really, it's not even noon, and I think that's Paris time."

"So? It's got to be getting-drunk time somewhere." Nikki brushed angrily past him.

"Using alcohol to cope with emotional issues is one of the signs of addiction."

"I'm having a bad day, OK? I don't think I'd be any fun. You want someone who would be fun."

Kit leaned closer, scrutinizing her face. "Have you been crying?" he demanded.

"No!" exclaimed Nikki, blushing and wiping at her cheeks.

"Yes, you have. What happened?"

"Nothing," answered Nikki, avoiding eye contact.

"Was someone being mean to you? It was Brandt or one of his bastards, wasn't it?" He waved a hand back toward the hotel. "'Cause I'll fire them like that." And he tried to snap in his mittens, but it didn't work. Nikki laughed a little.

"No, it wasn't them. It was my boyfriend. My ex-boyfriend." His head tilted to the side inquisitively, and Nikki gave in. She had to tell someone.

"We were supposed to spend Christmas vacation together in Mexico, but he called at the last minute and canceled—again. And I got mad and I kind of broke up with him and he didn't call back and so I came here, but now, one of my . . . coworkers gave me this . . ." Nikki pulled out the picture of Z'ev and Nina.

"She's hot," he said.

"She's not me," said Nikki, glaring at him.

"But that's him?" he asked. Nikki nodded and wiped at her face again. "I guess now we know why he canceled."

Nikki opened her mouth to excuse Z'ev, to explain that he was working, but stopped. What was she going to say? Z'ev had betrayed her secret and canceled their vacation to go make out, and probably more than that, with Nina Alvarez.

"So you were serious about the getting-really-drunk thing?" he asked. She nodded. "You don't want to do that," he said.

"Yes, I do," said Nikki with a sniff.

"No, you want to do that later. Right now, you want to see the sights of Paris with me."

"I won't be any fun," said Nikki halfheartedly.

"No, it'll be good," he said, squinting into the distance and nodding as if he could see the future. Nikki shook her head, but she could feel herself giving in.

"Come on," he said with his impish grin. "You said I needed backup; sounds like you could use some too. We'll back each other up."

"Yeah?" she asked. "Like partners?"

"Good cop, bad cop," he answered.

"OK," said Nikki, and they started to walk away from the hotel.

"I get to be the bad cop," they said at the same time, and laughed.

"We're going to have an absolutely brilliant time," he said, tucking his arm through hers and then back into his pocket. "I can tell."

They strolled arm in arm down the Champs-Elysées, past the Louis Vuitton store, past the Virgin Megastore, past the movie theater, and toward the enormous circle of the Ferris wheel that marked the entrance of the Tuileries, the gardens outside the Louvre. Around them tourists of all kinds marched with wondering eyes or irritation according to their disposition. Kit kept his hat down and his collar up, pulling it down only to point out a particularly remarkable specimen of tourist.

"I think this is where they light off fireworks at New Year's," said Kit, gazing up at the Ferris wheel.

"Really? I would have thought that they would do it from the Eiffel Tower."

"I think that's for Bastille Day. This is what they'd show on the TV when I was a kid. The Ferris wheel and the Arc in the background." He turned around, walking backward and holding up his hands to make a square screen. "Yeah, this is it. This is where the party is. Too bad we won't be here."

"I guess so," answered Nikki, realizing that another holiday was creeping up on her. She felt a moment of panic. It couldn't be New Year's yet. She wasn't ready! She hadn't even had Christmas!

"You know where I want to go?" asked Kit as they entered the gardens, dodging past the Africans wanting donations and a signature for one cause or another—usually the cause was their pocket.

"I'm not sure we should be going anywhere really," said Nikki, having doubts about her impulsive escape from the hotel.

Kit's face immediately formed a pout. "I've been to Paris four times and I never get to do anything."

Nikki looked at him and reconsidered her position. If the bad guys didn't know where they were going, then no one else would either. It was safety, of a sort.

"Well, what's on your list?" she asked cautiously.

"I want to ride on the bat-boats."

"The what?"

"The bato-thingies?"

"The Batobus?"

"The boats with the clear roofs, right?"

"Yeah."

"Yeah, I want to ride on one of those. They're in all the movies. And then I want to see the Eiffel Tower and the Arc de Triomphe."

"I think those will probably have really long lines."

"Oh." Kit's face fell.

"But we can get off at the Eiffel Tower on the Batobus and see it from the ground."

"That'll have to do!" said Kit, bounding back. "Are you hungry? I'm hungry."

"Let's get hot dogs then," said Nikki, pointing to an octagonal hut tucked among the expanse of paths.

"Where are we?" asked Kit, looking around.

"The Tuileries," said Nikki, leading the way toward the hot dog stand. "That's the Louvre over there."

"I suppose the lines will be long for the Louvre too."

"Definitely. No *Mona Lisa* for you today."

They threw themselves in line for hot dogs, and twenty minutes later they were carrying their meal toward the river.

"This is not a hot dog," said Kit as they walked across the bridge and down to the quay for the Batobus.

"No, it's better," said Nikki, biting into the cheese-covered

French bread that contained two hot dogs. The cheese had melted across the top to form a light brown crust.

The Batobus pulled to a smooth stop, and they bought a half-circuit pass, taking them down to the Eiffel Tower. The other passengers looked up in mild curiosity as they entered and Kit nervously pulled his cap lower on his face and turned up the collar on his windbreaker. But no one commented or noticed that a pop superstar was among them.

They rode in silence for a while, admiring the towering skyline and the bridges that crossed the Seine.

"I ought to remember more," she said, thinking out loud.

"Hmm?" answered Kit.

"I was here in high school. I ought to remember more about Paris, but all I get is a vague feeling of familiarity."

Kit gave a short laugh. "I feel that way about almost every city I've ever toured in."

They fell back into silence, each contemplating their own miseries. Nikki's thoughts inevitably turned to Z'ev. She'd known, hadn't she? That it would all end in disaster. That he hadn't really wanted to be with someone like her in the first place.

"You ever go to a house party and go looking for a friend, but every time you go into a room everyone says, 'Oh, you just missed him,' and you're stuck wandering around all night looking for him like an idiot?" asked Kit suddenly.

"That sounds like every house party I ever went to," said Nikki. "I would have thought you would have had more luck than I did."

"No, I'd usually go get high in the bathroom and save myself the embarrassment," said Kit. "You weren't the popular girl?"

"Bottom tier of popular," said Nikki. "On the cheerleading squad, but not the captain. Frankly, I always felt like a fraud." Kit laughed. "But at the same time, I always felt like one of the problems with Z'ev and me was that I was too much of a popular girl, you know?"

"Well," said Kit, "he's an idiot. Anyway, his loss is my gain. But my point was . . . I had a point." He paused, brow furrowing.

"Losing people in a house party," said Nikki.

"Right!" he exclaimed. "That's how I feel about Christmas this year. I keep wandering in and people are all, 'Oh yeah, it was great, should have been here.'"

"I know what you mean. I was on a plane for Christmas, and now I feel like everywhere I go, I've just missed it, and if I could just get to the next place fast enough I could catch up," said Nikki, eyeing a sparkling red JOYEUX NOËL banner hanging from a building.

"Only it's worse than that!" he exclaimed. "It's like walking into a room and everyone not only says that you just missed him, they all have great pics of the fun they had without you."

"Yeah! That's it. I never thought I was that into Christmas, but I really am missing it this year. Even though I was going to miss it anyway," she said sadly. "I was going to be in Mexico with Z'ev."

"It's one thing to miss things because you planned on it, but another thing altogether to have things taken from you."

"I suppose. But you know, even if I was home I think I'd still be missing something. Is it possible to miss something you've never had?"

"Definitely," said Kit, nodding. "I miss my brain constantly. No, seriously"—he continued around Nikki's laugh—"I miss having parents. I mean, my mom loves me and all, but she isn't exactly June Cleaver and mostly I grew up with Nan anyway. I remember once I went over to a friend's house when I was about eleven, and his mom was running around getting dinner ready, his sister was making a mess, the dog was barking, and I actually got light-headed I was so jealous. It was nothing but everyday life and I wanted it so bad. I appreciate my family and everything, but it's not the same."

"My parents split up when I was pretty young. I used to wear these really short skirts over to my friend Tanya's house because her dad would always yell at me to go put some clothes on. He wouldn't let us out of the house until I borrowed a pair of Tanya's pants."

"How insane is it that we would want to be yelled at?"

"If they're yelling at least you know they care."

"Does that mean you care about me?"

"Oh, come on," said Nikki, feeling suddenly embarrassed by her outburst on the bus.

"No, I'm serious. I can't always tell how people feel about me."

"What are you talking about? You've got girls screaming your name. You know everyone loves you."

"Mmm, no. They love Kit Masters, the product. And a product is something you can leave on the shelf. I can count the number of people who care about Christopher Masters on one hand."

"All right, do it," said Nikki, challenging him.

"Nan, Mom, Trista, and Brandt."

"What about Duncan?"

Kit cocked his head thoughtfully. "Yes, you're right. Duncan has done a few things that went beyond a paycheck."

"Beyond a paycheck? That man loves you."

"Duncan?" Kit blushed. "Nah, he's a real tough guy. It's his job to look after me and he takes his job seriously. That's all."

Nikki laughed. "You have been out in the spotlight too long."

The Eiffel Tower loomed into view, like the corpse of a giant iron praying mantis. Its four latticework legs clamped into the cement, and the body was swarmed by hungry worshipful ants. They walked off the bus and tilted their heads back and then farther back as they tried to take in the entire structure. Climbing the stairs, they crossed the street and looked at the line snaking in S-curves across the expanse of cement beneath the tower.

"Kit Masters could get to the front of that line," he said thoughtfully.

"If he wasn't trampled to death by hundreds of screaming teenagers first."

"Mmm," said Kit. "Besides, Kit Masters is too cool to come to a place like this. He's probably holed up in some posh hotel snorting coke off a high-priced hooker's midriff."

"I think that was more information than I wanted to know," said Nikki as they ventured into the throng. There was an uncomfortable silence between them.

"I've never been with a hooker!" burst out Kit, drawing a strange look from a passerby. "No, really." He reaffirmed it in answer to Nikki's raised eyebrow. "I mean yeah, I've done the thing with the coke, but I never had to pay a woman to sleep with me."

"I believe you," said Nikki, and he blew out a gusty sigh of relief.

"I forget not everyone knows when I'm joking."

"Well, when you're not joking about the coke, how am I supposed to know you're joking about the hookers?"

"I . . . I don't know. I guess I just didn't think you'd think I was the kind of person to use a hooker."

"You're a rock star!" said Nikki.

"No, I'm me. We've been talking about this in my meetings. We all get caught up in what we are. Our label. Sometimes it's our job or what are friends tell us we are, sometimes it's our addiction. I guess I'm probably more susceptible to it than most people since I get to see everyone else's opinion of me printed in a newspaper, but mostly we do it to ourselves. We put ourselves in this little box. At first the box is comfortable, but after a while . . ."

"After a while you feel stuck."

"Right! And it starts to crush you."

"How do you get out of the box?" asked Nikki quietly.

"One inch at a time, I think," he answered. "I tried other substances, but apparently they don't work." He winked and Nikki smiled. "It's funny, though, the more you try to get out, the more you realize you're out already. We never fit entirely into one thing."

"We just get used to thinking of ourselves that way," murmured Nikki.

"Yeah," said Kit, and then stopped to look around. "Wow!" he said, turning back to look at the Eiffel Tower. It spiraled up toward the winter sky above the crisp carpet of bright green grass. He took a slim digital camera out of his pocket and snapped a photo. "Here, let's take one of you!"

Nikki posed and then returned the favor, then made him squat a little and put up his hands so it looked like he was wearing the Eiffel Tower as a hat for the next picture.

"Oi! Excuse us!" said Kit, interrupting a pair of middle-aged German tourists, plump around the middle and friendly in the face. "Can you take our picture?" He was practicing his American accent, but after starting with "oi" Nikki couldn't believe anyone would buy it.

"Do you know, you look very much like the English pop star Kit Masters?" asked the German man as he handed back the camera. Kit and Nikki exchanged glances.

"Y'all keep sayin' that," responded Nikki. "We've never heard of this Masters fella."

"He is a singer here," said the woman cheerfully. "Very famous! All the girls love him!"

"Well, I guess I'll have ta make sure no one tries ta steal my guy," answered Nikki, taking a possessive hold of Kit's hand.

"Thanks for the photo," said Kit.

"*Ja,*" said the woman, and waved cheerfully as they walked off.

"I can't believe they bought that," said Nikki, pulling Kit toward Les Invalides and Napoleon's Tomb. The museums were at the end of a long expanse of grass down from the Eiffel Tower and worth a look, if Nikki remembered correctly.

"You know, I know the clouds have kind of come up, but I keep thinking the sun's shining over there." He pointed to the golden dome atop Les Invalides. It radiated the kind of glow usually reserved for movie special effects.

"Sometimes it just seems like a sunny day," said Nikki. "Even when it's not."

PARIS VI

Le Gator

"No, wait, wait. You girls stay up here," Kit commanded the three giggling teenagers. Nikki couldn't imagine why; they had just butchered "Brand New Key." Their Tears for Fears had been OK, but Nikki decided that the French should not be allowed to sing American seventies kitsch.

"I'm going to need some backup singers," Kit explained, rushing around the stage to set up an extra mic for the girls. "All right," he said, standing in front of his own mic. He hitched up his jeans in an embarrassed gesture that still managed to look sexy. "This next song"—he was still pushing the American accent—"is for my friend Nikki. The very drunk redhead out there."

"Whoo-hoo!" yelled Nikki, throwing her hands up. The crowd of bar patrons cheered too, but whether it was for her or for Kit or for drunk redheads in general, Nikki couldn't tell.

"Nikki recently caught her boyfriend having a public snog"—the accent was slipping—"with a South American heiress."

The crowd booed, and Nikki joined in wholeheartedly.

"No, actually," said Kit with a serious expression, "it works out well for me 'cause I want into her pants and the only way I stand a chance is if she's drunk." The crowd laughed, and Kit laughed back.

"But seriously," said Kit, the Sinatra accent back in full force as he grabbed the mic stand and leaned it way down like one of the old-time crooners, "Nikki, this song's for you." He snapped his fingers at the DJ, who launched the music for Aretha's "Respect." The bar roared its approval; Kit had them eating out of his hand. Awed, Nikki realized that being a rock star wasn't about getting paid to sing before thousands. It was this, the ability to take a room full of people and make them into an audience—into one single voice, a single mind. She felt that she should have known this, but like everything else they had done that day, it was surprising.

They had skipped Napoleon's Tomb, with the myriad families and children that were too close to Kit's demographic, and found the Rodin Museum. The quiet museum house and gardens had proved the perfect distraction and Kit had spent an entirely blissful few hours contorting himself to match the poses of the statuary. Nikki snapped pictures and laughed till her sides hurt. Kit had demanded Notre Dame next, fans be hanged.

Notre Dame was Notre Dame; impressive and Catholic and filled with the incessant murmur of a few hundred tourists pretending to be quiet.

"I thought it would be more sacred," said Kit, looking around at the massive columns and the overhanging rose window. But as they stopped in front of a quiet alcove chapel, Notre Dame sneeked up on them, and they felt it anyway—the tug of a million prayers layering over each other thicker than leaves in fall. Kit dropped a Euro into the offering box and lit a candle.

"For my dad," he said, crossing himself, and then looked at Nikki with a half-embarrassed smile. "I suppose you think it's silly?"

Nikki shook her head and lit a candle of her own. "For my father, wherever he is," she murmured, and crossed herself as well.

It seemed a thousand years since she'd watched the Catholic mass with her father's mother or felt the old woman's gnarled hand as they walked toward the white-robed priest waiting with the blood of Christ. Nell had never liked the church; she said it was a guilt trip designed to keep women under the domination of men. But looking up at the vaulted ceiling and light gray stone turned dark by eight hundred years of smoke and the touch of human hands, Nikki felt a new appreciation for the church. Notre Dame was a home for any Catholic who walked in the door; Nikki felt a swell of envy for everyone who knew they belonged somewhere. Kit took her hand as they walked back toward the doors, and it felt comforting.

Their solemn mood lasted only as long as it took them to cross the water into the Latin Quarter. A bustling hive of commerce and the historic site of the camps of France's Roman conquerors, the Latin Quarter had long been the seething home of students, revolutionaries, tourists, and all things ineffably Paris. Barkers stood at the doors of the restaurants and called people in like carnies at a sideshow. Everyone was selling something, and just about everyone was buying. The air was briskly cold, and their breath came out in white puffs, but in among the crowded, narrow streets it didn't seem so cold.

By seven o'clock darkness was falling and the cafés were filling up. Nikki and Kit followed the crowds winding toward the restaurants. Soon they had settled into the corner table of a steamy café and were sharing a traditional bowl of onion soup.

"I feel a bit silly," he'd said, poking a hole in the crispy golden crust of Swiss cheese and dipping a slice of bread into the soup, "but French onion soup is what you're supposed to eat."

"We're being tourists today, so we have to. I think it's a law."

"Right!"

After dinner they began to chat with the twentysomething French couple at the next table. It took only a few moments of Kit flashing his smile around before the couple swooned and invited them to Le Gator.

"All right, so the plan is I order water and I stick with it," Kit muttered into her ear as they approached the bar. "If you see me with anything else, you grab me and get me the hell out of there, OK?" He looked at her with worried eyes and Nikki felt his hand tense inside his mitten.

"OK," she said, and smiled encouragingly.

Le Gator was a karaoke bar swarming with singles and people who weren't single but sure acted like it. Then came the drinks. Marci and Jean were the soul of hospitality and their friends were friendly, or at least smelled fresh blood. The drink offers began to stack up.

"*Non, merci,*" answered Kit for the fifth time, and then Nikki caught the sparkle of wickedness in his eye. "But my friend, she would love one."

After that the drinks came straight to her, which, on reflection, was how Nikki came to be dancing to Kit's version of "Respect" with a burly Frenchman. After that the night was a blur; eventually the tired DJ was asking for the last song requests of the night. Nikki had flipped through the book but hadn't turned in any of her slips. She loved singing in her car, but the idea of singing in front of people terrified her.

She felt her phone ring in her pants pocket, and she dodged

out of the crowd to answer it, feeling a sudden quickening of her pulse and the slight tang of guilt as she recognized Jane's number.

"Jane!" exclaimed Nikki eagerly.

"Nikki!" answered Jane. "I'm with Astriz."

"You're OK then?"

"Er, yeah . . ." There was a popping sound in the background, and Nikki could hear the squeal of tires. "More or less," said Jane, sounding breathless. There was another sequence of sounds—beeps and clicks—and Jane swore under her breath. "We've got a piggyback. Nikki, I'll be at your location tomorrow. Contact you then."

The phone went dead, and Nikki felt the blush of fear. She looked around for Kit, fighting the feeling of alcohol. They needed to leave. They shouldn't have been here in the first place. She dove back into the club, swimming against the crowd.

"Nicole, Nicole Lanier," announced the DJ over the loudspeaker, and Nikki's head snapped around.

"Your turn!" yelled Kit, pushing her onto the stage.

"I didn't turn anything in!" yelled Nikki over the commotion of the bar.

"Did it for you!" he yelled back.

Nikki stared into the spotlights in a blind panic. She looked back at Kit and shook her head; he nodded and grinned.

The music started with a twangy guitar and almost country sound. Nikki knew the music and licked her lips nervously as the words began to scroll across the TV in front of her. It was a song about Mexico and letting go. It wasn't a common song; Kit had obviously picked it out just for her. She didn't know whether to be mad or grateful. She resisted thinking about it, closed her eyes, and sang.

Mere minutes later, they were exiting the club with a wave of other club-goers. Nikki felt high from singing in public; she wondered if this was how Kit felt all the time.

"Hey, mister, got a light?"

Kit paused, and Nikki, who had her arm through his, swung to a red-rover stop, still humming her song. Her panic over Jane had subsided. After all, Astriz was with her. What could go wrong?

"Sure," answered Kit, fumbling in his pockets for his lighter and pulling out his American accent to match the stranger's.

Even in her inebriated state Nikki felt a flare of worry. No one would see through a fake American accent faster than a real American. She tugged at Kit's arm, wanting to leave. Kit waggled his eyebrows at her, ignoring the warning tugs, and lit the stranger's cigarette.

"Thanks," said the man as Kit lit his own cigarette.

"No problem," answered Kit, allowing Nikki to pull him away.

He jogged a few steps to catch up to Nikki's pace, and he put his arm around her shoulders, slowing her down. They staggered for a moment on the uneven flagstones until their strides synchronized. Nikki giggled at their ineptitude. The tall stone buildings were jammed together around them and seemed to lean into the yellow pools created by the streetlights, absorbing the sound of Nikki's laughter and sending back the smallest trill of an echo. Behind them most of the other karaoke singers were heading the other way. In front of them Nikki could dimly see a few figures in the mist walking toward the Metro station.

"You say you're going to leave," Kit sang into her ear, quoting his own song "Devil May Care"; it was practically the only song that hadn't been sung that night. Nikki laughed again, louder this time.

"You say you're going to leave, but I know you won't. He promises forever, but I don't. Sweet sin, slipping in. The devil may care," they sang together. Kit paused, spreading out his arms to belt out the last line to the overhanging streetlight. His voice reverberated off the stone around him, and Nikki shushed him, covering her mouth to stifle her own giggles.

"But I don't," sang Kit, finishing the line, but quieter this time and looking at her.

Nikki stared at him. Z'ev hadn't ever promised forever. There had never been any guarantees. Maybe this was just the way things were supposed to be: she and Kit on a cold Paris night under the soft glow of a streetlamp. Nikki found she was holding her breath. What if he tried to kiss her? He took a step closer. What if he didn't?

Out of the corner of her eye, Nikki caught a swift movement in the shadows. One of the other bar patrons? Nikki couldn't be sure, and suddenly she realized that they were standing in the middle of the street in a huge pool of light, twelve feet from any decent cover. Nikki felt a chill stab of fear and an inrush of cool adrenaline blowing away her drunken fog.

"The Metro closes at twelve-thirty," said Nikki, reaching out a hand.

"Who cares?" he asked, blowing out smoke and flicking ash off his cigarette, changing his mood as swiftly as she had. Nikki smiled. He reminded her of Val when he smoked. They had the same way of using their cigarettes as visual punctuation.

"Duncan will," said Nikki, still holding out her hand. He shifted his cigarette into his left hand and reached for hers with his right.

"And we wouldn't want Papa to worry, now, would we?" he asked, pulling her close to him. Hand in hand, they walked toward the Metro station. In the shadows, Nikki thought she heard the scuttle of movement.

They reached the blocky square structure that marked the

entrance to the Châtelet Metro stop. Its cavernous maw sucked them in, whisking them along in a wind created by the tunnel that stretched for what seemed the entire length of Paris. They hurried down a ramp, anxious to get away from the biting wind that shook their hair and tried to sneak inside their jackets. Huddling together, possibly for the warmth, Nikki watched their breath come out in white puffs that hung in the air before dissipating. The lower they went the less white there was. By the time they reached the turnstile, their gloved fingers fumbling to feed the tickets into mechanical slots, the puffs had disappeared altogether. A few more feet and she felt as if they were in a sauna compared to the outside.

Nikki and Kit wound their way farther into the warren of the underground, pausing at a map to find the platform they needed.

"We want the one going toward La Defense," said Nikki, fingering the map. Kit nodded and oriented himself to the multicolor signs pointing in various directions.

The square, cream-colored tiles that lined the hall reflected sound oddly. From somewhere deeper in the Metro wound the sound of an accordion and violin playing a sad song, but whether the music was originating from ahead or behind them Nikki couldn't say for certain. Occasionally, they passed another late-night traveler, but they all avoided eye contact, hurrying in their own homeward directions.

"A bit more of this and I'll be taking off my jumper," muttered Kit, stripping off his windbreaker as they reached their platform. Nikki scanned the empty expanse and wished the train would hurry.

"Your what?" asked Nikki, distracted from her surveillance.

"My jumper," he repeated, flapping his oatmeal-colored sweater to create a breeze while Nikki continued to stare blankly.

"Why, what do you call it?" he asked, still flapping the sweater—it was of the heavy, woolen variety and looked handmade.

"A sweater," she replied. There was something familiar about the sweater, but she couldn't quite put her finger on it.

"Well, yeah, it's that too. It's not that funny," he said when Nikki laughed.

"A jumper is like a pinafore," said Nikki. "Something school-girls wear."

"Hmm," Kit said, looking down, as if trying to picture himself in a pinafore. "Kinky, but I think I could pull it off." And he posed, strutting in his imaginary pinafore. Nikki laughed.

"I like making you laugh," he said, dropping the pose.

"You don't have to, though. You know that, right?" she asked, frowning. "You don't have to entertain me."

"You have a good laugh. I like to hear it."

"But you don't have to. I mean I laugh because you're funny, not because . . ."

"Not because I'm paying you?" he said shrewdly.

"Well, you're not actually paying me for anything."

"Well, I bloody well should be. Nobody does makeup for the entire band for free. If you're not getting paid, you should really have a talk with Brandt."

"No. Well, yeah, I am, but I mean it's not my normal job; I work for Carrie Mae. So I'm here because I want to be, is all I'm trying to say." Liquor was making Nikki's tongue stumble over itself.

"That's funny, I thought I had to talk you into letting me tag along."

"I think I may have been slightly mistaken about not letting you come along today. I had a good time."

"So that would make me, what? Right? Oh, yes, I think so." He threw his hands up in a rugby referee's signal for a goal.

"A girl can make mistakes," said Nikki, laughing.

"Can I be one?"

"You wouldn't be my worst one ever," she answered truthfully.

"Hell, I could be your best mistake ever," he said, and leaned in to kiss her. Their lips brushed, a kiss that was soft and firm at the same time and might have gone farther if it hadn't been for the bullets flying past them.

PARIS VII

Subway

Nikki tackled Kit into the subway well. Above them on the platform, two ski-mask-wearing men ran toward them, firing pistols. Huddled under the meager shelter provided by the lip of the platform, Nikki tried to force her brain into a plan.

One of the men jumped down, nearly on top of them, and Nikki went from planning to reacting. She threw Kit's windbreaker in the man's face, shoved Kit to the left, and dove right as the man fired through the fabric. Popping upright, she unbuckled her Carrie Mae belt and yanked it through the belt loops. The coiled steel slid through the loops with ease and straightened with a snap on the gunman's arm as he turned to aim at Kit. Whipping it around, she snared the foot of the second gunman, who was still above them on the platform. The end of the belt pulled him off his feet. Bullets sprayed in an arc at the ceiling as he went down. Swinging the belt overhead, she brought it slapping down on his wrist, sending the gun skittering away from both of them. The first man came back at her, but Kit surprised him with a diving tackle.

"Kit!" she yelled, grabbing him under the armpit and pushing him toward the other side of the platform. Kit took a final stomp at the man's groin before allowing himself to be dragged away.

Vaulting onto the opposite platform, they sprinted down the hall, heedless of the direction.

"Kit," gasped Nikki, hearing the sound of a train arriving.

"Which way?" he demanded.

"This way, I think," she said, and ran down the tube in time to see a train pull up on their side of the platform. They dashed down the ramp and hurtled into the train car. Throwing Kit down into a seat compartment, she followed suit.

Then the train didn't move. And didn't move. Nikki wrapped her belt around one fist and concentrated on willing the train to move. The door slid shut with agonizing slowness, and Nikki breathed a sigh of relief as the train pulled away from the platform.

"Did we lose them?" asked Kit, gophering up to look around.

"Wait till we clear the station," she growled, yanking him back down.

The train chugged into the tunnel, the compartment lights flickering a little as the train picked up speed.

"Who were those guys?" asked Kit, sitting up in the seat.

"I don't know," said Nikki, sitting opposite him.

The train swayed back and forth. Nikki could see through the glass of the connecting door into the next compartment and, when the cars were aligned, into the one beyond that.

"I . . . wow." He ran a hand up into his hair. Then he shook himself all over like a dog getting out of a bath. "I can't believe they actually shot at us."

"Yeah," said Nikki, thinking that there hadn't been much *us*. Mostly they'd been aiming at Kit.

"I . . . wow," he repeated. His fingers were drumming rapidly on his knees.

They rode in silence. The train slid into a stop and Nikki considered getting off, but a glance out the window at the treacherously empty platform changed her mind. She decided to wait a few stops, checking the names against her mental map of Paris—they were heading north. Whoever was after them would have to guess which stop they would get off at, and she wanted as much distance from their pursuers as possible.

"Look, Kit," said Nikki, determined to set a few ground rules, "next time something like this happens, just run, OK?"

"What do you mean, run? And what do you mean next time?"

"If you get a chance, run. Don't come back and try to help. I mean, I appreciate it, but don't worry about me, just get out. Do you understand?"

"No, I don't. Those guys had guns. Am I just supposed to leave you there? No way. Besides, we agreed we were partners. Can't leave my partner behind."

"I like partners, but honestly, Kit, just let me worry about my own skin, OK?"

"No," he said, smiling cheerfully around his stubbornness. "But don't let's argue. With any luck, it's not an issue that will come up again."

"You're going to give me a heart attack," muttered Nikki. Hadn't Z'ev said those same words to her not so very long ago?

"Let me know when your left arm starts tingling," replied Kit unrepentantly.

"Mmm," murmured Nikki, avoiding further argument and trying not to think of a similar argument with Z'ev. That was totally different, right?

"Do we even know where we are?" Kit asked. He got up to

stare at the Metro map above the doors. "I think we're on the four," he said, swaying slightly with the train. "But I don't know which way we're going. I should have looked at the sign on the last stop. It's either toward Gare du Nord or Montparnasse."

Nikki winced over his pronunciation of Montparnasse; he put the "T" in. She looked up, meaning to correct him, and glanced out the back window as the train jogged the cars into an unprecedented straight line.

"Kit, get down!" she commanded.

"What?" he said, looking around but not moving.

"They're on the train," she hissed, hauling him down onto the floor.

"Where?" he asked, trying to stick his head up and look around.

"About four cars back," she said, maintaining a firm grip on his collar. "And heading our way."

"Did they see us?"

"Don't know," Nikki answered tersely. "We'll get off at the next stop."

"Do we know what the next stop is?"

"Gare du Nord," answered Nikki, shoving him to the front of the car.

The train slid into Gare du Nord, and even at this hour the international train station was liberally populated. Nikki held Kit tight, waiting to get off the train until it was almost chugging away from the platform. The two men entered their compartment, and Nikki and Kit dashed through the doors just as they slid closed.

"Up the escalator," Nikki yelled to Kit, who was leading. They ran up the moving stairs, jostling late-night travelers and arriving on the main level out of breath and disoriented.

"Did we leave them on the train?" he demanded, looking down the escalator.

"I doubt it," answered Nikki, leading them past the lines of trains. The cold night air circulated through the enormous vaulted space, hinting at snow. "All right, here's what we're going to do: we're going to find the nearest gendarme, tell them you're an international rock star and you need protection from some crazed psycho in the subway."

"Um . . . Can we not?"

"People are shooting at you, Kit."

"And I'd rather not have that on the front page of the *Star*."

"You'd rather have 'Kit Masters Dies in Mysterious Metro Shooting'?"

"Can't we just get a cab and go back to the hotel?"

Nikki looked to the exit and saw a black-clad man standing dead center, talking on a cell phone; his head swiveled back and forth as if searching for something.

"I don't think so," said Nikki, tugging Kit away.

"What'd these guys do?" whined Kit as they hid behind a reader board of train times. "Get a special at the all-black clothing store?"

A train arrived with a screeching of brakes and disgorged a flock of weary-looking passengers. Ducking behind a tall man with a red beard, Kit and Nikki walked toward the exit.

"I'm just a tourist, nothing special about me; I'm just walking here," muttered Kit as they walked, drawing strange looks from the train passengers.

The crowd passed through the entryway, past the man in black, and began to descend the shallow steps toward the street. They were nearly away when they heard a shout from behind them.

"Don't look back," commanded Nikki, "just keep walking." They picked up speed, trying for the title of Most Casual Hundred-Yard Dashers.

"Hey," called someone from behind them, and Nikki whirled around at the sound of running feet. A girl of about sixteen was running straight toward them, her friend trailing a bit behind.

"Hey, you're Kit Masters, aren't you? You are, aren't you? Oh my God! I can't believe it's Kit Masters!" She jumped up and down excitedly, clapping her hands. Behind her Nikki could see three men in black converging on them. Apparently, they hadn't left the two on the train after all.

"Yes, he is. Do you want his autograph?" Nikki asked. Kit's expression managed to be both disgusted and amazed at the same time.

"Oh my God! That would be brilliant! Oh wait! Wait. I have my camera." The girl searched frantically through her bag. "Liz," she said, turning to her friend who'd just arrived, toting a backpack and looking slightly out of breath. "Do you have my camera?" Liz was staring at Kit openmouthed. "Camera, Liz?" Liz closed her mouth and shook her head, then, jerking one arm out straight, she pointed toward the street. "My boyfriend has my camera. I mean, he's not really my boyfriend, we can see other people," said the girl fanatically.

The men in black were within twenty feet now, hanging back, waiting for the teenagers to leave; the two from the train had their ski masks rolled up on their heads.

"That's OK!" said Nikki genially. "We'll go over there." She could hear Kit's teeth grinding.

They all followed the friend's signpost finger toward where two motorcycles were parked curbside with two glowering young men.

"Brandon!" screeched the girl, running ahead, leaving them with the uncomfortably smiling Liz. "Brandon, get out my camera! It's Kit Masters."

Brandon's dour expression didn't change. But Liz's young man stepped forward eagerly.

"Kit Masters! Wow! I have all your albums. I even have the @last albums. I must have listened to 'Sub-Zero Fire' about fifty billion times. This is so brilliant!" The kid pumped Kit's hand up and down.

"Thanks," said Kit with an awkward smile.

"And your new album, *Devil's Kit*? Awesome!"

"That's Dean," said the first girl dismissively. "He's Liz's SO. I'm Sara and this is Brandon." Brandon gave a careless wave as if Kit was the last thing of importance. Brandon was clearly far too mature to be impressed by a mere rock star.

"Great," said Kit.

Nikki stole a quick glance behind them. The three men had fanned out, covering them from all angles.

"That's a nice bike," said Nikki, looking speculatively at Brandon's motorcycle. It was a small, smooth check mark of liquid orange over a V-twin engine. The passenger seat was an afterthought, the fairing nonexistent, and the windshield tiny.

"It's a Buell," said Brandon proudly, his face lighting up.

"Yeah, the Harley-Davidson sport bike, right?"

"Yeah!" said Brandon, falling in love.

"Vance and Hines after-market muffler. You wrapped the pipes."

"I think it looks cool." Then he said with more honesty, "Plus, I tipped it and scuffed the pipes." Nikki nodded. The wrapping gave the bike a slightly *Mad Max* effect; it wasn't a bad solution. But her attention was on the two men she could see in the bike's rearview mirrors. She flicked her glance upward and spotted the third and largest edging closer to their position.

"How's it run? I heard the Buells tend to be temperamental."

"No, it runs great. Totally keeps up with Dean-o's Triumph." Nikki sized up Dean-o's black Triumph SLR; it looked a little more passenger-friendly.

"It's a great bike, really runs good," said Brandon, putting the key in the ignition, preparing to prove his statement.

"Who cares about motorcycles?" interrupted Sara, pouting. "We've got a rock star here! I found my camera." She snapped a picture to prove it, and everyone blinked in the flash.

"Great," said Nikki. "What if we get a picture on the bike?"

"Yeah," said Brandon, perking up, "that would be cool!"

"You can sit on my bike, Kit!" said Dean, chiming in.

"Sure," said Kit, glancing at Nikki. She jerked her chin in a minute nod, just as the big man in black pushed through Liz and Sara, reaching for Kit. Nikki grabbed the man by his shoulders, yanking him back as he reached for Kit. The man leaned forward, trailing his arms, and dove out of Nikki's grasp, leaving her holding his coat. Liz and Sara screamed. Kit turned around and swung a punch into the man's gut; the big guy ate it like a hamburger and bounced it back like a burp. Kit recoiled, shaking his hand. From behind, Nikki tossed the coat over his head and hauled down. His hands scrabbled at his coat, trying to scrape it away from his face. Nikki pulled harder; he teetered for a moment, on the edge of falling backward, on the edge of recovery.

"Hi-yah!" yelled Liz, and kicked the man in the chest. He went down with a thump that shook the cobblestones.

"Hey!" yelled the second man, reaching into his jacket.

"Kit!" yelled Nikki, tossing the jacket aside and jumping on the Buell. Brandon hadn't lied. The orange bike started on the first try, sputtering to life with the familiar loud growl of a Harley-Davidson. Kit was barely on the back when Nikki twisted the throttle and roared into the night.

"They took Dean's bike!" Kit yelled into her ear, twisting around to look behind them. Nikki glanced in the mirrors and saw the bug-eyed dual headlights of the Triumph behind them and farther back Liz, Sara, Brandon, and Dean, standing in the street yelling.

Nikki took a quick right and then a left, cutting between the blocks, swooping around the errantly parked cars. The Triumph kept pace with them, dogging their every move, never more than a block or two behind.

They were heading steadily uphill, and, between the houses, the sacred heart of Paris was revealed at each break in the skyline. The Church of the Sacré-Coeur stood at the top of the hill overlooking the Pigalle district and the denizens of its porn shops, prostitutes, and nightclubs with the saddened dignity of an old man looking over a disappointing family. Nikki set her course by the white church, trying to lose the Triumph in the twisting back streets. The winding roads led her to the carousel that lived at the foot of the stairs leading up to Sacré-Coeur. The higher-pitched hum of the Triumph's motor echoed somewhere below them, cruising the small shops that had been shuttered for the night.

"Off," she told Kit.

"What are we doing?" asked Kit, getting off as commanded. "They're still down there!"

"I know," answered Nikki, gunning the engine. "I'll be right back."

She rode toward the sound of the Triumph, homing in on the sound. The Triumph returned the favor, working its way up toward her. When they were too close for comfort Nikki flipped a U-turn and rode back toward the carousel, pulling the black bike with her.

When the carousel and Kit appeared in her headlights, she slid the bike to a stop, wearing a few millimeters off the sole of her boot as she yanked the bike ninety degrees to point its nose down the hill. This had to be timed just right. Kit stepped forward to ask her something, but she pulled away and began her descent. She kept the brakes on, not allowing too much speed, but at the halfway point, she hit the brakes hard. This was going to hurt. She swung her leg over, riding standing up, one leg dangling, one on the foot peg. Then she stepped off the bike. Her feet were under her for a second, and then the speed caught up with her and she went down, tucking her chin as she rolled. She sat up just in time to see the orange Buell T-bone the black Triumph. A few seconds later, Kit came running down the hill.

"Nikki!" he yelled, scanning the wreckage.

"Over here," said Nikki, sitting up on her elbows.

"Jesus, Nikki. Are you insane?" Nikki tried to stand up as Kit reached out a helping hand. She thought about checking on the rider but changed her mind.

"Come on, let's get out of here," she said, limping a little as she led them southwest away from the wreck, aiming for a main street.

"You could have been killed!" he exclaimed after a few blocks, as if it had struck him afresh.

"Actually, I think I'm getting better."

"Better at what?" he asked with a disbelieving stare.

"Crashing, mostly." They approached an intersection, and she scanned the corners of the buildings, looking for street signs. "We need to find someplace to hole up for a few hours."

"I think I've been here before," said Kit, looking around. "There's a hotel here somewhere."

Nikki surveyed the surroundings. The Pigalle district, far from the fashionable tourist areas, sported a patina of grime and bitterness that would probably last longer than the winter. It didn't seem like the kind of area that would have a hotel where a rock star would stay.

"Yeah, it was on Rue des Abbesses. I remember thinking it was a good joke I was getting laid on a street named after nuns." Nikki raised an eyebrow, and Kit shrugged. "I was high at the time," he said. It was Nikki's turn to shrug. "It's just down here. I think." He frowned.

"Well, your guess sounds better than mine," said Nikki. "Lead the way."

It began to snow as they walked: huge fluffy flakes that melted at first but then accumulated on windowsills. Nikki brushed them from her hair, feeling the wet and cold start to seep in, knowing she'd be black and blue tomorrow.

"There it is!" exclaimed Kit. "I can't believe I actually found it."

The hotel was marked by a single, navy-blue, vertical banner that was lost between the neon-lit signs of two sex shops and a pharmacy.

Tromping into the lobby, Kit slammed his hand down on the bell, waking the desk clerk.

"*Bonsoir, monsieur,*" said Kit. "We would like a room."

PARIS VIII

I Need TV When I Got T. Rex

Nikki flipped the lock on the hotel room door and did a quick sweep of the room. Outside the window a neon green pharmacy cross dimly illuminated the flurries of snow.

"Why didn't we go back to our hotel?" asked Kit, dropping tiredly into one of the narrow armchairs near the window.

"They'll be watching the hotel," said Nikki, closing the drapes behind him before turning on a light.

"They were shooting at me," said Kit as if he'd only just now noticed.

"Yeah, I know."

"Why?"

"I don't know," she answered. "We'll call Duncan in the morning and go straight from here to the airport."

"No," he said firmly. "I've got a concert."

"Kit, someone's trying to kill you. Now is not the time to

worry about some concert. You didn't even want to do the concert two days ago."

"People paid money to see me," he said miserably. "I'm going to be seen. I may not always like my job, but I get paid very well to do it. It's time I stopped behaving like a spoiled brat and actually do the things I say I'm going to do. Isn't that what you said?"

"Now you're going to listen to me?"

"I have a job to do, and some thug in a ski mask isn't going to scare me away from doing it. Why would someone attack me anyway?" he asked plaintively.

"I don't suppose you left any outstanding debts or anything when you went into rehab?" asked Nikki. She didn't really think it was true, but it might as well be crossed off the list.

"No, I bloody well didn't!" he shouted. "Besides," he said, visibly controlling his voice, "maybe they were after you. You seem a little overly capable in the bad-guy department—seems like you've had experience."

"Yeeeeah," said Nikki, hesitating. "Here's the thing. Your mom and I work for the same company."

"Carrie Mae, so what?"

"Well, have you ever noticed that your mom's gone a lot? Ever noticed any unusual skills in unarmed combat? Excessive interest in firearms?"

Kit's eyes narrowed. "Mom always had a gun when I was growing up. But what are you trying to say? Carrie Mae's just the front for some international terrorist organization?"

"Don't be ridiculous!" exclaimed Nikki. "Carrie Mae is dedicated to helping women everywhere. It's just that sometimes helping requires a little extra . . ." She hesitated, looking for the right words. Why hadn't she ever had this conversation with Z'ev? "Firepower," she said at last. "Camille and I are with the, uh . . .

security division of Carrie Mae. We deal with some of the more dangerous situations faced by our ladies."

"Trista judo-flipped this fan who got too close one time," said Kit. "What about her?"

"She's retired," said Nikki.

"My mom pushed me really hard to hire her," said Kit. "It seemed weird at the time."

"Well, she was worried about you. She wanted you to have someone you could rely on."

"Or she could rely on," said Kit bitterly. "Trista's probably been spying on me for her this whole time."

"Trista loves you," said Nikki firmly. "And I may not know your mom that well, but when she heard about Cano . . . she flipped out and wanted to come see you immediately."

"Who's Cano?" demanded Kit, and Nikki bit her lip. She hadn't meant to say that bit.

"Well, your mom has made a few enemies along the way. It happens in our line of work. And Cano is one of them; he escaped from prison."

"You think he's trying to kill me because of Mum?" asked Kit, and Nikki nodded.

"That's why you're here. I should have known," he said, laughing bitterly. "I should have known you didn't really care."

"Hey," said Nikki, grabbing him by the chin and forcing him to look at her. "I sang karaoke for you."

He finally returned her gaze and Nikki felt her breath catch; his eyes were blue like sapphires. She swallowed hard and stood up, nearly turning over the chair, and went to the window. He began playing with his hair, twisting it into the devil's points that Nikki had assumed were a stage affectation but was now realizing were a nervous habit.

"Are you bleeding?!" she demanded abruptly, noticing a suspicious stain spreading across the back of his shoulder.

"Oh shit," said Kit, twisting around, like a dog chasing a tail, "I've been shot! I've been shot! Why didn't you tell me I was shot?"

"Why didn't you tell me you were hurt?" retorted Nikki. "Into the bathroom. Take off your shirt now."

He stripped off his shirt and sweater and sat down on the toilet seat, looking white.

"It's really starting to hurt now," he said.

"Don't be a sissy," said Nikki severely, feeling her heartbeat speed up. She yanked the threadbare washcloth off the towel bar and placed it over the bleeding gouge on the back of Kit's shoulder.

"Thanks for the sympathy," he said, anger bringing a flush back to his face.

Gingerly, Nikki withdrew the washcloth to take a look at the damage. His shoulder was gouged, probably from a bullet or piece of shrapnel in the Metro, but it wasn't deep. Nikki wet down the washcloth with warm water and began to clean the area.

"Ow!" he exclaimed as she pulled away a sweater thread that had been glued to his skin with blood. "What are you doing back there? How bad is it?"

"It's not bad," said Nikki. "Just a scrape."

"Can I see?" He stood without waiting for permission and went to the mirror, twisting around to look at his shoulder. "Well, that's going to leave a mark," he said, eyes slightly big.

"Meh, chicks dig scars," said Nikki, pushing him back onto the toilet.

"Your bedside manner leaves a lot to be desired, you know," complained Kit as she continued cleaning.

"Sorry," said Nikki, "but it's really not that bad. And just think, now you can tell everyone you've been shot."

"That's true," said Kit, smiling again. Kit's mercurial mood changes confused her, but they did make her laugh. Once she had washed off anything that looked like it shouldn't be there, she rinsed the washcloth and put it back on the skin, applying pressure. She stood there, wondering if she should go pick the lock on the pharmacy across the street or whether she ought to just rip up the bath towel for bandages. Her eyes wandered as she contemplated and she found herself tracing the contours of Kit's naked torso with her eyes. With his shirt off, she could see that his skin was almost as pale as hers and seemed oddly luminous in the bizarre tint of the bathroom light. A light that threw his chest and ab muscles into chiseled relief. She found that the hairs on her arm were standing up where they brushed up against him—as if his whole body were electrically charged.

Attempting to distract herself, she stared at his tattoos. It was the first time she'd been close enough to get a good look at them. Whirling out from his shoulders and trailing down onto his chest and back, the tribal designs and Celtic knots gave him a decidedly wild appearance. Bending over him, Nikki realized that her breasts were at his eye level. Embarrassed, she glanced down at him, but his eyes seemed firmly, if rather forcefully, fixed on the far wall. He was being good. Involuntarily, she smiled at him and saw her smile echoed back.

"'Love forever,'" she said, reading the one incongruous tattoo buried in a complicated nest of trailing Celtic vines.

"Sure," he answered, a puzzled frown crossing his face.

"Your tattoo," she said, laughing and tracing her finger along the words.

"Oh!" He looked down at his shoulder. "Oh, right. That was my first. It looks silly now, but I believed it at the time." As he looked down she caught the heady scent of his body mixed with his shampoo.

"You don't believe it now?" she asked, putting his hand on the washcloth to continue the pressure. She took the bath towel and began the process of ripping it into lengths.

"Things change," he said, apparently unaware of his effect on Nikki. "Are you sure you know what you're doing? Maybe I should I be going to hospital."

"I'm a highly trained specialist, I'll have you know!" she exclaimed.

"Yeah, for a makeup company," he fired back.

"I've had additional training," she sniffed.

"I hope so," he said, looking doubtfully at the towel.

"Love's not the worst thing to believe in," she said, changing the subject.

"Look who's talking. Your boy takes a walk with a total Salma Hayek and you don't even lift a phone to get him back."

"We broke up," said Nikki. "I told him not to call me and he hasn't. How am I supposed to call him up and say, 'Yeah, I know I said don't call me, but oh, by the way, stay away from other women or I'll gouge your eyes out'?"

"Ouch, straight to the eye gouging? You're not still into him or anything?"

Nikki sighed. "It doesn't matter. We're better off not being together. It's complicated and hard and he thinks . . ." She trailed off. "It's just better," she said firmly.

"In rehab they say relationships are the hardest thing to do."

"But should they be?" asked Nikki. "Shouldn't they be more . . . fun? Like you and I—we had fun today. And it was . . ."

"Easy?" he said, smiling. "That's me. Mr. Easy." His expression added the double entendre.

She laughed and began to bandage his shoulder; his skin felt warm under her palm and she fought the urge to let her hand trail down his chest.

"I just meant that I have enough hard things in my life. I'm not sure I should fight for something that might be destined for disaster anyway."

"Well," said Kit, "as a professional disaster creator, survivor, and addict, I gotta tell ya—disasters aren't that bad."

"You seem pretty sure you're going to survive this," said Nikki, her eyes twinkling.

"Well, if it looks gross in the morning, I'm going to go straight downstairs, hire a cab, go to the hospital, and stiff you with the hotel bill."

"Nice to have a backup plan," laughed Nikki, finishing her final knot on the makeshift bandage.

"But that's what I'm figuring out," he said, easing upright to go look at her handiwork in the mirror. "I used to think that there was only one plan, and if it didn't work then everything was over. But it isn't over. The only over is if those guys had actually managed to shoot me. As long as I'm breathing, then there's always another plan. There is another chance. If I screwed up today and got drunk at that bar or whatever, I could start fresh tomorrow."

"Tomorrow is another day," said Nikki, borrowing Jenny's accent for a bit of Scarlett O'Hara.

"Laugh if you want, but I spent too much of my life worrying about what I was going to do when the world ended. And then it did. They told everyone I had mono and was recuperating in Switzerland. But really I had OD'd in some shithole in Bern. Duncan had to scrape me off the floor and carry me to the hospital."

Nikki stared at Kit as if seeing him for the first time. He looked happy, as if this were a good story. Her heart hurt at the idea of him cold on the floor. Instinctively, she covered his heart with her hands and he put his hand on top of her hers. She could feel his heart beating steadily into her palm.

"I OD'd, Nikki. I was dead; my heart literally stopped. They had to use the machine to restart my heart. And you know what I did the day I got out of hospital? I went out and bought some coke. I diced up three lines on a mirror I used to keep around for the purpose, and in the mirror I could see the burn marks on my chest from the heart paddles. Which is when I realized that whatever I was afraid of couldn't be half as hard as where I was now."

She kissed him. She hadn't been meaning too, but something about the fragile courage in his eyes, the warmth of his skin against hers, the way his mouth looked when he'd said her name, just pushed her into him.

Their lips met and for a moment Nikki almost lost herself in the heat between them. His arms wrapped around her, holding her the way she wished Z'ev had done.

"Where we're going can't be half as hard as where we are now," repeated Kit, pulling away from her. "Shit, I gotta write that down—that's a good line."

She leaned back and laughed, feeling a sudden sense of relief. If Z'ev had done something like that, she would have been pissed, but it was just so . . . Kit. She couldn't be mad at him.

"I'll write it down later," said Kit apologetically, reaching for her again.

"No," said Nikki. "You go write it down now. Don't want to lose the thought." He nodded, shuffling away to go find paper. Nikki settled down on the bed and watched him. He didn't seem to mind.

"I missed the boat, didn't I?" he asked twenty minutes later, looking up at her, tapping his jaw with the pen. "With us, I mean."

"But you wrote a song," said Nikki with a shrug.

"Sort of," said Kit. "The bridge is giving me trouble and I need at least another verse."

"You'll get it figured out," said Nikki with absolute faith. She got up and went to the window, checking the street. Trying to distract herself.

"It's too soon, isn't it?" he asked. "You're still into him."

"Probably; I don't know," said Nikki honestly. "But jumping into bed with you probably wouldn't clarify anything."

"You don't know till you try," he said, giving her a rakish grin that made her laugh as he went into the bathroom.

"I'll think about it," she said with a flirtatious smile. The door shut and Nikki flopped back down on the bed, trying to calm the flutter in her stomach. Kit was right; she was still into Z'ev. Even lying on a crappy hotel bed in Paris, she could conjure up his smell, the way he would feel lying next to her. She tried to remember the last time they'd been together. She hadn't thought it would be the last time.

Nikki returned from kickboxing and headed straight for the bathroom, taking the Tiger Balm out of the cabinet and unscrewing the top. The potent, spicy smell filled up the small space of the bathroom, making her eyes water as she gingerly applied the greasy stuff to the huge knot on her shin. Someday she was going to have to invest in shin guards. Lumpy shins were so not attractive. She felt the soothing buzz and tingle that told her the ointment was working and relaxed a bit.

She changed into her pajamas and took the Tiger Balm with her as she limped into the kitchen. Popping a bag of popcorn into the microwave, Nikki mixed a drink and prepared for total sloth.

She was relieved that Z'ev wasn't coming back till tomorrow.

Between the Tiger Balm and sweat she knew she must be putting out a stink that would knock over a skunk. Her hair was in the residual waves of a ponytail and she had dug out her most comfortable, least sexy flannel pajamas from the back of the dresser. Her entire evening's plan consisted of sitting on the couch, drinking something Z'ev would characterize as frilly, nursing her bruises, and feeling lonely.

Nikki had settled into watching *Strictly Ballroom* and was reaching for the popcorn when she absentmindedly rubbed her eye. She had barely pulled her hand away when she realized the stupidity of her actions.

"Damn! Damn, damn, damn," yelped Nikki, running blindly toward the kitchen. The residual Tiger Balm from her fingers stung the thin, sensitive skin of her eyelid, sending tears leaking down her cheeks. She rinsed her eye in the sink and carefully scrubbed her lid with a paper towel.

Nikki made her way back to the couch. She blinked, weepy eyed, at Scott and Fran on the TV. Her mood had not been improved by her own stupidity. She finished the bag of popcorn and went to the kitchen for another cosmo. As she returned, carefully toting her drink, the doorbell rang. She sighed and looked longingly at her couch. It was probably just her crazy neighbor, who was going to accuse her of stealing his geraniums again. Although what he thought she was doing with his geraniums was a mystery. Nikki dragged herself to the peephole and looked through. It was Z'ev.

Nikki opened the door and they stared at each other. He was leaning tiredly against the apartment wall.

"I caught an early flight," he said.

Nikki opened the door farther. He walked past her, taking the cosmo out of her hand and downing it in one gulp. Kicking off his shoes, he dropped his bags and slid out of his jacket on his way to the living room, where he dropped onto the couch. He sat staring vacantly at Scott and Fran dancing the fruuuuuiiiiitttyyy rumba.

Nikki shut the door and went into the kitchen for another cosmo and a beer. When she returned to the living room he was still sitting in the same place, still staring. Fran got self-conscious and fell down. Nikki handed Z'ev the beer and sat down next to him, carefully curling her feet up under her, trying not to jostle him. After a moment, he unbuttoned his shirt.

"Help me out of this, will you, baby?" he asked, trying to wrangle out of the shirt. Nikki noticed there was a bandage on his left arm. She helped ease him out of his shirt, and he leaned his head against the back of the couch and closed his eyes. Another minute went by and then he pulled her close to him with his right arm.

"Did you hurt your arm?" she asked, trying not to sound prying.

"Only a little bit," he said after a while. "Fell off something."

"Mmm," said Nikki, which wasn't an answer, but it was the best she could do without totally freaking out about her boyfriend falling off God knew what and nearly getting himself killed.

"You smell good," Z'ev said, his eyes still closed.

Nikki giggled, turning her face into his chest to smother the laugh. "It's the Tiger Balm."

"Smells like you used the whole jar," he said, kissing the top of her head.

"Not quite, but I kind of overdid it on the working out the last couple of days."

"Got any left?"

"Yeah. Why, do you need some?" She raised her head and scrutinized his face, but his eyes were still closed.

"Maybe just a little on my shoulder," he said, opening his brown eyes and smiling into Nikki's worried gray ones. Nikki reached over and retrieved the small jar off the coffee table.

"The left shoulder?" she asked, dipping her fingers into the jar. He nodded and sat up a little straighter for her. She leaned forward against the solid mass of his chest. She started at his neck, reaching behind him, kneading her fingers into the thick muscle that joined his collarbone to his shoulder. She leaned closer to him, her breasts brushing against his unclad skin. She ignored the subtle thrill from the contact, intent on easing the tension she could feel under her fingers. The heat of his body radiated against her cool fingers and his breath stirred the hairs on the back of her neck.

Unexpectedly, he leaned forward and gently kissed her neck. Nikki caught her breath as he kissed the little hollow behind her jawbone and then her earlobe.

"Nikki," he said, resting his forehead against her temple. Nikki didn't let him finish, turning her mouth into his. He wrapped his arms around her, pushing her backward into the couch.

Nikki ran her fingers down his chest while he fumbled at the hem of her shirt, wanting to take it off but not wanting to stop kissing her. Nikki pulled it up for him; as she tried to wriggle further out of the shirt it got hung up in her hair, and raising her arms over her head, she yanked it furiously off. Z'ev put his hand down on the shirt, pinning her arms inside, and went back to kissing her, the thumb of his other hand running in lazy circles over her breast. Nikki moaned as he bent to kiss her nipple. His tongue ran over the tip and Nikki let out a small gasp.

Finally freeing herself of her shirt, she twisted down and nipped his earlobe. Z'ev laughed and returned his attention to her mouth. Nikki ran her hands down his sides, feeling every curve of muscle and bone. The pungent smell of Tiger Balm filled the air as Nikki undid his belt buckle and pulled the belt slowly through the loops. With languorous enjoyment Nikki dropped the belt on the floor while Z'ev trailed kisses down her neck and onto her breasts.

The button of his pants came next, then the zipper. She slid her hand down the small of his back and into his pants, intending to work her way to the front.

Abruptly, Z'ev grabbed her hand and pulled away.

"I think," he said, as Nikki stared at him in surprise, "before we go any farther, that it might be better if you washed your hands." Nikki glanced down at their naked torsos and the faint sheen of Tiger Balm, only then noticing that tingling she was feeling was not entirely a reaction to Z'ev. She began to giggle. She couldn't help it.

"This wouldn't be funny if you had kept going," he said, grinning.

"Not for you anyway," said Nikki around giggles.

She woke up with a feeling of overwhelming sadness and knew that Z'ev wasn't beside her. And neither was Kit. Nikki sat up, only then realizing that the light was on under the bathroom door. She checked her watch; she'd been asleep for about two hours. Getting up, she knocked on the bathroom door.

"Did I wake you?" responded Kit, sounding concerned; she opened the door and peered in. He was sitting fully clothed in the tiny square bathtub, the pad of hotel notepaper on his knees.

"You don't have to hide in the bathroom," she said, and he blushed. She sat on the toilet, watching him with bemused curiosity. She'd never seen him embarrassed before.

"I was going to, but when I came out you were asleep and then I worried that the light might wake you. So I thought I'd just stay in here till I finished up, but I have to admit that my feet are starting to freeze."

"You're never going to get a song written with me around,"

said Nikki, laughing. "Come out and write at the desk like a real person."

"Nikki," he said seriously, "I was starting to think that I couldn't write any more songs, that all my creativity had gone the way of the dinosaurs. With you around, I'm pretty sure I could write lots of songs."

"So you're saying I'm a dinosaur? You are so romantic," she said, tweaking his hair, refusing to be serious. "Is this how you get the ladies? You compare them to T. Rexes?" She pulled her arms into her body, making little T. Rex arms, and waved them in the air until he laughed.

PARIS IX

Work Ethic

December 31

The morning arrived with a creeping, smothered light. Kit lay sprawled on top of the covers next to her, the pen still clutched in his hand. He was smiling in his sleep, and Nikki found herself smiling back at him even though he couldn't see her.

Nikki blinked, thinking over the details of the last twenty-four hours. Had she lost her mind? She had done exactly what Camille had wanted her to do. Well . . . She probably hadn't wanted Nikki to go running off with Kit. But she had definitely wanted Nikki to abandon her duties.

And then there were the masked men with guns. What had happened there? Nikki tried to piece together the events. Jane had said her call was being . . . what? Piggybacked? That might have meant it was being traced. And then Jane had hung up. Whoever had been tracing the call must have sent those thugs after her. Jane had been in Germany looking at Voges, who led to Cano, who had gone straight for Kit. Nikki tried not to groan out loud; she should have taken Kit and left right after the phone call. Somehow, in her inebriated state, she had missed that. She remembered feeling panicked, but she hadn't remembered the next step. How many other steps had she missed because she'd been too wrapped up in her own problems or too drunk to pay attention? What if Kit hadn't made it through last night? Nikki felt a surge of adrenaline and a fluttering of butterflies in her stomach.

Rising quickly to stop the thoughts circling around her brain, she dressed and peered out the window. The gray clouds hung heavy on the horizon, the rising sun coloring their bases yellow and gold. The effect was short-lived, and soon the clouds were merely dirty gray like the street. Cars zoomed through slush, their windshield wipers slapping at the still falling snow. The rising dome of the Sacré-Coeur could be seen in the distance, marking the skyline as unmistakably Paris. Even in the depressing light of winter it looked romantic, in a tragic sort of way.

Nikki checked her phone. No calls. At this point, she was afraid to call Jane, and Mrs. M wouldn't appreciate being nagged. But she needed help! She dialed Jenny and got her voice mail. Ellen's number was the same story. Nikki felt herself flush as she realized that they probably knew about Z'ev and Nina Alvarez. They probably weren't answering because they didn't want to tell her about it. She felt a hot wave of humiliation wash over her.

Breathing deeply, Nikki tried to control herself. She needed to maintain control. People were counting on her. She cracked the curtains and scanned the street. No thugs in evidence, but she spotted a familiar bulk lurking in the leeward side of the pharmacy. She glanced back at Kit, who was sprawling out to take up her side of the bed, burying his head under a pillow to avoid the light she was letting in the room. Nikki let the curtain swing shut and looked around for something to write on, finding only Kit's chicken-scratch-covered hotel stationery.

Where we're going can't be half as hard as where we are now / I was dying, but I've been saved from the final bow . . .

Various permutations of the lines evolved across the page. Farther down, some new lines sprang up.

There's a price you pay for greatness, there's a cost for all this fame, / And they tear a hole in my soul every time they scream my name.

Followed by: *And I've been needing something, better than I had before / A new way to fill this emptiness, a better kind of cure.*

There were arrows moving the lines and words around, and a few other phrases, followed by a crabbed set of musical bars and notations that Nikki couldn't read. Feeling slightly guilty for peeking, she flipped the sheet over and wrote her own note.

Everything's fine. Just stepped out for a minute. Don't go anywhere.

She paused to consider and then, feeling bold and slightly whimsical, wrote, *Love forever, Nikki.*

The window at the end of the hallway overlooked the back alley, and Nikki had carefully noted the night before that it opened onto a fire escape. She opened the window, climbed down the fire escape, and dropped into the snow. The sudden updraft blew a cold current of air up her pant legs, and she shivered. Huddling into her scarf and jacket, Nikki walked briskly down the alley and around the corner, circling the block. She forgot the chill as she rounded the corner and came within view of her quarry. She took her hands out of her pockets, swinging them loosely at her sides, stalking her target.

Buried under a knit cap and Helly Hansen jacket, the man leaning nonchalantly against the wall of the drugstore could have been almost anyone, but there was a certainty to his stance that Nikki recognized. She walked quietly, letting the flurry of pedestrians mask her approach. She would come up on his blind side and surprise him.

"Do you think this is the first time I've pulled him out of a sleazy hotel with some tart?" he called out when she was still five feet away. Nikki paused. So much for the blind side.

"The hotel isn't that bad. And I am not a tart," she said, realizing that she probably should have started with that and then gone on to the hotel.

"No, you're Carrie Mae." He finally turned to look at her, and his pale blue eyes bored straight through her skull. Nikki found that she was holding her breath. "I keep him safe. Do you really think I wouldn't know that?"

"Do you really think I don't know you're his uncle?" Nikki fired back. His stark silence told her she'd made a hit. He pushed away from the wall and in two swift strides had cut the distance between them. "I searched your room; I found a picture of Declan and Camille. You look too much like Declan not to be related, and so does Kit. Declan's dead. That just leaves one missing uncle. What is it you want from Kit?"

"Missing . . ." Duncan gave a bitter barking laugh. "I was in prison when Declan was killed. But Camille blamed me anyway. She said I ratted Declan out to Cano."

"Did you?"

Duncan's eyes flicked to hers; he was clearly startled by her bluntness. "No. I think Declan told Cano himself. Declan wanted to bury the hatchet. Put it all to rest so that he and Camille could raise their baby in peace. Didn't work out that way, and when I got out Camille threatened to kill me if I went near Kit. I lost myself in Africa after that and when I came back . . . It was like I'd never existed. Camille had moved Kit and my mother to London and sworn everyone to secrecy about our past. Then I saw Kit on TV one day and I thought I'd tell him. I'd worked up my courage. I figured, damn Camille, I'd just tell him. Called Mum; she told me where he was at. Only when I turned up they thought I was applying for the bodyguard position and I . . . I chickened out. And now, five years on, here we are."

"How does Camille not know?" groaned Nikki.

"She doesn't visit that often. I can usually just call in sick or schedule a vacation. Mum helps."

"Ellen is going to eat it up with a spoon," muttered Nikki.

"I don't want anything from Kit. I just want to make sure I don't lose him the way I lost Declan," said Duncan, as if he hadn't heard her. Nikki frowned, not sure whether to believe this. "But just what is it that you want from Kit?" he asked, looming over her.

"Same thing as you," she said, holding her ground. "To keep him safe."

He relaxed a bit and backed up half a step.

"You want to keep him safe?" He seemed incredulous. "So you decided to take him to a bar and do karaoke? He doesn't need help falling off the wagon; he can do that on his own." He paced to the drugstore wall and back.

"He didn't drink, but that's not what I'm talking about. Someone is trying to kill him."

Duncan paused in his pacing. "The tour bus? The stage? Those were Trista and Camille," he said dismissively.

"And yet you didn't do anything about them," said Nikki accusingly.

"And what was I supposed to do?" said Duncan. "'Oi, Kit, your favorite auntie Trista is trying to scare the shite out of you. She's part of an international ring of female spies, and she's probably under orders from your mother, who wants you to hang up the rock star gig to become an accountant. Oh, how do I know? Well, I'm actually your uncle and I knew them when I was in the IRA.' Yeah, that'd go over like a lead balloon."

"And maybe you didn't say anything so that you'd have the perfect fall guy when you had Antonio Cano kill him."

Duncan's face went white. "C-cano knows about him?" he stuttered.

"I saw Cano meeting with someone who was carrying a Hotel Hell backstage pass five days ago. I chased that person back to the concert, which is where I lost them. Someone on the tour is in league with Cano and I've been trying to figure out who. That's why I'm here."

"I thought Camille sent you," said Duncan, sagging against the wall. "I've been trying to figure out your angle. When you told Kit about the stage accident . . . I couldn't figure it out."

"What does Kit's look like?"

"He's not going to bloody need a will!" roared Duncan, bursting upright. "I will *not* let anything happen to him!"

"You misunderstand my question," said Nikki, trying not to flinch. "I'm asking who stands to inherit if he dies."

Duncan checked. "You're asking about suspects. No, that doesn't follow. It's Camille and Mum and Brandt. Maybe a couple of other bequests, but no one with any reason to kill him."

"What about Camille?" asked Nikki, and Duncan snorted in derision.

"She may not be the most hands-on mum, but she loves him. She'd never let anyone touch her precious baby."

"OK, so assuming that's all true, we've got a problem. Because someone is definitely trying to kill him. Someone on the tour is tied to Cano. And if it's not you or Trista, then I'm fresh out of suspects."

"Another accident?" repeated Duncan, frowning. "How? Trista's not here."

"Thugs in the Metro last night," said Nikki, shivering a little in the biting wind.

"That was you!" he exclaimed, pushing off the wall and into her space again. "I saw a report on the news. Is Kit OK?"

"He's fine," answered Nikki, suppressing the desire to back up. "I'm fine too, thanks for asking."

"How do you know they weren't after you?" he asked, going back to pacing.

The wind was kicking up, and it blew flurries of sleetish snow against her back. The gray light from the Parisian dawn gave everything an odd, ambient, shadowless look.

"I don't have any enemies," said Nikki with a shrug.

"You're young yet," he said with a snort.

"And besides," said Nikki, talking over his sarcasm, "they weren't aiming at me."

Duncan walked to the drugstore and back twice before stopping in front of Nikki, his hands behind his back—a military pose from a nearly forgotten past.

"Right; it doesn't matter who or why, because here's what we do. You go get him; I'll call a car. We'll go straight to the airport and straight back home to Ireland. I've got friends there. I can protect him."

"He won't go," said Nikki, shaking her head.

"London then. I can make that work."

"He won't go," repeated Nikki. "He wants to do his show. He says people paid to hear him sing and he's going to sing."

"Now he gets a work ethic?" demanded Duncan.

Nikki shrugged. "If not now, when?"

Duncan threw his hands into the air. "I'll talk him out of it," he said firmly. "Let's go see him."

Nikki shrugged again but followed Duncan into the street.

"You won't tell him, will you?" asked Duncan. "That I'm his uncle."

"I won't," said Nikki, considering briefly as they dodged cars in the crosswalk, "but you should. He deserves to know. He deserves a family."

"Yeah, a family, but I'm not that. I'm not much of anything. And besides, his mother . . . If she found out . . ."

"She'd totally freak?" Nikki filled in for him, and Duncan nodded. "I hear that, but if you don't tell him soon, I will. He deserves to know."

Duncan reluctantly nodded. "I'll tell him. Afterward. If we don't keep Kit alive I guess none of it will matter anyway."

"Nikki," said Kit, yanking open the door at her knock and sounding slightly panicked. "What's he doing here?" he asked, seeing Duncan.

"Next time look through the peephole, Kit," said Nikki, entering with Duncan trailing after her. "Duncan's not the sort of person you want to be surprised by." Duncan grinned and then took good stock of Kit's shirtless state and bandages.

"Jaysus, son!" Duncan exclaimed, his Irish accent sweeping in, as it usually did when he swore. "What'd you do? You said he was fine!" he shot angrily over his shoulder at Nikki.

Kit's eyes lit up, and he ran to the mirror.

"Do I look rugged and tough?" he asked, peeling off the bandages.

"No, you don't," said Duncan heavily. "You look like you should be in hospital. We're going back to London."

"Bollocks," said Kit. "I've got a show to do."

"People are trying to kill you!" exclaimed Duncan.

"I know, but that's why I've got you and Nikki."

"We can't catch everything. Why put yourself at risk?"

"Because," said Kit, pulling on his T-shirt and sweater, "I want to sing."

"What'd you do?" Duncan demanded, turning to Nikki.

"I didn't do anything!" she exclaimed, protesting.

"She gave me dinosaurs," said Kit, unexpectedly kissing her on the temple. "Come on, we've gotta check out, so I can get to the venue for rehearsal."

"What is he talking about?" asked Duncan. Nikki shrugged.

"I'm writing again, Duncan," called Kit from the hallway. "It turns out that creativity is a renewable resource. Dinosaurs dropping dead every minute—more oil on tap."

"Writing?" Duncan chased after him. "Wait, he's writing again?" he asked, turning to Nikki, who was bringing up the rear.

"He had some stuff he was working on last night," answered Nikki with another shrug.

"Oh," said Duncan. Then he smiled, and even underneath the mustache Nikki could see that his smile was twin to Kit's. How had no one noticed? "Well, that'll do then." His face straightened itself out, and Nikki realized no one had noticed because Duncan didn't smile.

"That'll do what?" she asked.

"That'll bring the lad round. He hasn't written a note since rehab. To tell the truth I thought he'd go back to the drugs just to get the words back, but if he's writing again . . . Well, things are all right, aren't they?"

"Yes, they are!" shouted Kit from ahead of them.

"You're both nuts," said Nikki.

“But you love us anyway,” said Kit, walking backward so he could see her. “Forever, right?”

Duncan stopped to see her reaction. Nikki sighed, looking at the pair of them. They were a ragtag little family, clinging together in spite of all their secrets, lies, and faults. Who couldn’t love that?

“Forever,” she said, rolling her eyes and wondering just what she’d gotten herself into.

PARIS X

You Turn the Screws

"Jeez," said Kit as they got into Duncan's car. "I turn off the phone for a couple of hours and all hell breaks loose. Mum's in town and freaking out because she can't find me. Brandt's freaking out because he can't find me. Ditto on Angela. It's pretty much a mass freak-out. Ahhhhh, freak out!" He added the last part in a disco falsetto.

"Your mom's in town?" repeated Nikki, ignoring the vocal flourish and exchanging glances with Duncan.

"What? Nothing on that one? That was good, that was." Kit sighed and then answered her question. "Yeah, she's called about fifteen times. I think she's waiting for me at the hotel," said Kit offhandedly, still poking at his phone.

"Uh, well," said Nikki, just as hers rang. They all jumped at the sound. "Sorry." She apologized as she picked up. "This is Nikki."

"Ah, Nikki," said Mrs. Merrivel. "It appears that you are having some problems with our Paris friends."

"Uh, yes, problems," said Nikki, and Mrs. M clucked her tongue.

"So unfortunate." Nikki held a sigh in; understatement was Mrs. M's métier. "Well, since Madame Feron is being extremely difficult I'm officially ordering you to suspend activities while I work on matters."

"But—" said Nikki, startled.

"Which is such a shame, really"—Mrs. M continued talking over her half-formed protest—"since Jenny and Ellen will be arriving shortly on flight 784."

"But—" Nikki tried to begin again.

"But maybe the three of you can pal around for a few days."

"Pal around," repeated Nikki numbly.

"Certainly," said Mrs. Merrivel calmly. "There's no reason why you shouldn't continue to associate with your friends. They can't really order you out of the country."

"Ah," said Nikki.

"Yes," said Mrs. M.

"Well, I've made some new friends while I've been here. I might introduce everyone," said Nikki.

"You girls have such active social lives," said Mrs. M pleasantly. "I don't know where you find the energy. Just remember you are absolutely to stop all activities relating to Cano."

"All right," said Nikki. "We'll just, uh . . . pal around and maybe go to a concert."

"Excellent, excellent," replied Mrs. M, but there was something in her tone that said she had ceased to listen. "Well, you girls have fun. It's been lovely chatting with you. Please let me know when you're back in country."

"Of course," said Nikki.

"We'll talk more then," Mrs. M promised.

"Bye," said Nikki, realizing that she was already talking to empty air.

"Kit," said Nikki, turning to stare at the rock star.

"Hm?" he asked, still looking at his phone.

"Are we friends?" she asked.

"Yes," he replied promptly, and then looked up suspiciously. "Why?"

"Just needed to clarify," said Nikki. "We may need to pal around later."

"Pal around?" he asked, amused and puzzled by the phrase. Her phone rang again; this time it was Astriz.

"Nikki," said Astriz without preamble, "the cluster-screw continues."

"Your director is suspending you from the case?" asked Nikki.

"Yes!" Astriz's strident anger came through the phone speaker clearly.

"Yeah, me too."

"Meanwhile," said Astriz, "I've put your other friend on a train to Paris. She seemed most eager to see you. And also something about not wanting any more sausages. But what are you going to do if you're suspended?"

"Well, they can't actually force me out of the city, so I'm going to be in Paris for a few days longer, taking in the sights." There was a pause while Astriz considered this. "Yes," said Nikki, "I shall be with a few friends who happen to be in town."

"I think I'm out of vacation days," said Astriz. "On the other hand, I could be coming down with something." She faked a cough.

"Don't worry about it," said Nikki, laughing. "I've got backup flying in; keep yourself out of trouble."

"Are you sure?" asked Astriz.

"Positive. Thanks for all your help, Astriz," said Nikki.

"Meh," said Astriz. "I did what I could. It should have been more."

"And I appreciate it," said Nikki. "Come out to L.A. sometime. We'll drink to Val."

"And spit on her grave!" said Astriz.

"And spit on her grave," echoed Nikki.

"Good luck, Nikki," said Astriz.

"Thanks," said Nikki. "I'll be seeing you."

"Maybe," said Astriz. "You never know." The line went dead and Nikki grimaced at it.

"Good-bye," she muttered at the phone. "It's not a hard word. Why do none of my coworkers use it?"

"I need breakfast," announced Kit from the backseat.

"Sure," said Nikki, rolling with the change of topic.

"I think we should go back to the hotel," said Kit. "Mum's there and I want a shower. Plus, I should probably call Brandt too."

"Er," said Nikki, glancing at Duncan, who was staring through the windshield. Nikki ran through a dozen possible lies; none of them sounded convincing. Wasn't this the part where her training in subterfuge kicked in? Why did she suck so hard at lying? Why did she have to lie anyway? Kit ought to know about Camille and Duncan.

"We probably shouldn't go back to the hotel," rumbled Duncan. "Everyone knows you're staying there. It's a security risk."

"Yes," said Nikki, nodding fervently.

"OK, well, the problem is that I will need my clothes for the show tonight. So eventually someone will have to go back to the hotel."

"I'll go later and pick stuff up," said Nikki, texting the girls to arrange a pickup time. "I need to pick up my friends at the airport anyway; I can swing by and grab a few things."

"More Carrie Mae women?" asked Duncan sourly.

"You need all the help you can get, pal, so don't complain," retorted Nikki, and Duncan grunted.

"I've got a friend who might be able to put us up for a few hours," said Duncan, changing the subject and glancing at Kit in the rearview mirror.

"You have friends? I had no idea," exclaimed Kit. "Who is he?"

"She," said Duncan, correcting him. "Her name is Antoinette. And she's a bit . . . Well, just don't inquire what she does for a living, OK?"

Nikki and Kit exchanged glances. This sounded promising.

"All right," said Kit. "But is it for my protection or hers?"

"Both," said Duncan as he put the car into gear.

Antoinette lived in an ancient third-floor walk-up, accessed only by a twisting staircase.

"I've got to quit smoking," mumbled Kit, leaning against the railing and coughing as Duncan knocked on the door. The door opened a fraction of an inch and then sprang all the way open.

"Duncan!" exclaimed the woman. "You're alive!" She was a wispy blonde of about Duncan's age. She was dressed in a long day dress and wore a beaded necklace and bangles that rattled as she rushed to embrace Duncan. "Who are they?" she demanded, seeing Nikki and Kit.

"This is Nikki Lanier; she's Carrie Mae. And this is Christopher."

"Not Declan's boy!" she exclaimed, seizing Kit by the shoulders and looking him over. "Yes, he looks like his father." Kit seemed suddenly frozen.

"You knew my father?" he asked hoarsely.

"Of course, I knew the whole family. The community was so much smaller then."

"Antoinette!" growled Duncan.

She continued as if Duncan hadn't said anything. "But we don't like to talk about that, do we? Come in, come in. I was just about to make breakfast."

"Actually, I would like to talk more about that," said Kit, following her in.

"What?" hissed Nikki, narrowing her eyes at Duncan. "Are you hoping she'll spill the beans and save you the trouble?"

"No!" said Duncan. "I was looking for a place to go where we wouldn't get shot."

"Uh-huh," said Nikki, and entered the apartment. She had the overall impression of small rooms and large, looming furniture. Most of the pieces were covered in some sort of gauzy scarf; it was as if a hippie had thrown up on an antique store.

"So you knew my father before the car crash?" Kit asked as Nikki and Duncan entered the kitchen.

"Car crash?" repeated Antoinette as she pulled out a cast-iron pan. Duncan cleared his throat significantly. "Absolutely," said Antoinette. "The car crash. Such a tragedy."

Kit looked from Duncan to Antoinette suspiciously.

"Time for breakfast!" she said cheerily.

"Yes, please!" said Kit. "I'm starving."

"You don't have to cook for us," said Duncan.

"Christopher said he was starving," said Antoinette, pulling ingredients out of the cupboards. "I was thinking omelets."

"I don't suppose you've got any bacon?" asked Duncan, sounding hopeful.

"In the icebox," she replied. Duncan began to root around in the minifridge as Antoinette turned on the tiny gas stove and set a knob of butter to melting in the pan. "So," she said brightly, turning around to survey the room, "what brings all of you to my humble home?"

"Someone's trying to kill me," said Kit cheerfully.

"Oh dear!" exclaimed Antoinette, raising her eyebrows. "How vexing!"

"I think it's Antonio Cano," said Nikki.

"Ah," said Antoinette. "Yes. He escaped. Someone called to say."

Now Kit looked from Nikki to Antoinette. "Why do I feel like everyone here knows something I don't?"

"How about those West Ham boys?" said Duncan, interjecting "What do you think their odds are against Leeds this season?"

"I am going outside for a smoke, so you can all talk about me," said Kit with a bitter smile, stepping grimly from the room.

"You had to bring up Cano?" demanded Duncan.

"You had to bring him here," retorted Nikki. "He's out on the balcony. Why not just go tell him the truth?"

"Yes," said Antoinette, cracking eggs. "He should be told. I am not ashamed of what we did."

"You may not be," said Duncan, "but I damn well am. Declan was right. We hurt people. True change cannot be brought about through pain."

"*Viva la revolución,*" she said, smiling sadly. "Things change. Even us."

Duncan grunted and slapped the bacon down onto the counter. "Be right back," he muttered, following Kit.

"They're probably going to be a while, aren't they?" said Antoinette, looking at the eggs in her pan.

"I'm still hungry," said Nikki.

"Me too!" said Antoinette cheerfully.

Nikki leaned back in her chair, trying to catch a glimpse of Duncan and Kit out on the balcony. At least they were talking. Antoinette buzzed around the small kitchen, setting the table and adding ingredients to the pan.

"What did you say your name was again?" asked Antoinette, setting down the plates and returning with glasses.

"Nicole Lanier."

"Lanier? That seems familiar." She squinted at Nikki as she set down a jug of orange juice. "Do I know your mother?"

"I doubt it," said Nikki, smiling. "My mother doesn't really like to travel."

"Hmm," said Antoinette, looking puzzled. "Still sounds familiar." The toast popped and Antoinette brought it to the table. She filled the plates with omelet and sat down, crossing herself in silent prayer before she picked up a fork. "Lanier!" she exclaimed just as Nikki was taking her first bite of omelet. Nikki began to choke, and she reached for the pitcher of orange juice and a glass.

"I knew I remembered Lanier from somewhere. Redheaded, too, come to think on it."

Nikki continued to pour orange juice into a glass, pleased to see that her hand wasn't shaking.

"It was back in my gun-running days," said Antoinette, smiling reminiscently. Nikki gulped the orange juice. "He used to run a boat up the Congo. Good smuggler—really professional. A Frenchman I think." Antoinette looked lost in the past, and Nikki held her breath.

"What was his given name? Paul?" Nikki breathed out. "No. It was Philippe, practically positive," she said at last as Kit opened the door and stepped inside. The two women eyed him cautiously for signs of fracture.

"Need toast," said Kit, putting bread in the toaster, staring blankly at the machine. Nikki reached over and pushed the lever down. Antoinette handed him a glass of orange juice, which he drank reflexively. The toast popped eventually, and Kit slathered it with butter, added a slice of the ham-sized bacon, and turned it into a sandwich as he returned to the balcony.

"Philippe is my father's name," said Nikki, watching as Kit gently shut the door and turned to say something to Duncan. "He was French-Canadian."

"Maybe that was him then!" said Antoinette blithely.

"Maybe," said Nikki.

Duncan came in next, mopping his brow as if he'd been sweating.

"How's it going?" asked Antoinette, pushing a plate his way.

"I dunno," said Duncan. "He's being so damn calm. I'm just not sure if it's sinking in."

PARIS XI

La Vie en Rose

Nikki surveyed the dressing room. Trista's equipment had been set up in orderly rows and columns. Nikki warmed up the airbrush and plugged in the bottle of premixed paint. She tested it a few times on a magazine with Kit's face on the cover. She gave him devil horns and then a mustache, goatee, and glasses. She stepped back and surveyed the results with satisfaction. She might not be as smooth as Trista, but it wasn't bad.

Nikki arranged her brushes and sponges from biggest to smallest and, in a Z'ev-like fit of straightening, arranged the tubs of stage makeup from biggest to smallest as well. She had the makeup sketches taped to her mirror and a list of instructions from Trista just below it, but she was pretty sure she had the sequence down. Nikki had the pattern for the evening set in her head, but she went over it again anyway. She started with the dancing girls, did basic stage makeup for the rest of the band, then Kit, and then everyone went onstage. They did their song and dance—three songs, to be precise, from eleven fifteen to eleven forty-five. Duncan would have the car waiting. She would send Jenny off with them while she, Ellen, and Jane got down to the business of men with guns. She had the feeling that Kit wasn't going to like being sent away, but she had to have him safe before she went to work.

Her phone calls with Astriz and Mrs. M had been reassuring. The multiple security checks on the way into the opera house had been reassuring. Even Kit's blind cheerfulness was reassuring. She counted up her reassurances and wished the list were longer.

Nikki struggled to feel in command. Yesterday, she'd been a little off. Z'ev had thrown her for a momentary loop, but she was not thinking about that. She was thinking about how to keep Kit safe for the next—she checked her watch. It was noon now, and they were flying out directly after midnight, so, the next twelve hours.

Kit came in, with Duncan a solid shadow only inches behind him. He slumped directly into the makeup chair by Nikki. He seemed drained. A million miles away from the morning's devil-may-care Kit. Maybe it hadn't been such a good idea to tell him that Duncan was his uncle. He'd been silent since then.

"Ahhhh, freak out?" asked Nikki.

Kit looked up, confused, and then smiled. "Maybe a little; *le freak, c'est chic.*"

"Well, hey," said Nikki, "on the bright side, now you can move up to 'We Are Family.'" Kit snorted through his nose, and a sparkle appeared in his eyes as he began to sing the refrain of the disco hit.

"What the hell is this—a free concert?" asked Brandt, striding into the room. "Look, sweetie, you're here to do makeup. Let's go, chop chop." He snapped his fingers at Nikki, who ground her teeth.

"Brandt," said Kit uncomfortably, "please don't talk to my friends that way."

"Your friends? Come on, Kit! No offense, love," he said, sparing a glance at Nikki, "but she isn't your friend. She's your employee. I'm your friend. Besides"—he checked his enormous watch—"we have a limited amount of time for practice here. We don't have time to mess around."

Kit frowned but said nothing as Brandt flopped into a chair and pulled a small black case from his pocket and took out a cigar. He efficiently snipped the end off with the little cigar guillotine that was too close to finger size to make Nikki comfortable.

"Brandt, I have to sing tonight," said Kit cajolingly, but Nikki heard the underlying seriousness in his voice.

"I just said that," said Brandt, the cigar between his teeth as he fumbled for a lighter.

"Well, I have to sing, so do you mind not smoking that thing?"

"Oh, come off it, Kit, you smoke like a chimney. Have done for years."

"And it messes up my voice. I've decided to cut back."

"You've cut back?" said Brandt incredulously.

Kit looked a little embarrassed. "No smoking the day of a concert."

For a moment Nikki thought Brandt was going to tell Kit where to get off, but he abruptly tucked the cigar away and stood up.

"Whatever you say, Kit; you're the star."

And there it was. Someone had finally said what had been bothering Nikki. Kit was the Star. Everyone's behavior was dictated by his. Their attitudes, their jobs, everything, changed at his whim. Even Brandt, who seemed the most likely to tell Kit no, still set his course by Kit's star. It wasn't a matter of Kit thinking their worlds revolved around him; they actually did. Nikki wondered how power-hungry Brandt felt about that. Not good, she was betting.

"They're ready for you now. The rest of the band is waiting onstage," said Angela, walking into the room.

"The band," repeated Kit with dissatisfaction. "We really do have to find them a name."

"I think Richie's still pulling for the Purple Weasels," said Nikki.

"I don't know about *that* name," said Kit, getting up and leading the way out of the room. "But we do need something."

"What's wrong with using 'the band'?" groused Brandt grumpily, following Kit.

"That one's taken," answered Kit, winking at Nikki as he left.

Angela was on the phone again, walking around the room, picking up and discarding objects, unstraightening everything Nikki had so recently straightened.

Nikki checked her watch; the girls would be arriving in a bit. She could hear the distant thump of Burg on the drums. She quickly recognized the backbeat of "Devil May Care"; Kit's songs were like musical crack. She watched Angela in the mirror. The blonde was standing near the airbrush and fiddling with it in an absent-minded way while nodding to her phone.

"You know," said Angela hanging up the phone and picking up the airbrush, "I always wondered how these things worked." Nikki leaned against the counter and watched her without response. Angela was being suspiciously friendly. "Do I just push this button right here?"

Angela turned the airbrush on Nikki and held down the trigger. Nikki reached out on instinct and caught the other woman's hand in a firm grip, but not before a gust of red paint had covered Nikki from waist to face.

"Oops," said Angela, sounding far from apologetic. Nikki applied extra pressure to the woman's wrist, bending the wrist down and the hand up until the other woman buckled at the knees, then she wrenched the airbrush away. "Ow!" shrieked Angela. "What'd you do that for? It was an accident!" She jumped back and glared at Nikki, nursing her injured hand.

"Sure it was," said Nikki, shaking droplets of red paint from her hand. "Why was your phone off the day of the bus accident?"

"I don't know what you're talking about," she answered stiffly, trying to step around Nikki. Nikki stopped her, placing one red hand on the woman's chest, right below the collarbone, knowing it would leave a mark.

"Your phone is never off. And yet, when Kit tried to call you, you didn't answer. It was, in fact, off."

"Don't be ridiculous," said Angela, nervously licking her lips, still holding her hand. "It must have been bad reception. Why would I turn my phone off?"

"I can think of a few reasons," said Nikki calmly, scooping red paint out of her eye and wiping it on Angela's blouse. Angela recoiled as if Nikki were wiping burning coals on her. "That's a Ralph Lauren jacket, isn't it?" asked Nikki, fingering the lapel and leaving red streaks. Angela flinched again. "Tell me about the bus accident, Angela."

Angela was breathing hard.

"This is complete nonsense," she said, her voice rising. "I don't know what you're talking about. I don't have to stay here!" Pushing Nikki away with panicked force, Angela ran out the door, and Nikki stared after her.

With a sigh, she turned back to the mirror and saw that she was covered in red paint from eyebrows to belt. She used the makeup remover to scrub at her face, but the paint was everywhere, seeping through her shirt and caking in her ears. This was going to take more to fix than a sponging off in the bathroom sink. Dejected, she went to find Kit and Duncan.

"Bloody hell," said Duncan when he saw her. Out onstage, Kit was being charmingly stubborn with the show's director. "What happened to you?"

"I had a run-in with Angela. I can't prove it, but she's in this somehow."

"Angela? Why would she do that? Besides, she's not that . . ." Duncan trailed off.

"Bright?" said Nikki, and Duncan nodded. "Someone's telling her what to do."

"But who?"

"Brandt springs to mind," she said, but Duncan shook his head.

"He and Kit have been friends for over ten years. Not to mention the fact that Kit is his top-selling artist; he wouldn't kill the goose that lays the golden eggs."

"Maybe, but I wouldn't leave Kit alone with either of them, just in case."

"Easy enough. Brandt left a while ago and Angela stormed out just now. Looked plenty pissed, too. What'd you say to her?"

"We just talked about fashion," said Nikki with a shrug.

Kit came offstage, started to speak, and then caught sight of Nikki.

"What happened to you?" he asked, laughing.

"There was a slight incident with the airbrush," Nikki said, trying to wipe the surliness out of her voice but not entirely succeeding.

"You'd better go change," he commented.

"All my stuff is back at the hotel," said Nikki, grumpiness taking over even further.

"Even better," he said persistently, refusing to give in to Nikki's attitude. "I need my stage outfit for tonight anyway. So you can go back and get a shower"—he dug into his pocket and handed her his hotel room key-card—"and be back by teatime."

Nikki glanced doubtfully at Duncan.

"You said you needed to pick up your friends at the airport anyway," said Kit, and Nikki reluctantly nodded. "If you stay here, you'll be sitting around watching me sit around. The director wants me to sing an @last song, and I'm not doing it, so he went to call Brandt and complain. Go get changed; Duncan and I can watch TV in the dressing room with the rest of the band. Besides, you look like some sort of mad footballer. I do have an image to protect, you know?" Nikki looked to Duncan, who shrugged and twitched his head toward the door.

"You're not going to go anywhere, right?" she asked, eyeing the proffered hotel key. "You're going to stay here?"

"I can't go anywhere without my tour guide."

"Well, all right," she said conceding with a smile. "I'll be back in an hour. Don't do anything stupid while I'm gone and don't listen to Burg."

"Oh please. I can keep myself out of trouble."

"Just be alive when I get back and I'll be happy."

"Yes, ma'am," he said, throwing her a mock salute, and Nikki grinned.

"Yeah, well, I'm counting on you," she said to Kit, but made eye contact with Duncan, who nodded his understanding.

PARIS XII

Have to Answer to Us

Nikki entered her hotel room and saw that Holly's natural-disaster mode had spread to the bathroom. There was stuff everywhere. It shouldn't have bothered her, but it did. She needed an orderly space for some orderly thoughts. Speculatively, she eyed Kit's key-card to the penthouse suite. Penthouse usually meant a giant bathroom. With giant showerheads and fluffy towels. Ignoring the twinge of guilt, she scooped up her luggage and headed for the elevator.

Once in the penthouse, Nikki dropped her purse and jacket by the door and pulled out Kit's clothes, laying them out next to her luggage in the bedroom. She was planning on taking the specialty items and ditching most of the rest. She stripped as she made her way to the shower. She was really looking forward to the multiple showerheads. She had to admit that rock star living had its perks.

As Nikki exited the shower, tucking one of the coveted velvety towels into place and running a comb through her hair, she opened the door to the living room, intending to get a glass of water.

"Well, this is a surprise," said Brandt. "You are most definitely not Kit. Angela really is incompetent. You wouldn't think an instruction like 'send Kit back to the hotel' would be hard to follow, now, would you?"

Nikki smothered a startled reaction and leaned against the door frame, staring at Brandt. Brandt tossed aside a magazine and showed all his teeth in an Angela-type smile. His .38 rested on the coffee table in front of him.

"She was a little distracted," said Nikki. "I think she got some paint on her jacket."

"Not the new one from Ralph Lauren? Tsk. She'll be devastated. You know, I can see now why he likes you. You are pretty."

"Smart too," said Nikki, wishing she were clothed. "You're the one who gave that groupie the drugs. You set up the semitruck accident. And you were the one who met with Cano in Stuttgart."

"You can't prove any of that," replied Brandt, but his smile was a little too wide, and the glint in his eye sparkled with acknowledgment.

"Why do you want to kill him?" asked Nikki, hoping to keep him talking.

"I don't," said Brandt, stretching out one arm along the back of the couch. "Well, I didn't at first, anyway. All I wanted was to get him back in the studio. Faustus needed a hit record, and since he can't seem to make music sober, I had to do something. But he's been remarkably resistant to my little temptations. Who knew Kit would actually stick with it this time?" Brandt was aggrieved, as if Kit's sobriety were a matter of personal insult. "He doesn't really have a backbone, you know. The only thing he's ever stuck with was music, and if the girls didn't scream for him, how long do you think that would last? Frankly, I thought between writer's block and the damn drugs I've been throwing at him, he'd break in a minute. But Duncan proved to be a bit too good at his job."

"So what changed?" asked Nikki. Brandt seemed eager to explain himself, or at least tell her how smart he was; Nikki decided to let him. "Why the gunmen?"

"The economy crashed. The banks are calling in their loans and suddenly a hit record wasn't enough. I needed to get creative."

"The letters," said Nikki, taking a guess, and Brandt narrowed his eyes. "The threat letters to Kit."

"It's funny what we'll do when the pressure's on, isn't it?" he asked. "I spent all that time trying to get a record out of him when I should have remembered about the contract. I wrote it after all. Kit was my invention, so why should his 'heirs' get the money? All those royalties and rights? Mine. I'd nearly forgotten it myself, but the ol' gray matter kicked in eventually." He tapped his temple with his index finger. "One day Angela walked into my office with the latest batch of crazy letters and I figured, one of them has got to be serious. So I reached out to a few of the top contenders, and I got Antonio Cano. This guy has such a hard-on for killing Kit that he actually broke out of prison when I said I would help. Can you believe it?" Brandt laughed as if Cano were the sucker.

"Money?" asked Nikki, returning to the bathroom and brushing her hair in the mirror, trying to look calm. She scanned the bathroom, searching for a weapon. All her clothes and gadgets were in the bedroom. "That's seriously it? You're killing your best friend for money?"

"You don't get it," said Brandt disgustedly. "This is about business. I'm trying to save Faustus. And I told you . . . I need something bigger than a hit record. I need a sensation. If Kit dies, I retain ownership of his entire back catalog and unproduced songs, all future royalties, everything. I can put out greatest-hits albums from now till the end of time. I was planning on having him die here in a mysterious shooting; that would have really kept things selling. But since he's not here, I suppose we'll have to improvise. Terrorist incident maybe; we'll see what Cano says. By the time I'm done, Kit will be bigger than Selena. I probably can't really hope he'll be as big as Tupac, but I can dream." Brandt took out a cigar and snipped off the end with his little cigar cutter.

"You think it's callous, I suppose. But do you know how much I spent, of my own money, to buy Kit out of that ridiculous @last contract? Not to mention all the drugs and the stint in rehab. I didn't regret it because I knew my horse was a winner. And Kit, he was right there with me. Faustus Records was our dream. We were going to conquer the world—the two of us together." Brandt laughed at his own youthful pretensions. "Now at the last furlong my horse has come up lame. Faustus is hemorrhaging and Kit's not lifting a finger to help."

"Does he even know?" asked Nikki, unwilling to believe that Kit wouldn't help his friend.

"I shouldn't have to tell him!" shouted Brandt. "Used to be, he would have known. Now, what? He gets sober and suddenly he's too good for us? Won't come around to hang with the old friends. Won't get back in the studio. Won't release old tracks. Walks out of concerts. Oh no, Kit won't help. Kit just wants to play with makeup artists." Brandt ended on a nasty note, his eyes sliding over Nikki's body. "Not that I blame him, of course," he said, sitting back and becoming the big-time record exec again. "Like I said, you're cute. But fun time's over."

He paused to light his cigar.

The bathroom was disgustingly bare. She ran over the usual ideas. Toilet lid? Too heavy to throw and it wouldn't beat Brandt's gun. Shampoo to sting the eyes? There probably wasn't enough left in the mini shampoo bottles, even if she had the time to stand them head down, so the dregs dripped to the top. That left toilet paper and a hair dryer. Not exactly her weapons of choice. The bathroom was a Jack and Jill style, connecting both to the hall and to the bedroom closet. She wondered if she could make it into the bedroom before Brandt shot her.

Brandt checked his watch and then stood with an easy grace. Nikki put down the brush and tensed, waiting for her moment. There was a soft knock and Brandt opened the door.

"Right on time," said Brandt to a man with his hand raised, on the point of knocking. "Sadly, our quarry is decidedly not at home. Not to worry though, we do have a consolation prize." He turned back to Nikki and smiled. "Cano, meet Nikki. She's a nosy makeup artist with Carrie Mae. Nikki, meet Antonio Mergado Cano. He's a—"

"A Basque separatist," Nikki said, finishing for him.

"Anarchist," said Cano, correcting her. "I no longer support the Basques. They are weak."

"Why beat around the bush?" asked Brandt. "He's a terrorist." Cano frowned but said nothing. "He's also, for a very nominal fee, willing to kill Kit."

"Among others," said Cano with a small smile.

Cano was short, no more than Nikki's height, but with a squat, powerful build. His dark brown eyes burned out from under a tousled mane of black hair. A three-day stubble coated his chin and he wore a spotted white-on-black tie over a black shirt and suit. The effect was mod with a tinge of mob. He carried a long coat over one arm, and the way he draped it over the back of the armchair told Nikki that the coat held something of a higher caliber than pocket change. He radiated a malignant destructive quality, and Nikki knew at once who had been responsible for the men in the Metro.

"Whatever," said Brandt, returning to the couch, seemingly oblivious to Cano's threat.

"Finally going to get your vengeance on Camille?" asked Nikki, and Cano smiled.

"The whole family, really. I hear that Declan's brother is with him also."

Brandt looked from one to the other, puzzled, but didn't say anything.

"And of course, I am always happy to kill any of you Carrie Mae women. So meddling. But it seems I'm about to get my payback."

"Trust me, having to look at that tie is payback enough," drawled Nikki.

"Tough girl," laughed Brandt.

"Even tough girls bleed," said Cano in the same thoughtful, calm voice. It was starting to creep Nikki out. "Where is Christopher?"

"He's at the venue. Angela was supposed to get him here, but apparently that didn't go as planned."

"Then I will go to the venue also," said Cano.

There was another knock at the door. Cano opened it without taking his eyes off Nikki, and two men slunk into the room. One was tall and wiry, with an olive complexion gone pasty and a bird beak of a nose. His eyes were fixed on her in an overbright, cunning stare, like a mongoose staring down a cobra. The second one was shorter and had a soft, slick face, like he didn't really have bones, just rounded edges. He wore his black hair greased back; it gave him a ferret-like appearance. Nikki recognized both of them from the Metro; they looked like they remembered her as well.

"We will meet at the opera house. You will get us in," said Cano. It was a statement rather than a question.

"Yeah, OK," said Brandt, looking slightly uncomfortable, "but wait till after the event's started. Security lightens up after that. I'll get you in then. Say in"—he checked his watch—"about two hours?"

Cano nodded.

"Count on it," muttered Mongoose.

"Well," said Brandt, stubbing out his cigar in the heavy marble ashtray on the coffee table. "This is where I get off."

"Go away," said Cano.

"Believe me, I am," said Brandt smoothly, and left the room. Nikki stared at Cano and his weasels; they were both grinning the same nasty, leering smile.

"You're going to kill him too, aren't you?" she asked after Brandt closed the door.

"After we get the money," hissed Ferret.

"After we kill everyone," said Cano. "The world should not have forgotten about us."

"What 'us'?" said Nikki tauntingly. "There's just you and a bunch of thugs. The Basques have publicly denounced you. The Irish have given up bombs. There is no movement anymore."

"There will be when I'm done," said Cano.

"*La chance mauvaise pas seul vient,*" murmured Nikki, walking toward the coffee table. It was a favorite proverb of her father's that roughly meant that bad luck never came alone.

"Do not speak French!" yelled Cano. Nikki looked at Cano in surprise. And then slowly the realization dawned. Cano was Basque. The Basques had been crushed by the Spanish and French governments for decades and were fiercely proud of their language and heritage. Speaking French wasn't going to earn her any points here.

"*La mala suerte no llega sola,*" said Nikki, switching to Spanish. She reached down for Brandt's cigar and braced for impact. Spanish wasn't going to go over any better.

Cano hit her. A backhanded strike, hard but not meant for anything more than punishing pain. Nikki took the hit and bounced up off the coffee table with the marble ashtray in one hand and the still smoldering cigar in the other. Striking out with the ashtray, Nikki caught Cano a glancing blow under the chin, sending him reeling backward. Ferret made a grab for her, and she jabbed into his outstretched palm with the still smoldering cigar. He yelped and pulled back.

Slower to react, Mongoose made a diving tackle but got nothing more than her towel. Cano stumbled forward, one hand outstretched, as she gained the bathroom; she slammed the pocket door on his arm and then cranked his arm backward against the joint. Cano howled and put a foot through the door. She let him yank his hand back, slammed the door closed, and locked it. Racing naked through the closet and into the bedroom, she knew that the flimsy door would hold him only slightly longer than tissue paper.

She grabbed a coat from the closet—something long and black—and she reached for her bag just as Ferret came charging through the open bedroom door. There was a rending of wood, and Nikki knew it would be only seconds before she had Cano breathing down her neck. She grabbed the strap of her bag and swung it into his face; he jumped back, throwing the bag away from him. Nikki reached for it as Mongoose yanked at her other arm. She swung around and missed the bag by a fingertip length. Using the momentum of Mongoose's grab, she spun and elbowed him in the ear. He let go and stumbled into Cano, who came charging through the closet.

Nikki dashed for the door and sprinted across the parquet floor with Ferret right behind her. He made a grab for her wrist as she reached for the door. She twisted out of his grasp and scooped the vase of flowers off the decorative table with the other, smashing it into his face. Then she was out the door and sprinting down the hallway.

She slammed into the elevator and thumped the "close door" button repeatedly, watching as Cano came stomping down the hallway, pulling what looked like an antiaircraft gun from under his overcoat. The doors slid shut as Cano pulled the trigger on his shotgun. Nikki heard the explosion and scattered impact of the pellets on the four inches of steel that shielded the elevator.

She hit the button for the lobby but then realized that all they had to do was run down the stairs a few floors and stop the elevator. She punched the button for the next floor and got out, dodging a woman in an expensive fur. Dashing into the stairs, she heard a shout from above her. Risking a look upward, she saw Ferret leaning over the railing. Running faster now, she leaped down the last few stairs and jumped over the railing onto the next flight down. The sound of footsteps echoed in the hollow stairwell, and Nikki used the sound to cover her escape onto a random floor. She skidded to a stop on the plush carpeting, tightening the belt holding her coat together, and tried to get her bearings. She heard the stairwell door open and sprinted toward the elevators.

The elevator was already crowded, and she received a few dirty looks as she wedged herself in, but the looks weren't half as nasty as the one Cano gave her as the elevator doors slid shut in his face again.

"Nasty-looking fellow," said someone.

The elevator was playing a Muzak version of a song that Nikki recognized but couldn't place.

"He's probably with the band," someone sniffed.

"The band?" asked the first fellow.

"That Kit Masters is staying here. The guy is probably with the band. You know those rock and roll types. Never bathe."

"Is this the Clash?" asked a third voice from the back corner. Everyone paused to listen to the music.

"I say, that's a bit sacrilegious," said the man who had insulted Cano's looks.

"It is," said someone from the left. "It's 'The Guns of Brixton.'" He began humming in time to the music. The entire elevator was humming along thoughtfully now.

Nikki looked around and wondered how it was that she, standing barefoot and naked in a packed elevator, wearing nothing but a trench coat, had managed to be the normal one of the group.

"It really shouldn't be allowed," said the first man as the elevator doors opened onto the lobby. "It's the Clash!"

"You don't have to tell me," said his friend. "I was at the Rock Against Racism concert in '78." Nikki followed the nostalgic duo toward the front door, but Cano was there ahead of her.

"Check outside," he told his two rodents. Nikki was pleased to see that Ferret was bleeding slightly from cuts on his face. "One of you get around back. I don't want her slipping past us."

Cano turned to the interior and began to survey the lobby. Nikki ducked behind a group of giggling teenagers and followed them into the bathroom. Apparently when someone kicked down her front door she wasn't going to come out with hands on her head or with a gun; she was going to be found hiding in the bathroom. This was not Carrie Mae behavior.

PARIS XIII

Underneath Your Clothes

Rushing into the bathroom, Nikki pushed the teenagers out of the way and pulled herself up to look out the window for an escape. Mongoose could be seen hovering at the mouth of the alleyway. The window itself was locked and painted shut. She dropped down and found the girls staring with baffled expressions.

"Hi," said Nikki.

"You're not wearing any shoes," replied one of the girls, her accent distinctly UK.

"Hell, I'm not wearing any clothes; shoes are the least of my worries." She opened the bathroom stalls, one after the other, vainly hoping someone had left something useful behind. Her search exhausted, she turned back to the girls, who were all dressed too provocatively and toting satchels that looked crammed full of potentially useful items.

"I don't suppose you could lend me a little something?" she asked with a winning smile.

The girls exchanged glances. There were three of them, but

they all looked to the one who had spoken first—the most Goth-looking one.

"Maybe," the dark-haired girl replied, hiking up her low-cut corset top.

"Come on, girls, are you going to help me or not?" Nikki did a pull-up and peered out the bathroom window again. Ferret had joined Mongoose and they were effectively blocking any alley escape. She dropped back down and felt the icy cold tile under her feet. If the tile was cold, the cement was going to be freezing. She needed clothes and shoes, even if she had to take out every single one of these girls to do it. She looked back at the three girls.

They were huddled around the Goth vampire queen again. Naturally pale, the girl was actually making her massive amounts of coal-black eyeliner and candy-apple lipstick look cool, in a porn-star kind of way. The tubby one wasn't having as much luck with her eyeliner, which was smearing, and the other one was chewing her black nail polish to pieces.

"Not so fast," Vampirella said. "What can you do for us?"

She could take them. Tubby might be a bit hard to drop without permanent damage and the short one looked like a biter, but she could do it. Nikki wrinkled her nose at the thought. It seemed so . . . un–Carrie Mae–like. *Something is going to have to be done about this,* said a little voice in her head that sounded suspiciously like Mrs. Merrivel.

"Kind of naked here, girls," Nikki snapped impatiently. "Not exactly carrying wads of cash."

"I know, but Tanya says she saw you get off the tour bus with *him*." Vampirella's voice throbbed on "him." "That means you can get us backstage." Biter nodded an affirmation.

"Look, kid, if I don't get to *him,* there won't be a backstage to get to. Give me the clothes and your names and I'll see what I can do." Biter and Tubby nodded their agreement, but Vampirella held up her hand, stopping them in mid-nod.

"Not good enough. We're going to need some sort of assurance that you'll come through."

"Like what?" demanded Nikki.

"That is your problem," answered Vampirella airily.

Nikki shoved her hands into her pockets, trying to think of something, and felt a ray of hope. Slowly, from her pocket she pulled a dog-tag chain and pass and watched their eyes widen as she did.

"Would a tour pass do it?" she asked. They were all nodding now. Vampirella reached out for the devil-head badge with trembling fingers. Nikki yanked it out of her reach. "Seems to me a tour pass is worth a lot. I'm going to need cash and shoes too."

Vampirella chewed her bright red lips.

"How much?"

"One hundred bucks," said Nikki. That ought to get her out to the airport and back. The girls exchanged glances.

"Fifty," countered Vampirella.

"Fifty-five," said Nikki, just to be mean, "and shoes."

"Done," said Vampirella, reaching for the pass.

"Clothes first," snapped Nikki.

Vampirella turned sharply to her followers. "Cough it up, girls."

There was a flurry of activity as the girls rifled through their satchels. Nikki pulled on clothes as they were handed to her. A black miniskirt, a red push-up bra, and a bizarre fur-rimmed belly-button-baring turtleneck. The mottled fake fur tickled her stomach.

"No underwear?" asked Nikki, feeling incredibly exposed in the short skirt.

"We've been here four days," said Biter. "They're all dirty." Nikki nodded, disappointed, but understanding.

"What size shoe?" asked Biter.

"Seven and a half." The girls exchanged confused glances.

"What's that in proper sizes then?"

Nikki squinted, trying to remember her size in English shoes.

"How the hell should I know?" she said at last. "One of you has got to have a pair of shoes that fit."

"Hold out your foot," said Vampirella. One by one they held up their feet to Nikki's, trying to find a match. Nikki cocked her head to one side, trying to shake the vague feeling of Cinderella-ness.

"That's you then, Sandy," said Vampirella to Tubby.

"No," said Tubby stubbornly. "My boots are the only spares I have."

"You can't walk properly in them anyway," said Biter. "You look like a horse." The other girl nodded and Tubby's head sank. Reluctantly, the girl reached into her bag and pulled out a pair of enormous boots with thick black rubber soles; tall, square heels; and black laces through heavy metal eyelets.

"Those are going to take forever to get on," said Nikki doubtfully, eyeing the laces.

"Oh no, they've got zippers," said Tubby. Nikki looked into the girl's round face and saw a desperate neediness underneath the baby fat. "See?" The girl displayed the zippers that ran up one side of the boots.

"Well, they are pretty cool," Nikki said, and smiled a little extra.

"I've got socks too," volunteered Tub—Sandy.

Nikki pulled on the red socks and then the boots. The long, black trench coat came next, which did a little something to alleviate Nikki's feelings of exposure. She flipped her hair out of the coat and turned to look at herself in the mirror. Goth Cinderella looked back. Her hair, without blow-drying, had gone a bit wild, and the black knee-high boots gave her a decidedly dominatrix appearance.

"You need makeup," said Biter.

Nikki looked at her fairy god-teens and gave in to temptation. If she was going to wear the boots she might as well wear the eyeliner too. Five minutes later Nikki was fully made up. Risking a glance out of the bathroom door, she saw Cano still standing by the front door.

"Uh, girls," she said, ducking back into the bathroom. "I don't suppose any of you have a hat I can borrow? There's a guy out there I'm not too anxious to meet, and while this outfit might fool him, my hair is a dead giveaway."

"I don't think so," said Vampirella, looking at her followers.

"Oh, wait!" exclaimed Sandy, thumping down her satchel and digging through it. "Here!" Sandy pulled a newsboy cap from the bottom of the bag, dusting off crumbs, eyeliner shavings, and lint. "Forgot I bunged it off my brother."

"Cool," said Nikki, taking the cap; it reminded her of Astriz. She rolled her hair in a French twist and pulled the cap on over it, tilting the brim to a rakish angle.

"You look cool," said Biter. Vampirella nodded in vigorous agreement.

"Come on," said Vampirella, picking up her bag, "we'll walk you out." Nikki shook her head.

"Thanks, girls, but this guy's dangerous. I don't want to get anybody hurt."

"He's looking for you, not all of us," said Vampirella reasonably.

"And if you're with us he won't even see you," said Sandy.

"Particularly in that outfit," said Biter in agreement. Nikki narrowed her eyes, considering the proposal; it did make sense.

"All right, but if I say run, you all run. Understood?"

"Understood," said Vampirella in her position as group spokeswoman.

They left the bathroom and walked toward the front door, the girls giggling nonstop. This was the most fun they'd had *ever*. Nikki held her breath as they passed Cano. His eyes roamed over them, stopping on Vampirella's legs and Biter's breasts, and then continued on past them.

The girls waited with her until the doorman presented her with an open cab door, his eyes glued to a spot inches above her head, determinedly not looking at her legs. The cabbie had no such compunction and actually swiveled in his seat to watch her get in the cab. Nikki pulled the long folds of her trench coat over her legs.

"*Au revoir,* girls," she said, turning back to her Gothic woodland sprites.

"See you at the concert," they crowed, waving farewell.

"Charles de Gaulle," she told the cabbie. "And try watching the road."

PARIS XIV

Paris, France

Nikki stalked through the broad halls of Charles de Gaulle international airport, the heels of her boots making a hard smacking sound on the tile. The sound seemed the perfect expression of her mood.

Nikki saw the Air France sign and walked down the rows of placards until she got to number four. Ellen was sitting quietly against the window wall across from number four with her bag and a long, square, bulky case at her feet. Dressed in a gray skirt and green peacoat, Ellen seemed the epitome of middle-aged affability. As Nikki approached, Ellen picked up her bags and fell into step just behind her. Ellen gave her outfit a once-over and then kept noticeably, tactfully quiet.

They passed a brasserie selling overpriced water and pastries. Without acknowledging them, Jenny rose from one of the small tables, swallowing the last of a croissant and dusting off her hands with a napkin. She slung her bag over her shoulder and ambled into formation next to Ellen. As usual Jenny carried her father's old military duffel bag and dressed with her mother's sense of style. Her thigh-length black jacket and slacks were perfectly complemented by her black beret and shining blond hair.

"Nice outfit," Jenny commented with deadpan sarcasm. Nikki flipped her the bird.

"We expecting anyone else?" asked Ellen.

"Jane," answered Nikki tersely. Ellen and Jenny exchanged twin expressions of surprise.

Nikki walked briskly toward the train depot; neither Jenny nor Ellen commented on the pace. Nikki pushed out into the cold air and refused to shiver as the biting wind took aim at her exposed legs. Jane stood below a sign, head swiveling back and forth, apparently trying to read the train schedules. She was dressed in an enormous, full-length, quilted down coat of pale yellow and a bright orange knit cap. Nikki heard Jenny stifle a laugh. Jane did look something like a baby chick—all puffed up and confused. They walked toward Jane and were less than four feet away when Jane finally spotted them. Nikki jerked her head, and a startled Jane scrambled to grab her bags.

"Nice outfit, Nikki," Jane said.

"Speak for yourself," retorted Nikki. "Don't you think that coat's a little bright for a Goth?"

"No one told me it'd be so freaking cold!" exclaimed Jane. "It was all they had at the shop! Besides, not all of us can pull off boots like that."

Nikki glanced suspiciously at Jane, but she was breathlessly draping herself in her carry-on, laptop, backpack, and camera. Her comment had apparently been serious.

"Did you fly into a different airport, Jane?" asked Ellen, puzzled.

"No, I took the train," mumbled Jane, sorting through her bags.

"Took the train from where?" asked Jenny, suddenly noticing the discrepancy.

"Germany," muttered Jane, burrowing farther into her bag.

"Since when does Jane go on assignment?" asked Jenny, and Jane blushed.

"She doesn't," replied Nikki, leading the way to the cab stand. "She's on vacation."

"Vacation!" exclaimed Ellen suspiciously. "What kind of vacation?"

"The kind where I . . ." mumble, mumble, "Voges."

Nikki waved for a cab again. None of this really mattered to her and she knew that it didn't really matter to Jenny and Ellen either. Jenny was going to think it was cool; Ellen would be shocked. They would bicker about it for five minutes and then it would occur to them to ask why they were here and what the plan was.

"You're going to have to speak up," said Ellen. "I'm getting older and it sounded like you said you went to take down Voges, the gun supplier."

"Er, well . . . ," said Jane.

"Jane! That was very dangerous!"

"Way to branch out!" said Jenny cheerfully.

A cab pulled to a halt in front of them and the driver popped the trunk.

"You could have been killed!" said Ellen.

"But I had to," said Jane. "I owed Nikki for my screw-up in Colombia, and it turned out to be very important!"

"Er, speaking of Colombia," said Ellen, looking sheepishly at Jane. "We kind of had to spill the beans to Mrs. M."

"Ellen!" exclaimed Nikki. Jane blanched.

"We didn't tell everything. We just said that we accidentally walked in on Nikki while she was on the phone and we thought that Z'ev might have overheard us talking about Nina Alvarez. We made it a group thing," explained Jenny. Nikki pinched her lips together, dissatisfied. "It's OK, though," said Jenny. "Mrs. M had already guessed as much because of—" Nikki turned just in time to see Ellen giving Jenny "abort" signals.

"Because of what?" asked Jane, oblivious.

"Because Z'ev was already in Colombia," said Nikki.

"No!" exclaimed Jane, horrified.

"We saw him making out on the beach with Nina Alvarez," said Ellen.

"Oh my God," said Jane. "That bastard!"

"From the chatter we picked up it sounded like they were trying to lure Alvarez into making a personal attack on Z'ev. You know how he never leaves the compound without ten guys . . . We figure they were trying to make him angry enough to do something foolish so they could pick him off," explained Jenny.

"And what if his foolish move was to kill Nina?" demanded Nikki, outraged. "What was he thinking? How could Z'ev put her at risk like that?"

"We kept someone on her the whole time," said Jenny reassuringly. "We didn't pull out until they were moving her into protective custody. But he did seem to have things covered."

"I don't believe him!" said Jane, always willing to voice her emotions. "I can't believe he canceled your vacation to go make out with Nina Alvarez! And didn't you tell him it was a secret? And if that was why he went, why not tell you?"

"Yeah, well, all that aside, once Mrs. M saw him, she was pretty sure we'd blown it somewhere," said Ellen.

"Was she really mad?" asked Jane, looking depressed.

"She said we needed a refresher in professionalism. To tell the truth . . ." Ellen hesitated.

"To tell the truth, what?" asked Nikki.

"She seemed glad you and Z'ev had broken up," said Ellen.

Nikki took a deep breath and let it out. What was there to say to something like that?

"OK," said Nikki, then she turned to Jane. She could feel Jenny and Ellen exchanging meaningful looks but ignored them. "Well, I'm glad she let you come in spite of that. What did you find out from Voges?"

"Ooh!" Jane bounced up and down in excitement. "You'll never guess what Voges sold Cano!"

"Oh, right!" said Jenny, slapping her forehead as she dropped her duffel in the cab. "That was the real reason we flew out here. You sent us that contract. Took us forever to decipher it. Had to run it past Mrs. Merrivel to have her fill us in on your case. The long and short of it is that if Kit Masters dies control of his music goes to his management company, which is run by—"

"I was talking here," said Jane.

"But ours is important," said Jenny reasonably.

"So's mine! I got shot at and I had to eat hotel sausages!"

"What do sausages have to do with it?" asked Ellen, lifting her bag into the trunk.

"Brandt," said Nikki, opening the car door. "It's Brandt Dettling."

The girls followed her into the car, Ellen taking the front seat and Jenny and Jane squeezing onto either side of Nikki.

"How'd you know?" asked Ellen, clicking her seat belt on. "Mrs. Merrivel said we had to fly out and tell you immediately."

"A phone call wouldn't have done?" asked Nikki, confused.

"*À où?*" asked the cabbie.

"I told you that was weird," said Jenny. "Why should we fly all the way to France to deliver a message? It was a Merrivel thing. I told you."

"*L'opéra,*" said Nikki, and he nodded.

"Yes, you're very smart," said Ellen, rolling her eyes. "Nikki, just what kind of trouble are you in? Mrs. Merrivel was being very mysterious."

"I have been officially ordered to suspend activities regarding Cano," said Nikki.

"Ah shit," said Jenny.

"You can't stop!" exclaimed Jane. "Because what Voges sold Cano—"

"Well, considering that Cano and Brandt just tried to kill me and Cano is on his way to kill Kit, I can tell you that I sure as hell am not going to suspend all activities."

"Good!" said Jane. "Because it was a bomb."

That stopped the conversation.

"Voges set Cano up with some mercenaries, some guns, and a bomb," Jane said, reiterating.

"Ah, crap," said Ellen. "How big of a bomb?"

"Pretty big," replied Jane, looking worried.

"It's got to be the awards show," said Nikki. "He's going to blow the whole thing. He said there would be a movement and that must be what he's trying to do—make his first statement."

"I'm confused," said Jenny. "I thought this Cano guy just wanted to kill Camille and her family. And I'm still not sure why he wanted to do that . . ."

"Well, back in the day, Camille married Declan, Kit's father, and got him to quit the IRA, and at the same time the IRA stopped associating with Cano. Cano blamed Camille for the separation and when Declan arranged a sort of peace summit, Cano tried to kill both of them. Camille thought Duncan, Declan's brother, had betrayed them to Cano and blamed him for Declan's death, so she told him to stay away from Kit. But he really wasn't to blame, so he came back and has been secretly working as Kit's bodyguard for the last five years. Meanwhile, Cano thinks all of them betrayed the revolutionary cause, so he wants to kill Kit to get revenge on Camille and make a terrorist statement. And then he wants to kill Duncan and Camille, you know, just to kill them."

There was silence in the cab.

"This is better than *One Life to Live*! Why didn't you call me earlier?" exclaimed Ellen. "We've been running training missions and sitting on our asses in Colombia. And you know I can't understand a damn word of their soap operas!"

The girls burst out laughing.

"That's what you do when you go on vacation, isn't it?" asked Jenny. "You lock yourself in your apartment and watch all the soap operas."

"Actually, I usually go visit my daughters. And I mean, I love my grandchildren, but after the twentieth poopy diaper, shooting people starts to sound like a wonderful idea. My eldest daughter actually said the words 'It must be so exciting for you to get out of the house.'"

"What do they think you do?"

"I don't know. It's possible they think I sit at home waiting for them to call."

"Don't they notice that you're never home when they call?"

"Well, I tell them I screen my calls and the messages get forwarded to me, so I just call them back from wherever."

"You mean they don't know you're out of the country?" asked Nikki, slightly shocked. It had never occurred to her to not tell Nell where she was going.

"I don't think so." Ellen shrugged. "It's one of the benefits of living four states away. They don't usually pop 'round for a visit unexpectedly."

"I hope I'm as cool as you when I grow up," said Jenny, and Ellen chuckled.

"Well, you're a long way from that, but we're getting distracted from the point."

"Yes," said Jenny, "the point is that you should call us much earlier when you're having this much fun."

"Actually," said Ellen, "I think the point was that you were going to tell us the plan."

"Right," said Jane, "the plan."

Nikki looked at their expectant faces and felt a sinking feeling in her stomach. She probably should have figured that out on the cab ride to the airport.

"The plan . . . right. I was going to tell you the plan." Nikki racked her brain. "Well, the plan is . . ."

PARIS XV

Assault on the Opera

"Do you really think this is going to work?" asked Ellen. The four women stood at the foot of the broad stairs that led up to the Paris opera house.

"Well, since Kit isn't answering his phone and security is refusing to let me in, it's pretty much going to have to work," replied Nikki. "Besides, it's a concert. Universal laws apply. There's bound to be a scalper. As long as we have cash, then someone will have tickets."

"Uh," said Jane, clearing her throat, "does anyone actually have cash? I've got a few Euros, but I didn't stop at the cash machine before I left. Kind of hard with the car chase and whatnot."

"I've got about seventy-five," said Jenny.

"Me too," said Ellen.

"You guys!" said Nikki. "That's going to get us about one ticket." Nikki sighed and adjusted her plan. "OK, one of us goes in the front. The rest of us will find some other way in."

"Aren't you like Mrs. Kit Masters now? Can't you just walk us into the back?" asked Jenny, sounding annoyed.

"I told you, the regular tour guys aren't working this. I don't know any of the crew here."

"Who gets the ticket?" asked Jane, skipping the argument and moving to the pertinent question.

"Ellen," said Jenny and Nikki at the same time.

"Right," agreed Ellen. "Ante up, girls." Ellen held out her hand, and Nikki handed over the remains of her fifty-five euros. Jane chipped in fifty in bills and a handful more in coins, and Jenny handed over her seventy-five. Ellen pushed the money into one uniform stack. "All right, off you go." Ellen waved them away and climbed the stairs toward the door.

"Why Ellen?" asked Jane as they walked away.

"The mom factor," replied Jenny. "She gets away with a lot just by looking like someone who gives good hugs and knows where they keep the comfort food. She can talk her way past people we'd have to club over the head."

"But we're pretty girls!" declared Jane, shocked.

"Moms trump pretty girls every time," answered Nikki, leading them down the sidewalk toward the artists' entrance. "Everyone knows pretty girls can be evil." She stared at the roped-off area, waiting fans, bustling delivery vans, and security guys. "So that's where we want to be."

"Well, that is just going to be about as easy as skinning a frog."

"I can't tell if that was sarcasm," said Jane. "I don't know how hard it is to skin frogs."

"I think I recognize those security guys from this morning; they might remember me," said Nikki.

"But they won't remember either of us," said Jenny.

"What are you thinking? Deliveries or security?"

"Catering," said Jenny, and Nikki nodded. "I'll take Jane with me."

"Take Jane where?" asked Jane. "I'm confused. What are we catering?"

"It's a surprise," said Jenny, smiling her beauty-queen smile.

"Just go with her, Jane," said Nikki. "I'll meet you at the door in ten?" Jenny was already nodding her agreement as she walked away. Jane trailed behind, casting a lost look over her shoulder. Nikki began to work her way through the crowd of fans toward the security gate. The crowd was packed thick and was about equal parts girls and boys. The fans of various artists had grouped together. The Kit Masters fans wore devil's horns and seemed to be bullying the Craig David fans.

She was nearly to the door when she saw Biter heading her way. Nikki ducked her head, but it was too late; the teenager was already waving vigorously.

"Nikki!" exclaimed the English girl, drawing near. "We were looking for you! Gladys said you'd be here." She turned and waved to someone else in the crowd; Vampirella and Tubby hurried over.

"Kind of in a hurry here, girls," said Nikki, sparing a minute to marvel that Vampirella's real name was Gladys. No wonder the poor girl wore so much makeup.

"We know!" said Gladys, taking over. "And we were on our way in, but then . . ."

"But then what?" asked Nikki, suddenly afraid.

"Those men. The ones who were chasing you. We saw them go inside. We tried to warn security, but they just laughed at us and said they were with Kit Masters's private security force. Which is absolutely ridiculous!" the girl exclaimed, sounding outraged. "Anyone who knows anything about Kit knows he only travels with one bodyguard. He doesn't want a whole squad!" She sniffed in fierce disapproval.

"Do you have the tour pass with you?" asked Nikki, focusing on her immediate issue. Biter flashed the tour pass briefly from her pocket, keeping it mostly covered and looking around nervously. Through the fence, Nikki could see Jenny wearing a burgundy catering jacket and pushing a heavy cart toward the entrance.

"All right, give me the pass." A security guard was making a beeline for Jenny as she wheeled the cart up the ramp. "And as soon as I'm at the gate, do you think you two can start a ruckus?"

"What sort of ruckus?" asked Sandy.

"Anything big that'll draw attention." Tanya looked nervous, but Gladys nodded.

"No problem."

"Great. Leave your names and numbers at the ticket office. I'll make sure that you guys get tickets for this, I promise."

"We just want Kit to be safe," said Sandy proudly.

"Me too," said Nikki, but she was privately amazed at the girl's fervent love for someone she'd never met. She draped the pass over her neck and approached the gate.

"Hey," she said, flashing the pass at the guard. "Let me in. I do makeup for Kit Masters."

"I'll bet you do something for . . ." the guard started to say, eyeing her short skirt. Behind him Nikki could see Jenny arguing with another guard.

"Craig David does not sing better than Kit Masters!" screamed Biter from somewhere back in the crowd. There was an immediate uproar as the Kit Masters fans went after the Craig David faction.

"Ah hell," said the security guard. "Inside quick," he added, waving Nikki inside the gate. The other security guards were running toward the fence. Outside the fence the Craig David fans were taking a pummeling; she saw Tanya, Gladys, and Sandy sprinting away and smiled. She was going to have to get all their names and put them on the Carrie Mae watch list. Those girls had potential.

Jenny was pushing her cart into the building as fast as possible. Nikki caught up to her and held open the door. They found a deserted hallway and parked the cart.

"OK, out you come," said Jenny, sliding open the cart panel. Jane peered out, swaddled in her down coat. She had been packed into the cart like breakable china in bubble wrap.

"I think I'm going to need some help," said Jane. Nikki pulled on Jane's lapels until she burst forth onto the floor.

"Mazel tov," said Jenny. "Quick, smack her on the bottom."

"We are infiltrating a highly secured facility," said Jane primly. "I hardly think now is the time to be making jokes."

"Well, I'd hate to break with tradition," said Nikki. "Come on, we don't have much time. Cano's already inside."

"How'd you find that out?" asked Jane, shouldering her bag.

"Same way I started that riot out front. Girl power."

Jane made a face, and even Jenny winced a bit.

"I hate that slogan. It's so incredibly lame, and it reduces us all to some sort of unadult status. We are women, damn it. Subcategorizing our power implies that it is a lesser power." Jane straightened her coat with an irritated jerk.

"Jeez, read many self-help books lately?" asked Jenny.

Nikki interrupted before Jane could reply. "Actually, these really are girls. Fans of Kit's. Got my clothes from them."

"So they all hate you is what you're saying?" asked Jenny.

"Don't start," said Nikki, punching the button for the elevator. "Besides," she said taking off her hat and fluffing her hair in the reflective panel of the door, "they thought I looked cool."

"You do," said Jane. "You don't think she looks good?" she asked, turning to Jenny as the elevator closed them inside its echoing belly.

"I don't think we have time to discuss fashion," said Jenny. "We are infiltrating a highly secured facility . . ." Her voice trailed off as the elevator slowed and then stopped. The elevator went black and then after a moment, the backup lights came on with a flickering fluorescent hum.

"That's not a good sign," said Jane.

"I agree," murmured Jenny.

"Well, it's nice to know we all agree on something," said Nikki.

They all watched the ceiling intently, as if they could somehow see up the elevator shaft. After a moment, Jenny got up on the side rails and popped open the elevator hatch, pulling herself easily out into the elevator shaft. Nikki and Jane heard a bit of stomping around, and then Jenny's face appeared in the hole. Her soft blond hair fell forward into the elevator and swung gently around her face, tantalizing in its randomness, like some sort of willful cat toy.

"We're about two floors down from where we need to be, but there's a ladder. It shouldn't be a problem."

"Good," said Nikki, nodding. "Jane, up you go."

"Uh," said Jane, "I think I might need a boost." Jenny sighed and stopped just short of an eye roll. Nikki made no comment but simply cupped her hands for Jane to step into.

"Give me your hand," commanded Jenny, reaching down.

Nikki heaved upward as Jane stepped into her hands and Jenny reached down, grasping Jane's arms and pulling upward. There was a brief scramble at the edge of the hatch, and Jane's feet disappeared into the darkness.

"Your turn, Nikki," said Jenny, looking in. Nikki tossed up Jane's bag, which Jenny neatly caught. Nikki jumped upward and caught the edge of the hatch. Hanging for a moment on the edge, Nikki wondered, briefly, why pull-ups never seemed to get any easier.

"Will someone tell me why I seem to spend half my life dangling off things?" asked Nikki, managing to pull herself onto the roof of the elevator and still keep her knees together.

"Hardly half," answered Jane. "It's probably less than one half of one percent."

"Thank you, Jane," said Nikki sarcastically.

"It just seems like half when you're hanging there," said Jenny distractedly, looking up the elevator shaft. "What do you think, Nikki?"

"I think it seems like forever when I'm hanging there."

"No, I mean what about the elevator? Did it break or was it jammed?"

"Oh." Nikki looked at the cable and brakes. "No, the way the power went out? I think it was turned off."

"Why would someone turn off the elevator?" asked Jane.

"To make it more difficult for people to get up or down when something goes wrong."

"Well, we'd better hurry if we want to be in the nick of time; let's get moving. After you, chief," said Jenny, gesturing to the ladder set into the wall of the elevator shaft.

"Er, no," said Nikki. Jane and Jenny stared at her. "I think I should go last." Nikki tried to pull her skirt down a little lower.

"O-kay," said Jenny, pulling out the syllables. There was more staring and Nikki broke under the pressure.

"I'm not wearing any underwear, OK!"

"In that skirt?" asked Jane, shocked. Jenny snickered.

"I didn't plan it this way," responded Nikki, outraged. "I just got caught—"

"With your pants down?" interjected Jenny.

Nikki sighed. "Coming out of the shower," said Nikki, finishing her sentence. "There were these guys with guns in the hotel room. They chased me out of the hotel. I had to swap the girls a tour pass for some clothes."

"Why were guys with guns in your hotel room?" asked Jane.

"When are guys with guns not in her hotel room?" said Jenny.

"It wasn't my hotel room," said Nikki impatiently. "It was Kit's. They were there to kill him."

"She was naked in the rock star's hotel room," said Jenny, looking significantly at Jane.

"She was using his shower," answered Jane with a nod.

"Oh for God's sake!" shouted Nikki, and then ducked as the echo reverberated around their heads. "Will one of you just climb the damn ladder?" she whispered.

Jenny grinned impudently and started up the ladder.

"Dudda-da-dum," said Jane, giving a shimmy and singing the opening bars to "The Stripper." Jenny giggled and Nikki sighed.

"My friends," muttered Nikki. "My very dear friends."

PARIS XVI

Fork in the Road

"Ah crap," said Nikki, pulling herself through the heavy, wedged-open elevator doors. Down the hall she saw Duncan run past.

"The dressing rooms are up that way," she said, pointing to the right. "Jenny, go find Kit and the band. Get them the hell out of Dodge if you can. Jane, go find the control booth and get the elevator turned back on. I'm going after Duncan. I'll catch up with you." She was already running as she spoke.

"Duncan!" she yelled, catching a glimpse of him ducking down a hallway that led up to the offices.

"Duncan!" she yelled again, rounding the corner and slamming into his back. They both stumbled and caught their balance. Then Nikki saw the reason for his abrupt halt. Camille was waiting for them, a gun in one black-leather-gloved hand. She was wearing a beautiful black suit and mile-high stilettos. Her makeup managed to hit just the right note between mystery woman and all business. She looked exactly how Nikki knew she ought to look.

"Ah crap," said Nikki again. Duncan didn't say anything but shot her a look of frowning disapproval. Apparently, "ah crap" lacked appreciation for the emotional drama playing out before her.

"Nikki," snarled Camille. "I should have known you were responsible for this mess!"

"We don't have time for this," snapped Nikki.

"What did you do, Matthew?" hissed Camille. "Betray Kit to Cano, just like you did your brother?"

"I did not betray Declan," said Duncan evenly. "Why won't you believe that Declan went to Cano on his own?"

"Liar!" shouted Camille.

"Dude, we do not have time for this. Kit is in danger." Nikki knew it was a gratuitous use of Surfer Dude, but Camille, with her perfect British accent and perfect lady-spy outfit, made her feel Keanu-ish.

"Don't have time?" repeated Camille, the gun never wavering in her hand. "Like you care about Kit. You used him for bait. I read Astriz's preliminary report. You were waiting for Cano to take another shot at him!" Nikki noticed that under the perfect application of what had to be false eyelashes, she looked pale and pinched. "I should have known." Disgust dripped from her voice. "Partners follow partners. You're a traitor, just like Valerie Robinson."

Nikki didn't stop to think, she just pushed herself forward. Forgot about the gun, forgot about Kit, forgot about everything. Just walked in on Camille until they were standing inches apart. She could smell the peppermints and coffee on the older woman's breath.

"Say that again." She was dimly aware that she had curled her fingers into fists. Camille took a few steps back, trying to bring the gun up between them. Nikki smacked her hand down with an angry slap. "Valerie Robinson was twice the agent you'll ever be. Don't you come at me with your stupid accusations. I do my job." She advanced again, and Camille backpedaled another step. "Hell, I'm doing your job. And if you were half as smart as you think you are, you'd know that."

Behind them a door sprang open and rebounded off the wall. Nikki glanced over her shoulder, really hoping to see Jenny. Instead, she saw Ferret framed in the doorway, balancing an enormous shotgun on one hip like a big-game hunter.

"Well, look who it is," said Ferret. "Pretty girl and Matthew O'Deirdan. I heard you were dead."

"Gentza?" said Duncan, and Nikki heard the breath catch in his throat.

"He's with Cano," said Nikki.

"Ah crap," said Duncan.

"Oh, don't pretend you didn't know!" yelled Camille. "You brought him here to kill Kit!"

"I'm not going to kill Kit!" Duncan yelled back.

"Well, I am," said Ferret, and raised the shotgun to his shoulder. Nikki tackled Camille as Duncan dove for an open office door. Ferret fired off a blast; the sound was deafening in the enclosed space.

Camille scrambled across the hall and into an office. Ferret fired after her, showering her in wood chips and plaster dust. In the hallway, Nikki spun around on her back, grabbed Camille's gun, and fired six shots dead center into Ferret's torso. Ferret looked down dumbly and collapsed to his knees, then went face-first into the floor, like a building imploding.

"Come on," yelled Duncan, reappearing to pick her up bodily off the floor and pulling her with him. Nikki dropped Camille's gun.

"What about Camille?" asked Nikki, looking back over her

shoulder at Camille, who was already reloading the abandoned weapon.

"Forget her!" answered Duncan without stopping. "We need to find Kit!"

"Don't you go near Kit!" screamed Camille after them.

"Is she insane?" asked Nikki, trotting to keep up with Duncan's long strides.

"She has her good points," said Duncan, sliding to a stop at a corridor junction and peering cautiously around the corner. "But listening to reason isn't one of them. Besides"—he dashed across the hallway and Nikki followed—"she feels guilty."

"For what!?"

"She broke in on Cano and Declan's meeting. Rumor has it, that's why it went south. Personally I think Cano would have killed Declan anyway. It doesn't matter, but if you were Camille, wouldn't you always wonder?"

"It's been twenty-five years. How long can guilt last?" panted Nikki.

"A lifetime and more, if you believe the priests," said Duncan.

Nikki shook her head. "It has to stop somewhere," she muttered.

Duncan shrugged. "Kit should be going to the stage about now. We've got to get him out of here before Cano finds him."

"Or Brandt."

"Brandt?"

"He found Cano through the hate mail Cano was sending Kit. He's paying Cano to kill Kit, with the bonus that he'll get to kill you, too."

"The past always comes back to bite you in the ass," Duncan said, leaning against the wall and looking sick. Nikki shrugged; what little past she had was well behind her.

"Let's keep moving," she said, leading the way into the back-stage area. "We want to find Kit before anyone else does."

"Too late," said Cano.

He had the director, the director's assistant, and Ewart, the donut-eating stage tech, all lined up against the wall at gunpoint. The assistant was cowering in the director's shadow. The director, on the other hand, was puffed up in outrage. Ewart, meanwhile, was trying to dig through the wall with his shoulder blades. Flanking Cano were three more thugs and Mongoose.

"By now Gentza and his team have your precious rock star and are waiting for my signal."

"Gentza's dead," said Duncan calmly.

"You're bluffing!"

"Call him yourself," Duncan said, taking a step forward. Nikki faded to the right, trying to get closer to the large cement pillars and cut the angle on the gunmen. Cano hit a button on his phone and it burbled just like in the commercials.

"Gentza!" Cano paused, waiting for a response. "Gentza," he snapped again.

"Oh, I'm sorry," said Duncan, edging forward again. "Looks like ya lost your man."

Nikki looked around for a weapon. The only thing within reach was a table full of canapés and champagne. Nikki wrapped her hand around a magnum and dropped it discreetly to her side. Timing was going to be important here; she had to wait for the right moment. From the stage area the sounds of a restless audience could be heard, then the sounds of ragged cheering.

"Hold it right there!" yelled Camille, charging into the room. There was a burst of gunfire from one of the more nervous weasels, and the room erupted in confusion. Nikki tossed her bottle of champagne, flinging it end over end at the nearest gunman, who went down like a three-inch kewpie doll. One of the men charged, and she upended the ice bucket on his head, then spun, slamming him into a concrete pillar. Cano and Duncan were locked in a grudge match and Camille was fending off a large brute with a neck thicker than his head. Mongoose fired his TEC-9 at Nikki as she ducked behind the pillar. Diving for the ladder directly in front of her, Nikki pulled herself up the rungs, heading for the gangway above the stage.

"Oh no you don't," snarled Mongoose, catching at her foot as she reached the top rung. Nikki stomped on his fingers and he fell the next few rungs, yelping. She gained the gangway and raced toward the other side of the stage, intent on getting to Kit before any of Cano's men did. But looking down she realized it was too late.

Down below, Jenny was trying to lead the band across the stage, but she was hampered by three more black-clad thugs. Nikki looked around, hoping to spot something useful. The stage was framed by pulley-controlled curtains, which gave her an idea—the only problem being that Mongoose was swinging a bony fist at her face. Nikki slipped the punch, coming in with a hook to the gut. The gangway swayed with their movement, throwing them into a tangle. She caught a blow in the stomach, which pissed her off. She threw a flurry of punches, felt his nose crunch slightly, felt her knuckles sting as they connected with brow bone, felt the weird shift of flesh as her fist raked his lips across his teeth. Then she stuffed a front kick into his chest and watched him stumble back, making the wheezing, gasping sound that told Nikki she had knocked all the air out of him. Nikki cocked her head to the right and considered her next move.

Her next kick sent Mongoose crashing through the guardrail. Flailing, he grabbed for one of the ropes and began a rapid descent to the stage floor. She watched the other end of the rope, weighted with a large sandbag, rise toward her. Nikki took a step back and then launched herself off the gangway. There was the heart-stopping moment of free fall, then she was fighting for a clean hold on the sandbag. Everything balanced for a moment on the pulley and then slowly she began to sink down toward the floor. There was a jerking stop, and looking up, she saw Mongoose wedged into the pulley. Nikki dropped the last six feet, knowing she looked cool as she landed in a crouch with a huge flapping of black coat, only remembering about the underwear issue a second later. She took a peek at the front row, hoping she hadn't just given someone a total *Basic Instinct* moment, but they were all staring at Kit and the band as they fought their way across the stage.

Jenny was doing her best, but every time she made progress against their adversaries, Hammond would trip, or Burg would try to tackle the bad guy and miss. The melee swayed in her direction, and Nikki spun around on the ball of one foot, sweeping out her other leg and wiping out one of Cano's men. Burg let out a huge Tarzan bellow and led the band in a mass tackle. Jenny dove for the one on the left, leaving just Kit and the remaining villain. Kit's style of fighting was schoolyard vicious—all elbows, knees, and biting. It was effective for football scraps and barroom brawls, but he was outweighed and outmatched. Nikki picked her moment, waited until Kit was shoved free, and then tapped his partner on the shoulder. He spun around and ran his chin into Nikki's fist. His wore an expression of surprise as he crumpled.

"Come on!" yelled Jenny, charging toward the wings.

"Not that way!" yelled Nikki. But it was too late. The band and Kit and Jenny were heading straight for Cano.

PARIS XVII

Basque Standoffs

The band had scattered, returning to their natural state of helplessness. The director was still yelling. Ewart and the assistant were back to cowering. Jenny had found a gun. She and Camille were aiming at Cano. But it didn't matter because Cano had his gun pointed at Duncan's head.

"I'm getting out of here. You're going to put down your weapons, or I'm going to put a bullet in his ear."

"Go ahead," said Camille coolly.

"No!" shouted Kit from behind the pillar, shaking off the restraining hands of Burg and Richie. "No, Mum, give him whatever he wants. Just don't let him hurt Duncan!"

"Forget about Duncan," snarled Camille without taking her eyes off Cano.

"He's saved my life," yelled Kit. "I am not forgetting him."

Startled, Camille looked over at Kit. Cano seized the opportunity; his gun swung away from Duncan and aimed at Camille.

"No!" yelled Duncan, wrenching at Cano's arm. The pair

wavered for a moment, struggling with the gun, then there was a muffled pop from somewhere above them in the scaffolding as Ellen did her job, and Cano reeled back, gun still in his hand. Duncan reached for the gun, but Cano was already pulling the trigger. There was a flash and Duncan crashed to the floor. Camille screamed and Nikki snatched the gun out of her hand, charging Cano. She brought the gun butt down across his face just as he looked up.

The blow split his eyebrow and sent him stumbling backward, blood streaming down his face. Nikki kicked him in the gut, sitting him down hard, and put the barrel between his eyes.

Cano looked up at her, and she stared into his eyes. In her peripheral vision, she could see his fingers tightening around his gun. "Do you really think I won't pull this trigger?" she asked, pushing the gun until it tapped against his skull. "I don't even have to aim at this distance."

She pushed the thought of what she would do if he kept moving to the back of her mind, but the question flittered around the back of her brain, trying to make its way to the front. Slowly, his hands rose into the air. She kicked the gun out of the way. "Roll onto your stomach and put your hands behind your head," she commanded. The words were rote. They were out of her training script, but she felt a disconnect in her head. All she could think was that behind her Duncan was dead. The knowledge loomed over her conscious mind like the monster behind the door, but there were a lot of monster back there. She didn't dare turn around to look.

"Somebody bring me something to tie him up with," she demanded.

"Here," said Jenny, producing a pair of handcuffs and tossing them to Nikki.

Nikki rolled Cano over and shoved him against the wall. The director was screaming obscenities in hoarse howls of rage about how *his* show was ruined. Acting with a decisiveness that Nikki had to admire, Camille kneed him in the balls and went to help Duncan. Kit and the band scuttled after her. The band was spouting piffle and pretending they weren't scared. It was all very British.

"It's Jane," said Jenny, handing Nikki her cell phone.

"Go," said Nikki bluntly, taking the phone.

"I got the elevators and power back up, but I ran into a slight problem," answered Jane. "Well, first there was some girl named Angela."

"She's the tour manager. I hope you beat the crap out of her."

"Well, I kind of did, actually," said Jane, sounding slightly embarrassed. "And then I locked her in a supply closet. But she's not the problem."

Cano was starting to move and Nikki kicked him.

"What's the problem?" said Nikki to Jane. "Will someone call an ambulance?" she said to the band, covering her phone speaker.

"Nikki, you're not listening," protested Jane.

"I'm listening, Jane," she said, turning her back on the gabbling voices. "What's the problem?"

"I found the bomb."

"Shit," said Nikki, glancing around at the band. "Call Ellen, get her to your location. I'll call you back. 'Kay? Bye." She flipped off the phone and shot a glance at Jenny, then looked back at Cano. Jenny nodded. Grabbing him by the collar, they dragged him behind a pillar.

"Talk to us about the bomb, Antonio," said Nikki.

Cano smiled. "The world is finally going to remember me," he said. Ellen's bullet had gone through his shoulder, and Nikki shoved her finger into the wound. Cano gasped in pain. Out of the corner of her eye Nikki saw Jenny shift nervously.

"I don't really care about you, Antonio," said Nikki. "I care about a whole building full of innocent people."

"Innocent?" spat Cano. "I see no innocents here. All I see are willing participants in a bankrupt culture that ignores its obligations. That culture of globalization—a culture of homogenized, pasteurized slaves—is creating a world of dead souls. People need to remember—"

"Remember what?" snapped Nikki, wiping her finger on his tie. "That evil men can kill their children? Pretty sure they already know. Are you going to tell me about the bomb or am I going to shoot you?"

"Carrie Mae doesn't kill," said Cano, smiling smugly.

"You've been in prison for a while, so I'll forgive your ignorance, but guess what? Times have changed." She leveled the gun at him and waited.

"Nikki," said Jenny sotto voce. "Not really sure this is a good idea."

"It doesn't matter," said Cano. "I'm prepared to die for my beliefs. You kill me or the bomb kills me—it is all the same to me. My manifesto is already on its way to the news service. I will be heard, even if I die."

"Nikki!" hissed Jenny again. Nikki relaxed her hand.

"Jenny, what's the number for that reporter you dated a while ago? The one with the British AP news."

"Toni?" repeated Jenny, looking confused. "What for?"

"I'm going to call Toni and I'm going to let the world know that there is a bomb in the Paris opera house that will strike a blow for al-Qaeda."

Cano struggled to sit upright, rage coloring his face.

"He won't give me what I want, so I'm going to make damn sure he doesn't get what he wants," said Nikki, smiling. "Kit!" she yelled, looking around the pillar. "Give me your phone!" Kit tossed it over without looking up from Duncan.

"They won't believe you," said Cano, glaring.

"Sure they will. What sounds more realistic? A relic of the Basque separatist movement killing a bunch of Parisians or al-Qaeda doing what it's been doing for years?" She dialed Jane and waited for her to pick up.

"Looks like Toni's number is still in my phone," said Jenny. "I'm dialing now."

"How do I defuse the bomb, Cano?" asked Nikki, poking at his shoulder wound. "Talk to me, Jane," she said as Jane picked up.

"Um . . . ," said Jane.

"You're all going to die," Cano spit out, thrashing in the handcuffs.

"Yes, but it doesn't have to be today. If you go back to prison there's still a chance you can make your statement. If you let this thing ride, it may be that we can stop the bomb or maybe we can't, but either way you are not getting credit for it."

Cano ground his teeth.

"It's ringing," said Jenny.

"Jane?" demanded Nikki.

"Uh, best guess says it's either the green wire or the red wire. I was hoping you would have more information?" Jane said, ending on an optimistic note.

"Hey, Toni," said Jenny cheerfully. "Guess who? Yeah, it's been a while, but I've got a story you might be interested in."

"Green or red, Cano?" asked Nikki, and Cano swallowed hard. "I speak six languages; I can be a very convincing Muslim terrorist over the phone. No one is going to read your manifesto, let alone believe it, by the time I'm done."

"Green," he said at last with a violent shrug.

"Red wire," said Nikki to Jane, and Cano jerked forward in fury. There was silence over the phone and Jenny watched her with wide eyes.

"Problem solved," said Jane cheerfully. "Thanks, Nikki. Gendarmes and paramedics are on their way; should I call anyone else?"

Nikki sighed. "Probably ought to alert the Paris branch; they're going to be pissed as hell, but we're going to need their help."

"Got it," said Jane, and hung up.

"I'm going to kill you," said Cano. "I'm going to kill both of you and your families and anyone you ever loved."

"I'll keep that in mind," said Nikki, pushing her way off the floor.

"How'd you know he was going to lie about the wire?" asked Jenny.

"I would have if I were him," said Nikki. "We hadn't told anyone about the al-Qaeda thing yet; clip the green wire, the bomb blows, he wins."

"What if you'd been wrong?" asked Jenny, looking horrified. Nikki shrugged; she didn't want to think about that right now. They dragged Cano back around the pole to where the band was still arguing about Kit's family situation. Camille had bandaged Duncan's shoulder, and she and Kit looked up at Nikki with twin expressions of concern.

"He needs a doctor," Kit said.

"The paramedics are on their way," said Nikki.

"Um, I say," said Richie, interrupting. "We just want to be clear. Your mum is a spy and your father was IRA? And your bodyguard is your uncle?"

"Declan was quitting," said Duncan and Camille at the same time, then exchanged rueful glances.

The director had recovered enough to crawl toward his headset, which was making little tiny yelling noises.

"Mum is with the security department of Carrie Mae. Duncan is my uncle and used to be with the IRA. He's been masquerading as my bodyguard to protect me."

"Holy shit," said Hammond, mopping sweat off his brow. "I'm going to have a bestseller."

"I need to stop smoking hash," said Richie.

"Kit's mom's kind of hot," said Burg.

"Shut up, Burg," said Holly, and smacked him in the back of the head.

"Great!" interjected the director, clawing his way up a table leg and onto his feet. "That's all taken care of then. You"—he grabbed Burg out of the middle of the group and threw him toward the stage—"out onstage."

Burg went with the shove, tumbling in a somersault out onto the stage. There was a burst of applause.

"I don't think the instruments are plugged in," said Ewart, coming out from under a table.

"You two next." Richie and Hammond went flying out after Burg.

"I can't play," said Kit. "I have to go to the hospital with Duncan." He stopped and turned to Nikki. "I don't know what to do. I can't play. Everything's different." He shook his head, clearly confused.

"You've got to play," said Duncan, opening his eyes. "That's what we did all this for, wasn't it? So you could play?"

"Well, that's a bloody stupid reason," answered Kit, looking shocked. "Forget about it. I'll go with you."

The director was reaching for Holly.

"You want to spend some time on the floor again?" she demanded.

"Right, right, whatever, just move!" hissed the director. Holly looked at Kit with a shrug and walked onto the stage under her own power. Kit looked around the room, at Duncan and Camille, at the pleading director, and finally at Nikki.

"We'll be here when you get done," said Duncan.

"We'll be at the hospital," corrected Camille.

"What they said," said the director, and began to push Kit toward the stage.

"Mr. Masters," said Ewart, interjecting hurriedly. "Maybe you don't remember me . . ."

"Sure, you're Ewart, you handle the mechanical stage," said Kit numbly, still leaning against the pushing hands of the director. Ewart blinked; he hadn't been prepared to have his name remembered.

"Yes, only Mr. Dettling fired me, because of that little snafu the other night. And I swear that wasn't my fault! But Nikki said that if I came here I could talk to you and maybe—"

"Now?" screamed the director. "You're asking about your job now? My entire career is on the line and you are worried about your job!"

Kit looked at the director and Ewart and then at Nikki.

"What do I do?" he asked.

"Whatever you want," she said. "Same as always."

"Damn free will," Kit said. Then he nodded and walked away from the director so abruptly that he nearly fell over.

"The instruments still aren't set up," said Ewart, pointing to the disconnected cables that ran from the sound system to the instruments.

"Well, go fix them!" screamed the director.

"You'd better go," said Nikki as Ewart looked to her for further instruction. "You wanted your job back, and the band can't play without instruments."

"Right," said Ewart with a startled nod. "The show must go on." Crouching over, he ran out onto the stage; he was going to save the day.

Kit walked out onto the stage to a smatter of applause. The audience had been confused by the stage fight, uncertain if it was real or part of the entertainment. Kit looked at his band; they stared back in pie-eyed panic. The crowd was murmuring restlessly. Kit looked back at Nikki, who grinned encouragingly.

"Well," said Kit, walking to the mic and adjusting the height. "Needless to say, this isn't going like it did in rehearsal." That got a nervous laugh from the audience. Ewart ran out onstage and dove under the drum kit to fiddle with some cords. "Um . . ." Kit looked back at Burg, who shook his head and shrugged. "Sorry about this, but things got a bit screwy backstage. I think someone just tried to kill me."

He hadn't intended it to be, but his deadpan delivery and cockeyed confusion made the line funny, and there was a wave of snickers from the audience. A squirt of white noise came from the speakers.

"Almost there," muttered Ewart, running by.

"So," said Kit, turning to the audience again and smiling brilliantly. "I've been on the road with these guys for about half a tour now, and some for more than that, and we still don't have a band name. Richie over there"—he pointed to Richie, who strummed a soft chord on his guitar; the speakers picked up halfway through and Richie turned his test chord into a melodic riff—"thinks we should be the Purple Weasels."

The audience cheered. The band began to test their instruments. Ewart was running back and forth like a chicken with its head cut off, and the next instrument to be heard distinctly was the keyboard.

"Hammond, our resident socialist, thinks we should be the

Communist Synthesizers." Hammond's fingers ran down the keyboard in a waterfall of notes and settled into a funk rhythm to the cheers and hoots of the audience.

"The eternally lovely Holly, our bass player and backbone, thinks we should be the Rhythm Method." Holly worked the strings in a *bumpa-bumpa-bumpa* funk that moved up down and then settled down to match Hammond. The crowd roared their approval.

"And Burg . . . What were you shooting for? Dead Mimes?"

"The Egregious Philibins!" yelled Burg, and hit the skins with a flourish.

"So we've got the Purple Weasels"—cheers and a screaming riff—"the Communist Synthesizers"—louder cheers, and Hammond let fly with hands like Jerry Lee Lewis—"the Rhythm Method"—the crowd went wild as Holly ran and slid to center stage on her knees, rocking the bass line—"and the Egregious Philibins!" Burg nearly drowned out the cheers with a thunderous fusillade on the drums. The band had clicked in now, music had filled in the holes dug by fear, and they had started to jam.

"But I bet you want to know what I want. Do ya?" Kit was leaning out over the crowd now. "You want to know what I want?" He almost sang the words over Holly's bass line, and the crowd screamed. "Do you want to know what I want?" He reached out to the crowd, and they reached back.

"We are the Devil's Horde!" Kit threw his fist up in the air and struck a pose as the Horde rocked into "Devil May Care." The crowd was on their feet and screaming.

"Did anybody clock that?" asked Nikki, looking around. "That was complete disaster to absolute miracle in like two point six minutes."

"I want his children," said the director fervently.

"You do find the sexiest guys," said Jenny, shaking her head.

PARIS XVIII

After 2+2 Is 1+1

Kit was rocking into his second song when the paramedics arrived, with Jane and Angela following close behind. Jane had a metal briefcase in one hand and was dragging Angela by the elbow.

"Where's Ellen?" asked Jane breathlessly.

"Hopefully, she's hunting down Brandt," said Nikki. She eyed Cano for signs of suspicious movement, but he had lapsed into sullen silence. "Where's the bomb?"

Jane raised the heavy-looking briefcase in response. "The police and the Paris branch are both on their way. I brought her along; didn't know what to do with her."

"Sit her next to Cano," said Nikki, "and can you call down to security and make sure that the police are expected?"

"I should have known you'd be behind all this," snarled Angela.

"Isn't that my line?" asked Nikki, confused. She shoved Angela down next to Cano.

"This is your fault!" screeched Angela. "Brandt is going to destroy you."

"Apparently she didn't know about the bomb," said Jane, watching Angela with a skeptical expression.

"Bomb?" repeated Angela, looking at Cano and at the rest of the bodies. "Brandt said it was just supposed to be Kit—to save Faustus."

"Brandt is a moron," said Cano, and Angela made an angry squeak.

"Take care of security, Jane," said Nikki, shaking her head.

"I'm on it," answered Jane. "You," she snapped as she snatched a headset off the assistant director, and he jerked to attention. "What are the security codes?"

As Jane walked away, Nikki looked around the backstage area. Jenny was making sure Cano's gang was well secured, and the director was obliviously stomping among the bodies, shouting directions into his headset. For the moment everything seemed under control. Nikki leaned against a pillar and waited for the next emergency.

Svenka arrived next. Throwing off her scarf and exchanging kisses with Nikki, she looked positively delighted.

"Oh, Nikki, this is marvelous! I saw Camille on the way out—she said she would call Madame Feron and clear everything up. And here you have Cano! You are superb! I rushed to be the first on the scene. I wanted to help!"

"Yeah, well, I'm going to need some help once the police arrive. Can you help with that?" Nikki looked hopefully at Svenka, who beamed.

"Of course! I was a law student before I was Carrie Mae. I know how to handle things!"

"Good," said Nikki with relief.

"What are we telling the gendarmes?" said Svenka. "They are going to want someone."

"Feed them Cano. That should keep them busy; just make sure Carrie Mae doesn't get mentioned. We also haven't got the linchpin in this whole fiasco: Brandt Dettling."

"Kit's manager?" asked Svenka, sounding surprised. It was Nikki's turn to nod.

"We've got his assistant." Nikki nodded in Angela's direction. "Brandt hired Cano to kill Kit, so he could sell off his back catalog and save his record company. I've got a teammate on him, but I haven't heard from her yet, so I don't know his whereabouts at the moment." Svenka nodded again. "Meanwhile, I want Jenny and Jane"—she pointed to her friends—"to get out of here before the gendarmes show up. If anyone asks, they were groupies the band picked up, and nobody knows where they've gone."

"Nikki, the police are on their way up," said Jane, appearing beside her.

"May I say that I'm representing Mr. Masters?" asked Svenka, and Nikki shrugged.

"Sure, it can't hurt, and I'll tell Kit he's hired you when he gets offstage." Svenka blinked and glanced at Jane, who smiled smugly.

"Very well," said Svenka, stripping off her gloves. "You may leave this to me."

Jenny arrived to stand next to Jane. Nikki smiled at the two of them. Jenny ran a hand over her hair, smoothing the one flyaway strand, and then dropped her hand to rest on her hip. Jane's hair was ruffled, her Bettie Page bangs had separated and were sticking up, and her T-shirt was untucked and protruding from under her sweater.

"So the Swedish volleyball team seems to have things under control," Jenny commented.

"She does," said Nikki. "Why don't the two of you split? Find Ellen; regroup and meet me at Kit's hotel."

"Will do," said Jenny, tugging on Jane's sleeve.

"Thanks, guys. I really appreciate this," said Nikki.

"Wouldn't have missed it for the world," said Jenny as they strolled away.

The cops arrived and within seconds had draped everything in yellow tape. Svenka was handling everything with an adroitness that surprised Nikki. Svenka had untapped talents. Cano and his friends were being marched out of the room as Kit began his third song. Nikki sighed and leaned against the pillar again. Things were going to be messy at work. She'd probably be on desk duty for months. Why was everything she touched such an enormous mess? Could she not make things run smoothly, just once?

A French detective arrived on the scene; he was a tall man with a rumpled trench coat and weary eyes over a curving French nose. Nikki watched him watch Svenka verbally muscling the gendarmes around. The gendarmes were demanding to speak with Monsieur Masters, or see Monsieur Masters, or possibly just get Monsieur Masters's autograph. Whatever they wanted, the "Monsieur Masterses" were flying fast and furious. Nikki watched the tall detective prepare to swoop in on Svenka, and Nikki squared her shoulders, redying herself to help. She marched toward the yellow police tape that surrounded the area. Just as she was about to duck under the tape, the band came running offstage to the sound of thunderous applause. Nikki changed direction and grabbed Kit.

"All right, everyone, get your stories straight," Nikki hissed to the sweating band. "Jenny was just some groupie you picked up. The blonde over there is Svenka, Kit's new assistant. You don't know who attacked you or why. Got it?"

"Wait, if our story is that we don't know anything, does that mean I actually do know something?" asked Burg.

"Trust me, Burg, you know nothing," said Hammond.

"Great. That's settled, off you go," said Nikki, and shoved them in Svenka's general direction. Nikki made as if to follow, but Kit grabbed her hand and pulled her away.

"Don't go out there!" he whispered, peering around the pillar. "I've heard my name six times in the last minute. I may not know French, but I know that's not good."

"Well, between the gunfight and the escaped Basque convict I think they want to ask you what the hell is going on."

"You know very well that I don't know what the hell is going on," said Kit. "Come on, we're getting out of here."

Pulling her by the hand, Kit wove through the throngs of confused backup girls, celebrities, and crew. He paused briefly at the refreshments table, running his fingers over the bottles until he found one he liked.

"It's not champagne," he said, tossing the bottle to Nikki, who caught it neatly, "but it'll have to do."

"Where are we going?" asked Nikki, holding up the bottle to read the label. It was nonalcoholic sparkling cider.

"We're going to do what everyone else in Paris is doing," he said, looking back over his shoulder. "We're going to see the fireworks!"

Nikki checked her watch. It was twenty minutes till midnight.

"We'll never make it," she said as he tossed open the front doors of the opera house.

"We're just a few metro stops away," he yelled, bounding down the stairs. "We'll make it if we run!" Nikki followed after him. They dashed up the street to the nearest turnstiles. The Metro, free all night long on New Year's, was still nearly full of last-minute travelers. They scrambled into a car as the doors slid closed and joined a giddy crowd that was singing along to an accordion player's catchy tune. Kit's face pulled into a puzzled expression and then he turned to Nikki, who laughed, recognizing "Devil May Care" set to an accordion and being mangled by French teenagers. One of the teenagers ripped open a bag of noisemakers that unrolled in flickering foil tongues.

"*Bonne année!*" yelled the girl, and the car answered back. She shoved noisemakers at Kit and Nikki. The car filled with the hollow frog voices of the noisemakers, and the accordion player matched the beat with a new song, something zydeco-ish that Nikki didn't recognize. The train pulled to a stop and the party moved up the stairs and out into the streets.

"Come on," Kit yelled over the din of the crowd. "We're going to miss it." Reaching back, he grabbed Nikki's hand and began to run. He dodged people with a ruthless determination, leaving a trail of squished toes and jostled elbows in their wake. He came to a stop almost directly under the enormous Ferris wheel. Nikki skidded to a stop, laughing breathlessly and clutching their bottle of sparkling cider. Around them, people milled with alternating moods of disinterest and drunken revelry. Somebody had a small radio that was cranking out tinny French pop.

"Would you look at that?" he asked, looking back the way they had come and wrapping an arm around her waist, hugging her close.

Nikki looked up the Champs-Elysées to Napoleon's glowing arch of triumph and understood the awe in Kit's voice. The six-lane road divided by a generous median was usually crowded with zooming cars, and the sidewalks, wide as most roads, were normally sprinkled with shoppers. But tonight, the entire street was a sea of humanity, swaying and twisting, warming the air with their presence—nothing but people as far as the eye could see.

"I can't believe I'm here," said Kit.

"It is kind of unbelievable," answered Nikki, watching as a circle of Australian backpackers began to bounce, chanting something catchy and probably rugby related.

"No, I mean me. I can't believe that I'm here. I should be dead." Nikki looked into Kit's face, seeing more seriousness than she was used to. "I would be dead if it weren't for you."

"It wasn't exactly single-handed," said Nikki, trying to joke him out of his mood; she wasn't very good at seriousness. "I had a little help from Duncan and the girls."

"Right, from my uncle. That's a hell of a thing."

"A good thing?"

"I . . . yes." Kit nodded. "But talk about a total shocker. I just feel like . . . I'm not at all who I thought I was. No wonder Mum wanted me to be an accountant. And no wonder I always wanted all the thrill-seeking crap—with my genes they're lucky I didn't become a soldier of fortune. So much stuff makes so much more sense now! Like no wonder Nan always seemed so fond of Duncan. She kept knitting him socks." He shook his head, still seeming perplexed.

"You're still the same person," said Nikki.

"Yeah, I guess, but I just wish I'd known before. I feel like I would have done stuff differently. It's a total shift of perspective on my own life."

"Well," said Nikki, quoting him back to himself, "where you're going can't be half as hard as where you are now."

"I'll drink to that!" he laughed, reaching for the bottle of cider. He barely had the wire cap and paper off when the plastic cork exploded from the bottle in a cider-propelled arc. They watched in awe as the cork went up and then ducked as it came down on a man a few feet in front of them. Still ducking, they shuffled to the left.

"I think it's OK," she said, poking her head up cautiously.

"That's all we need tonight," said Kit, popping up next to her like a prairie dog. "'Kit Masters Blinds French Man with Cider Cork.'" He read off the imaginary headline; Nikki grinned.

"You know, I take it back," he said. "I think you're the biggest surprise of the week. I didn't know there was anyone like you. Actually, I don't think there is anyone like you. You're pretty amazing."

"I could say the same about you," answered Nikki.

Behind them the BONNE ANNÉE sign lit up, and the crowd began to cheer.

"Happy New Year, Nikki," said Kit warmly, and leaned in for a New Year's kiss that became something more. Nikki was dimly aware of flashing lights, and when she looked around again the sky was awash in fireworks.

"It's not the same, is it?"

Nikki looked at Kit, knowing that he was talking about Z'ev.

"Cider," he said, holding up the bottle and taking a drink. "It's not the same as champagne."

"We can't have champagne," answered Nikki.

"You could."

"I'm happy with cider."

"But you're thinking of champagne."

Nikki opened her mouth to deny it but found she couldn't. Kit shrugged and looked back up at the fireworks. Nikki sighed and took his hand, leaning against his shoulder.

"Sorry," she said, knowing it was inadequate.

"I have an actual family for the first time in my life. I'm sober for the first time in ten years, and I've written a new song. I think maybe I can live without champagne."

"You're going to be fine," said Nikki, and Kit looked at her as if he were going to say something and then laughed instead.

"Happy New Year!" he shouted to the passing crowd.

"*Bonne année!*" shouted Nikki, not to be outdone, and the crowd roared back.

PARIS XIX

The World According to Brandt

"I suppose we should go around back or something," said Nikki as they reached the hotel. There were mobs of people in front, but Nikki couldn't tell if they were fans or homeward-bound partiers.

"Screw it," said Kit. "I'm not in the mood. I want to go in the front for once." He forged a path to the door, and the doorman opened it as they approached.

"Mr. Masters," murmured the doorman, identifying them with the superhuman skills of recognition that only doormen possess.

"Maybe not the wisest choice," whispered Nikki as the sound of Kit's name brought a screech of identification from two fans on the sidewalk.

"Since when has wisdom been on my résumé?" asked Kit, grinning. "I pay other people for that." Nikki laughed again as the doorman hastily closed the doors behind them.

"I don't suppose you still have my room key?" asked Kit, and Nikki shook her head.

"I left in a bit of a hurry," she explained.

"Front desk it is then," he said with a shrug.

"Ah, Monsieur Masters," said the concierge, his face lighting up when he saw them. Nikki saw him take in their interlocked fingers with a flickering glance that betrayed no emotion. "I am glad to see you. There seems to have been some upset at the *Bonne Année* show?"

"Er, yes," said Kit with a glance at Nikki. "Lost my room key in the process. Don't suppose you can give us a spare?"

"Of course," said the concierge, sliding a key-card across the desk. "But I believe your band is there, waiting for you." He paused slightly and cleared his throat. "You may have known this already, but I did not wish you to be surprised."

"Uh, OK, thanks," said Kit, taking the key with a shrug. "That's fine. We probably need to talk to the band anyway," he said, turning to Nikki, who nodded. Out of the corner of her eye she saw the primly mustached concierge watching them with a kind of paternal glow. She wondered if Kit really failed to notice such things or if he was just used to it.

"After we talk to the band, let's go to the hospital and find Mum and Duncan," he said as they got in the elevator. "Or my uncle, or whatever." She watched his eyebrow twitch as he tried to come to grips with the idea of family.

"You'll get used to it," she said, and he looked over, surprised.

"Will I?"

"Reality shifts, and it takes the mind a day or two to catch up, but it does eventually. It's like jet lag for your brain."

"You sound like you speak from experience."

"My reality seems normal to you?"

"No," he answered. "Not if this is an average week for you."

"I wouldn't say average, but let's just say it's not the weirdest week of my life."

"I don't think I like brain lag," he said as the elevator doors folded back on themselves.

"Well, if you can survive being a rock star, I expect you can survive having a family." He laughed and reached out with the key-card, but the door was yanked open before he could slide it into the slot.

"Where have you been?" demanded Burg.

"We have been worried sick about you," said Richie.

"I wasn't," said Holly, not rising from the couch.

"We came back and found this place in utter shambles, with Nikki's clothes all over the floor, and you weren't here! You said you were going to meet us back here!"

"I told them he was with you," said Jane, lounging in the bathroom doorway, "but that didn't seem to stop them from worrying." Ellen was sitting just outside the bedroom door, filing her nails, and when she caught Nikki's eye, she jerked her head subtly toward the bedroom.

"They didn't really get the full import of that statement," said Svenka, smiling from the wing chair next to Holly.

"And I admit that I did not find it all that illuminating either," said a tall police detective in the trench coat from his position in the bedroom doorway.

"Nikki, Monsieur Masters, I'd like you to meet Inspector Javier of the Paris police," said Svenka with a social smile. "I'm afraid he's very insistent about taking Monsieur Masters's statement tonight."

"I don't have much of a statement to make," said Kit, giving Nikki a worried glance.

"Well, if you could just answer a few of my questions," said

Inspector Javier, stepping forward, "I'm sure that things could be cleared up in a matter of minutes."

"Questions?" repeated Kit. "Didn't the band answer all of your questions?"

"There were a few blanks that the band and your new assistant could not fill in," answered Javier, and Kit frowned slightly, trying to puzzle out who his "new assistant" was.

"And there's another thing," said Burg, sounding aggrieved. "You might have mentioned hiring Svenka. I really think hiring hot Swedish chicks deserves a mention."

"Sorry," said Kit, flashing a brilliant smile, "but it was a bit of a last-minute decision. Nikki only introduced me to Svenka the other day." Javier's eyes narrowed as he watched Kit improvise. Nikki didn't think they were fooling him.

"Well, Mademoiselle Nicole," said Javier, turning the glittering beam of suspicion on Nikki. "You must be the makeup lady," he said with notable disbelief.

"Well, yes, and then again no," said Nikki. "My name is Nicole, but I am not a makeup lady."

She saw Svenka stiffen and heard Jane make a small, quickly smothered gasp.

"I told you she was a spy!" hissed Richie to Burg.

"I work for a private security agency hired by Kit's mother, Camille Masters. Camille was concerned about the recent behavior of Kit's manager, Brandt Dettling, and asked that my agency provide added protection as well as investigate any peculiarities I might come across."

"And did you come across any of these . . . peculiarities?" asked Javier, still looking skeptical. Behind him, Svenka and Jane were texting furiously, probably setting up her new identity as she invented it.

"I'd say nearly being killed by a group of terrorists counts as pretty damn peculiar, wouldn't you?" said Kit.

"Perhaps, but I'm not sure what one has to do with the other," answered Javier, turning his head slightly to point his mouth at Kit but not taking his eyes off Nikki. "Do you have any proof of your employment?" he asked, turning back to Nikki. "Or of your charges against Mr. Dettling?"

"My identification was unfortunately mislaid during the attack. However, you may ask Camille Masters, and I can have papers sent from the home office within the hour," said Nikki steadily. Jane glared at her, probably for offering to have paperwork within the hour. Some poor tech-support girl back at the office would be working overtime.

"Well, finally!" said Burg. "That makes so much more sense than being a makeup girl."

"I told you," said Holly smugly.

Nikki continued ignoring the band. "As for Mr. Dettling . . ."

"Yes, what about Mr. Dettling?" asked a smooth voice from the doorway of the suite. "What's all this nonsense? Christ, Kit, can't I leave you alone for two minutes?"

Brandt Dettling came out of the bedroom and into the already crowded living room. Brandt's sleek blond head turned, surveying the room and its occupants. The band shuffled sideways, almost as if not wanting to breathe the same air as the manager.

"Perhaps you did not know that Monsieur Dettling was here?" asked the detective smugly, clearly hoping to surprise Nikki.

"Absolutely shocked," said Nikki. No reason to let them know that she'd had Ellen following Brandt.

"Kit, what sort of nonsense is this girl filling your head with?" asked Brandt. His hands busied themselves with the business of taking a cigar out of the case, but his eyes were sweeping the room. "I've seen it a hundred times. Kit will hit on anything in a size two and heels. Sorry, pal, but you know it's true. And these girls think it's true love; they don't realize they're only going to be around till Kit gets bored."

"That isn't true," said Kit fiercely.

"Kit, come on. It's no big thing. You're a rock star. People expect you to have a few flings; it gives them something to read when they're in line at the grocery store. You just can't get tied up with people like her." He gestured at Nikki with his cigar. "You have to remember who really matters in your life. You have to remember who your real friends are." His voice slipped through the air, sliding like poison into the ear of a sleeping king. Nikki watched Kit's eyes dull, turning inward, doubting.

"Faustus is in financial difficulties," said Nikki. "Originally, he wanted Kit back in the studio to create a hit record, and he tried to tempt Kit into relapsing to make him easier to control. When that didn't work, he decided to kill Kit to gain control of all of Kit's unreleased material and back catalog."

"Oh my. What shocking accusations! I suppose you think I should be fleeing the country?" asked Brandt, leisurely snipping off the tip of a cigar.

"Antonio Cano had been sending Kit hate mail. Which is how Brandt contacted him. And when Brandt offered Cano the chance to kill Kit, Cano broke out of prison to take Brandt up on his offer."

"Interesting. Would you care to respond, Mr. Dettling?" asked the inspector, eyeing them both suspiciously.

Brandt took out his lighter and snapped the fire into being with a flick of his wrist. "What are you, nuts?" he asked through teeth clenched around his cigar, the flame of his lighter still flickering in his eyes.

"You sent Cano to kill Kit," said Nikki.

"Says who?" He grinned around his cigar. "You?" he asked, blowing out a cloud of smoke. "Do you really think he's going to believe you over me? Trust me, Kit," said Brandt, waving away the words in a trail of smoke. "What is she? Nothing. I'm the one you count on. You and I, we've been through everything together. We have things all arranged between us, don't we? I make the decisions and you do what you do best: you get to be a star." The room held its breath. Kit started to turn to Nikki. "Don't look at her," snapped Brandt. "I'm the one who matters!" He stood up and walked across the room to Kit, dropping heavy hands onto Kit's shoulders.

"I'm your brother. I'm your family. Who else would take you, if it wasn't for me?"

Kit looked up into Brandt's face.

"I have a family," he said crisply, and straightened his spine. "And I make my own decisions."

"Since when?" asked Brandt, straightening Kit's collar, smiling all the while.

"Since now. You've had Angela sending booze to my greenrooms. And that groupie in Stuttgart—you gave her the drugs. It's been you the whole time. I just didn't know why."

"You didn't know why?" Brandt's smile relaxed into reality, and he laughed lightheartedly.

"Faustus is failing," said Nikki. "And you're his cash cow."

"Shut up!" said Brandt, turning on her savagely. "Faustus is not failing! I do not fail!" He screamed the last words, his face flushing and then going pale. He stood in the center of the room quivering with rage. "If it's me, Kit, then it's always been you. You would be dead in a gutter somewhere, forgotten, a drunken has-been—no, a drunken never-was, if it weren't for me. And now suddenly you think you can run your life, make your own decisions? You don't exist without me!"

Kit opened his mouth to speak and then closed it again and shook his head.

"I can't be what you want me to be anymore," he said at last. "I'm sorry, Brandt." Kit seemed close to tears. "I can't live that way anymore. I'm really sorry. I didn't want to disappoint you. I didn't want to disappoint anyone. I'll help with Faustus. At least, I'll try, but I can't be what you tell me anymore. I need more than that."

Brandt stared at Kit, mouth agape, then with a wordless howl he lunged for Kit. Nikki reached forward, intercepting him, seizing him by his collar and one outstretched wrist. Pivoting on the ball of her foot, she let the momentum of his lunge carry them to the floor. Keeping hold of his arm, she wrenched it around until all his fingers were pointing back down at his head and her weight was driving his arm into the floor. Brandt screamed in pain.

"Yes, well, mademoiselle, if you will just hold him there . . ." Inspector Javier walked forward, casually snapping out a pair of handcuffs.

"Not a problem," said Nikki through gritted teeth. "I've got things under control."

"Apparently so," said Javier.

PARIS XX

Home Again

January 1

"I thought we'd have more time," said Kit, looking vaguely around the first-class lounge, which was mostly empty save for the few travelers foolhardy enough to fly with a hangover. Jenny, Ellen, and Jane were staring out the window and giving them the pretense of privacy. Svenka and a Carrie Mae–supplied bodyguard were waiting outside the lounge.

"I guess the holidays are all we get," said Nikki with a weak smile.

"The paparazzi were crazy this morning, huh? You'd think everyone would have something better to do on New Year's Day."

"Guess not."

"I told Svenka to track down those poor kids we stole the motorcycles from, and I sent those tickets to those girls you said I should."

"Oh good," said Nikki. "They were really helpful, and tickets and a note from you will blow them away."

"You're really good at taking care of your team," said Kit.

"I'm not sure teenage groupies who give me clothes count as a team," said Nikki.

"You have lots of teams," said Kit. "You're just a natural leader. You find people and make them into a team. Makes us all feel safe."

"Oh dear," said Nikki. "You do know I don't know what I'm doing half the time, right?"

"From where I was sitting you looked like you had it all under control," said Kit, smiling.

"Well, if it comes down to under control, then you should try looking in the mirror. Your band and crew would follow you anywhere."

"That's just . . . ," said Kit, shrugging uncomfortably.

"That's just because you're their leader. Remember after the bus crash? You were the man with the plan."

"I don't feel like I have a plan," said Kit plaintively.

"You think I do?" retorted Nikki, and Kit laughed ruefully.

"You don't think you can stay?" he asked, changing subjects and picking at the seam on her carry-on luggage.

"Well, the French branch is kind of pissed at me in general. And my company doesn't really like publicity."

"And I'm all about publicity."

He studied their feet for a long moment.

"I think I actually am going to offer Svenka a job," said Kit reflectively, shifting his gaze to the ceiling. "She's so efficient. Do you think your company will mind that?"

"No, they're pretty flexible, just private."

"I like having you around," he said at last.

"You do keep me on my toes," said Nikki.

"Yes, but you know you had fun, too," he said, a twinkle in his eye.

"Of course," said Nikki. "I was with you."

"I'm going to miss you," he said.

"I'm only a phone call away."

"Not the same."

"No, it's not."

"So, I'm going to be stateside in a month or two for a concert. The publicity will have died down by then, and no one knows me in the U.S. anyway. I don't suppose . . . I mean, provided things don't work out with you and the jerk, that maybe you and I could go out on a date that didn't involve someone trying to kill me?"

Nikki laughed. "I'm not sure I'd know what to do on a date where people didn't shoot at me."

"You make out," said Kit with a self-assured nod.

"Oh, is that what happens?" she asked, laughing. "I didn't realize. Well, call me when you get to L.A.," she said impulsively. "We'll see what happens."

"Count on it," he answered with a wink, and leaned in to kiss her. After a moment she heard Jane cough discreetly. "Apple juice can be good," Kit pointed out, and Nikki reached out to ruffle his hair.

"I never said it wasn't."

A stewardess bustled over to the counter and announced their flight.

"That's us," said Nikki.

"You'd better go, then," he answered.

Nikki hefted her luggage and walked to join Jane and the other passengers queuing for the plane. Looking over her shoulder, Nikki caught a last glimpse of Kit before they walked into the belly of the plane. His hair was sticking up in devil's horns and he waved good-bye with the ghost of a smile.

"I am so glad to be going home," said Jane, sinking into her seat, "I don't think I've had a full night's sleep since Colombia."

"Tell me about it," said Nikki fervently. "You managed to get all that paperwork to Javier really fast," she said, changing the subject.

"Wasn't me," said Jane. "It was Svenka. She really came through."

"I think Kit might offer her a job," said Nikki.

"Really?" asked Jane, making a face. "I don't think that's a good idea. The company needs people like her."

Nikki shrugged. "Yeah, but sometimes dealing with all the bureaucratic BS makes another job look tempting. Like Colombia. If I had to work under Camille, I'd be out the door."

"Speaking of Camille," said Jenny, "does anyone know what she's going to tell Mrs. M? She smoothed things over with the Paris branch, but Mrs. M might still be a little pissed depending on how shit goes down."

"Why?" asked Jane, ignoring the safety video and rifling through the SkyMall magazine.

"I don't know; misappropriation of resources, your little vacation to Germany, disobeying a direct order. I'm sure she can think of more," said Jenny.

"Meh," said Nikki. "She sent you two to help out. Plus, Kit said he'd make sure Camille didn't make waves. She might still be mad about Colombia, but since we pulled everything out OK here . . . I think it'll turn out to be a wash. Plus, she seems sort of calmed down now that everything's out in the open with Kit."

"I'm going to get these lawn flamingos with the nine interchangeable holiday outfits," said Jane, pointing at the picture in the SkyMall magazine. Nikki thought of a bird whorehouse and smiled.

"You don't have a lawn," Jenny said.

"I have a very large planter."

"OK, then."

"And I'm thinking about the wall-sized crossword puzzle."

"Do you do crosswords?" asked Ellen.

"Not really, but it could be a fun party thing."

"What kind of parties are you throwing?" asked Nikki in disbelief.

"I'm a geek, Nikki; I associate with other geeks and that's who comes to my parties. The fact that I get to hang with you and Jenny and Ellen is just a quirk of fate."

Nikki leaned back in her seat as the plane threw itself skyward. "Fate. Yeah, she's quirky all right."

Jane looked over with a sympathetic smile and patted Nikki's knee. "Chin up, young person. The day's not over yet."

Nikki closed her eyes and prepared to sleep away the flight. She was too tired to keep her chin up.

L.A.

Work Related

January 2

Nikki wearily climbed into her car. Her post-mission debrief with Mrs. M had not gone well. Mrs. Merrivel had been politely expressive on the nature of professionalism.

"Carrie Mae's very existence is a monument to the discretion of our agents," Mrs. Merrivel had said, smiling slightly. "Although I wish to push our agency into the modern age, I don't think we should do so at the expense of the values that made us what we are today. Don't you agree?"

"I agree entirely," said Nikki firmly. "The incident with Z'ev was entirely accidental."

"Mmm . . . yes. And what about Kit Masters?"

"What about Kit?" asked Nikki, confused. Mrs. Merrivel sighed and pulled a tabloid newspaper from her briefcase.

"The French branch sent me an advance copy of the *Star*—it's only in the European version, thank God."

"Oh dear," said Nikki, staring at the picture of her and Kit on the cover with a horrified fascination. "I don't know what to say."

"You do have a penchant for choosing the most inconvenient men," Mrs. Merrivel said. "I mean, with Kit's mother being an agent, he might be considered well within the dating pool, but don't you think that his being an international pop star might make being a part of a secret organization a bit difficult?"

"Yes," she said dejectedly. "I'm sorry."

"Well, I can't be too mad," said Mrs. M, her eyes twinkling. "Cano is back in prison, Kit has actually donated a significant sum to the Carrie Mae Foundation due to your performance, and Camille has requested a leave of absence to spend time with Kit. And I understand that she's also reconciled with her brother-in-law?"

"Duncan," said Nikki. "She's finally realized he loves Kit as much as she does."

Mrs. M nodded as if well satisfied.

"I wasn't sure you'd be happy about that, to tell the truth," said Nikki. "Since it means losing a branch director for a while."

"Jane wasn't the only one who needed a vacation. When Camille returns she'll be much more effective. How was Jane's vacation, by the way?"

"Uh . . . ," said Nikki.

"Should I be sending her out for some additional training? Or do you think attempting to take on Voges alone was a one-time event?"

Nikki held her breath for the count of one—just long enough to make her decision.

"Knowing Jane? Send her for additional training. Having gotten away with it once, she's only going to try it again."

Mrs. Merrivel nodded. "Just what I was thinking. I should warn you that there may be some fallout from the Nina Alvarez situation, and you seem to have annoyed the Paris branch director as well."

"What kind of fallout?" asked Nikki, dreading the answer.

"Undetermined at this time," said Mrs. Merrivel. "And it may yet be avoided. You know, although I didn't wish for it to happen, politically, it's probably better that you broke up with Z'ev."

Nikki nodded numbly. Yeah, politically, it was better.

Mrs. Merrivel continued. "Anyway, go home. Get some sleep. We'll worry about all this tomorrow."

Once in the Impala, Nikki rolled down the window and let the warm California breeze sweep across her face. L.A. in January wasn't so very warm, but it was definitely warmer than France. She was nearly home when she was startled by her phone.

Glancing at her phone, she saw her mother's name on the display. With a sigh she pushed the "answer" button.

"Hi, Mom."

"You never called back," said her mother icily. Nikki felt her guilt meter surge.

"I've been busy, Mom," said Nikki. "Besides, I told you my phone was broken."

"Did your fingers break too? You could have picked up any phone and dialed my number. I'm assuming you remember it?"

"Yes, Mom, but . . ." Nikki started to say.

"But you were too busy cheating on your boyfriend with another man? Was that it, hmm?"

"Ah crap," said Nikki. Kit Masters was definitely something that she had been intending to keep in the "mother doesn't need to know" file.

"Front page of the *Star*, Nicole. Stacey Marlick went to Canada for the weekend and guess what she brought back? Guess, Nicole."

"A copy of the *Star*?"

"That's right. She trots it into the office this morning and says, 'Isn't this your daughter?' And I look at it and sure enough, there's you, in what can only be described as, and I quote, 'a passionate lip-lock.' When I was a girl we called that playing tonsil hockey. Then I read the article and it says this guy, who they claim is famous but who I've never heard of, was spotted earlier in the week at a bar, singing karaoke and generally 'behaving very much like a couple' with the 'mysterious redhead.'"

"Oh dear," said Nikki when her mother paused. She'd been hoping the *Star* had limited itself to just the picture. Apparently, there was an entire article as well.

"'Oh dear'?" repeated her mother. "That's all you have to say? Who is this guy, Nikki?"

"Kit Masters. Biggest thing since Robbie Williams."

"Who's Robbie Williams?"

"Um, he's kind of like Che Guevara: someone everyone but Americans knows about."

"Who the hell is Che Guevara?"

"He was a South American revolutionary."

"You're dating a South American revolutionary?"

"No, Mom, he's a pop singer. I'm just saying . . . Sorry, never mind, forget I said anything. I just went a little left-wing on you there."

"Well, don't. It's not funny."

"Sorry," said Nikki, pulling into her parking spot and resting her head against the steering wheel, feeling too tired to defend herself.

"What about Z'ev?" asked Nell. "You know you've totally blown it if he sees a copy of this, right? He's going to know you've been cheating on him."

"I broke up with him, remember? It's not cheating," answered Nikki, head still on the steering wheel, one hand reaching for the trunk release. She heard the trunk pop and with a sigh opened her door, swinging her legs out onto the cracked cement of her parking lot. She rested there another moment, gathering her strength for the final trek to her apartment. She was looking forward to crawling into a bed that didn't smell like a hotel.

"Uh-huh. Bet it didn't feel a thing like cheating, what with you still being in love with him," said her mother.

"Mom!" She couldn't believe her mom had mentioned the L-word. "I never said I was in love with him. And besides, are you telling me you don't like a rock star better than an ambassador?"

"Well, rock stars do make more money, but really, they're not very dependable, and the *Star* says he has a drug problem."

"He went to rehab," said Nikki, feeling defensive on Kit's behalf. "He's very committed to his recovery."

"Committed to his recovery and every groupie in his immediate area," said Nell, talking over her. "And so Z'ev cancels a few plans? At least he's got a steady job. And he sent me a card for my birthday and he was very polite on the phone. Although"—Nikki could hear the sound of the *Star* being riffled through on the other end of the phone—"this Kit Masters is kind of cute. What's this about some masked-gunmen publicity stunt?"

"Oh, it was just a thing at the *Bonne Année* show," said Nikki carelessly. Back on the job, she got up briskly and opened the trunk, pulling out her backpack and carry-on.

"I thought you were in the UK," whined Nell. "Why didn't you tell me you were going to Paris? I would have asked for stuff."

"Don't worry," said Nikki. "I got you the perfume you like."

"Hmm," answered Nell. "Why were you even with this guy? I thought it was a work thing."

"The foundation was hoping Kit would donate a lot of money, and his makeup artist broke her leg. So I did a little pinch-hitting in the makeup department and got the donation," answered Nikki glibly.

"Really?" Nell sounded impressed. "Are you sure that wasn't all you were hitting?"

"Mom!" exclaimed Nikki, slightly outraged.

"Sorry," said Nell, sounding unrepentant. "Have makeup bag, will travel, I guess. I wish my work would send me to exotic places." There was a pause while Nell flipped a few more pages and Nikki tried to get her purse and carry-on into synchronous orbit. Nikki staggered to her mailbox and opened it; mail burst forth as if it had been waiting to ambush her. With a sigh, Nikki bent down to sort through the pile on the floor. Junk, three bills, and two Christmas cards from Thailand. Nikki smiled, recognizing Laura Daniels's address and Lawan Chinnawat's careful script. She jammed the mail in the outer pocket of her bag for later perusal.

"When are you coming home?" asked her mother, apparently losing interest in Kit. "The flights are really cheap right now. I have Christmas presents for you."

"I was thinking at the end of the month," said Nikki, mentally reviewing her calendar and feeling guilty. "I have presents for you too."

"Are you going to see the rock star again?" asked Nell.

"I don't know, Mom," said Nikki, marching up the stairs to her front door and shoving the key into her lock. "He'll be in L.A. in a couple of months, for a benefit concert or something, but I might be traveling again."

The door swung open and hit the wall with a Sheetrock-denting crash. Her carry-on slipped down her arm, tangling with her already dangling purse. She half kicked the bag, half shuffled into the entryway, lugging the backpack after.

"Mom," she said, looking into her living room. "I'm going to have to call you back. I have company."

"How can you have company? You just got home."

"Believe me, I'm aware of that."

"OK, well, fine. Call me later."

"You bet," said Nikki.

"Bye."

"Bye."

Z'ev sat comfortably in the Swedish armchair reading a copy of the *Star*. It was a testament to the photographer that the picture was better than the usual grainy mess of a slouching celebrity, actually veering dangerously close to artwork. Kit had one arm around her waist and the other gently clasped around her neck. The Ferris wheel glowed behind them and a shower of fireworks illuminated them in a golden wash of light. Her coat hung open, revealing the micromini and mile-high boots, not to mention quite a bit of Nikki's thighs. The cider bottle dangled negligently from her hand, and around them the crowd had blurred the photograph with movement. Only Nikki and Kit had held perfectly still. The photo seemed to capture everything a Paris New Year's ought to be.

"Have a nice New Year?" asked Z'ev, putting the *Star* down.

Nikki dropped her bags on the hallway floor with a thud. "How'd you get in?"

"I picked the lock."

"Lovely," said Nikki. "Is there something I can help you with or were you just in the neighborhood?"

"Yes, you can help me understand what my girlfriend is doing on the cover of the *Star* with a British pop star."

"I don't know, how was your South American vacation?" answered Nikki spitefully.

"We didn't go to South America."

"One of us did!" Nikki shot back.

"No, I didn't." But he seemed less righteous in his denial.

"Oh!" Nikki was too outraged for words and could only sputter. "Liar!" she said, reaching into her purse and pulling out the picture of Z'ev and Nina Alvarez. "This isn't you, then?" She waved the picture in front of his face. He snatched it out of her hand, frowning.

"Where did you get this?"

"I work for Carrie Mae, Z'ev; we have franchises in fifty-seven countries! And Nina Alvarez is one of our contributors."

"It was work related," said Z'ev through clenched teeth, crushing the photo into a ball.

"You looked up Nina Alvarez, didn't you? After I told you that information was confidential, you looked her up."

"All right, fine—yes, I did. And you were right, she needed help."

"She needed help and you . . ." Nikki wanted to say "wouldn't let me take care of it" but remembered herself in time. "And you canceled our vacation?"

"You don't think that rescuing a woman, crushing a drug cartel, and stabilizing a region was worth canceling a vacation for?" he demanded.

"I might have if you'd told me what was going on!" yelled Nikki.

"I can't talk to you about work!" he yelled back.

"Oh, this is working?" demanded Nikki, picking up and straightening the picture of Z'ev kissing Nina. "You're seriously telling me that the CIA made you kiss her? Yeah. No wonder you can't talk to me about work."

"Really?" asked Z'ev. "You really want to go there?" He held up the *Star*.

"It was work related," repeated Nikki sarcastically, her hands on her hips.

"Yeah, right. How?"

"When you canceled our vacation they decided to give me a last-minute assignment," said Nikki, repeating her story in its now well-practiced format. "The foundation was hoping Kit would donate a lot of money, and when his makeup artist broke her leg I did a little pinch-hitting in the makeup department and got the donation." She crossed her arms across her chest and glared at him, daring him to call her bluff.

"I'll just bet you got a donation."

"It wasn't like that!" Nikki shrieked, outraged. "I was just filling in for someone."

"Filling in?" he repeated in disbelief. "This is filling in? What were you doing? Adjusting his eyeliner with your tongue?"

"Why I am even explaining this? We broke up, remember? You canceled our vacation, like you cancel everything else; I broke up with you and you didn't call me back."

"I did call you back!"

"No, you didn't!"

"Yes, I did. It said your phone was out of service."

"Oh," said Nikki, dropping down from the height of justifiable anger. "Right. It got broken. I just picked up my replacement today."

"Oh." Z'ev ran his fingers over his head and paced the length of the room and back. "I don't want to break up," he said bluntly, stopping in front of her.

She looked up, startled. His brown eyes were set deep over a prominent nose and held an expression she couldn't identify.

"But how are we supposed to stay together?" she asked softly, sitting down on the coffee table.

"You know why I had to break into your house?" he asked. "It's because I don't have a key."

"It doesn't make sense for you to have a key," she said dully. "I always pick you up at the airport. You're not here if I'm not."

"That's what I'm saying. I had a lot of time to think about this over the last week. We don't share anything. You live here; I live in Chicago. And since both of our jobs are prone to last-minute traveling we don't actually have any time together. How can we have a relationship if we're not in the same town long enough to see each other for more than two days in a month?"

"Well, thanks for pointing that out, Captain Obvious," said Nikki bitterly.

"I put in for a transfer to L.A." he said.

"What?" asked Nikki, blinking up at him. He couldn't really be saying that. He couldn't really be trying to get back together. That would be . . . unprecedented. Men left. They didn't come back.

"I want to live here. I want us to be together. At least in the same city, anyway. I want to meet your mom. Well, not really, but on general principle I probably should. I want you to meet my parents. I'm not sure I'm expressing this very well, but we can't keep doing what we've been doing."

"You want us to be a real couple?" asked Nikki. She wanted to laugh. Or cry. She wasn't sure which. It was as if he were repeating all her thoughts for the last week.

"Yes," said Z'ev, his shoulders relaxing.

Nikki felt as though a whirlwind were whipping around her brain. Mrs. Merrivel wouldn't approve. She'd promised Kit they could go on a date when he came to L.A. Z'ev was politically inconvenient.

But Z'ev was here. He had come back for her. Some small panicked voice was shouting in the back of her mind that she should kick him out, make him leave. It was the smart thing to do. She stared into his brown eyes and felt her own shoulders relax. What was she going to tell the girls? She was going to be in such trouble.

"Do you really want to break up?" Z'ev asked.

"No," said Nikki. "I don't."

They stared at each other for a long moment.

"Did you sleep with that guy?" he blurted out. "Never mind, I don't want to know."

"No," said Nikki, suddenly very, very glad she hadn't slept with Kit. "Did you sleep with Nina?"

"No."

"You really tried to call?" she asked. She had to be certain.

"About fifty times," he said with that Boy Scout look in his eye that made her trust him.

"Well," said Nikki, standing up and smoothing her skirt, "I guess I retract my breakup then."

Z'ev's laugh boomed around the living room, echoing off the ceiling. "Oh good," he said in his customary gravelly voice. "That means I get to do this."

He kissed her then, and Nikki felt the champagne bubbles popping all around.

Acknowledgments

In the making of this book, I first have to acknowledge the contributions of the city of Paris—research has never been so fun or tasty. Although, frankly, I could have done without that riot (which is a story for another day). Second, but much more fervently, I must thank family and friends for their unfailing support and love. And last, but certainly not least, I thank my editor Sarah and my agent Theresa for their considerable help and insightful editing. You have all been great sources of inspiration and expertise on this journey—*merci*!